Becky Ward has worked in magazine publishing for over twenty years on titles including *OK!*, *New* and the *Daily Express* supplements. She's had hundreds of travel features, show and restaurant reviews published.

She wrote her first book – a choose-your-own-adventure – at the age of ten and more recently self-published an illustrated children's book to raise money for charity. *The Dance Deception* is her first published adult novel.

THE Dance DECEPTION

BECKY WARD

Published by AVON
A division of HarperCollins*Publishers*
1 London Bridge Street
London SE1 9GF

www.harpercollins.co.uk

HarperCollins*Publishers*
Macken House
39/40 Mayor Street Upper
Dublin 1
D01 C9W8

A Paperback Original 2023
1
First published in Great Britain by HarperCollins*Publishers* 2023

A catalogue copy of this book is available from the British Library.

ISBN: 978-0-00-860934-4

Typeset in Birka by Palimpsest Book Production Limited, Falkirk, Stirlingshire

Printed and bound in the UK using
100% Renewable Electricity by CPI Group (UK) Ltd

THE Dance DECEPTION

Chapter 1

When you spend several hours pressed up against the muscular torso of a drop-dead gorgeous professional dancer, I promise you it will cross your mind how it might feel if there weren't two layers of clothing separating your bodies. And that's exactly what's going through my mind now, a couple of hours into my first training session with Merle Picard, the ridiculously attractive French dancer from the *Fire on the Dance Floor* team, as he walks me through our first routine together.

I imagine running my hands over his rock-hard abs, trailing my fingers across his smooth, tanned skin and working my way down . . .

It sets off a light tingling sensation between my legs and an involuntary sigh escapes from my lips.

'Ça va?' Merle asks.

'Oh yes, sorry, all good.' I snap back to attention. 'I was just . . . never mind. You were saying?'

He goes back to explaining what his various hand signals mean – a double shoulder tap for a body roll, a lowered hand to prep for a turn – but despite my best efforts to stay focused, I slip back to picturing us getting more intimately acquainted.

This time when he asks if everything is okay, I reply, 'Oh, *oui*,' with a shy smile.

'How about now?' he asks, taking both my hands and pressing them firmly against his chest.

I glance up and see the intense look in his dark brown eyes.

'Um, better.'

He takes my hands and moves them to his hips, curling my fingers round onto his taut buttocks.

'And now?'

'Very good.'

He puts one of his hands over mine and slides it round to the front so I can feel him getting hard through his gym tights.

'And now?'

My cheeks flush as my brain scrambles to formulate a response that won't sound corny, but he saves me by planting a kiss firmly on my lips, his tongue pushing into my mouth to find mine . . .

'Kate, are you still with me?' the real Merle asks. 'I know it's a lot to take in on your first day. We can go a little more slowly if you'd like.'

'Sorry, sorry, sorry,' I babble, blushing. 'I've got this, I promise.'

'Why don't we take a few minutes to regroup? Grab

yourself some water, use the bathroom if you need to, nip out and get some fresh air. Let's get back to it in ten, fifteen minutes. Okay?'

'Good plan,' I agree.

A splash of cold water might help me focus. In five days' time we're going to be dancing in front of a live studio audience, as well as however many millions of people are watching on the telly, so I've got to pull myself together and start getting to grips with our routine. I'm here to learn, not to lust after my instructor. Even so, I can't help hoping he's into redheads.

'All set?' Merle asks when I head back into the studio. And I nod, because I don't trust myself to speak. I just can't get over how achingly handsome he is.

He walks towards me and places his hands on my shoulders, giving them a squeeze.

'Just try to relax,' he says. 'To be a good dancer, you need to release all this tension you're carrying up here.'

But it's hard to relax when his fingers feel so warm and inviting against my skin. I fight the urge to close my eyes, tip my head back and sigh with pleasure. *He's just trying to help me become a better dancer*, I remind myself. But what I really want to do is tell him I know the perfect way for him to relieve any tension.

'Let's try some breathing exercises,' he suggests, stepping back and turning to face the mirror. It's not exactly what I had in mind.

'Take a deep breath in and raise your arms up above your head, like this,' he says, showing me the move, then watching me to make sure I'm following his direction.

3

'Then exhale as you bring them back down in front of you, like this. And again . . .'

I can't stop looking at his sculpted biceps as he repeats the exercise, and I notice he doesn't take his eyes off me, either. And it feels like something changes between us in that moment, because afterwards he reaches for my shoulders again, to see if I've loosened up, and this time I'm certain his hands linger for longer than is necessary.

But just as I'm convincing myself this is not just wishful thinking on my part, he steps away again.

'That's much better, Kate. See how your shoulders are much softer now?'

'I do,' I agree, even though they don't feel any different to me.

'Great, then you're all set. And now, let's dance.'

It quickly becomes apparent that Merle is something of a perfectionist. There's barely time for any more chat as he walks me through the first steps of our routine – he's too focused on showing me exactly how he wants us to look and making sure I really understand what we're trying to achieve. I hadn't realised he'd be so competitive, but I get the impression he really wants to win the show.

He goes into minute detail about the timing and the musicality and how this hand should be here and this foot there. It turns out there's even an optimum way for me to flick my hair – who knew? But I certainly know about it now. We go over and over it, because Merle wants our performance to be flawless.

'Try to give it more *swoosh*,' he instructs, as I roll my head stiffly and my ponytail flies clunkily over my shoulder.

'It should be sexy, seductive,' he purrs.

When I still haven't got it after the twentieth attempt, he suggests we give my neck a break and starts showing me some of the footwork instead, reminding me continually to lift my chin up, hold my back straight and keep my steps nice and small.

I don't know how I'm supposed to take it all in when I'm having to concentrate so hard on keeping my eyes from drifting to his bum cheeks, which are impossibly pert in his clingy gym tights. I've never seen a body like his before – not in the flesh, at any rate. It's like his torso has been carved out of rock.

I knew he was going to be attractive before we met for the first time at the studio this morning because I googled him when I found out who l was going to be dancing with. There were only a handful of news stories about him online, detailing the various bachata championships he's won, but there were photos of him holding his trophies and he looked gorgeous in every single one of them. And yet somehow I still failed to anticipate how infatuated I'd become with him – and how quickly.

A few short hours ago I was feeling sick with nerves just at the thought of training with him. My only dance experience is the three weeks of pre-show classes I took with the other contestants ahead of my appearance on *Fire on the Dance Floor*, and I was convinced I was going to make a total fool of myself in front of him. But now all I can think about is how fit he is and how much I'd like to have sex with him. Like a teenage crush, with an X-rated certificate.

I'd like to be able to say I impress him with my progress throughout the afternoon, but I'm not sure my wild hip-swinging and arm-flailing could be classified as dancing at this stage. I suppose by the end of the week I might look less like I'm trying to shake out a spider that's fallen down my T-shirt, but I'm definitely not there when Merle announces it's time for us to call it quits for the day.

'We don't want to overdo it,' he says. 'This is just the beginning of a long journey.'

I nod enthusiastically, because I don't want to look defeatist. But based on today's efforts, it's going to take some kind of miracle to get me through the first live show, never mind all the way to the final.

'Are you feeling okay?' he asks. 'No aches and pains? Anywhere feeling a bit tight?'

I do a mental assessment of my body parts. It's so tempting to tell him I've seized up all over and that the only possible cure would be a top-to-toe massage. But of course, I don't. 'I think I'm good for now. I guess I'll find out for real in the morning.'

'Make sure you have a hot bath tonight,' he advises. 'It will help, to a degree. That's what I'll be doing when I get home.'

I blush at the thought of him naked in the tub.

I find myself dawdling as I change out of my dance shoes, wanting to prolong my time with him. When I glance up for one last surreptitious look at that glorious body of his, his bag is already flung over one shoulder, ready to go – and he's watching me fiddling with my laces. My heart flips, knowing I've been caught in the act, and I hastily scramble to my feet. 'So, er, same time tomorrow?' I stammer.

'Of course.' He smiles and leans towards me to kiss me goodbye – one cheek then the other, in the way the French do.

Only it doesn't quite work out that way. I've never known whether you're supposed to go left then right, or right then left, and somewhere in the middle I accidentally brush my lips against his. We both freeze and for a second we just stand there, not looking each other in the eye. The moment seems to drag on forever, my heartbeat pounding in my ears.

Then his bag slides off his shoulder and crashes to the floor, his mouth finds its way back on mine, and as we kiss I squeeze my eyes shut and wonder if I've entered a parallel universe where all my fantasies turn into reality. I know I've been thinking about this for most of the day and there have been one or two times when it's felt like we've been sharing a moment, but I did not, for one instant, expect the day to end like this.

He raises a hand to my cheek as his tongue tangles with mine, and I can't help reaching round to touch his buttocks. So *solid*. How can buttocks be that solid? He responds by kissing me harder and I feel him stirring in his gym tights. Has this been on his mind all day, as well, then?

I don't know how long it lasts – not as long as I'd like it to – before we eventually break away. We look at each other again and I hold my breath, not really sure what to do. But then he smiles again and says he's really pleased with how things have gone today. Dancing aside, I couldn't agree more.

'I'll see you tomorrow, Kate,' he says as he turns and heads for the door.

I stare after him, catching my breath, not quite believing what we just did. But suddenly I can't wait for our next training session.

Chapter 2

When my alarm goes off in the morning, my first thought is that I've got nine more blissful hours alone with Merle today. I can't think of anything I'd like more. I want to look my best, so I've given myself extra time to do my hair and make-up. I have a good feeling about the day ahead.

I need a coffee before I start getting ready and my flatmate is waiting in the kitchen with a mischievous smile. 'So have you come back down to earth yet?' she asks.

'Not really,' I laugh, reaching past her to check if the kettle's still hot.

She nearly choked on her wine last night when I told her what happened at the studio. Given that she practically had to bundle me out of the flat and frogmarch me to the train station to make sure I didn't bottle out of going, she was as surprised as I was by the way things turned out.

'So will there be more of the same today, do you reckon?' she asks with a twinkle in her eye.

I laugh again as I fill my mug. 'I can but hope.'

'You might fall in love,' she says dreamily. 'It happens on *Strictly* all the time.'

'To celebrities,' I remind her. 'Not to twenty-three-year-old nobodies.'

'You're not a nobody,' she says sternly. 'You're a gorgeous soon-to-be TV star who deserves her *Dirty Dancing* moment. You could even end up marrying him.'

I roll my eyes, but I have to admit I can't wait to find out if there'll be more kissing with Merle today. The dancing part is still giving me palpitations – I just can't imagine ever being good at it – but the prospect of another close encounter with a gorgeous sex god is certainly a strong incentive to get me back to the studio.

If there's more kissing today, and the next day, and maybe even every day for the whole five weeks of the competition should we make it right through to the final, who knows what might happen after that? Could it become something more?

'So, are you going to tart yourself up before you go in today?' Lucy asks. And there's no point trying to deny it – she knows me too well.

She waves her favourite leggings in the air and asks if I want to borrow them. They're black with mesh cut-outs running all the way up the sides and I always think she looks amazing when she's wearing them. I grab them from her eagerly.

'Enjoy,' she says with a wink, as she retreats to her bedroom to get ready for work.

I take a long sip of my coffee and thank my lucky stars

that I never have to go back to the crappy admin job I left to be on *Fire on the Dance Floor*. Lucy loves it at the fancy ad agency she joined a couple of months after university, and it's hardly surprising – her office even has its own bar. But I just took the first job I was offered because I thought it was important to get some work experience on my CV – then I stuck at it, even though I was bored senseless, because I didn't want future employers to think I had no staying power.

My plan had been to hang in there for a year then sign up to all the job alert sites and move on to something better. That's not how it panned out, though. Before I'd even been invited to an interview, I was hit by a bombshell at work that completely floored me, when one of the girls in the office calmly broke the news to me that she'd been seeing my boyfriend behind my back since I introduced them at a company get-together a month earlier. The shock nearly made me vomit.

Our two-year anniversary was only a few weeks away. We'd got together at university and were still going strong almost a year after graduation. Or so I thought. I don't know how I managed not to fall apart in front of my colleague as she tried to make it sound like she was doing me a favour by telling me – which she was, of course, but I couldn't see it at the time.

When I had it out with Ed, he didn't even apologise – he just said he'd post any stuff of mine he found at his flat back to me when he got a moment. His lack of emotion was another punch in the stomach. It was like I'd never meant anything to him.

11

After that, my hunt for a new employer didn't go well. As I battled with my misery, I was so convinced no one would want to hire me that I struggled to convince anyone they should. And as I didn't have enough money saved up to hand in my notice without another job to go to, I just had to put up with the torture of seeing that girl at the office every day, knowing she and Ed were now together and that everyone else at work knew it.

So you might wonder why it took so much arm-twisting to get me to eventually jack my job in and join the *Fire on the Dance Floor* line-up. The show offered the escape route I wanted and the chance to win a sizeable cash prize that would mean I'd never need to feel trapped in a job I hated ever again. But having only just suffered such a monumental humiliation, it felt like the last thing I needed was to make a fool of myself trying to tango in front of millions of people.

I had absolutely no intention of applying to go on the show when I first showed Lucy the call for contestants I'd seen on Twitter and joked about putting myself forward. But Lucy, being Lucy, had other ideas.

'This is the perfect way to get over Ed,' she declared. 'You've been moping over him for long enough. It's time to start living your life again.'

'It's only been six weeks,' I protested, but she wasn't deterred.

'This could be your new career,' she enthused. 'And if not, it would look great on your CV.'

Then she really turned on her powers of persuasion. 'And just imagine the look on your colleague's face if you told her you were leaving to be on the telly. That would stop her being so smug.'

When I still refused to apply, Lucy sent in a video application without telling me. It was a clip of me prancing around our flat when I was several bottles of champagne into a New Year's Eve celebration. It would hardly have had Beyoncé quaking in her boots.

I was furious with her when I got the email from Channel 6 asking me to come in for a meeting at their office in Hammersmith. She knew how down on myself I was feeling – it was hardly the time to be baring my soul on national television. But Lucy was adamant it would do me good to take myself out of my comfort zone and have something else to focus on.

'You've got nothing to lose by just talking to them,' she insisted. Then she turned on the persuasion again. 'They wouldn't want to meet you if they didn't think you had potential.' And, 'You'll always wonder what might have happened if you don't go for it.'

In the end I agreed to meet the show's producer, Shane Mitchell, just to get some peace. I'd go, explain why it wasn't for me, then that would be the end of that.

But Shane had an answer to every obstacle I tried to put in my way. When I told him frothy ballgowns weren't really my thing, he said that wouldn't be a problem because the show wasn't including any of the ballroom classics, only lively urban and Latin dances, in a bid to appeal to younger viewers. When I admitted I couldn't afford not to work for months on end just to take part in a dance competition, he told me they were sticking to a short run for the debut series – five weeks, so the viewers don't lose interest – and that the contestants would be paid five thousand pounds each for participating. More than I earned in my actual job.

When I asked him why on earth he thought people might be interested in seeing someone like me learning to dance, he smiled warmly and said that was exactly the point: having regular people like me on the show rather than celebrities would make it more relatable for the audience. And after that I was out of excuses. I fell silent, my head spinning while I chewed my lip until I actually tasted blood.

'We're so excited about this project and we'd really like you to be part of our success story,' Shane said, with such enthusiasm that it was hard not to be swayed.

And then something just clicked. Yes, it felt a bit like I'd be throwing myself off a cliff and just blindly hoping there weren't any rocks beneath the sea's surface. And after the way things ended with Ed, I had serious doubts about my ability to make good life choices. But I was also sick of feeling miserable. That moment when my colleague told me Ed was cheating still haunted me every single day and I wanted to stop being reminded of it. So, before I could think of any other ways to talk myself out of it, I signed on the dotted line.

I still had to suffer through my four-week notice period at work, but it was easier to handle knowing it was coming to an end. And then, before I knew it, I was free – and thrown into a whirlwind of group rehearsals, where there was so much to learn, so much to think about, that I didn't even have time to wonder if I'd done the right thing.

And here I am now, wondering why I ever hesitated.

I'm itching to get to my second day of kizomba practice with Merle – and so thankful Lucy decided she knew what was best for me.

'Gorgeous,' Lucy declares when she sees me caked in make-up and with a swishy new blow-dry. 'He won't be able to resist you.'

I hold up crossed fingers. 'I hope you're right.'

But on the way to our Kensington studio, my bravado starts to falter. What if Merle has decided kissing me was a mistake? What if I turn up looking like this while he just wants to forget all about it? The doubts crowd my mind as the Tube clanks its way across London.

By the time I reach the studio, I'm almost as nervous as I was yesterday. And I nearly jump out of my skin when I swing the door open and step inside, because he's crouched down right beside the entrance, pulling his dance shoes out of his bag.

He straightens up to his full height, studies my face and says, 'You look tense again. Are you thinking about me or are you thinking about dancing?'

I feel like I've been hit by a bolt of lightning.

Before I've even contemplated an answer, his lips are on mine and he's fighting my tongue with his. He pulls me tight against him and buries his fingers in my hair, crushing his mouth against mine. It's the most passionate kiss I've ever experienced.

'I've been thinking about that all night,' he says when we finally come up for air.

'I'd be lying if I said it hadn't crossed my mind too,' I admit breathlessly.

He pushes my hair back from my face and runs his thumb over my lips. 'We'll have a good session today, I can feel it. I think we're going to have a lot of fun together, you and me.'

I break out in goose bumps at the thought of it.

Then he switches back into teacher mode, delivering instruction after detailed instruction about the next part of our routine to ensure I get every element just right. At least this time, they're interspersed with knowing smiles and the occasional squeeze of my hand. He even uses the word 'beautiful' when I'm working on my hair flicks. I know I still haven't cracked it so I think he's just being polite, but still . . .

When we break for lunch, he pulls a salad box from his bag and sits cross-legged on the floor. I lean back against the mirror and try not to feel embarrassed about the giant ham and cheese baguette I picked up on the way here.

While we're eating, he asks me how well I know the other dances we may have to perform during the course of the competition – the salsa, rumba, bachata, cha-cha, merengue and Argentine tango. I was taught the basics during the pre-show training with the other contestants, but I can't say I know any of them well – and I still feel like an idiot when I'm trying to dance them.

I doubt this is the answer he was hoping for, so I hastily change the subject – I don't want him to focus on my shortcomings. I ask him what made him want to be a dancer in the first place.

He shrugs. 'I never wanted to be anything else. And I was fortunate. In Paris, where I lived, I had access to the best performing arts schools. I won my first competition when I was ten.'

'Ten? Wow. That's impressive.' I think my greatest achievement at that age – and possibly even since – was not coming last in the obstacle race on school sports day.

'I trained every day,' he says, his voice full of passion. 'I wanted to be the best.'

'So what made you want to do *Fire on the Dance Floor?*' I ask – then instantly wish I hadn't. Because he replies, with a certainty I don't think I've ever felt in my life, 'It's something I haven't won – but I intend to.'

I struggle to swallow the bite of sandwich I've been chewing. Much as I'd love for that to happen, he must be able to see I'm not really up to the task. I change the subject again before even more self-doubt can take hold.

'It must have been exciting, growing up in Paris. I've been a few times on the way to my sister's and I love it. It's pretty where she lives, down in the south-west, but there's so much to see and do in Paris.'

'Paris is cool, but London is my home now. I've lived here for nearly six years.'

'Oh, which bit?' I find myself hoping it's near me. 'I'm in Balham. I moved there with my mate Lucy after we graduated last summer.'

'You're not living with a boyfriend, then?' he asks, which makes the hairs on my arms stand up on end. Why else would he enquire unless he was considering himself for the role?

Still, my voice cracks just a little when I tell him I don't have a boyfriend. Ed and I had been talking about getting a place together before we split up. We might even have moved in by now if he hadn't run off with someone else. It hurts to think he might now do that with her instead.

Thankfully, Merle doesn't seem to notice my wobble. Keen to get back to rehearsing, he claps his hands, jumps to his feet and declares it's time to get back to business. And I do a pretty good job of following his lead as he teaches me the next section of the routine. I can't brood about Ed while I'm focusing on my dancing – and on the bewitching way Merle moves his body.

When my concentration does slip, I'm sure he must know that's what I'm thinking about, because it always happens when we're in one of the close contact parts of the dance or when his hand is on my lower back – lower, I'm sure, than it needs to be.

At one point, his hand brushes against my boobs. It's my fault, though I can't say I'm sorry. It momentarily throws us off our rhythm, which makes us both laugh, and I'm sure I catch him looking at them several times after that. It makes me want to stand a bit taller and invite his attention. I want him to look. It feels like the first time in ages that anyone has wanted to.

All too quickly, it reaches closing time at the studio, and once again I don't want to have to say goodbye to Merle yet. While I won't be sad to slip my aching feet out of my dance shoes and into my trainers, I want to get to know him better and I definitely want to kiss him again. There'd be nothing accidental about it this time round – not on my part, anyway.

But I can't quite find the courage to broach the subject

directly, in case he doesn't feel the same way, so I settle for asking if he fancies grabbing a bite to eat before we head home. I've secretly got it all mapped out in my head – the two of us chatting over a pint and some dinner at the pub next door, then heading back to mine afterwards for 'dessert'.

'Ah, but I can't, I'm sorry,' Merle says, crushing my little fantasy. 'I have an arrangement already.'

I know I must look disappointed, because he puts his hands on my shoulders and says, 'But we'll make up for it tomorrow.'

He massages me gently and once again I can feel the warmth of his hands through my T-shirt. 'We'll work on loosening more of this tenseness, so you can really relax into the dance.'

Then he pulls me into an embrace and I can't stop a moan escaping from my throat as his lips find mine. Never before have I been so turned on by just a kiss. It certainly wasn't like this with Ed.

I press myself into him and run my hands up his back. He slides his down to my bum and pulls me tighter against him so I can feel him stirring. Then he moves them to my breasts and rubs my nipples through my T-shirt with his thumbs, which makes me want to rip it off and feel him skin on skin.

As if he can read my mind, he reaches up underneath and pushes his fingers inside my bra, making me groan with pleasure. It's like it's the first time anyone has ever touched me there.

'I'm so sorry I have to run off this evening,' he says between kisses.

It's some time after that before he withdraws his hand.

'I have to go,' he says eventually, stepping away and reaching for his bag. 'I'm sorry,' he says again, as he walks backwards to the door. '*À demain*, Kate.'

Until tomorrow. I'm already counting down the minutes.

Chapter 3

That evening, after I've delighted Lucy with all the details of my day, she persuades me to go to our local pub, Balham Bowls Club. A guy she likes from work is going to be there and she's hoping they'll get talking away from the prying eyes of her colleagues.

We find a table in the main bar and I'm determined to go easy on the alcohol, what with rehearsals tomorrow, but Lucy has other ideas. She buys a bottle of Sauvignon Blanc and sloshes a large measure into each of our glasses.

'Steady on!' I hold my hand out to stop her pouring me any more.

'I need the Dutch courage,' she says. 'If I feel brave enough, I might ask Aiden out tonight. If you're going to get all loved-up with Merle, I need to find myself a man quick, before I've got no one left to hang out with.'

'I wouldn't say loved-up, more like in lust. But you've had a crush on Aiden for ages, so you should definitely go for it.'

As for Merle, it's true that I can't stop thinking about him. I keep imagining us glammed up on a night out at a fancy wine bar, snuggled up in a booth together while all the other girls look on with envy. Or at my flat, him padding round the kitchen in his boxers as we make breakfast together after a night of steamy sex – like Ed used to do when we first got together.

Even better, we could skip breakfast altogether and just stay in bed, naked, for a whole weekend, doing nothing but enjoying each other's bodies. Ed and I never did that. Could it happen?

'Here he is.' Lucy grips my arm and nods at the door as her colleague walks in. I can see straight away why she likes him. His whole face lights up with a beaming smile when he spots the friend he's meeting. They bump fists, then the friend waggles his half-empty glass at Aiden, who turns and makes his way to the bar.

'Go!' I urge Lucy. 'Go and talk to him.'

She nudges in beside him and I watch ten minutes of hair swinging and exaggerated laughter before she returns to our table with another bottle of wine.

'Well?' I ask.

'Well, I couldn't go to the bar then not buy anything, could I?'

I roll my eyes. 'But did you ask him?'

'No! It's too early for that.'

'But you really like him?' I don't really need to check – it's so obvious. She never usually loses her cool around guys.

'I do,' she admits.

So before she has time to stop me, I walk over to Aiden and his friend and invite them to join us. They don't hesitate and pull up chairs, Aiden squeezing in next to Lucy and saying 'Hello again,' as he flashes his infectious smile.

'This is Warren,' he says, introducing his friend.

'Kate,' I say, shaking hands. 'And Lucy, of course,' I add, pointing at my startled best mate. I know she'll thank me later.

'Looks like you ladies are planning quite a session,' Warren says, indicating the two bottles of wine on the table.

Lucy finds her tongue. 'We're celebrating. Kate's going to be famous this weekend.'

'Not famous,' I correct. 'Just on the telly.'

'Ooh, what are you in?' Warren asks.

'It's a new show called *Fire on the Dance Floor*. It's a bit like *Strictly*, but with real people rather than celebrities.'

'Wow, so you're a dancer?' He suddenly seems very interested in me.

I laugh. 'I'm working on it.'

He wants to know everything – how I came to be on the show, who I'm going to be up against, how I rate my chances of winning – and just talking about it makes me shiver. It suddenly hits home just how utterly flat I've been feeling since breaking up with Ed. But a hint of my old self might just be returning, thanks to *Fire on the Dance Floor*.

'I'll be up against six other contestants this week,' I explain to Warren. 'Then one of us will be eliminated every week until there are just three left in the final.'

'Who's the biggest threat?' he asks.

That's an easy one. 'A girl called Emilia. None of us really believe she's never danced before. She picked up all the steps on the first attempt during training – the rest of us didn't. One of the other contestants, Tammy, even smacked straight into me on the first day, because she turned the wrong way. We laughed about it though. It broke the ice and we ended up going for coffee afterwards.'

'It doesn't sound like she'll be in the running.'

'Oh, Tammy's got some moves,' I assure him. The one I feel a bit sorry for is a guy called Liam. He did okay in the group classes, but he did struggle to look graceful because he's built like a tank, whereas the other two guy contestants are really lean and flexible.'

'That must be annoying for him,' Lucy says.

'He's such a nice guy, he took it all in his stride. He just really wants to win so he can use the prize money to open a gym. He's applied for every show you can imagine – *Love Island*, *Who Wants To Be A Millionaire?* – but this is the only one he heard back from.'

'How much do you get if you win?' Warren asks.

'Twenty-five thousand.'

His eyebrows shoot up. 'Seriously? Wow! That's a decent wedge. What would you do with that kind of money?'

Of course I've asked myself the same thing, even though there's not the remotest chance of me walking away with the prize money. Hypothetically, aside from sticking a load in a savings account to give me a security blanket for my future, I'd spend a portion of it on travelling. My sister did a round-the-world trip a few years back and has always raved about how amazing it was. So I tell him I'd chuck some clothes in a backpack and head overseas for a couple of months.

'It isn't very likely though,' I hastily add. 'I haven't even got through the first week yet.'

'And how's that going?' he asks.

Lucy stifles a giggle and I shoot her a warning look. I'm not about to share those details with a complete stranger.

'It's intense, but I'm loving it,' I tell him, and leave it at that. He doesn't need to know exactly what it is I'm loving about it.

Talk then turns to what everyone else would do if they won £25,000 and at some point another bottle of wine appears. I don't really notice the room is swaying until the bell rings for last orders and I have to hang on to the back of my chair to stand up.

By this point, Lucy and Aiden are leaning into each other and it looks like things are moving in the right direction there, so I tell them I think it's time for me to go home. Warren stands up to leave with me.

'Stay,' Aiden says. 'It's still early.'

'It's midnight and it's closing,' Warren points out. 'And we've got work tomorrow. You can stay for one more, but we're heading off.'

'Okay, sure, see you later,' Aiden replies. Then he asks Lucy, 'One for the road?' and her grin gets nearly as wide as his.

Outside the pub, Warren takes my hand and asks if there's any chance I might fancy extending the evening back at his place. I'm flattered, but although I might have been tempted if he'd asked me just three days ago – it's the first time since Ed that I've clicked with someone so well conversationally and I've enjoyed our flirty banter – I tell him it's a no. Because the only person I want to extend my time with right now is Merle.

Chapter 4

It feels like someone is hammering nails straight into my skull when my alarm goes off the next morning. A hazy memory of the previous evening claws its way to the surface. Was there a fourth bottle of wine after the first three? Did we remember to eat anything? I did say no to Warren, didn't I? I fling my arm across the other half of the bed and am relieved to find it empty. That's a complication I could do without.

I sit up, then promptly lie back down again. How the hell am I going to get through today feeling like this? I'm not sure I can even make it out of my bedroom.

Spurred on by thoughts of Merle, I drag myself in the direction of the kitchen. When she hears me moving, Lucy comes bounding out of her room with the biggest grin on her face. I hold my hands up.

'Stop moving so much,' I plead. 'It's making me queasy.'

She takes the kettle from me and points me towards the table, where I flop into a chair.

'Why do you look so . . . so normal? I feel terrible!' I wail.

'Aiden and I went for pizza after the pub, to soak up some of the booze. Then we snogged on the doorstep for about an hour, like sixteen-year-olds. And then he asked if he could take me out on a proper date this evening. How cute is that?'

I'm thrilled for her and want to find out more, if only I could stop my head throbbing. I can't believe I got so carried away at the pub – I'm such an idiot.

Lucy puts a steaming cup of coffee in front of me and follows it with Marmite on toast, and gradually the world starts to feel less wobbly. A blast of ice-cold water in the shower goes some way towards clearing my brain fog and two more slices of toast help my stomach settle down. By the time I leave the flat I'm still far from top form, but I'm at least a paler shade of green.

I arrive at the studio before Merle, which is a relief because it gives me more time to compose myself. While I'm waiting for him, I catch up with the messages on the "Fire Dancers" WhatsApp chat that I set up with Liam, Tammy and another of the contestants, Beth, on the last day of pre-show training. By then we'd got into the habit of having lunch together every day, so when it was time to go off for our individual classes we promised to post regular updates.

'*How's everyone's first week going?*' Beth has asked.

'*Hard work,*' is the reply from Liam. '*I probably should have spent less time at the pub over the weekend.*'

A sentiment I currently identify with all too well.

'*I've never sweated so much in my life.*' This is from Tammy.

'*And I've got muscle aches in places I didn't even know I had muscles. I'm progressing much quicker than I did in the group classes, though.*'

'*Yeah, I'm learning loads. My teacher is so nice,*' Beth has written. '*Is everyone happy with their first dance?*'

When we finished the pre-show practice, we were each given a sealed envelope containing details of our first dance, the name of our instructor and how to find our individual studio. We were asked not to share this information with anyone before the live show, but we were all in agreement that the Argentine tango is the dance none of us wants in week one – it's by far the hardest.

'*It's not the tango,*' is Liam's response, followed by a '*ditto*' from Tammy.

'*No tango for me either,*' I type. '*Thankfully! I've made a bit of headway this week – I think. But I'm still no Emilia.*'

'*I think that goes for all of us,*' Tammy replies. '*We all know she's going to kill it on Saturday. I've been stalking her on Instagram – is that bad? I don't think she'll notice though, she's got about five thousand followers.*'

'*Five thousand?*' I repeat. That makes my ninety-four look feeble.

'*I guess that's what you get when you add a new picture every fifteen minutes,*' Tammy writes. '*Really, though, I don't care how amazing she is on Saturday. I just don't want it to be one of us who's eliminated. I know it's mean, but can it just be Dean or Theo please?*'

'*I don't think they'd be too happy,*' Liam chips in. '*I saw them together on the last day of training. I think they might have secretly got together.*'

'*What! Why didn't you say?!!!*' Tammy writes. '*That's a brilliant bit of gossip. The first FOTDF romance. I wonder if there'll be any more.*'

'*Not for me,*' Beth says, before I have a chance to say anything about Merle. She's been with her boyfriend for two years and is desperate for him to propose.

'*Well I'm definitely on the lookout,*' Tammy writes. '*My dance partner's out – he's loved-up with his wife. But there must be someone on the production team or in the audience who's single and looking to mingle. Ooh, speak of the devil, here he is. Time to get to work.*'

'*Yep, me too,*' Beth adds. '*The dance floor's waiting. See you soon, guys. Miss you!*'

My Merle revelation will have to wait.

He arrives soon after that, striding purposefully across the dance floor and smothering me with a kiss, seemingly ready to pick up where we left off yesterday. But just as quickly, he pulls away and fixes me with a look so deep it feels like it's penetrating straight into my soul. *Oh no –* please don't tell me that means he can still taste the booze on my breath. I brushed my teeth three times, and I'm sure I put on enough concealer to hide the bags under my eyes.

'I find you very hard to resist,' he growls, which is music to my ears – even though it still blows my mind that someone as gorgeous as him could be into me.

'Then don't,' I whisper, conscious of the tremor in my voice. I might be feeling a bit fragile, but I fancy him more than I've ever fancied anyone in my life. Yes, Ed was handsome in his own way, but with Merle, there's a magnetism I just can't get enough of. It makes my whole body ache.

He runs a hand down my cheek and tilts my chin up towards his. Then he brings his mouth to mine again, this time so delicately it's like he's scared I might break.

'We should get started,' he murmurs, letting his hand trail tantalisingly down my body. And for a moment I think he's talking about something other than dancing, until he says, 'We've got a lot to get through today.'

I bite back my disappointment as he turns away to change his shoes. Doesn't he realise the effect he has on me? It's almost more than I can bear.

As soon as he's ready, Merle gets us working on a section of the routine where, to put it bluntly, it feels like we're dry humping for quite a few seconds. I don't know if it's deliberate, but it makes me so aware of his body rippling against mine that I can't think about anything else. With a different instructor I would have found it painfully embarrassing, but with him I just want to lose myself in the moment.

He keeps his voice soft as he tells me when to lean into him and away again. For my arm positioning, he just guides me with his hands, running them from my shoulders to my wrists to make sure I'm fully extending, then using his thumbs to create a slight bend in my elbows before returning to my hands to tease each finger into position. My skin tingles from his touch, even after he's moved his hands away.

There's a half-spin midway through the sequence and when I'm facing away from him, I can feel his breath hot on my neck. He holds each position for longer than we will in real time – to give my muscle memory time to develop, he says. Because he can't tear himself away from me, is what I want to believe.

Once we're facing each other again, we barely break eye contact. His irises seem to have turned a shade darker and the intensity of his gaze makes my knees feel weak. I don't think anyone has ever looked at me so deeply: like nothing matters in the universe but me. I can't tear my eyes away from his. I've never felt so captivated – or so captivating.

I think I might explode when he murmurs huskily, 'I want you, Kate.'

'I want you too,' I whisper, my heart pounding. My God, do I want him.

Without another word, our mouths crush together and we're pulling each other closer, one of his hands moving straight to my breasts, my own quickly finding their way under his T-shirt.

He sighs when I trace the lines of his six-pack, and steps back to pull his top up over his head. I try not to stare as he drops it onto the floor behind him. I know I've been thinking about this since the second I laid eyes on him, but I can't believe it's actually happening, right here in the studio.

It occurs to me that I was with Ed for more than a month before we saw each other naked, whereas I hardly know Merle. But for once, I don't care. I'm so attracted to him that I don't care if we're moving at the speed of light. As he comes closer and helps me lift my vest top up over my head, it feels reckless and exciting. Look where waiting got me, anyway.

His eyes drink in my breasts before he starts caressing them through the lace of my bra. I push them towards him and he groans and reaches behind me, releasing the catch and letting it fall to the floor. Then he brings his thumbs back to my nipples and my hangover becomes a distant memory.

He spins me round to face the mirror and stands behind me, kissing the back of my neck and reaching round to tweak my nipples. I watch our reflection and feel the heat building between my legs.

When his hand drops lower it sends a million currents through my body. He rolls my leggings down and lifts my feet to free me from the material, then he runs his hands back up my legs, strokes my waist, moves back up to my breasts, taking his own sweet time.

I try to turn back towards him, but he shakes his head no and continues to run his fingers all over my body, bringing every nerve to life as I watch in the mirror. The longer he takes, the more urgently I want him, but at the same time I don't want him to ever stop touching me.

When he eventually works his way back to my clitoris, he stays there for a deliciously long time, circling with his fingers while he grinds himself against my naked backside. Then he replaces his hands with mine and urges me to carry on.

'Let me watch you touch yourself,' he says, stepping back to free himself from his gym tights.

I stroke myself tentatively. It's not something I've done in front of someone before – Ed would never have suggested it. But when I see how Merle can't peel his eyes away, I push aside my self-consciousness and move my fingers faster. It's not long before he moves back in behind me and places his hands over mine.

I can feel his erection against my back as he uses a finger to push my own up inside me, guiding my movements like he's choreographing a dance. It makes me gasp. How could I not have known I could feel this aroused?

'You're so wet,' he whispers, as he withdraws his hand and trails it back up my body. He runs his fingers over my lips, pushing one into my mouth, and moans softly when I suck on it. Then his hands are back on my breasts, squeezing and teasing while he watches me respond to his touch.

Taking my hands again, he places them against the cold glass and I think he's going to enter me from behind, but he drops to his knees and spreads my buttocks, taking my breath away as he starts licking me in a way I've never experienced before.

I nearly come like that, steadying myself on the mirror as he pulls me onto his face. But before I do, he draws me down onto our discarded clothes with him and straddles me as I lie on my back. He pushes two fingers up into me, using his other hand to mirror the movements on the outside, and we don't break eye contact as a back-arching burst of pleasure rips right through me. Having him watching me writhe in ecstasy as I come makes it feel even more intimate, like I'm showing him a part of me that no one else knows.

When he starts stroking himself, I reach up to take over, but he blocks my hand and says, 'Let me.'

I watch the muscles contracting in his stomach as he finds his rhythm and gets closer to orgasm. He doesn't take his eyes off me when his hips start juddering. He comes above me with a quiet roar.

When he runs his hands over my body one last time it feels like we've shown each other all our secrets.

Chapter 5

'So, how's it going with the sexy dance teacher?' my sister Dee asks innocently later that evening, when I log on for our weekly Skype chat. She's squashed in between my parents on the sofa and I can hear my niece and nephew playing in the background.

'Great,' I tell her, hoping they don't notice me blushing. 'I'm learning new things every day.'

And I don't just mean how to have the best orgasms of my life. It turns out getting intimate with Merle did wonders for my dancing. All my inhibitions went out of the window after being so open with him, so the stiffness I struggled with on the previous two days completely vanished for the rest of the rehearsal. I can only hope it won't be back tomorrow.

'That's good,' Mum says. 'So are you feeling confident about the live show on Saturday? We do feel terrible that we're not going to be there.'

Every summer my parents go to France for the holidays.

They're both teachers, so it's the only opportunity they get to spend a reasonable chunk of time with Dee and the grandkids. They did offer to cancel when I told them about *Fire on the Dance Floor*, but I wouldn't let them. I know how much they love their summers there and they can see me any time. It hasn't stopped them feeling guilty, though.

'You don't have to worry, Mum. I'm in good hands with Merle. He's a professional, so he knows how to make me look good. And Lucy will be there to support me on the night – and Rach from school.'

Each contestant is allowed two guests for the live shows so I've invited my best friend and my oldest friend.

'Well, we'll be cheering you on remotely,' Mum says. 'And I'm glad you're getting on so well with your teacher. Have you been socialising together, too?'

'Not yet.' Not in the way she means, at any rate. 'But I'm sure we'll do something on Saturday night after the show.'

I would have postponed tonight's Skype chat if Merle had been up for sharing a bottle of rosé in a sunny beer garden, but he'd had another appointment to get to. At least he told me before I asked this time, though, so while I was disappointed after everything that had happened earlier, I didn't feel rejected.

'That'll be nice,' Mum says.

'And how are the old nerves holding up?' Dad asks.

'Hm, so-so.'

Before I left the studio this evening, Merle reminded me that a camera crew will be joining us tomorrow to film us rehearsing. The footage they capture will be edited down into a three-minute segment that will be played on the live show.

'So we'll have to be on our best behaviour,' he warned.

It made me realise I've been in complete denial about the fact that there's going to be an actual show at the end of all our practices. There weren't any cameras during the pre-show training, so it was easy to pretend I was just doing a few Zumba classes with my mates. And what I got up to with Merle this morning hardly felt like something that's going to be watched by thousands of people. But with the video team coming to our studio tomorrow, it suddenly feels a bit more real.

'You're bound to feel a bit anxious,' Dad says. 'But hopefully Merle can find a way to help you relax.'

My cheeks start burning again when I think about the way he's found. Thankfully, my niece and nephew choose that exact moment to squeeze in front of the screen to say hello to their Auntie Katie, so I don't have to respond to Dad.

'Hi Nathan! Hi Daisy!' I give them a wave. Then the conversation gets chaotic as the kids run in and out of the room, wanting to show me their latest drawings and the cupcakes they made earlier.

'Hi Kate!' Dee's husband Pete sticks his face in front of the camera. 'Just clearing up in the kitchen. I'll join you in a minute.'

He disappears again and is replaced by a big hairy nose as their dog decides to give the screen a good sniff to see what all the fuss is about.

'Ah, I wish I was there,' I sigh, suddenly missing the craziness of a full household.

'Come over as soon as you've finished with the show,' Dee says. 'The kids would love to see you. We all would.'

'I will,' I promise.

We chat for another hour until it's time for her to get Nathan and Daisy to bed. Mum signs off by sending me a virtual hug, telling me how proud she is of me and making me promise I'll keep her updated on my progress.

'And good luck for Saturday. We'll all be rooting for you.'

I switch off my laptop, feeling bathed in a warm family glow. But as soon as I climb into bed, my thoughts drift back to Merle and the show and the day of filming that lies ahead. I usually try to avoid being filmed – it tends to result in cringey videos like the New Year's Eve one that became my audition tape. And that was only a minute long. My stomach churns at the thought of having a camera on me for hours.

I wonder if I'll get any alone time with Merle afterwards. When I think back to this morning, I can almost feel his hands on my body, touching my breasts, caressing my bum. I picture him going down on me and start feeling aroused. I wish he was here now.

I roll over and bury my face in my pillow, trying to clear my mind so I'll be able to sleep, but I can't stop thinking about it: his tongue between my legs, my body juddering until I can take no more. I reach for the vibrator in my bedside cabinet, wondering what has come over me.

The intoxicating tingling quickly builds up as I picture us back in the studio. He comes towards me, lifts me up and wraps my legs around his back.

'I need to be inside you,' he whispers, resting my back

against the wall. Then he pushes up into me, making my whole body feel alive.

My breasts bounce against his chest as his thrusts get faster. I can feel myself tightening around him as my orgasm creeps closer, making us both groan with pleasure.

'I'm going to come,' I whisper, feeling myself starting to lose control.

Then my body bucks against the bed in a powerful climax till I collapse against the pillow, my head in a delicious spin.

Chapter 6

I wake up with a gasp, followed by a sigh of relief when I realise the giant camera relentlessly chasing me up a steep hill is just a bad dream – a classic anxiety-fuelled nightmare. If this is what the thought of filming in our little studio does to me, what on earth am I going to be like when the live shows start?

While I'm doing my make-up, Lucy raves about her date with Aiden. He took her for a fancy meal and they're going to meet up again on Friday for a movie night. Seeing her so happy gives me hope for my own romantic future.

'And how was it with Merle yesterday?' she asks.

'Incredible,' I grin, shivering at the memory.

'Ooh, does that mean things have progressed?'

She claps her hands with increasing enthusiasm as I give her a rundown, then she peppers me with questions about the size of his penis, whether he shaves his balls and what his come face looks like. Typical Lucy.

But I'm happy to replay all the details. I can't stop going

on about him and how he makes me feel like a goddess. He's unveiled a side of me I didn't even know existed.

'I'm glad I've got Aiden or I'd be dying of jealousy,' Lucy says, taking over the styling of my hair when she sees me struggling with the back. She twists it into long, loose waves so it bounces round my shoulders.

'Is it too much?' I ask when we look at the finished result. I'm worried I look like I'm going clubbing rather than to a daytime dance rehearsal.

'Not at all. Why shouldn't you look fantastic? It's your TV debut.'

'This bit is just us in training, though.'

I don't want to look stupid or over the top.

'Merle will love it,' she assures me. 'Do you really want to tone it down?'

And the truth is, I don't. I want Merle not to be able to take his eyes off me. I know we won't be able to rip each other's clothes off while the cameras are there, but I still want him to be thinking about it. And when they're gone . . .

Merle, however, barely glances up when I arrive at the studio, because he's busy telling the three people who I assume are the camera crew where he wants them to put their equipment so it's not in our way. I try not to let this upset me – I can see he's in work mode – but I can't help feeling a bit put out after the effort I've made.

When he does come over and greet me, it's a courteous peck on each cheek that feels awkward and formal. I want the other Merle back. There's a very different atmosphere in the studio with the other three present – it definitely feels overcrowded.

'This is really weird,' I whisper to him.

'Don't worry.' He pats my arm in the way a colleague might, not a lover. 'We just do our thing and they do theirs.'

'All of our thing?' I ask, with what I hope is a seductive smile, wanting some reassurance that things haven't changed between us since yesterday.

'No!' he says sharply, making me flinch. But then his expression softens. 'We'll save the best bits for after they've gone.'

And my alarm dissipates. He hasn't had a change of heart after all. He's just being professional while the camera team is here, that's all.

'Come and meet the others,' he says. 'This is the shoot director Sarah. Steve and Andy here are on lights and mics. Everyone, this is Kate.'

We shake hands and say hello.

'It's nothing to worry about,' Sarah says, making me think I must still look a bit shellshocked from my exchange with Merle. 'We'll just film a bit of you dancing, a bit of you talking about how things are going so far, then we'll chuck in something funny at the end to give the audience a laugh. We'll probably need an hour or two of your time at the most. Sound okay?'

I take a deep breath to steady my nerves. 'Sounds perfect.'

I want to get this over with as quickly as possible.

'Okay, let's start by filming you arriving,' Sarah suggests. 'We're going to pretend it's still Monday and that this is the first time the two of you have met, so try to look excited when you come through the door.'

I leave the room and try to convince myself this is perfectly normal. I'm just walking into the studio. How hard can it be?

But it doesn't feel natural, and apparently it doesn't look it either, so we end up having to film it again. And then a few more times, while my cheeks flush redder and redder with embarrassment. In between each take, Merle wants to watch a playback on Sarah's laptop, which takes ages because she has to remove the memory card from the camera, transfer it to her MacBook then wait for the file to download. And every time, Merle shakes his head and points out something he's not happy with.

'Again please,' he says for what feels like the hundredth time, and I realise it was wildly optimistic that the filming would only take a couple of hours. I'm not sure it's ever going to end.

'You're doing great,' Sarah tells me. 'Just try to relax a bit more, and don't look directly at the camera. I know it's hard but try to pretend it's not there. And remember to smile. Right, one more time . . . '

When Merle is finally satisfied, we move on to filming part of our dance routine. Even though Sarah is the expert, Merle has his own ideas about where the camera should be to capture our best angles, which results in a few animated exchanges. Standing awkwardly while they bicker, I tell myself it's a good thing that he wants us to look our best.

Merle continues to watch each take on the laptop and find fault with all of them. A lot of it's because I'm so tense that he can't lead me through the moves properly. I find myself wishing he wasn't such a perfectionist and I suspect Sarah feels much the same way. I think we both breathe a sigh of relief when Merle finally gives one of the clips a nod of approval.

Thankfully, the part where she films us chatting is easier, because Merle jumps straight in and does most of the talking, so I don't feel like I'm messing things up. There's no more breaking into a sweat every time he wants to start over; I just keep a smile plastered on my face and nod enthusiastically while he talks about the amazing progress we're making with our kizomba, even if I think he's exaggerating.

Sarah wants to finish up by having us do something that shows how much fun we're having. There isn't much in the way of props in the studio, but she brings a chair into the middle of the room, finds some music on her phone and proposes a game of musical chairs for two.

She has us dancing round in a circle till she stops the music, then racing to be first onto the seat. On the first attempt, Merle crashes into me and makes me tumble to the floor.

'Cut!' he demands stroppily as he hauls me up.

'Are you okay?' he asks, brushing dust from my leggings. It's the first intimate gesture of the day. I nod. I'm mildly mortified, but I'm not hurt.

'Are you sure this is a good idea?' he asks Sarah.

'Can we just try it one more time?' she says.

It takes nine more attempts before Merle is happy with the scene Sarah has captured – of him and me both ending up on the chair, back to back, nodding at the camera with our arms folded across our chests. If I'm honest, it seems a bit cheesy to me, and I feel a flicker of unease about the show on Saturday night, but Merle doesn't appear to share my concerns, and neither does Sarah, so I must just not be seeing whatever it is they're seeing.

'I think that's it then,' Sarah says. 'We've got everything we need.'

I want to hug her. I've been dying to hear those words for hours. I watch impatiently as she starts packing up her gear with Steve and Andy.

'Thanks for your perseverance, everyone,' she says when they're done. 'I know it's been a bit of a slog, but I think you'll agree it was worth it.'

It's all I can do not to cheer as Merle pushes the door closed behind them. I can't believe how long it's taken and how little of the day we have left – although I'm not sure how much fun the remaining time will be if Merle doesn't drop his professionalism. I breathe a sigh of relief when he tucks a loose strand of hair behind my ear and kisses me the minute we're alone again.

'Today has given me an idea,' he says, taking my hand and leading me to the middle of the dance floor. 'There's something I want to try to help you feel the steps and not just step them.'

'Sounds intriguing.' I smile. I think I know what's coming next, and I'm so ready for it.

He pushes my arms into the air and slides my top up over my head, making my smile double in size.

'Close your eyes,' he instructs, and I shiver with anticipation as I do as he says.

I hear him crossing the room and rummaging around in his bag. Then he walks back to me and slides something silky over my eyes. It's a scarf, which he ties in a loose knot behind my head, blindfolding me.

I hold my breath, not sure I like being so vulnerable, but as he trails his fingers over my skin, I realise I want him to do whatever it is he has in mind. I don't doubt he'll make sure I enjoy it.

He releases the catch on my bra and lets it fall to the floor. I wait for the feel of his hands on my breasts, but it doesn't come. I force myself to be patient.

He lifts my feet one by one, to remove my shoes, and places my bare feet back on the cool wood. Trailing his hands up my leggings, he pauses on the waistband, then he rolls them down over my hips, lifting my feet again to free me from the material. As he repeats the process with my underwear, I'm so conscious of my nakedness that my heart starts pounding. But his hands still don't explore my body.

Just as I'm about to beg him to do something, anything, he takes my arms and moves them up to his shoulders, nudging his leg between mine – the starting position of our dance. My nipples brush against the smooth material of his T-shirt, sending currents through my body as he starts walking us through the steps, slowly at first, then a little faster until we're eventually at the full speed.

The sensation of his clothes brushing against my bare skin is so arousing. As he uses his body to guide mine, I feel like I've become an extension of him, moving wherever he wants me to go.

He breaks away twice, once to put our music on, so we can dance to our song, and the second time I don't know what for, until he slides my blindfold off and I realise he was filming us.

'Merle! What the hell?'

'Don't be angry, please,' he soothes. 'I just want you to see how you look when you're truly feeling the dance.'

'But you should have asked; it's not—'

'Trust me,' he says, pressing the phone into my hands and moving round behind me so he can watch over my shoulder.

'Just watch it once,' he whispers when I hesitate to press play. 'Then we'll delete it, I promise.'

'From the Cloud, too?' I can hear the anxiety in my voice.

He puffs his breath out. 'I never store anything. Why open yourself up to the risk of hacking?'

And I waver. Instinct tells me to delete it immediately – he can't film me naked without my permission and just assume it's okay. But curiosity gets the better of me. What do I look like when I'm nude, exposed, but engrossed in our dance and so ridiculously turned on? I kind of want to know.

So I take a deep breath and start the video, telling myself it's happened now, so I might as well see it. And what I don't predict is how indescribably erotic it is watching myself pressed up against him while we move across the dance floor. We look completely immersed in each other and our routine looks all the better for it. I had no idea I could look like that.

As the recording plays out, Merle reaches for my breasts and I moan softly as my nipples harden under his touch.

'Play it again,' he whispers huskily as he moves his hands downwards and starts working his magic down below. It's suddenly harder to concentrate on the screen.

As the routine comes to an end for the second time, he takes the phone from me and drops it into his bag, finally pulling me into a full embrace. We kiss for a long time until he steps back to strip his own clothes away.

'I came prepared this time,' he says, pulling a yoga mat out of his bag and unfurling it on the floor. We lower ourselves onto it and he smothers me with kisses before rolling on top of me.

I move my legs up onto his shoulders before he enters me, so he can push in deep, and in an instant all the earlier frustrations of the day evaporate from my mind. All I can think about now is that one part of my body where everything is happening – the glorious, all-encompassing sensations that are already taking over me.

I can't take my eyes off Merle as his forehead creases in concentration and his biceps bulge from the effort of supporting himself. I move my hands to my breasts, thinking back to how sexy I felt before when he watched me touch myself, which makes him lose his rhythm and slam against me, sending waves of pleasure rocketing through me.

Sensing I'm about to come, he pulls away and drops my legs back to the floor, burying his face between them till I lose control under the expert flicks of his tongue. But he keeps going, stretching my orgasm out for longer than I ever knew was possible.

Pulling away again, he deftly flips me over and draws me up onto my knees so he can enter me from behind. My head spins lightly and my arms feel weak as he slams against me, but I don't want him to stop. I don't want this feeling to ever stop. My nipples are tingling and I can feel my wetness everywhere – on my thighs, between my buttocks. He grabs my hips and crashes against me one final time as he lets out his now-familiar roar.

'I knew my idea would work,' he says when we're lying side by side afterwards, catching our breath. 'I think you feel it now. I think you're ready.'

And for the first time, I let myself believe he might be right.

Chapter 7

When I tell Lucy about it over breakfast the next morning, I leave out the video detail, not wanting her to judge me or think badly of Merle. I know she'll think he was way out of line because that was my first thought, too. But I don't know if she'll understand that after I watched it, I was glad Merle had done it – because the girl in the video was sexy and adventurous and that's what I needed to see. And he promised to delete it, so there's no real harm done.

'It all sounds so raunchy,' she sighs. 'I bet you're gagging to get back to the studio today.'

'If they hadn't booted us out to close up last night, I'd probably still be there,' I laugh.

'You must be getting pretty close to each other now, too, with all the time you're spending together.'

'Closer,' I concede, 'but we haven't actually done that much talking. We're either dancing or sticking our tongues down each other's throats. Before we left last night, Merle said I'm a much better dancer after sex. So I told him we'd better do a lot more of that.'

She grins. 'You'd better get going then. You don't want to miss out.'

But I don't think there's any danger of that. After the last two days, I'm confident today will not be rated PG.

Merle doesn't whip his clothes off as soon as I arrive at the studio, though, which I'd half been expecting. We kiss, and I can feel him getting aroused as I run my hands over his buttocks, but then he breaks away so we can get stuck into our last rehearsal. Our kizomba may be looking pretty slick now, and Merle is confident we won't be eliminated from the competition tomorrow, but he still wants to use every available second for a bit more practice.

Given that finessing the intricate details mostly involves him running his hands up and down my body, folding me into a back bend with his leg between mine and pulling me tight against him in a rippling motion, the day is not without its provocative moments. But it's not until midway through the afternoon that things get really steamy again.

It starts when Merle sits on the chair we used as a prop yesterday to retie one of his shoes and I take a moment to stretch my legs, bending over and locking my hands behind my ankles to relieve my hamstrings. When I straighten up, he's checking out my bum, a lustful look on his face.

'Come here and do that again,' he suggests, widening his legs and beckoning me to stand between them. A smile spreads across my face as I walk towards him.

I don't do what he proposes, though. Yesterday I let him have all the control and I feel a sudden urge to take some of it back. I push his knees back together and straddle him, lifting his chin so I can kiss him, then I take his hands and move them to my breasts, feeling his smile grow wider as I push my tongue into his mouth and rock gently in his lap.

When I pause to yank my top over my head, his eyes shift straight to my breasts. I'm wearing a push-up bra that I know makes them look huge, especially from this angle. I guide his hand inside the material and smile as he starts playing with my nipples.

Feeling him stir down below, I slide backwards off his lap and down into a crouch between his knees, telling him to raise his hips so I can pull his gym tights down and out of the way. Then I take him in my mouth, and watch his knuckles whiten as he grips the chair while I slide my lips all the way to the base.

He pushes himself towards me, hovering halfway off the seat until I put a hand on his chest to stop him.

'I'm doing this my way today,' I say firmly, and he sinks back into the chair, happy, it seems, to let me dominate.

Eventually I stand up to continue undressing and he doesn't take his eyes off me, stroking himself while he watches. Then I push his knees back together and straddle him again, facing him so I'll be able to watch him come. When I lower myself towards his lap I do it slowly so that only his tip enters me. Then I push a fraction deeper with every bounce till he's all the way inside me.

He reaches under my bum to lift me again and this time

I slam against him, making the chair scrape backwards on the floor. He buries his face in my breasts as I roll forwards and backwards in his lap, then he raises me and crashes me against him again. I wonder if the chair is going to hold out.

'Again,' he pleads, and I rise and fall above him, my breasts bumping against his chest. The chair slides further back with every thrust.

Merle throws his head back and growls as he fights not to come too quickly, but he's so hard inside me I know he's close. He moves one hand to my breasts and finds my clit with the other, circling and flicking in a ragged rhythm that makes me bounce even faster until we're both crying out as we climax at the same time, something I've never experienced with anyone before. It makes every orgasm I had before meeting Merle pale into insignificance.

For a moment we cling on to each other, breathless and panting, then I close my eyes and lean my head against his, feeling the tremor in my thighs and the smile creeping onto my lips. God, I love having sex with this man.

Gradually his breathing gets less heavy.

'So,' he says eventually. 'Our last few hours of practice. Shall we continue?'

Back to work it is, then.

It's not until he catches me massaging my thighs, which are tired from the sex as well as the dancing, that he decides we should call it a day.

'We're in good shape for tomorrow,' he says. 'And we don't want to risk being too tired to give our best performance when it matters.'

With that in mind, I don't even think about suggesting a quick drink to round off our first week of rehearsals. It's going to be a long day at Channel 6 tomorrow – they want us in at eleven a.m., even though the live recording doesn't start until seven p.m. – so any socialising is definitely best left till after the show now.

If we make it through to the next round, and I so hope we do, we'll celebrate afterwards. And as Sunday is a rest day for all the contestants, there'll be no rehearsals to get up for, so there's no reason not to make a night of it.

I'm not even allowing myself to think about what might happen if it doesn't go well in front of the cameras. I can't bear the thought of waking up on Monday and not having another week of private coaching with Merle to look forward to. I want to be back in our cosy Kensington studio with him even more than I want to win the *Fire on the Dance Floor* prize money.

'This week has really been something,' Merle says, tilting my chin up to kiss me goodbye. 'Let's keep up the momentum.'

And I play these words over and over in my head on my way back to Balham, breaking into a grin every time I think about what they mean. He's just confirmed what I was hoping for all along – that this is just the beginning.

Chapter 8

It's still dark when I open my eyes the next morning, but I can't get back to sleep. I've got that same buzz of anticipation I used to get as a kid on Christmas Day. But by the time Lucy and Aiden surface and join me in the kitchen for breakfast I've had too much time to think and my stomach is doing somersaults.

Even though I know the routine off by heart now, even though I trust Merle completely and am confident his sultry choreography will impress the judges and the audience, even though I feel like we couldn't have done any more to make our performance perfect, I can't stop fretting about all the things that might go wrong today. What if I get stage fright and freeze on the dance floor? What if I tread on his toes? It's one thing dancing in a private studio behind closed doors with no one watching, but what if I make a total mess of things in front of everybody?

To make matters worse, Rachel has been called away with work at the last minute, so I haven't even got a full support team for my *Fire on the Dance Floor* debut. I doubt I'll find a replacement at this short notice.

'I'm not going,' I tell Lucy, shaking my head. 'I can't go through with it.'

'Oh no. What's changed? You seemed quite relaxed about it yesterday.'

'I've had a reality check. I'm not ready to put myself out there.'

'But you've got this,' she says, squeezing my shoulders. 'You're going to be brilliant. You've been working so hard.'

'You're bound to have pre-show nerves,' Aiden adds. 'I bet all the others have, too. I'm sure they'll all be just as worried as you are.'

'But Merle's not going to let you do anything stupid,' Lucy reassures me. 'So you don't need to worry. I think you're going to blow everyone away. I can't bloody wait to see you up there doing your thing.'

'Rachel's not coming either,' I tell her.

'What, again?' Lucy frowns. It's not the first time Rachel has let me down. 'What's it this time? Her job again?'

I nod sullenly.

'Well, I'm sure Aiden will step in if you want him to,' she suggests. And there's such hope in her voice that I tell him he'd be welcome. Not least because it saves me trying to find someone else at the eleventh hour – the last thing I need right now.

'So you are going!' Lucy claps her hands triumphantly. 'I knew you'd see sense. Tell you what, I'll jump on the Tube with you when you're ready to go. We've got no plans today till we come down for the show later.'

'You don't have to do that.'

'I want to make sure you get there. I've put a bet on you to go through to the next round so I don't want you to bottle out en route,' she laughs.

'Lucy!' I put my head in my hands. 'Like I need any more pressure.'

'I've got faith in you.' She gives my arm an encouraging squeeze. 'You're going to smash it.'

I'm glad one of us is so sure.

My palms sweat for the whole Tube journey and my anxiety is off the scale by the time we arrive in Channel 6's sunlit atrium. The thought of seeing Merle is making me just as jumpy as our imminent performance. How will he act? How will I? Will he just play it cool like he did in front of the camera crew?

I'm greeted by an enthusiastic girl with a clipboard, who 'can't wait to take me through to where the rest of the dancers are having a morning coffee before things get exciting'.

'Good luck,' Lucy calls after me, but my confidence dissolves even further as she waves goodbye. I was crazy to think I could pull this off. I'm not a dancer or a TV star. I'm just Kate who works in admin. I don't know why I let Lucy talk me into it. I should never have agreed to take part.

My heart races as I follow Clipboard Girl through a maze of corridors, recognising parts of it from my first visit here to meet Shane. But instead of heading to his office, she leads me to a reception room lined with red velvet seating, where a few small groups of people are sitting chatting. I can barely take it all in as she ushers me into the room and tells me to make myself at home, pointing out the drinks machine and telling me to help myself to refreshments.

It's a relief when I realise two of the people chatting in a corner are Tammy and Liam. Seeing their familiar faces briefly makes everything feel a fraction less terrifying. I can't wait to get over there and talk to them.

Clipboard Girl explains where I can find the toilets and the fire exits and tells me she'll be back when the last few people have arrived. I practically sprint across the room to Liam and Tammy as soon as she's gone.

'I think I'm having a panic attack,' I announce by way of greeting. 'I'm hyperventilating.'

'Whoa, girl, take a breath,' Tammy says. 'It is mad finally being here, isn't it? I think we're all feeling the pressure.'

'I brought some Dutch courage with me,' Liam confesses, showing us the hip flask in the top of his rucksack.

'Liam!' Tammy exclaims. 'You can't get pissed before you go on TV.'

'I won't be pissed. Just a little looser around the hips. I might as well tell you now – I've got the salsa.'

'Nice,' Tammy nods. 'I've got the merengue. What about you, Kate?'

'Kizomba. It's going to be so weird doing it in front of an actual audience.'

'It will, but I'm excited,' Tammy says. 'Elijah seems happy with what we've rehearsed and he knows what he's talking about. That's my pro partner, by the way. When he's not doing this he's teaching classes at Bar Salsa on Charing

Cross Road, so this is a big deal for him. He can't wait to get out there.'

Beth comes running over, out of breath and sloshing her coffee over the side of her cup.

'My bloody train broke down – I thought I was never going to get here. That was not what I needed this morning. How's everyone feeling? What have I missed?'

'We're all fine, and you haven't missed anything,' Liam assures her. 'We're just waiting till everyone is here then we'll find out what happens next. You're not even the last one.'

'Oh, phew.'

She turns to scan the room to see who we're still waiting for and I do the same, although it's really only Merle I'm looking for. And there he is. He has his back to me but there's no mistaking his broad shoulders and pert bum. He's talking to a guy and a girl I don't recognise, but they must be two of the other pro dancers judging by their physiques. I don't know whether he's seen me or not, so I try not to feel upset that he hasn't come and said hello. God, I hope I don't let him down today.

There's another group who look like pro dancers chatting by the drinks machine. And Emilia is standing nearby with Theo, although she's ignoring him and scrolling through her phone. It looks like only Dean is missing.

'That's my partner Valentina,' Liam says, pointing towards a dancer with long brown hair.

'And mine, Gabriel, the one next to her,' Beth says. 'That's not his real name though – he's really called Clive but he's using Gabriel to sound more exotic. You can't tell anyone else though – he'd kill me.'

Before I can point out Merle, Clipboard Girl arrives with Dean, and once he's joined Theo on the other side of the room the day officially begins. She introduces herself as Olivia and explains how the schedule is going to work. We'll go to hair and make-up two at a time and while some people are there, another person will go to the costume department and someone else will head to the studio for a dress rehearsal with their pro partner. After each element, we're to return to this room so she can tell us where we need to be next.

'It's a strict timetable, so we all have to be where we're meant to be when we're meant to be there,' she says.

'She's fierce,' Liam whispers. 'We'd better do what we're told.'

'Shh!' Tammy nudges him with her elbow.

'The reason we've got you in so early today is because we've got a lot of prep to get through,' Olivia continues. 'But you will find there's a fair bit of hanging around, because we have all the pro dancers to get ready too, so we ask you to wait in this room whenever you're not due to be anywhere else. Please don't stray too far in case we need you for something – and because this building is a bit of a maze, it's easy to get lost. A light lunch will be served in here between one p.m. and two. If you've got any food allergies please come and let me know.'

'I'm already starving,' Liam mutters, patting his stomach.

'Shh!' Tammy and I whisper simultaneously, making us giggle.

Olivia sends a stern look our way then continues. 'And now I'm going to introduce you to all the dancers. You'll obviously know your own, but over there we have Gabriel Romero, who's dancing with Beth Atkins, and there is Daniele Sala, who's partnered with Theo Edwards.'

They raise their hands to identify themselves as their names are called out in turn, and my heart flutters when she gets to Merle.

'Next up is Merle Picard – give everyone a wave, Merle!' Olivia instructs.

'Holy crap, is he real?' Tammy mutters.

'Jesus,' Beth whispers. 'Someone got lucky.'

'Merle is dancing with Kate Wareing,' Olivia announces, and my cheeks flush as they both turn to look at me.

'Is he single?' Tammy asks. 'He's a god!'

'Hands off, he's all mine,' I laugh.

After introducing the rest of the dancers, Olivia calls out my name and tells me I'll be first to get my hair done. Theo is coming too, 'so his skin can be made camera-ready'. Olivia tells us she'll come back to collect us when we've both been beautified. I guess I'll have to catch up with Merle later.

For the next hour, Theo and I make small talk while Hannah the hair lady backcombs some volume into my hair and Layla from make-up buries Theo's face under layers of foundation and powder.

'It's so the lights don't wash you out,' she explains.

Afterwards, we swap places and Layla applies more make-up to my face than I would usually get through in a month, but I have to admit the end result is impressive. Dramatic flashes of green glitter frame my eyes, and the false eyelashes and lashings of eyeliner make them look huge. I'm not used to thinking of myself as alluring, but it's what I would say about someone else who looked like this.

Back in the reception room, there's just enough time for Tammy to tell me I look gorgeous before she's called away by Olivia for her own makeover. I sit drinking coffee with Liam and Beth while we wait for our next appointments. So far Beth has had her costume fitting and she's now dressed in a floaty ice-blue dress, and Liam has done his dress rehearsal with Valentina and tells us the set is spectacular, designed to look like the colourful streets of Havana. I can't wait to see it.

For the rest of the day, the other pro dancers come in and out of the reception room. Beth and Tammy spend some time chatting to their partners Gabriel and Elijah, and Liam even invites Valentina to join us for lunch. Not that any of us – except Liam – eat much. I'm far too nervous.

Merle doesn't even show up to grab a coffee. But the mystery of his whereabouts is solved when Beth comes back from hair and make-up midway through the afternoon.

'Apparently your one is a bit of a diva,' she says. 'Layla told me he's the only one of the dancers who's got his own dressing room.'

I try not to let on how hurt I am by this revelation, and the fact that he's chosen to hide away in there all day rather than spending any time with me. Surely he must realise I could do with a bit of reassurance to calm my nerves. I'd thought I could rely on him to keep me level-headed.

It's not till an hour before the live show that I finally get to see him. Olivia drops me off at the studio for our dress rehearsal and there he is, making himself at home in one of the judges' chairs – working out the best angle for us to start with, he later tells me.

'Thirty minutes max, okay?' Olivia says. 'We're behind schedule and the audience starts arriving at six-thirty sharp.'

'*Pas de problème*,' Merle replies, hauling himself up and holding his hand out towards me.

I ignore it at first, furious with him for abandoning me all day. But at the same time I'm so relieved to see him at last that all I really want to do is fling myself into his arms. Instead, I look around and drink in the huge space around us. It doesn't make me feel any better.

Behind the judges' chairs there are rows and rows of seats for the audience – which look daunting enough when they're empty, never mind when they're full of people. I try to convince myself it's nothing to worry about, but I couldn't be more intimidated. It's so different to our Kensington studio – it feels so exposed.

Kelly from costumes has put me in an emerald-green sequinned catsuit and I can feel my skin prickling with sweat beneath it. I'm glad I didn't eat any lunch – it's too tight to hide any lumps or bumps – but that does mean all the caffeine I've drunk on an empty stomach is making me even more jittery.

Merle's biceps are bulging under a skin-tight black top with a flash of green sequins across one shoulder. His black trousers hug his bum and thighs, and another green flash shines across one hip. He looks hotter than ever, but as much as that makes me want to kiss him, what I really need is a comforting hug.

He leads me out onto the dance floor and calls out 'music please' to a man I hadn't spotted at the side of the stage. As our track starts streaming through the giant speakers, he reminds me to keep my eyes on him while we're dancing, which isn't hard. But the rehearsal is a total disaster.

All the things I feared might go wrong do. I mix up the order of the steps and crack my knee against Merle's, making both of us wince and me lose the timing.

'Don't stop,' he says as I start to apologise, but I'm two beats behind him and I bump into him a second time, forcing him to strengthen his lead and practically drag me through the rest of the routine. It's the worst two minutes of my life and by the end of it, I'm fighting back tears of frustration.

'I'm sorry,' I sob. 'I can't do this.'

'Yes, you can. We'll go again.'

But when he sees the distraught look on my face, he takes me firmly by the hand and pulls me away from the imposing rows of seats.

'Don't smudge your make-up,' he says. 'Layla won't like it if she has to start all over again. Come with me. I know how to fix this.'

I follow him down the corridor and into a dressing room tucked away at the end.

'Is this your . . . ?'

'Shh,' he hushes me, pulling off his top as he walks me back towards the dressing table.

He lifts me onto it and pushes my knees apart, watching me intently as he finds my clit with his thumb. Even through the sequins he makes me tingle.

He steps in towards me and kisses me hungrily while he locates the zip at the back of my catsuit, which he pulls down, then pushes the material aside to expose my bare breasts. He presses his groin against mine as he reaches for them, so I can feel him getting aroused, and I sigh into his mouth as my nipples harden from his touch. This is exactly what I need to stop me panicking about our dance. All I can think about now is how much I want to feel him inside me.

In a flash he sweeps me off the table and spins me round to face the mirror, pulling the catsuit all the way down and moving one of his hands back between my legs. He tugs his trousers off with the other and our eyes meet in the mirror as he guides himself into me. I briefly wonder if we've got time for this, but I'm not about to stop it.

I press my hands against the table and grind my body back against his as he starts pumping behind me. His reaches for my breasts and I watch his eyes flick from my reflection to the real me and back again. I just can't get enough of how transfixed he always seems to be with me.

He clings to my hips as his thrusts take on an extra urgency, and his orgasm arrives quickly and with its usual roar. As his judders slow to pulses, he reaches for my clit again, to make me come too. It doesn't take long as I watch him stroking me in the mirror and he groans as I climax with him still inside me.

We stay like that for a minute, catching our breath, until we hear voices approaching in the corridor. Glancing back I realise Merle did not fully shut the door.

'*Merde*,' he mutters, withdrawing and hastily crossing the room to push it closed.

'Merle?' Olivia calls from outside. 'It's time.'

'Just coming,' he calls back, and the double entendre isn't lost on me as we scramble for our clothes.

He smooths down his hair and I check my make-up is still in place. When I'm ready, he reaches for my wrist and I realise he's taking my pulse.

'Much calmer,' he says. 'Follow me out in a few minutes.'

And with that, he's gone.

Chapter 9

The next hour passes in an absolute blur. The judges are in their seats, the spotlights are glowing on the set and the audience members are ready for some action, their eyes glued to the stage. I'm huddled in the area at the side with the other dancers as the show's host, Kimberley Ross, waits for her cue then welcomes everyone to 'the brand-new dance extravaganza that is *Fire on the Dance Floor!*'

She introduces herself and the three judges – Mariana Gomez from the prestigious Brooklands school of dance, four times UK salsa champion Sophie Shaw and Jacques Flores, a master of Argentine tango who has also won multiple accolades. Then she explains the format of the show – how there will be seven of us competing, each doing a different dance, how the judges will give their comments and critique, but it will be up to the audience to decide our fate.

She reminds us the whole thing is live, so the person who

comes bottom of the seven will be sent home immediately. Which makes my legs feel like jelly – although that might also be down to what just happened in Merle's dressing room.

Emilia is called out onto the stage first with her partner, Aleksis Lapsa, and she doesn't appear remotely fazed by the hundreds of eyes looking at her. She's all brilliant smiles and perfect posture, and while I watch her I find myself trying to unhunch my own shoulders. She did tell us during the group training that she'd been a gymnast at school. It has clearly stayed with her.

Kimberley introduces them to the audience, then the entire back wall of the stage lights up – I hadn't noticed before that it's a video screen – and a clip of their week in rehearsals starts playing. They look good, there's no denying it, even though they've been lumbered with the Argentine tango.

I realise I'm holding my breath as their actual performance gets underway. We might be rivals, but I don't want anyone to have a bad first dance.

I needn't have worried. Emilia breezes through it, looking like she's been dancing her whole life.

I can't help envying her cool composure while she waits for the judges' comments. Her cheeks are flushed from the dance and she's breathing heavily, but there's not a hint of concern in her expression. I guess she must know they're going to love it.

'What a brilliant opening to the series,' head judge Mariana beams, clapping her hands together in delight. 'It's not easy being the first one out on stage, but you took it in your stride. Your footwork was exceptional – you didn't miss a beat – and the lift at the end was graceful and controlled. Your kicks were nice and sharp, too, but there was still a smoothness to the whole routine. Great work, well done.'

'Thank you,' Emilia beams.

'And that's the first time you've ever danced the Argentine tango?' Jacques asks.

'That's right. Until a week ago, I'd never done this before.'

I still find this hard to believe, but Jacques doesn't seem to share my doubts. 'Then even more kudos to you,' he says. 'This is not a dance you can learn in a day and yet you seem to have mastered it in minutes. If I were still competing, I might even be worried about my title. Fantastic job, both of you, and great choreography, Aleksis. That's going to be a very tough act for the other contestants to follow.'

'It certainly is,' Kimberley says, 'But let's not forget it's the audience who get to decide who stays in the competition and who goes home. So audience, for the first time tonight, please pick up your keypads and enter your scores. It's time to see where Emilia and Aleksis come on our dance scale.'

A graphic appears on the video screen of a scale from one to ten. As the audience members enter their scores, the marker races up from the zero straight to the eight, then it flutters between the eight and nine before finally coming to a stop on 8.5.

Emilia shrieks and flings her arms round Aleksis. Kimberley congratulates them and the audience claps and cheers. Then, as they half-run, half-skip off the stage, Kimberley introduces the next couple, Liam and Valentina.

My heart goes out to Liam when he appears to have a mental block in the middle of his salsa routine. Valentina tries to save it with a bit of solo work while he catches up, but the damage is done – his timing is off and their dismayed faces say it all when the music comes to an end. They both know they've had a shocker. The judges don't go easy on them either.

'You fell apart under the pressure,' Sophie says. 'It was a good effort up to that point, but when something goes wrong you must never stop in the middle of a dance. Sadly I think you've put yourself in a very vulnerable position for the audience vote.'

I want to give Liam a hug as the scale appears on the screen and the audience gives him a measly 5.2. I don't know how he manages to keep smiling – I probably would have burst into tears. Valentina graciously tells him not to worry when he apologises to her for messing it up, but I can't help wondering if she's secretly fuming. It's definitely put them in a rocky position, unless someone else cocks their routine up as well. There's still a good chance it will be me.

Next up is Beth's cha-cha and she nails it. The judges are impressed with the amount of work she's put in, and the audience gives her 8.1. But Dean's rumba is not so well received. He's a bit wooden and is warned to work on that if he makes it through to week two. It results in a score of 6.8.

Theo pulls off a decent bachata, although his pro partner is berated for not being as creative as she could have been with the routine. The audience likes it, though, and he moves into third place with 7.7. It looks increasingly like Liam is in trouble, unless I completely fall apart.

Next up is Tammy's merengue, which is amazing. She's a ball of energy and the judges praise her sense of rhythm, saying she's one to watch. She looks like she might burst with happiness and I can't wait to congratulate her. So it's a shock when the audience only award her 6.9. She barely put a foot wrong. It's a sharp reminder to us all that whatever the judges might think, our fates are in the audience's hands.

And then it's my turn.

'The final couple to dance tonight is Kate Wareing and Merle Picard, dancing the kizomba,' Kimberley announces. 'Let's see how they got on with their routine this week.'

Merle, who's standing behind me, discreetly brushes his hand against my bum and gives it a light squeeze as our video starts playing, so instead of cringing about seeing myself on the screen, I'm thinking about the dressing room and his naked body moving against mine while the audience watches our three-minute clip. Despite being cheesy, I have to admit the musical chairs scene is kind of endearing.

Then Kimberley invites us to take our place in the centre of the stage, Merle grabs my hand and we're running out into the spotlights. He draws me into his arms and we're ready to begin.

I have the briefest panic that I haven't done my catsuit all the way back up, before I start wondering where Lucy and Aiden are sitting, whether Ed is watching on TV with my old workmate, what my mum and dad are up to right now down in France . . .

Before my concentration can slip any further, Merle puts his lips close to my ear.

'Just remember to feel me, the way I feel you,' he whispers. 'Just like on Thursday.'

He moves his leg between mine and I close my eyes to shut out all the people staring. When I open them for the dance, he holds my gaze as I let his body guide mine through the steps. I don't take my eyes off him. I don't even realise we've finished until I hear the audience clapping and whistling.

'Perfect,' Merle whispers, and I stare at him in complete astonishment.

'Phewee!' is the first word out of Mariana's mouth as we turn to face the judges. She fans herself with her fingers. 'That was pure passion. It was powerful, it was seductive, and I love how lost you were in the moment. I really felt your story. There's a real connection between you two – I loved it. Well done, excellent job.'

'I think you've got someone a little hot under the collar,' fellow judge Sophie laughs. 'And no wonder, that was seriously sexy. You can almost taste the chemistry between you. From the moment you started, it was like there was no one else in the room. It was mesmerising. I couldn't take my eyes off you.'

'We were looking for fire on the dance floor and you certainly brought it tonight,' Jacques adds. 'I loved the intensity and how every move seemed to have such meaning, such feeling. This is exactly what a kizomba should look like. It was glorious. What a perfect way to end the show.'

My brain races to take it all in.

'Thank you,' I manage. 'That means a lot.'

'And now it's time to see if the audience agrees,' Kimberley says. 'Audience, you've heard the judges' comments, and they certainly seem to be carrying a little torch for Kate and Merle tonight! But how did you find their kizomba? It's time to enter your scores.'

Adrenaline courses through my body as the dance scale flashes up on the big screen. The marker starts moving up, rising and falling as it calculates the average score. It hovers around the eight, pushes up past the nine, drops down, climbs again until eventually it settles on 8.7 and a cheer erupts from the audience – no doubt led by Lucy and Aiden. It's the best score of the night.

'Eight point seven!' Kimberley shouts. 'Which means Merle and Kate, you're at the top of the scoreboard this week and will definitely be joining us again next Saturday. Congratulations, you must be delighted. Ladies and gentlemen, I give you the winners of this week's show – it's Kate and Merle!'

There's another huge round of applause as we exit the dance floor and I feel as if I've left my body and I'm watching this happen to someone else. It's all so surreal.

I watch from the sidelines as Kimberley calls Liam back onto the stage.

'But sadly, that does mean we now know which couple we have to say goodbye to this week. Liam and Valentina, come over and join me. I'm so sorry, guys – I know you must be really disappointed with how things went this evening. It's a tough break when it doesn't go right on the night, and it's always hard to be the first to leave. How are you both feeling? We're all really sorry we won't get to see you again in the next round.'

'At the end of the day, someone has to go home tonight, and that someone just happens to be me,' Liam says. 'But I've had a brilliant week hanging out with Valentina, and the next time I'm at a club with my mates I'll feel a lot more confident about getting up to dance, so I'm glad I took part.'

'We've had a great experience and I'm so glad we got to spend a week training together,' Valentina adds. 'Liam is such a lovely guy and he worked so hard. But sadly we just weren't good enough on the night.'

'At least now I can relax and watch the rest of the show with a beer in my hand,' Liam says with a grin. 'I'm looking forward to seeing who wins.'

'It's been a pleasure having you both here,' Kimberley says warmly, resting a hand on his arm. 'Ladies and gentlemen, for the last time, give it up for Liam and Valentina!'

They bow and wave as they leave the stage, and Kimberley thanks everyone for watching and for taking part. Then there's a flurry of activity as the dancers are all herded into the corridor to be taken back to the reception room, while the audience is directed out of a different exit to be shown out of the building. I'm separated from Merle in the whirl of chatter, back-patting and sympathy for Liam as we make our way back.

'I'm sorry,' Tammy says. 'That was such bad luck for the first night.'

'I'm cool with it.' He smiles to prove he means it. 'I knew I wasn't on the same level as everyone else. I'll just keep up with the applications for the other shows and buying the lottery tickets. I'll get that gym one day. You guys were amazing, though. Beth, you looked so beautiful, and Kate – if I'm honest, I wasn't expecting that.'

'Oi! Although to be honest I really wasn't expecting it either. I still can't quite believe it – it all feels like a crazy dream. I don't know if I'll ever come back down to earth.'

'That's exactly how I feel,' Beth agrees, still charged with adrenaline too. 'But congratulations, Kate – what a result. And Tam, you were insanely good too. I'm dreading the merengue; it's too bloody fast!'

'My score wasn't great, but I loved it.' Tammy gushes. 'It was so much fun.'

'I thought you were robbed,' Beth says. 'I don't know what the audience were thinking. Although we were all wrong about Emilia coming out on top, too – despite her making the Argentine look like a walk in the park.'

'She's lucky to have got it out of the way. We've still got that to come,' Tammy reminds us.

I excuse myself to go and ask Merle if he knows what our next dance will be. I'm dying to relive the judges' comments with him, too. He must be delighted that we got such great feedback on the very first show.

He's standing near the table of drinks that has been set up in the reception room, sipping what looks like a pint of apple juice. I'm ready to hit the wine after today's emotional rollercoaster, so I grab myself a glass and raise it to his.

'Thank you so much for making that happen. It was amazing – the best feeling ever. I think I'm still in shock that we came first!' I gush.

'*Santé*, and you're welcome. I knew my methods would pay off.'

'They did – they *really* did.' I can't wipe the smile off my face. 'So let's celebrate. And perhaps you could show me a few more of your methods afterwards.'

He laughs. 'I have plenty more to share. But I also have a very busy day tomorrow. I have the choreography to prepare for next week, as well as some other business to attend to, so I'm going to have to head straight home from here I'm afraid. Sunday may be a day of rest for you, but sadly it's not for me.'

I feel my heart break just a little.

'I thought . . . ' My voice trails off, heavy with disappointment.

'You should celebrate with your friends tonight,' he says, nodding in the direction of Liam, Beth and Tammy, who are still chatting animatedly on the other side of the room. 'They must be wanting to go out and party. We can save our celebration for the studio on Monday. By then I'll have some new moves for us to try out. And I promise I'll make them worth the wait.'

He winks and kisses both my cheeks before walking away, and my eyes glisten as I watch him go. I'd been so convinced tonight was going to be our big night together. I don't want to wait until Monday before I can be with him again, even if he is planning something good.

'Everything okay?' Beth asks, noticing my gloomy

expression when I rejoin the group. 'It's not the tango, is it?'

I force a smile back onto my face. 'He didn't say, so I guess I'll find out on Monday. But never mind that – what's the plan for now? Is that two glasses of wine you've got on the go there, Liam?'

'I've got to make the most of it now it's the only free booze I'm going to get,' he says. 'I'm going to have to guzzle it, though – my parents are waiting outside for me and they came all the way down from Newcastle so I can't not go for dinner with them.'

'I'd better drink up too,' Beth says. 'Matt's taking me out for a meal tonight as well. It's our anniversary today.'

'I guess I should think about going to find my parents, too,' Tammy says. 'They're going to give me such a hard time about my score though, so I'm putting it off. Do you want another glass before we go, Kate?'

I tell her I do. I want to drown my sorrows. I was so sure I'd be spending the evening with Merle that I haven't made any other plans.

While Tammy's getting the drinks I dig my phone out of my bag and fire off a quick text to Lucy, ignoring the flood of messages that have arrived from friends and family after tonight's performance.

Any chance you're still local? Things are wrapping up here earlier than I expected, I write.

I'm in a pub just up the road with Aiden, she replies straight away. *The Golden Grape. Come and join us.*

'*Cool, thanks. I'll just scrub this make-up off then I'll see you there. Aiden won't mind?*'

'*Aiden never minds. He's the easiest-going person I've ever met.*'

Thank goodness for Lucy, I think as I put my phone away. The other messages can wait till I get home. It'll be something to read before bedtime.

Chapter 10

When I arrive at the pub, it's a typically busy Saturday night, but Lucy and Aiden have found a table next to a window and they've already got me a glass of wine.

'You were so good out there this evening,' Lucy gushes as soon as I sit down. 'You looked like one of the professionals. I knew you could do it. And that score – wow! Congratulations, buddy.'

'Yeah, it was really impressive,' Aiden agrees.

'Thanks!' I grin as we clink glasses. 'To be honest, I can barely even remember being told our score. It all flashes by so quickly.'

'We can watch it back later on catch-up,' Lucy says. 'Have you spoken to your mum yet? Or anyone else? You must have loads of messages from people. Have you looked at Facebook?'

'I haven't even started reading the messages yet. That's probably why we get Sundays off, just to reply to everyone.'

'Merle must've been pleased,' Aiden says.

'I didn't get much of a chance to talk to him afterwards, but yeah, I guess he was.'

Noticing the disappointment in my voice, Lucy moves the subject swiftly on. 'I felt so sorry for Liam. What a horrible way to go out of the competition.'

'He didn't seem too upset. He's already planning which show to try and get on next.'

'That's men for you,' Lucy says, and Aiden gives her a playful nudge.

As we carry on chatting, I notice a few people looking over at our table. I guess it's inevitable I'll be recognised now the first episode has aired. One of my friends went on a dating show a while back and for a few weeks afterwards people kept going up to her, not quite able to work out where they knew her from. Most of them thought they must have been at school together.

So I've been expecting a few looks here and there, maybe a few people wanting to come and say hello or take a selfie with me. It's just part of the process, although it's a bit surprising it's happening already. The people in the pub presumably haven't seen *Fire on the Dance Floor* yet, unless they were in the audience.

There definitely seems to be quite a bit of interest in our little group, though, and I notice a lot of the people are looking from their phones to me, presumably to check if I really am 'the girl from the dance show'. It's a very strange feeling – a bit of a thrill while also vaguely unsettling. Lucy has noticed the looks we're getting too.

'Your video must be up on YouTube already,' she says, and we reach for our phones. I've never googled myself before – it's quite exciting – but as the list of results appears on screen, the blood drains from my cheeks and I start feeling queasy.

A news story with the headline "*Kiz Kiz Bang Bang*" is trending, accompanied by a photo of me and Merle in the dressing room, clearly up to no good. There are related stories on other news sites titled "*Fire in the Dressing Room*" and "*It Started With a Kiz*".

I click on one of the links. Close-ups of our faces leap off the page alongside more dressing room images. They're blurry, but it's pretty obvious what's going on. I start reading.

"*Fire on the Dance Floor couple Merle Picard and Kate Wareing are sizzling off the dance floor as well as on it. Their chemistry was undeniable during their steamy kizomba on tonight's opening show, leaving fans wondering if the pair have become more than just dance partners.*

"*And it seems the passion we saw in their performance is mirrored off-stage. The couple, whose sultry dance bagged them a near-perfect score and secured them a place on next week's show, made little effort to hide how they feel about each other as they got hot and steamy in the dressing room ahead of their performance. They were spotted looking very close just moments before they walked onto the dance floor and . . .*"

'No,' I gulp. 'No, no, no.'

I click on the next story and it's more of the same. And the next. Those same photos are everywhere – Merle from behind, topless, me leaning back with my catsuit folded halfway down and my legs round his waist, his hands on my boobs, my face tipped back but clearly identifiable.

'Jesus, Kate!' Lucy exclaims. 'Your mum's going to see this.'

'*Everyone*'s going to see this,' I panic, dropping my phone on the table and taking a large gulp of my wine. 'I don't know how it could have happened. We would have noticed if someone was filming us. It's impossible.'

But then I remember the door hadn't been properly closed when Olivia came to tell us it was time for the show to begin. Someone must have stuck their head in before that and we were so busy we didn't even notice.

'I can't believe this is happening.' I drop my head into my hands. 'I've got to speak to Merle. I don't know what he'll be thinking. We might get kicked off the show.'

'You're not going to get kicked off the show,' Lucy soothes as I grab my phone again, scroll down to his number and hit dial. 'It's only a few photos.'

But Merle doesn't answer.

'Come on,' I plead, feeling increasingly anxious, but after two more tries he still doesn't pick up.

I switch to WhatsApp and notice that the number of messages waiting to be read has doubled, but none are from Merle.

'*CALL ME!*' I type, swigging more wine.

I flick back to the first news story and scroll down to the comments below it.

"*Lucky cow*", "*He's so fit*", "*I'd definitely go there*", people have written. The sentiment seems to be the same from most of the commenters.

Then . . . "*I feel sorry for his wife.*"

And the room screeches to a standstill. His wife? Merle,

who I've just spent all week getting intimate with, has a *wife*? I suddenly feel even queasier.

Seeing the rest of the colour drain from my face, Lucy takes my phone to see what I'm reading. 'Oh boy. That complicates things.'

'I didn't know!' I wail. 'He never mentioned anything about a wife.'

I hadn't even thought to check whether he was actually single. Why hadn't I thought to ask him?

'It might not be true,' Lucy says, the voice of reason. 'People write all sorts of things in these comments. It might just be someone trying to stir up trouble.'

I hope to God she's right. The photos are bad enough, without this on top. But tears pool in the corners of my eyes as a growing sense of dread creeps over me.

'Hey!' Aiden shouts at a neighbouring table, making me jump. One of the girls is filming us on her phone, but she puts it away when Aiden stands up as if he's going to go over and confront her.

'Let's get out of here,' Lucy mutters, taking in the distraught look on my face.

We don't even finish our drinks before we head for the door.

As we weave between the tables, it feels like every single person we pass is undressing me with their eyes. It's all I can do not to break into a sprint.

The chatter behind us seems to double in volume when we reach the door and I'm certain it's me they're talking about. I don't think I'm ever going to live this down.

Aiden orders us an Uber and when it drops us off at

the flat he doesn't come in. He knows I need Lucy to myself for the rest of the evening. She pours me a large glass of wine as I stare at the news stories on my phone and freak out about all the people who will have seen the photos. Never even mind all the total strangers, what about my friends and family? What about the other contestants? What are they all going to think?

The WhatsApp messages are really mounting up, but I can't face looking at them. I've never been more humiliated in my life. Lucy tries to convince me it will all blow over and that everyone will have forgotten about it before the week is out, but I can't be placated. I'm too busy going to pieces.

'Why hasn't Merle called me back?' I sob.

Lucy tops up my wine and tries to calm me down. 'He's probably just busy and hasn't seen your message yet. I'm sure he'll contact you soon.'

Beth and Tammy both ring me, but I let the calls go to voicemail. I don't want to talk to them. I don't want to talk to anyone but Merle.

'You'll get through this,' Lucy assures me. 'It'll simmer down and you'll put it all behind you. We'll probably even end up laughing about it one day.'

But I can't imagine that day right now. I just want to curl up and hide forever.

Chapter 11

There are approximately five seconds of peace between the moment I wake up and the moment I remember the horror of the previous evening. I lurch out of bed and reach for my phone to check if Merle has been in touch yet. He hasn't.

I finally force myself to read some of the messages that are piling up from friends, family, some of my old work colleagues and even uni friends I haven't heard from for months. The early ones are all congratulatory, but they soon adopt more of a shocked tone, with a few questioning whether what they're reading is true and others checking if I'm all right.

I'd optimistically allowed myself to think that maybe my parents might not have heard anything about it seeing as they're down in France, but a message from my sister puts paid to that idea.

'Um, we were just googling you to see if you're famous yet and we didn't get quite what we were expecting. Mum's on her third glass of wine. Call me?'

Oh God, oh God, oh God. I'm going to need more than three glasses before I'm ready to have that conversation.

I scroll to the Fire Dancers chat and open it, dreading what the others might have written – and breathe a sigh of relief when I see there's no judgement from them.

'*Ha ha, no wonder you came out on top last night.*' This is from Tammy. '*That's one way to get the heat into your dancing.*'

'*Woo! Go, girl!*' Beth has added. '*I can't believe you didn't tell us, you sly devil.*'

'*Yeah, I'd be shouting it from the rooftops. He's lush!*' Tammy has replied. '*I'm going to have to up my game next week to compete with that.*'

'*Oh yes, I didn't even think of that,*' Beth says. '*Unfair advantage alert! Has it been going on all week? I can't believe you kept it to yourself.*'

A little later she's written, '*Hey, are you ignoring us?*'

'*Yeah, let us know you're okay,*' Tammy has added. '*Saw the news this morning. What an arse.*'

I switch to the news feed and the trending story makes my heart sink. My prayers that a major world event would have grabbed everyone's attention and pushed me into obscurity have not been answered, and the headline of the number one story is "*Dance Cheat Shown Door by Devastated Wife*".

So it's true. He really does have a wife.

My heart pounds as I open the link. I'm confronted by a picture of Merle looking all brooding in front of an elegant Georgian townhouse. He looks like a model in a photoshoot with his perfect hair, stylish clothes and leather holdall by his feet. There's also a picture of his wife, whose name is apparently Sofiya. She's wearing big sunglasses that hide half her face but she's a similar build to me, just with light blonde hair rather than red.

Despite the piece firmly suggesting Sofiya has kicked him out of their marital home, Merle is quoted as saying, "*My wife and I have decided to take a bit of time away from each other, but we're going to work through this. I've made a terrible mistake, but I love my wife very much and I'll do whatever it takes to make it up to her so we can be the team we've always been. We're not going to let one silly mistake ruin everything.*"

His words cut through me like a knife. A silly mistake? If it was such a mistake why did he keep coming back for more?

A flash of rage courses through me. That this man, who's seen every inch of my naked body, who's touched me and kissed me everywhere and let me believe there was plenty more of that to come, has been married the whole time. The whole time! No wonder he always had to rush off after training.

And just as quickly I'm back to thinking how stupid I've been, and fretting about what people are going to think of me now. Someone that gorgeous? Of course he wouldn't be single. So how did I not see this coming? I'll probably be branded an idiot or an evil homewrecker. Possibly both. It makes me want to never leave the flat again.

My misery deepens when an email marked urgent pops up from Shane Mitchell at Channel 6, summoning me for a crisis talk tomorrow morning. It feels like I'm being hit by blow after blow.

I drag myself out of bed to go and find Lucy in the kitchen. 'They want me in at Channel 6 first thing tomorrow,' I tell her. 'I guess they're going to drop me from the show after all.'

'Do you really think they'd do that?'

'Haven't you seen the news this morning?' I hand her my phone.

'Oh,' she says, sinking into the chair opposite mine as she skims the article. 'So it was true. Bugger. But you didn't know, so you haven't done anything wrong. If anything, it's Merle they should be getting rid of, right?'

If only.

'I'd be much easier to replace than he would,' I sigh. 'The stupid thing is, I didn't want to do the show in the first place, but now I think they're going to get rid of me, I don't want to go. Not like this, anyway.'

I'd just started feeling like I was getting my mojo back after weeks of despondency. I don't want to say goodbye to it now.

I start welling up again and Lucy reaches over to give my hand a comforting squeeze. 'Have you heard from Merle yet?' she asks, her voice full of sympathy.

I shake my head and look away, determined not to cry.

'I'm sorry, Kate. I feel like it's all my fault for getting you into this in the first place.'

'Don't be daft – you couldn't have predicted this would come out of it.'

'I'm still sorry though,' she sighs.

'I just wish I knew who took those bloody photos.' I cross my arms and stare out of the window. 'I'd bloody kill them. All I can think about is all the people who . . . they'll be looking at my face when they're talking to me, but it's those pictures they'll really be seeing. It makes me feel ill.'

'You don't have to deal with it today,' she soothes. 'We can just chill out here and I'll get Aiden to bring a takeaway over later, if you like.'

'Yeah, that'd be good.' I offer up a weak smile. 'Thank you, Luce.'

'I know it feels really shitty right now, but you will move past this,' she says gently.

I so want her to be right, but right now I can't share her conviction. How does anyone get over something like this?

'And if you are cut from the show tomorrow, at least you won't have to deal with everyone there,' she adds, in a sweet attempt to lighten the mood. 'Every cloud, and all that.'

After that, she allows me to wallow. We spend the rest of the day curled up on opposite ends of the sofa watching films. Or sitting in front of films, I should say – they definitely don't have my full attention. My mind keeps drifting to those online stories, the email from Shane and that image of Merle's wife.

I know I should hate Merle, but my heart also aches when I think about how differently things could have worked out. It's the first time since Ed that I've been excited about someone, that I've opened myself up to the idea of getting close to someone again. I hadn't even realised how much I wanted that. Or how hard I'd been avoiding it since Ed, so I couldn't get hurt again. I can't believe I've managed to get it so wrong again.

Why couldn't Merle just have been one of the good guys? Like Aiden, who, bless him, arrives early with not just pizzas, but wine, chocolate and ice cream, too – everything a girl needs for this kind of crisis. And he doesn't bat an eyelid about the fact that I haven't even bothered getting dressed.

My mind is still turning everything over on repeat when I finally crawl back under my duvet. Did Merle really not give me a single clue he was married in the whole week we spent together? Was it really such a surprise that someone as attractive as him had been snapped up already?

But I wasn't looking for it, so I didn't see it coming. I was too dazzled by the fact that someone as hot as him was actually into me and busy daydreaming about all the amazing things we could do together. Even if all we actually did together was rehearse and have sex.

I find myself wondering if sex will ever be that good again – whether there's anyone out there who'll be able to make me feel like he did, but who'd be there for me in all the other ways too. And if that man does exist, will I ever find him? Or will he run a mile when he realises I'm that girl in the pictures on the bloody internet?

I push my hands into my hair and dig my fingers into my scalp, hoping that massaging it might stop my mind racing, but I can't stop wondering how long it will be before the world forgets about those photos. How I wish I could turn back the clock and start the last seven days again.

Chapter 12

By the time my alarm goes off at seven-thirty a.m. I've worked my way through the entire spectrum of emotions at least five times over – embarrassment, self-pity, anger, hurt, upset – and my eyes are red and puffy from lack of sleep and the odd tear of frustration.

I wear sunglasses on the way to my meeting with Shane – even on the Tube – and I keep my hood up for the whole journey, both to hide the state I'm in and in the hope that no one will recognise me. It attracts a few curious glances but at least no random strangers start making lewd comments or shouting abuse at me.

I try to convince myself they probably haven't seen the show anyway, so they wouldn't even care about the weekend's headlines, but it doesn't make me feel any less vulnerable.

I'm a nervous wreck by the time I get to Channel 6. I wouldn't have thought it was possible to feel more apprehensive than I did when I came to this building for my very first chat about *Fire on the Dance Floor*, or when I arrived for the opening show, but this is definitely worse. It feels like my heart is trying to beat its way right out of my chest as I wait for Shane in the atrium.

'Kate. Thanks for coming in,' he says as he strides towards me across the lobby. I hold my breath as I wait for him to deliver the blow before I've even had a chance to stand up, but he holds his hand out to shake mine as I scramble to my feet.

'Follow me – we'll head up to my office.'

So we're not going to do this in front of anyone else. That's something, I suppose.

'I'm sorry,' I start babbling as I follow him into the maze of corridors. 'I had no idea we were being photographed, really I didn't. Or that Merle was married. I know how bad it looks and I didn't mean to hurt anyone. I'm not like that. I just didn't know he had a wife. I'm really sorry. I really don't want to leave the show. I promise it won't happen again. I mean . . . '

'Whoa!' Shane stops abruptly and turns back to face me. 'No one's leaving the show.'

It takes a moment for this to sink in.

'Off the record, you've done us a favour,' he continues as we start walking again. 'There's a lot more interest in us now than there was a week ago. I'm getting calls left, right and centre. Advertising has rocketed. So no one's leaving the show just yet.'

And even though that means I'm going to have to deal with whatever looks and comments are thrown my way from everyone who works here, a weight lifts from my shoulders.

I'm still in the show! And when I leave, it will be because I'm not the best dancer and not because of Merle's infidelity.

But then I realise that staying on the show will mean another week alone in the studio with Merle. How's that likely to go? I can't just forget he lied to me and ghosted me, but will I still find him irresistible when I see him in the flesh? In spite of everything, a tiny part of me doesn't want to stop having sex with him. That's the trouble when it's so mind-blowingly good.

'Here we are, in we go,' Shane says, holding the door open for me.

I'm surprised to see Aleksis Lapsa, the Latvian dancer who's partnered with Emilia, already in the room. What on earth is he doing here? What's this got to do with him? He fixes me with an icy glare that almost stops me in my tracks. I don't know what his problem is, but if looks could kill . . .

'Take a seat,' Shane says, pointing me towards a chair. 'You know Aleksis, right? Aleksis, this, officially, is Kate Wareing.'

'Um, hi.' I give him an awkward little wave. Aleksis barely nods.

'So,' Shane says. 'That was something of an opening weekend. *Fire on the Dance Floor* was the most-watched show on catch-up yesterday. Our ratings predictions for next week have shot through the roof.'

He sounds delighted. It seems one girl's scandal is another man's lottery win. I glance over at Aleksis again, but he avoids my eye. Then Shane's tone becomes more serious.

'Now, I'm not going to lie to you, Kate; if I had my way, I'd be keeping you and Merle together as a pairing, because I think that's what the viewers will really want to see. They'll want to scrutinise your every move to try and work out if you're still, you know, *whatever*. However, Merle is refusing to continue with the show if he has to dance with you. He thinks a change of partner might be the only way he can smooth things over with his wife.'

I don't know why this news pains me, but I have to battle to keep my expression neutral. It's not like I've spent the last twenty-four hours thinking Merle is going to realise it's me he wanted all along and that we'll live happily ever after. But it's a biting reminder of being cast aside by Ed – and having to find out about that from someone else. I can't believe Merle didn't have the balls to be upfront with me, either.

'Now I'm not usually one to be held to ransom,' Shane continues, 'but on this occasion, I'm going to go with it. There's a lot of interest in the pair of you right now, so I want you both still in this show. And that means from today, Kate, you're going be dancing with Aleksis here instead of Merle, and Merle will switch to dance with Emilia. We know it's not ideal with the competition already underway, but we think it's the best solution.'

My mind whirls as I scramble to process this new bombshell. Does it explain why Aleksis looks so pissed off? Because he used to be paired with the strongest contestant and now he's got me? Although it was me who came first last week, not Emilia, so it surely can't be just because of that.

'We want to keep it to ourselves for the time being,' Shane is saying, 'so no putting anything out on social media – or telling anyone else who might put it out there. We don't want to lose the viewers who'll be tuning in just to see you and Merle, so let's keep everyone guessing.'

He pauses to make sure this has sunk in.

'In the meantime, we've found a new studio for the two of you to rehearse in – one where it will be easy for you to arrive and leave without attracting any attention. It's in Brixton – I hope that's not too inconvenient. It's a bit run-down, but it was the best we could do at short notice. You can go there straight after we're done here and get started on your next routine. And that's about it, I think. Are there any questions?'

I look over at Aleksis again and notice his jaw clenching, which seems to confirm he's not thrilled about this change of events, but he doesn't say anything.

How do I feel about it? I know I should probably be relieved that I don't have to confront Merle this morning, but instead I just have an irrational flare of jealousy that he'll now be dancing with perfect Emilia. Even though he's telling everyone he's determined to repair his marriage, I can't help wondering if he'll seduce her, too. Which somehow hurts more than finding out he was married. I thought I'd met someone who really got me. Now I'm not sure he was into me at all.

'Did Merle ask specifically to dance with Emilia?' I hear myself asking.

'That was his stipulation, yes,' Shane confirms.

Which even gets me wondering if it might have been

Merle himself who set up and exposed those dressing room photos. Was it all part of some messed-up plan to get him partnered with Emilia? But that doesn't make sense. No one would put their wife through that just to get a different dance partner, would they? I realise I'm being ridiculous.

'Anything else?' Shane asks.

I shake my head and Aleksis stands up to leave.

'Thanks for coming in then, both of you. And for being so understanding,' Shane says. 'I hope you have a good week.'

Chapter 13

Aleksis stares out of the window in silence as our taxi whisks us off to Brixton. He must be able to tell I keep looking over at him, but he refuses to meet my eye. It makes it impossible to start up any kind of conversation.

It strikes me that he couldn't be more different to Merle. Where Merle is dark-haired with a Mediterranean tan, Aleksis's hair is so blond it's almost white and his skin is as pale as a marble statue. He seems about as cold as one, too.

We eventually pull up outside a nondescript office block that looks ready for demolition and the driver tells us we've arrived. The second-floor studio inside is, as Shane warned, somewhat shabbier than the one I shared with Merle. The wooden floor is damaged in places and has been patched up with duct tape, and several sections of the mirrored wall have mottled with age. There's a battered ballet barre along the back wall, and a crack in the door that looks like it may have been made with an axe. I tell myself it's got character.

Aleksis surveys the room then dumps his bag in a corner and pulls out his dance shoes. Expecting to be dropped from the show this morning, I didn't bring mine with me, so I'll have to dance in my socks.

'We've got the salsa,' he says – his first words to me. 'You know the basics?'

I nod.

'Good, let's warm up then. Just watch in the mirror and copy everything I do.'

We spend the next few hours going over the footwork he wants me to learn. First without music, then with, then with arm movements, then again from the beginning, again with sharper turns, and again with more style. It's hard to keep up, and I don't feel like I'm really getting it, but he doesn't slow down or make any allowances for the fact that I'm still a novice.

And then, midway through the afternoon, he suddenly announces, 'Okay, we're done,' leaving me staring at him from the middle of the dance floor.

'But it's only three,' I point out. 'There's still loads more time.'

'Tomorrow we'll start partnerwork. We'll meet here at eleven,' he says coldly, snatching up his bag and heading for the door without even changing his shoes.

'But . . .'

It's probably a full minute before the shock subsides and I manage to react. I run to the open door and peer down into the stairwell, but he's nowhere to be seen. I go back into the studio and look out of the window, but I can't see him on the street below. I check the time on my phone, in case the clock on the wall is wrong, but it really is just three o'clock. He really has just walked out in the middle of training and I don't quite know what to do about it. All I can think is, *What the hell is his problem?*

For a few minutes longer I remain immobilised. At first I convince myself he must be pranking me and will come back any minute. When he doesn't, I try to go through the steps again on my own in front of the mirror, but my heart's not in it and I keep looking at the door every five seconds to check if he's come back.

Eventually I sink to the floor next to my bag and pull my trainers back on, feeling dejected. Was Aleksis really so annoyed about having to dance with me in this dingy little studio that he couldn't bear to stay here any longer? Was he worried I might try it on with him if he stuck around too long? Maybe he also has a wife and doesn't want her to think he might follow in Merle's footsteps.

I reach for my phone and pull up the dressing room photos on the screen yet again. Those bloody pictures. If it wasn't for them, none of this would be happening. I'd be back in the studio with Merle, I probably wouldn't know he was married and we'd probably be getting up to all sorts. All of which feels preferable to this.

There is absolutely zero chemistry between me and Aleksis. I'd even go so far as to say today's session has been downright depressing after the excitement of last week. I reckon if I'd been paired with him from the start, it would have been me, not Liam, who was voted out of the show on Saturday.

I'm amazed Aleksis managed to do so well with Emilia. Lucky for him that she's so talented. I flick to YouTube and search for their performance. I watch it twice, trying to figure out what it is she has that the rest of us don't. Are you just born a good dancer?

I try to copy one of her moves in the mirror from my position on the floor, but my arms refuse to look how I want them to, which makes me feel even more deflated. I know I pulled off a presentable kizomba last week, but realistically that came from Merle. What a fool I was to let anyone make me believe I had any talent. I drop my head into my hands and sigh through my fingers, feeling stupid and alone.

I can't help thinking how good Merle and Emilia are going to look together on stage next Saturday. I wonder which dance they've got. The more I think about them as partners, the more gutted I am about how things have panned out.

I'm sure Merle could have dragged a decent salsa out of me. I'm sure we would have focused on our partnerwork right from the start rather than the footwork drills Aleksis has fired at me all morning. The truth is, much as I hate what he's done, I wish I was still dancing with Merle.

With a sigh I grab my bag and head home, where I distract myself with the telly until Lucy gets home from work. She's dying to know what the outcome of my meeting with Shane was and I tell her everything. I know I'm not supposed to mention the partner switch to anyone, but I trust her to keep it secret.

'So you're still in the show *and* you don't have to dance with that arsehole any more? That's great!' she exclaims.

Then she clocks my glum expression and narrows her eyes. 'Only you don't look like you think it's so great . . . What am I missing?'

'Aleksis absolutely detests me. He walked out halfway through the session,' I sigh.

She looks alarmed. 'Why? What did you do?'

'I didn't do anything,' I protest. 'We were just going over our solo section for the umpteenth time and I thought we were about to move on to something else, but instead he announced we were done and just left.'

I fight back the urge to cry as I recall how hated he made me feel.

'That's so weird,' Lucy frowns.

'The whole thing was awful,' I confess. 'He was so unfriendly and he didn't make any effort to talk to me. I don't know how we're meant to look like we've got any kind of connection on the dance floor if this is how he's going to be with me.'

'Maybe he just needs a day to get used to the new partnership,' she suggests. 'It probably came as a shock to him too, right? I reckon he'll be fine about it once he's had time for it to sink in.'

'I hope you're right,' I sigh, but I'm not so optimistic.

'I think he's kind of cute,' she says sheepishly. 'I thought that at the show on Saturday.'

'What? Ew!' I chuck a cushion at her in horror.

'It's those eyes. They're so blue you just want to dive straight into them,' she laughs. 'And his body is easily as fit as Merle's.'

This makes me snort. 'He's definitely no Merle.'

'Even Aiden agreed he was attractive. Speaking of whom, I'm meeting him up the road later – do you want to join us? There's a band playing in the downstairs bar at Hagen and Hyde. Aiden won't mind.'

On any other day I would have loved to, but it was hard enough getting on the Tube today, wondering if anyone was going to say anything about the photos. The thought of being in a bar full of people – it makes me shudder just thinking about it.

'Thank you, but I'm going to stay in tonight. I've got the dreaded phone call with my parents to get out of the way. I have no idea how they're going to react after what they've seen.'

'They might surprise you,' she says.

'They might, but I'm already picturing the look on Dad's face and it isn't pretty.'

'They're your parents. They'll just want to make sure you're okay.'

And thankfully she's right. Although my heart races as I wait for them to log on to Skype, it isn't nearly as awkward as I expect. I can tell Dad is too embarrassed to even mention it and when Mum looks like she's about to launch into a mini lecture about the kind of behaviour that's becoming of a lady, Dee jumps in and steers us to safer ground – namely, what my next career move should be once I'm done with the show.

She's been talking to her friend, who works in events management, and she wants me to have a chat with her because she thinks it's something I'd really enjoy. And I'd actually be able to make use of my marketing degree, so it would feel more like a career role, too. She promises to set something up when I'm ready.

After that we talk about the kids for a while, who are in the other room watching telly, then Mum tells me she and Dad are thinking about cutting their trip short and flying back to the UK on Friday in time to come and sit in the audience for the next show – probably so they can make sure I don't do anything else embarrassing.

'Although it's not going to be easy watching you dancing with that man after what we saw,' Mum says. 'I hope you were taking precautions.'

'Mum,' Dee warns.

'Well,' Mum starts, but I interrupt her.

'You don't have to worry, Mum, we were using condoms. And that aside, I'm not going to be dancing with him any more. They've given me a different partner for this week.'

I'm aware I'm letting the cat out of the bag again, but who are my parents going to tell? And it will put their minds at ease.

'Oh,' Mum says, visibly relieved. 'Which one have you got now then?'

'Aleksis. The one who was with Emilia last week.'

Just saying his name brings back all the frustration from earlier today, but Mum doesn't notice me shudder.

'Oh, I liked him. I thought he was really good,' she beams, then her face falls. 'You're not going to sleep with him as well, are you?'

'Mum!' Dee and I shout in unison.

'No, sorry, of course not,' she flaps. 'Well, that's good to know. That'll make your dad and me much more comfortable.'

104

'There's really no danger of anything untoward happening with Aleksis,' I assure her. 'We barely even talk to each other. So you really don't need to ruin your holiday and fly back because of me. I don't want you to waste your time off sitting around at home just so you can see me on the show for one hour a week. Stay there and enjoy yourselves.'

'But we do worry about you,' Mum says.

'I know, but there's no need. Tell them, Dee.'

'She's fine,' Dee says.

'See?' I'm suddenly eager to finish the call. 'I'll check in again at the weekend, okay? With hopefully less drama to report than this weekend. In fact, definitely with less drama. It's just going to be a normal week this week, I promise. So I'll talk to you all soon. I love you all.'

'Love you,' Mum says. 'And we're here for you whenever you need us.'

I close my laptop with a sigh of relief. I don't want to have to talk to them about Merle ever again. I really should reply to some of the other people who sent messages following the events of the weekend, though, so I take a deep breath and start with the Fire Dancers chat.

Beth has asked how my rehearsal with Merle went today, after everything, and suggested us all getting together for a midweek drink if I want to talk about it. But I know I'll probably end up letting slip that I'm not dancing with him any more if I have a couple of glasses of wine with them, so I tell her rehearsals were fine but that I'm keeping a low profile for a few days because I'm not ready to discuss anything yet.

'I get that,' she replies. '*This can't have been easy. Just let us know if there's anything we can do.*'

I promise I will.

'*And if you feel up to it by Saturday, I was going to see if everyone wants to go out and party after this week's show. It was lovely going for dinner with Matt last week, but I can do that any time.*'

'*I'm up for it,*' Tammy writes. '*My two sisters are my audience guests this week and they'll definitely want a drink afterwards.*'

'*I'm in,*' Liam says. '*I can nab us a table at a pub near the studio while you're doing the show, then you can come and join me afterwards.*'

'*Great,*' Beth replies. '*Can we save you a seat, Kate? We'd really love you to be there too.*'

And I want to be – I don't want to miss out on all the fun. Plus, they'll know about Aleksis by then, so that will no longer be a problem. But can I get past my embarrassment about the photos? Can I stop feeling nauseous every time I think about anyone so much as mentioning them?

I'm going to have to face everyone at Channel 6 on Saturday anyway, so maybe I just need to swallow my fears and get on with it. Is it really so bad if people know I have an active sex life? Obviously I'd rather they hadn't had such a graphic insight into it, and that it hadn't involved a married man, but neither of those things were my fault. So can I stop torturing myself and just own it? I decide I owe it to myself to try.

'*Okay fine,*' I reply to Beth. '*Put me down for a chair.*'

Chapter 14

I allow myself a lie-in the next morning, given that Aleksis doesn't want to get started till eleven. With Merle it was always ten on the dot, half an hour for lunch and a six p.m. finish. I wonder how many hours Aleksis will put in today.

I'm still wondering when I've been at the studio for half an hour and there's still no sign of him. It occurs to me that I haven't swapped numbers with him like I did with Merle, so I have no idea if he's even going to show up and no way of contacting him to find out.

When he strides into the room at eleven-forty a.m., there's no apology.

'Right, let's get this done,' he says, leaving me too stunned to respond. Could he really be this rude?

'Partnerwork,' he announces when he's changed his shoes. 'Come here. We'll start in this position. Straighten your back, relax your shoulders, give me some tension in your arms, more, okay, now try to follow. Right foot first, one, two, three . . . '

I don't even utter a word as I follow his lead. I think I'm in shock. And when we break for a late lunch a few hours later, it takes me a while to realise that it's not a lunch break at all – he's decided he's had enough again and is not coming back.

'It's bloody ridiculous,' I fume to Lucy that evening. 'He's treating me like I killed his pet cat or something. I don't know what his problem is. I mean, I know he must be disappointed that he's not with the best contestant any more, but it's a bit over the top.'

'What is it with these dancers?' She's as incensed as I am. 'Aren't they meant to be professionals?'

'Beth and Tammy seem to be doing all right with theirs,' I sigh, my shoulders slumping. 'Maybe it's just me.'

'Don't be daft. It's not your fault Aleksis is so prickly.'

'It's making me not want to go back to the studio tomorrow,' I admit. In fact, when I think about it, it fills me with dread.

Lucy isn't about to let me be defeated, though. 'You're just going to have to have it out with him. He can't refuse to rehearse with you properly. It's his job, he's getting paid to do it. When you see him tomorrow, tell him if he doesn't start showing you a bit of respect, you'll report him to Shane. That'll make him pull his socks up.'

I know she's right, but the last thing I want is a blazing row with Aleksis to add to the trauma of the last week.

'I'm starting to think I should've stayed in my old job. I know it wasn't perfect, but at least it was less stressful than this,' I sigh.

At least there I could avoid Ed's new girlfriend as much

as possible. And when I did bump into her, I could make out I was way too busy for any kind of conversation, so there were no awkward confrontations. But I can't avoid Aleksis.

'Absolutely no way,' Lucy says firmly. 'Whatever happens with the show, you needed to leave that place. You've still got time to turn things around with Aleksis. You could still win the show. You could still even meet the man of your dreams. It just might be one of the camera crew or something, rather than your dance partner.'

I think about Steve and Andy and shake my head. Lovely as they both are, Steve is about twenty-five years older than me and Andy is so golf-obsessed I don't think he ever does anything else.

'Then maybe one of the people sliding into your DMs,' Lucy persists. 'I bet there are loads. Have you even looked?'

But when we check my Instagram, we discover my account has somehow stayed under the radar and I tell Lucy I'd prefer to keep it that way. Some of the news stories about me and Merle have attracted a few nasty comments since it came out that he's married and I don't want to open myself up to any further online abuse.

'I'm happy to stay off-grid for as long as possible,' I tell her. 'Once everyone knows I'm not partnered with Merle any more, hopefully that will take the focus off me and give them all something else to talk about. It better had anyway, because I've told Beth and the others I'll go out with them after the show on Saturday and I don't want a repeat of last weekend at the pub.'

'If anyone says anything to you, just tell them to piss off,' Lucy says defiantly.

'Will you and Aiden come too? I'll feel a lot better if you're there as well.'

'Of course we will. It'll be great to meet everyone properly.'

'It might be my leaving party at the rate things are going with Aleksis,' I sigh. 'I will brave that chat with him tomorrow though. I can't put up with his stroppiness for one more day.'

She gives my arm an encouraging squeeze. 'Good for you. I don't think you'll regret it.'

'Well, I don't think things could get any worse.'

But it turns out I'm quite wrong about that.

Chapter 15

Despite convincing myself I'm going to go in all guns blazing the next morning and confront Aleksis before he's even changed his shoes, I hesitate for a moment too long when I arrive at the studio and he starts dishing out instructions before I've had a chance to say anything. I almost lose my nerve completely, but we're not far into the rehearsal before he infuriates me enough to snap me back into action.

'Not like that, like this,' he says impatiently as I mess up a toe-tap sequence that he's had to show me five times already. I keep starting it with the wrong foot, which leaves my weight on the wrong leg for the next move. 'You're not listening to what I'm telling you,' he huffs, his voice dripping with irritation.

'Are you surprised?' I fire back, throwing my arms up in anger. 'I don't know what your problem is, but I'm sick of it. You either boss me around like a three-year-old or act like you'd rather be anywhere else but in this room.

Well, you might not care about this dance or the show or anything else, but I do.

'We've only got a few days before we're doing it live and I, for one, want to at least try to get through to week three. So for five minutes could you please just put the attitude aside and stop treating me like I've got the plague or something? Because if we carry on like this it will almost certainly be the end of the show for both of us.'

'And what a shame that would be,' he sneers, his eyes flashing with anger. 'But you don't have to worry about that, we won't be leaving the show just yet.'

'We will if we carry on like this.'

He shakes his head and glares at me.

'What?' I snap. 'What is it?'

'Did you know he was married?' he asks.

'Excuse me?'

'Merle. Did you know?'

'Is that what this is about? No, I didn't know, although I fail to see how that's any business of yours.'

'That's something, at least.' He looks away from me.

'Aleksis, I've had a shitty enough time dealing with all that crap without you wading in on it as well.'

'Oh, you think you've had a shitty time, do you?' he rages. 'How do you think Sofiya is finding it, seeing those images of you and him splashed all over the internet? And then having to put up with the press camped out on her doorstep day and night?'

I swallow, taken aback by the venom in his voice. 'I'm sure she's—'

'No, you don't get to comment on it,' he cuts in, his

voice biting. 'Because you've got no idea. And in answer to your earlier question, what does it have to do with me? I'll tell you what. That's my sister whose husband you've been screwing.'

I feel like I've been slammed into a brick wall. 'Your sister?'

No wonder he's so angry with me.

'That's right. So if you've been asking yourself why I don't want to be stuck here in this shitty studio with you, now you know. Do I want us to go through to the next round and have to do it all again with you next week? No. I can't think of anything I want less. But do you know what my consolation prize was for being forced to swap partners and dance with you? We're going through on Saturday, no matter what. They're going to make sure of it.'

'You mean they're going to fix the scores?' I don't want to believe it. Surely they wouldn't do that.

'Yes, if they have to. So there's really very little point in me wasting my time here trying to teach you this dance, because it's all bullshit anyway.'

When I fail to respond – my mind is reeling – he tells me he's leaving.

'I'll be here tomorrow, because that's when we have to film our segment for the show,' he says. 'And don't worry – I'll pretend I don't hate you for a couple of hours. But apart from that I don't want to talk to you, I don't want to be around you, I'll just tolerate you until this is all over.'

I can feel tears pooling in the corners of my eyes as I watch him stalk out of the studio. I don't think anyone has ever despised me so much. I can hardly blame him, either.

I just can't get my head round that fact that Merle's wife is his sister. And Merle obviously knew this when he suggested the partner swap, so he was well aware of what a horrendous position he was putting us in. Did he do it deliberately, knowing it would likely ruin any possibility of us being any competition for him on the show? Does he want to win that desperately? Or did he just want to be partnered with Emilia so much that he didn't care where that left me and Aleksis?

And on top of that, to learn the audience vote is going to be fixed. It makes me wonder if that's why I came out on top last week instead of Emilia, when she's clearly the better dancer. Is Aleksis right – is it worth us even trying to do well?

I can't believe what a nightmare this week has turned into. The thrill of being in the studio with Merle and our surprise Saturday night win are both distant memories. I'm not sure I even want to carry on with the show if this is how it's going to be from now on.

With nothing else to do I head back home, typing an email to Shane on the way to tell him I want to withdraw from *Fire on the Dance Floor*, and suggesting they could reinstate Liam in my place. But I don't send it. A part of me doesn't want to give up, no matter how uncomfortable it is with Aleksis and how bogus the scores might be.

I can't help wishing my experience could be more like Tammy's and Beth's. Why couldn't I just have been a regular contestant on the show, enjoyed my five minutes of fame, not had sex with my married dance partner, stayed in the competition for a couple of weeks, graciously lost out to Emilia just before the final and left with my head held high? Instead of this mess.

I don't know how I'm going to handle a day in front of the cameras with Aleksis tomorrow. He might be able to brazen it out, but I'm not sure I can. I don't even know if Lucy's words of encouragement can get me through this time, although she does her best to lift my spirits when I tell her what's happened. I get a pep talk from Mum and Dee over Skype too when I confess how badly the rehearsals have been going. And Mum offers to fly back yet again, so I backtrack and tell her it's not as awful as I've made out. There's no point both our weeks being ruined.

Ten more days of this, though – the thought doesn't exactly fill me with joy. With our free pass on this week's show, the earliest I'll be eliminated from the competition is the following Saturday. Can I tolerate Aleksis's hostility until then?

Chapter 16

I go to the studio early the next morning, because I don't
know what time the camera crew is coming. Aleksis
didn't tell me. But the lights are still out, so he clearly
hasn't rushed in to meet them.

While I'm waiting for everyone, I scroll idly through all
the news sites on my phone to see if anything else has
been printed about Merle or me. There are a few new
comments under the "*Kiz Kiz Bang Bang*" story – one or
two that are sympathetic to me, but the majority firmly
Team Merle. Which hardly seems fair – it wasn't me who
was married.

Hearing someone arriving, I glance up to see a strikingly
beautiful woman walking into the room. I leap to my feet
as I clock her pale blonde hair and realise it's Aleksis's sister
– Merle's wife. What the hell is she doing here? I thought
my week had already hit rock bottom, but now this?

My skin starts prickling as Aleksis follows her into the
room. I can't believe he's brought her here – or actually, I

can. He's probably loving this. My eyes dart between the two of them as I wait for a barrage of abuse to begin. But Sofiya holds her hands up in a conciliatory gesture. 'I'm not here to fight. I just want to say my piece then I'll be gone.'

Heart pounding, I glance over at Aleksis, who's now leaning against the mirror and observing me coolly, his expression unreadable.

'I had a visit from Aleksis yesterday,' Sofiya says, 'and he told me how things are going here.'

She pauses to look round the studio. 'Not too well, by the sound of things. I know how stubborn my brother can be.'

Another pause, then she turns back to me and says, 'But I don't want him to waste the opportunity he's been given with his first TV show. This could lead to a lot more work for him, so he needs to take advantage of it. I'm not going to let him throw away his chances because he's trying to be loyal to me.'

I swallow loudly, but I can't find any words.

'So I've come here today to show him I'm not angry with you. I know what Merle's like. I've known for a long time what Merle is like, but I've always hidden it from Aleksis, because it was Aleksis who introduced us and I knew how it would make him feel.'

'I'm really sorry,' I finally manage. 'I genuinely didn't . . .'

Another raised hand tells me she doesn't want to hear my side of the story.

'Let me finish.'

'Of course,' I whisper, unable to take my eyes off her. I wonder if she can tell my heart's racing.

'I was twenty years old when I fell in love with Merle. He was charming and gorgeous and made me feel like the most important person in the world. We were married within six months.'

She says this matter-of-factly, but it's clear there was a time when she thought her relationship with him would turn out very differently. Which I, of course, can relate to.

'But over time it became apparent I wasn't the only one he was making feel that way. His dance partner was the first. I didn't want to believe it – wouldn't let myself believe it. Then, when I couldn't lie to myself any longer, I confronted him and he broke down and told me what a mess he'd made of things. He promised to change, so I gave him a second chance and for a long time after that it went back to being perfect. Until it happened again.'

I glance over at Aleksis. This must be hard for him to hear. But he's looking down at the floor so I can't gauge what he's thinking.

'I still didn't leave,' Sofiya continues. 'Or the time after that. I simply hoped things would run their course then we'd get back on track again – and we did. And I thought I was happy, because when it was good, it was really good with him.

'But now I find myself back here again and this time, I don't know why, it just feels different. I don't know if it's because it's been so public with you. Or if it's just because while you're standing here realising you weren't the first, I'm here finally realising you won't be the last. And all of a sudden, enough's enough. I don't want this to be my life any more.

'So while Aleksis thinks he needs to protect me from the pain you might have caused me, in fact I'm grateful to you, for giving me the impetus to walk away at last.'

'Well, I . . . '

She shakes her head firmly. 'I'm nearly done. I need Aleksis to know I don't blame you for what happened. Merle didn't tell anyone at the show he was married in case it affected his chances. So why wouldn't you fall for him? What I want both of you to understand is that this is neither a great shock nor a desperate heartache for me. That reporter camped out on my doorstep, trying to get a picture of me looking devastated, is going to have a very long wait. I'm finally ready to draw a line under my relationship with Merle. And Aleksis, I want you to do the same.'

She says this last part in a tone that suggests it's not up for debate.

'All I want now is for people to see what a brilliant dancer you are. You deserve it. Which means the two of you need to put your differences aside and be the best you can be for the rest of your time in this competition. I'm not leaving until you agree.'

I wait in case there's more, but she seems to be done this time. I can hear the relief in my voice when I tell her this is absolutely fine with me.

'Aleksis?' she says.

My eyes drift his way again and he stares back at both of us for a long moment before giving a curt nod. I let out a breath I hadn't realised I'd been holding. Finally, the tension in the room dissipates.

'Then that's all I have to say,' his sister says, heading for the door. '*Lai veicas!*' she says over her shoulder as she walks out of the room.

I don't know how long I stare after her before Aleksis pushes himself away from the mirror and comes towards me.

'It means good luck,' he explains reluctantly.

I study his face, trying to decide if he looks any less like he can't stand the sight of me. It's impossible to tell.

'Well, that was unexpected,' I admit, feeling dazed. 'And, er, motivating.'

'It doesn't mean we're friends,' he says coolly. 'But we can work together.'

'Of course,' I backpedal. 'That's exactly what I was thinking.'

'Let's get started, then. The camera crew will be with us after lunch.'

I think his tone does get a fraction gentler as we start rehearsing, though, and he seems more patient. We even manage the odd smile when parts of the dance feel like they're going okay. I'd say I almost feel relaxed by the time Sarah, Steve and Andy arrive.

'Hi guys,' Sarah says. 'It's that time again. How are you getting on so far this week?'

'We're making progress,' Aleksis replies diplomatically.

'That's the most important thing,' she nods.

She gives our tatty studio a once-over while the other two unpack their equipment. 'We're going to need to do a lot of retouching on the background at the editing stage,' she sighs. 'But we'll make it work.'

When the camera and mic are set up, she tells us she'd like to start by filming us practising our routine. 'And while you're doing that, I'll have a think about where we can take it from there.'

What we end up mostly focusing on is Aleksis trying to teach me how to build up the number of spins I can do on the spot. To begin with, it's almost three – which isn't great this far into rehearsals – but eventually I manage six, although Aleksis has to catch me a few times and I have to stagger across the room and cling on to the ballet barre once or twice.

Sarah then decides I should have a go at spinning Aleksis. And as he can spin on the spot without me even touching him, we manage to make this look good. Sarah is pleased with how it looks on her monitor.

I notice Aleksis doesn't ask to see it, which is refreshing after all the interfering Merle did on our filming day. We might not like each other, but I find myself respecting him for trusting Sarah to do her job.

'This has given me an idea,' she says, rummaging around in her bag and retrieving a roll of duct tape. Seeing my quizzical expression, she explains that she wants it to look like Aleksis has spun me right through the floor. She pulls the old tape off one of the holes and gets Aleksis to pretend to fix it with new tape while I hold my shoe and look incredulously at the heel.

'I love it,' she declares when she's captured it all on film. 'Which means, you'll be pleased to hear, that's us nearly done for today.'

There's just a brief recording of us talking about our

week – both of us choosing our words carefully – before we say our goodbyes.

'Thanks for making our lives so easy this afternoon,' Sarah beams. 'And good luck for Saturday. Hopefully we'll see you again next week.'

I can't help noticing how much Aleksis's face changes when he thanks her with a smile of his own. The angles soften and there's a glimmer in his eyes. He almost looks nice. But the smile fades when he turns back to me, and the hardness returns to his features.

'We have a lot to do,' he says stiffly. 'Shall we?'

For the first time, we rehearse until the studio closes. The janitor even has to come and tell us to leave the building before we get locked in – just when it feels like we're finally making progress. I would happily have carried on for a few more hours if we'd been able to stay – not least because it's been much easier to have my arms round Aleksis when it doesn't feel like he wants to snap them off.

It's such a relief to get through a whole day with no hostility that I go home on a bit of a high. So when Lucy invites me to join her, Aiden and Warren for the pub quiz at The Grove – another Balham favourite – I seriously consider it. I'd as good as forgotten what it was like to feel upbeat and it seems a waste not to make the most of it.

Of course I haven't magically forgotten the anguish of the photos and I'm not sure I'll ever be a hundred per cent over them, but I'm suddenly determined not to let it beat me. With some extra encouragement from Lucy, I manage to convince myself it doesn't matter if a handful of people in the pub think they know things about me because of what they've seen. They can think what they like, but they don't know anything.

Fighting off any lingering doubts, I take a deep breath and tell Lucy I will be on their team. If people want to talk about me, let them. And if they stare, I'll deal with it. Lucy praises my newfound feistiness and reminds me that once this first outing is out of the way, it can only get easier. Then she hustles me out of the door before I can change my mind.

I have my first and only wobble when we're standing at the bar and the couple next to us start sniggering.

'Maybe I shouldn't have come,' I backtrack, even though it might not be me they're laughing about.

'Don't worry about them,' Warren says reassuringly. 'You're with friends, just ignore everyone else.'

'And you're here now, so you might as well stay,' Lucy adds.

'Plus Aiden's terrible at pub quizzes, so we really do need you on our team,' Warren says with a grin.

'Hey! I'm not that bad,' Aiden protests. 'But I do want you to stay. You can't leave me and Luce alone with this loser all night.'

'This loser who just happens to know the perfect way to fix this situation,' Warren says. 'Wanna hear it?'

'Go on,' Lucy prompts.

'Tequila!' Warren shouts.

'Now I wish I hadn't asked,' she laughs; then, 'Okay, I'm in.'

'Go on then, let's do it,' Aiden agrees.

And even though a small voice in the back of my head says, *This is a terrible idea when you've got another rehearsal day tomorrow*, I don't object. My salsa may not be anywhere near as polished as my kizomba was after all the time Aleksis and I have wasted, but it doesn't matter. We'll go through anyway. And as frustrating as it is that we won't be staying in the competition through our own merit this week, it does feel like payback for what I've had to go through with Merle.

'Screw them all,' Warren toasts as we tap our glasses together and lick piles of salt off our hands.

'Screw them all,' we repeat as we tip the tequila down our throats, wincing in unison as we feel the alcohol burning our throats.

'We'll take one more each,' Warren tells the barman as we suck our lemon slices. And no one protests.

We take the second round to our table with our other drinks and this time Warren simply toasts Thursdays, declaring it the official start of the weekend. He gives me a playful nudge and I can't help grinning back. It's nice to feel like he's got my back.

The quizmaster kicks things off and we get stuck into answering questions. At regular intervals Warren touches my arm and checks I'm okay. And I'm surprised to find I am – because when everyone around us is concentrating on picture rounds and music rounds and who the president was fifty years ago, no one is paying the slightest bit of attention to me. But it's really sweet of him and I appreciate it.

We order two more rounds of tequila in between sets of questions and it's no surprise to any of us that we're not one of the top five teams when the quizmaster eventually reads out the answers. But we weren't expecting to win the consolatory round of drinks that goes to the team who finishes right at the bottom, either. Thanks to all the shots, instead of being embarrassed we find this hilarious.

We're still giggling when Aiden comes back from the bar with four complimentary glasses of Baileys on ice. As we clink glasses, Warren puts his arm round me and asks, 'Are you glad you stayed out now?'

'I am,' I nod. 'It's been such a fun night.'

The truth is, I haven't laughed so hard in ages.

He lowers his voice and says, 'Listen, I know you didn't fancy it last time we met, but I've still got to ask – do you want to come back to mine for a bit after this? I'm not ready to call it a night just yet.'

And perhaps because I'm a bit giddy from all the drinks, but more because he's been so kind to me all evening, I tell him I do. I actually do. This is what I need in my life – a really nice, funny guy, not some arrogant dancer who doesn't give a damn about me. Plus there's the fact that I really want Merle not to be the last person I had sex with.

I'm pretty sure one thing will lead to another back at Warren's, and that will hopefully make me forget about the whole Merle situation once and for all.

Chapter 17

Warren shares a flat with a girl from his work and a guy from his football team. It doesn't have a lounge, because they're using it as the third bedroom, so we head straight to his room, which is dimly lit by the bedside lamp he must have left on before he went out. As soon as the door is closed behind us, he takes my hand and leads me towards the bed. Then we kiss standing beside it, a poorly coordinated effort that makes our teeth clash.

We kiss again and it's no less clumsy – we're completely out of sync with each other. But it doesn't matter. I'm kissing someone. Someone who isn't Merle. And that can only be a good thing.

I tug Warren's sweatshirt over his head, and he takes his T-shirt off himself. He's chunkier than Merle, but not in bad shape. Where Merle's chest was all hard muscle and waxed smooth, Warren's is toned, but softer, with a light covering of hair, which I run my fingers over.

'Oh yeah, that's good,' he says.

He guides my hands down to his belt but after several seconds of fumbling with the catch, he nudges me to the side and releases it himself, letting his jeans drop to the floor. He's fully erect in his boxer shorts and I reach for him, feeling the heat through the material.

'Oh yeah. That's it – touch it there . . . oh yeah, that's so hot – oh yeah,' he says.

He tugs his boxers off, then helps me remove all my clothes before pulling me down onto the bed with him and grinding himself against me with a flurry of 'yeah, baby's' that make me wonder if he's been watching too many seventies porn films. I fight back a snigger.

'You're so tight, oh yeah,' he says as he pushes a finger inside me. For all of two seconds. Then he breaks away to retrieve a condom from the bedside table. I rub my clit as he puts it on. He glances up briefly and says, 'Oh yeah, you make me so horny. I can't wait to get in there.' But then he turns his attention back to the condom.

Once in place, he asks, 'How do you like it – missionary or doggy style?'

It doesn't feel like the time to point out these aren't the only two options.

I tell him I like it doggy style. If he carries on with the 'oh yeah's, I'm not sure I can keep a straight face and at least this way he won't see if I get the giggles.

'Oh yeah, ooooh, mmmm, yeah,' he moans as he slips inside me, groaning louder and louder as he picks up speed. 'Oh yeah, I knew this would be amazing. Oh yeah, here it comes, oh yeah.'

The volume goes up another notch. 'Oh yeah, are you ready? Here it comes. Ahhh yeah. I'm ready. Are you ready? Ahhh yeah. Are you ready?'

I don't think I could tell him I was ready even if I wanted to. I'm too busy using the pillow to stifle my laughter. I wonder how many times his flatmates have had to listen to this, and whether they're cracking up in their rooms at this very moment.

That's not to say things don't feel good down below, but there's no way I'm going to come if Warren doesn't hit the mute button for a few minutes. It's clearly not a problem for him, though.

'Oh yeah, ahhh yeah, that's it baby . . . ahhh yeah, so hot . . . oh yeah!' he yells. 'Oh yeah, it's coming . . . oh yeah, I can't hold it . . . oh yeah, here it is, here it is . . . oh yeah . . . ahhhhhhhhhhh.'

With a final shudder he pulls away and collapses on the bed beside me, eyes closed and breathing heavily. 'That was so amazing. So good. Oh wow. Come here, beautiful.'

He pulls me down beside him and for a moment I think he's going to finish me off with his hands or his tongue – or both. But his eyes stay closed as he pulls me in for a cuddle.

'I'm knackered,' he says to the top of my head, and I'm not kidding, about ten seconds later he's out cold.

I reach down between my legs and stroke my clitoris again, but with Warren snoring lightly beside me, the moment has gone. A sigh escapes from my throat as I withdraw my hand. Instead of making me forget about

Merle, Warren has simply reminded me how good the sex was with him and how desirable he made me feel. He knew exactly how to turn me on and would never have left me hanging like Warren has. It's hard not to crave his expert touch again.

I close my eyes and try to sleep, but I can't drop off, and after I've been lying there for a while, sobering up and starting to think about the long day ahead in the studio, and how it will be a lot less awkward if I sneak out of the room now than if I have to do morning-after breakfast with Warren's flatmates, I decide to head back to my own bed.

Warren stirs as I quietly retrieve my clothes. 'Are you not staying?' he murmurs, without opening his eyes.

'I really need to get going,' I tell him, already pulling on my jeans. 'Rehearsals and all that.'

'I'll call you,' I add as an afterthought, because it seems like the polite thing to say. But as I pull the bedroom door closed behind me, I think we both know I probably won't. If I wanted a repeat of this evening, I wouldn't be running off into the night, would I?

We got on so well at the pub that I thought it was a good idea coming here afterwards. But instead of making me feel better about being dropped by Merle – and Ed, for that matter – I feel like I've hit a new low. Trudging home alone through the dark, deserted streets of south-west London after dismal sex with a guy I hardly know? It's hardly the stuff dreams are made of.

I stifle a yawn, suddenly exhausted. I know life is all about taking chances – as Lucy reminded me with *Fire on the Dance Floor* – and there was always the possibility that tonight could have worked out differently, but right now I wish I'd left the chance-taking to someone else.

Chapter 18

I doze on the train on the way to rehearsals the next morning, letting my mind drift over the events of the last twenty-four hours and the likely events of the next twenty-four.

Lucy looked crestfallen when I broke the news over breakfast that there won't be any double dating for us with Aiden and Warren.

'But you were getting on like a house on fire at the pub,' she protested, not yet ready to give up on the idea.

I explained we're not sexually compatible – and she asked if he's into something weird. Trust her to jump to that conclusion. She bit her knuckles when I did a quick impression for her, then she reluctantly accepted it wasn't ever going to be repeated.

I wish I could have told her we'd had the time of our lives and that my steamy studio sessions with Merle were now a distant memory. But in fact, sleeping with Warren has had the opposite effect. My traitorous mind even has me thinking how easy it would be to pick up where I left off with Merle now I know Sofiya doesn't want to save their marriage and there's no need to feel guilty. But I shake the thought away, angry with myself for even contemplating it. I'm better than that. I deserve better than that.

Bloody Merle. It's like the harder I try to push him out of my head, the more he intrudes on my thoughts. Why did he have to turn out to be such a liar and a cheat? And how the hell am I going to face him for the first time since it all blew up? I shudder at the thought of it. Will we talk about it? Does he blame me? Will there be a gigantic showdown in front of everyone at Channel 6? I hope to God there isn't.

Thankfully I don't have any more time to fret about it once I arrive at the studio. For the first time, Aleksis is there before me, keen to get cracking as we've only got one more day to practise before the live show. I throw myself into it as best I can, but because I've only had five hours' sleep, I struggle to remember all the things he tells me and a bit of tension creeps back into our rehearsal.

After the pep talk from his sister, he wants us to go out there and show the audience something amazing, but I find it hard to keep my spins consistent and my steps fast enough and he gets frustrated when I can't get it right. After I lose my balance during yet another spin, he snaps at me, and I hit back at him that if he hadn't wasted so much time at the beginning of the week, we wouldn't be in the shape we're in now. By lunchtime, we're barely speaking again.

It takes an apology and a peace offering to get us back on track. He offers me a Mars bar and says, 'I know I'm pushing you hard today; I'm sorry if it feels like too little too late. You have every right to be annoyed that I wasn't in it from the beginning. But I'm trying to make up for it now. I'm being tough on you because I want us to prove to everyone that we deserve our place in the show, that we don't need their fake score to get us through. We're better than that.'

'But you can't just click your fingers and expect me to be perfect,' I point out.

'I know and I'm sorry.' He looks me right in the eyes, which makes me feel unsettled, though I don't know why. 'We'll take it slower this afternoon,' he says, his voice softer, 'and I'll change anything that isn't working. By the time we leave here tonight we'll have a routine that works for both of us, I promise.'

And we do manage to pull together for the rest of the session, resulting in a routine that's perhaps not as dazzling as it might have been, but is good enough that I won't be embarrassed performing it. It's a huge relief after the way the week began.

I'm absolutely exhausted by the end of the day – physically, mentally and emotionally – and can't wait to go home and collapse on the sofa. But I'm feeling more positive too. While our dance isn't likely to blow anyone away, I don't think it would necessarily knock us out of the competition either, if our score were genuine.

I've warmed to Aleksis a tiny bit too, now we're talking more and he's stopped being vile to me. While he hasn't exactly apologised for his initial behaviour, he has more or less admitted he's to blame for our rocky start. He even offers some reassurance when I admit I'm anxious about tomorrow, which makes me see him in a slightly different light – one where dancing with him for another week might not be quite so unpleasant.

Safely buried among the cushions back at the flat, I fire off a message to the Fire Dancers group, to see how everyone's week has been.

'*Hey, stranger,*' Liam writes back. '*We were getting worried. We thought Merle might have murdered you or something.*'

He adds three laughing faces to show he's joking.

'*I'm still here,*' I type. '*Tough week this week. It's wiped me out.*'

'*I hear ya,*' Beth replies. '*I might as well tell you now, cos you'll find out tomorrow anyway, but I've got the Argentine this week. It's an absolute NIGHTMARE. I have a lot more respect for Emilia now – she made it look like a piece of cake last Saturday. Mine's more crumble than gateau.*'

'*I'm sure yours will be just as delicious,*' Liam writes. '*You did really well last week, you'll surprise yourself again. I can't wait to see all your dances. You're going to smash it.*'

'*And then we're going to get smashed,*' Tammy adds. '*Woohoo!*'

'*I've managed to reserve a table at a place round the corner from Channel 6,*' Liam writes. '*The Golden Grape. It's just a few minutes' walk away.*'

My heart lurches. Of all the places, why did it have to be there? But then I force myself to think about it rationally. The chances of the same people being in a London pub on two consecutive Saturday nights are slim. And if there are one or two who recognise me, I can handle it – especially if I'm surrounded by friends. I got through it last night, and I'll get through it again.

In fact, I'm grateful to have a night out with the whole gang to look forward to after the show. Before that I've got to get through the awkwardness of seeing Merle again and pull off a decent two minutes of salsa in front of the judges. I don't know which I'm dreading more.

Chapter 19

Tammy and Beth meet me at the Tube station in the morning so we can walk to the Channel 6 building together. Despite all my bravado about rising above photo-gate, they know I'm dreading seeing all the people on the show. It's way more daunting than facing a bunch of total strangers.

I still haven't told them I haven't seen Merle all week, though, and that I'm completely freaking out about it. So they have no idea just how grateful I am for their moral support.

Tammy waves as I come through the ticket barrier. 'So how are you feeling? Ready to do it all again?'

'I can't say I'm necessarily looking forward to the next few hours,' I admit.

'Just focus on your performance and try to ignore all the other stuff,' Beth says. 'If it's any consolation we're both feeling apprehensive too. I thought it would get easier as we went along and got more used to everything, but it

136

definitely feels like there's more pressure this week.'

'It's true. I feel like this could be it for me after my lousy merengue score,' Tammy adds. 'But I'm not going down without a fight.'

'I think we'll all feel better once we've got our sequins on,' Beth says. 'We just need to get in there and get in the zone.'

I listen to them swapping stories about their weeks on the ten-minute walk to the studio. They're both full of praise for their instructors – they haven't had a single cross word.

'Are you okay, Kate?' Beth asks as we approach the entrance. 'You're very quiet.'

And I know I can't keep my secret any longer. 'I have a confession to make.'

'I knew there was something,' she says. 'What's going on?'

When I stop walking they both turn round to face me.

'I'm not dancing with Merle any more,' I blurt out. 'I've switched partners with Emilia. I haven't seen Merle since last Saturday. I'm kind of shitting myself. I don't know how he's going to react to seeing me again.'

'Whoa!' Beth exclaims.

'That's big,' Tammy nods, wide-eyed.

'I'm sorry I didn't tell you, I was under strict instructions to keep it secret,' I explain. 'But you're going to find out in a minute anyway. So there it is. I'm dancing with Aleksis now. Merle is with Emilia. Oh, and I met Merle's wife. She came to one of my rehearsals. She's Aleksis's sister.'

'What?' they shriek in unison.

'Holy crap!' Tammy adds. 'You don't do things by halves, do you?'

Beth shakes her head in disbelief. 'No wonder you're on edge. What a nightmare. How's Aleksis about it all? I mean, is he all right? With you?'

'It's complicated,' I shrug. 'But we're getting by.'

Tammy still looks gobsmacked. 'His sister? What the hell?'

'She doesn't want us not to do our best on the show because of her, or because of Merle,' I explain. 'She gave us her blessing.'

'That's insane,' Tammy says.

'Tell me about it.'

Before I can share any more details with them, Olivia holds the door open and looks pointedly at us. 'Are you coming in, ladies? You're among the last.'

'Try not to worry,' Tammy says quietly. 'We'll be right there if Merle starts any funny business.'

'Thanks, I really appreciate that.'

We follow Olivia down the now-familiar corridors to *Fire on the Dance Floor*'s reception area and as soon as we walk in, I scan the room for Merle. I can't help it. And there he is, standing by the drinks machine with Emilia, his arm draped around her shoulders. My heart leaps into my throat.

Last Saturday, he didn't so much as glance in my direction in the reception room. Today he's hugging Emilia in front of everyone, and looking pretty smug about it too.

Does it mean they're sleeping together? I know I shouldn't care, but I hate the thought they might be. Seeing them looking so close reminds me how much I wanted that for myself, but I never got the chance. It doesn't seem fair.

Thankfully, I'm distracted by Aleksis coming over to say hello. He greets everyone then tells me to remember I have nothing to fear today.

'Ah, that's so sweet,' Beth says. If only she knew what he meant.

I turn away from her and Tammy and quietly ask him, 'Does Merle know about our special arrangement today?' I'd forgotten to ask before.

'He doesn't, and nor must anyone else, okay? I'd suggest you just stay out of his way today, and I'll be doing the same. Otherwise, I'll probably thump him.'

I realise I haven't given much thought to how hard this must be for Aleksis, too, and I feel a rush of sympathy for him. It makes me want to squeeze his arm, like Lucy does to comfort me, but I hold back. That's not the place we're in.

'I never liked him much,' Aleksis says, 'and I like him a lot less now. But my sister wants me to keep out of it. She prefers to fight her own battles.'

I offer an understanding smile, but he's too busy shooting daggers across the room at Merle to notice. When I glance at Merle to see if he's aware, he looks back at me at that exact moment. And winks. Or at least I think he does. It's so unexpected I'm not sure if I imagined it, but my skin breaks out in goose bumps.

Then Olivia bangs on her clipboard to get everyone's attention, and the moment has passed.

'Right, you lot, you know the drill now,' she says. 'We've

139

got a lot to get through today. Beth, Gabriel, you're first for hair and make-up. Theo, costumes. Emilia, Merle, rehearsals. The rest of you, don't go far. Does everyone remember how to get to their designated stations? You do, Gabriel? Great, take Beth with you. Merle, Emilia, you do too? Great, off you go. Theo? No? Okay, you follow me. Everyone else, I'll be back shortly.'

It's the last I see of Merle and Emilia till the show's about to begin.

Tammy keeps me distracted with stories of her week in rehearsals until it's my turn in costumes, where I'm dressed in a pink and orange tasselled minidress. It's not exactly something I'd choose, but it's bright and colourful and the tassels swoosh from side to side when I move, which will hopefully make my dancing look more fluid than it really is.

In hair and make-up, I'm relieved when no one says a single word about me and Merle. I wonder if the team has been briefed not to mention it, because if it was me I'd be dying to ask about it. But instead we stick to chatting about the latest things we've watched on Netflix and some of the other famous people they've had in their makeover chairs, so I manage to relax while they backcomb my hair and give me glittery eyes in colours that match my dress – which might look like I've been teleported back to 1984, but will stand out nicely on the dance floor.

My studio rehearsal with Aleksis is mid-afternoon and goes well. I make it through the whole routine without missing a step and he manages not to get his hands caught up in my tassels. He's been given a spray tan and I can't

140

help thinking it suits him. I'd even go so far as to say I can see why Lucy said she found him attractive. He's still not my type, though.

There are a couple more hours to wait until it's time for filming, which I mostly spend with Beth and Tammy, but Aleksis comes and joins us for some of it. And it turns out he's quite the entertainer when he wants to be, making all three of us laugh with tales from his days on the dance circuit.

'He's hilarious,' Beth gushes, when he's eventually called away by Olivia. 'You must be so happy you're dancing with him now instead of Merle.'

'Oh yes,' I nod, not wanting to admit to them how emotionally draining the week has been. Or how, in spite of everything, I can't help feeling gutted that Merle is paired with Emilia now.

I wonder if he even tried to patch things up with Sofiya after she found out about me, or if at any point Sofiya considered giving him one last chance. But she'd never be able to trust him again. I remind myself Emilia is welcome to him.

Chapter 20

When Olivia finally tells us she's ready to take us all to the studio for filming, there's an immediate buzz in the air. As we follow her down the corridor, she calls out the running order of our dances. Theo is kicking things off this week, with his partner Daniele. Aleksis and I will be second from last, presumably so they can make sure our score is high enough to keep us in the competition. Merle and Emilia will close the show.

My heart leaps as Merle falls into step beside me. 'You're still the most sexy,' he whispers into my ear as he passes. Then he strides ahead, with Emilia sweeping along behind him. She doesn't even glance in my direction.

I stare after him, pulse racing, thinking perhaps I imagined it. But I know I didn't mishear him and it throws my head into a whirl of confusion. Does that mean he regrets switching dance partners and wishes he was still dancing with me too? No, that wouldn't make any sense – he's the one who instigated the swap.

Could it be that he *is* now sleeping with Emilia, but it's not living up to what he shared with me? *No, that's just my ego talking*, I tell myself firmly. Although if I miss those moments, it's not too much of a stretch to think that he might as well . . .

Not that it matters, I remind myself. I'm not about to forgive him for the way he treated me. And the fact that he thinks that's an appropriate first thing to say to me after everything that's happened is the perfect reminder of why not.

But it doesn't stop his words tumbling round in my head as Kimberley Ross takes her place on the stage and week two's live show begins. My eyes keep drifting towards him, even though his back is now turned, and I know the jitters in my stomach are not just pre-show nerves.

'Ladies and gentlemen, welcome back to *Fire on the Dance Floor*!' Kimberley shouts to a cheer from the audience. 'There are just six couples left in the competition this week and we can't wait to see what they've got in store for us tonight as they battle it out for a place on next week's show.

'Sadly, last week, we had to say goodbye to Liam after his salsa failed to light up the dance floor. But sparks flew during Kate's saucy kizomba, which saw her and Merle get on top of the table. To the top of the table, I should say!' she laughs.

My cheeks flush as the audience sniggers at her joke. I thought the show would gloss over last week's antics, not highlight them in the opening minutes. I plaster a smile on my face to hide my irritation.

'So will the salsa be the dance that sees off another couple this week? Tonight, it's Kate who'll be showing us her hip-swinging moves – once again,' Kimberley smirks, with a conspiratorial wink.

'Jesus Christ,' I mutter when this gets more laughter. I'm not sure I can maintain my composure if Kimberley carries on with her innuendos. I want to grab the mic and lob it out of the studio. I nearly jump out of my skin when I feel Aleksis give my hand a supportive squeeze.

'But we've got a big surprise for you this week,' Kimberley says brightly, before chucking in one last cheap laugh. 'Because this week it's not Merle who Kate will be getting jiggy with, but Aleksis, former partner of Emilia, who has stepped in to take Merle's place. Merle, meanwhile, has joined forces with Emilia, and we predict they're going to be a force to be reckoned with.

'We can't wait to see what they bring to the dance floor this week. Will they be the ones who set our hearts racing tonight with their sensual bachata? Will Kate and Aleksis have the same chemistry she found with Merle? It's time to find out – so without further ado, let's bring out our first couple and start the fire on the dance floor!'

I have to concentrate even harder on my poker face as Theo and Daniele run onto the stage to a cheer from the audience. The bloody bachata? Of course, Merle would luck out with that for his first dance with Emilia. He lives and breathes the bachata, it's his speciality. It's bound to be brilliant. I can only hope that means it will at least take the focus off him and me.

Theo and Daniele score 7.9 for their cha-cha, so they're off to a good start. Tammy's kizomba comes next and I can see she's relieved when 8.1 flashes up on the screen. It's a huge improvement on her merengue score and means she's safe for another week. It's followed by Dean's merengue and although it's not as energetic as Tammy's was, he plays up to the audience and makes them laugh and it gets him a straight 8.

'That's it, we're halfway through,' Kimberley says, 'and as you can see it's really, really close this week. With their score of 7.9, it's Theo and Daniele who are in the danger zone at the moment, but there are still three more couples to dance and, as you know, it's you who get to decide their fate. Anything could happen, so let's see who's up next. Ladies and gentlemen, it's Beth Atkins and Gabriel Romero!'

I can tell Beth is nervous because she clenches and unclenches her hands over and over as the video clip of her week's rehearsals plays on screen. Then the spotlight lands on her and Gabriel, their music starts playing and their Argentine tango begins.

The rest of the stage stays darkened and the spotlight follows their slow journey round the dance floor. I think it looks beautiful, like they're dancing in moonlight, but the judges aren't quite so taken.

'I'm a bit lost for words,' Jacques admits. 'The tango is meant to be fiery and sharp and electrifying, but it felt like you were both sleepwalking across the stage. Where was the energy, the pizzazz? I think you maybe tried to use the staging to make up for the lack of drama in the choreography, but I'm afraid all you ended up doing is highlighting how misjudged this performance was.'

My heart goes out to Beth.

'Harsh words there,' Kimberley interrupts. 'Sophie, did you see anything you liked in Beth and Gabriel's routine?'

'Sadly I have to agree with Jacques – it was all a bit lacklustre. For me, it fell flat.'

'Some tough feedback tonight,' Kimberley says, turning to Beth. 'How do you feel about that?'

'I'm not going to lie, I really struggled with this dance,' she admits, 'so I think their comments are fair. I wasn't feeling confident and Gabe did have to slow it all down for me. But I still enjoyed performing it and if I get the opportunity to be up here again I'm going to do whatever it takes to win the judges over next time.'

'Good for you.' Kimberley smiles. 'And now, audience, it's time to deliver your verdicts. Do you want to see Beth and Gabriel dancing again on next week's show? Grab your keypads and let's find out.'

The scoreboard lights up and the marker starts moving, but it only creeps as far as the seven. There's an 'ooh' from the audience and Beth looks gutted. I wish I could give her a hug.

'Beth, you must be disappointed; but remember, it's not over yet. There are still two couples to come,' Kimberley says chirpily. 'Ladies and gentlemen, please give it up one more time for Beth and Gabriel. And next up, dancing the salsa, please welcome to the stage Kate Wareing and her new dance partner Aleksis Lapsa!'

And then we're out in front of the audience, watching ourselves doing spins and fixing the studio floor in our video clip, which thankfully gets another laugh – this time a welcome one. Then we're in position and everything else slips out of my mind as I concentrate solely on remembering the routine and not messing it up.

Two minutes later it's all over, and all I can think about is how mad it is that we practise for so many hours for just these few short minutes.

'Over to you, judges,' Kimberley says at the end.

Mariana is nodding. 'Not bad. There was just enough content there to keep it interesting. There was a little hesitation around some of the spins, and you fell behind on the timing just a fraction at times. But you recovered well, and overall it was a good effort.'

'I have to agree,' Sophie says. 'There were a few missteps here and there, and I felt you were maybe relying a little too heavily on Aleksis at times, but all in all I liked what I saw. Obviously you've had the added challenge of adjusting to a new partner this week, which is never easy, so well done for coping with that. Personally I hope you make it through. I think there's real potential in this partnership and I'd like to see what else you can bring to the competition.'

This gives me hope. Maybe they won't need to fix our score after all.

'And Jacques?' Kimberley prompts.

'Like Sophie says, this is a new partnership, so it's fantastic to see it already gelling. And if we compare this dance to the dances in week one, it comfortably stands up to the competition. But of course it isn't week one, and it wasn't perfect.'

My heart sinks again.

'If you go through, you're going to have to work hard to push yourselves up in the rankings,' he advises. 'But something tells me you can do it – so I wish you luck.'

'So it seems like the judges are keen to see Kate and Aleksis again on next week's show,' Kimberley says. 'But, audience, what about you? Do you want their salsa to shimmy to the top of the scoreboard? It's time to find out!'

My stomach twists in anticipation, even though I know we're safe from elimination. It might not be our real score, but I still want it to be good, especially after I finished in the top spot last week. I feel awful for Beth, though. With me guaranteed to go through and the only other dancer still to come being the best dancer among us, things aren't looking great for her.

And then our score arrives . . . 7.1. Just .1 above Beth, which makes me feel even worse. How I wish I knew if it was our real score or if the producers have tampered with it. But I doubt I'll ever know.

As we leave the stage, there's a murmur in the audience as Merle and Emilia take our place. Kimberley hushes everyone as their video starts playing on the big screen. It starts with Merle talking, while Emilia strokes his arm and gazes adoringly at him.

'As you know, it's been a tough time for me recently,' Merle says solemnly. 'I started this week thinking my wife, Sofiya, and I could work through it, but after some difficult discussions we've made the decision to end our marriage. It hasn't been easy to accept that we've grown apart, but we both feel much happier now we've mutually agreed it's time to move on.'

So she really has told him to sling his hook – and is sticking to her guns this time. I'm glad for her. I'm sure she'll be happier in the long run.

I can't believe Merle is going for the sympathy vote though. He obviously knows he's got some grovelling to do to keep the audience on side. In the video, he turns to Emilia and looks at her affectionately.

'But this one has been keeping my spirits up,' he says, taking her hand.

Yeah, I bet she has.

'She's been there for me every step of the way and has been such a rock for me these past few days. I can't thank her enough.'

He smiles at her and she tells him he's welcome, with a dreamy look in her eyes.

'Life is sometimes full of surprises and we've become so close this week when I was least expecting it,' Merle continues. 'We didn't plan it, and I know it will seem a little soon to some people, but I can't imagine wanting to spend my time with anyone else right now. I think this could be the start of something really special.'

Then they kiss on the lips. And there it is. Confirmation of what I suspected all along. My fists clench so tightly I can feel my nails digging into my palms. There was absolutely no need to put me through the partner swap if he wasn't going to work things out with Sofiya anyway. And to then replace me with Emilia without so much as a blink . . . am I supposed to just be okay with that?

'So I hope I don't let her down tonight,' Merle says. 'And I hope you won't judge us for anything other than our dancing. Emilia is a beautiful person and a beautiful dancer – and the best way for me to thank her for all the support she's given me this week would be for my choreography to take us through to the next round. She deserves nothing less.'

They kiss again as they fade from the screen and I swear I can actually taste the bitterness his fawning monologue has left in my mouth.

It turns out it's got nothing on how jealous their absolutely mesmerising bachata makes me feel, though. Merle and Emilia couldn't look more like star-crossed lovers if they tried, as they start their dance with their foreheads touching and her arms round his neck.

Her hair sweeps the floor as he dips her backwards then pulls her back in with a series of body rolls. I can't take my eyes off them as he drops to his knees to spin her, pulls her down to execute a perfect head roll, then runs his hands up her legs, drawing her up with him and lifting her up into a spin with the splits. They look like they've been doing this forever.

They end with her sitting on his knee, head tossed back, and his hands on her hips. Someone wolf whistles in the audience, then the judges are out of their seats, clapping, and Kimberley is fanning herself theatrically as she tells the audience it's one of the hottest things she's ever seen.

The audience responds by giving the dance a whopping 9.5. But it's Merle and Emilia's celebratory kiss that rattles me more than their score. My cheeks flush with frustration. Lied to, rejected, and to top it all off, this. More than ever I wish I'd never, ever been paired with Merle. Or Aleksis for that matter. A nice safe option like Tammy's partner Elijah could have saved me a world of pain.

'This couldn't mean more to me,' Merle gushes, his arms still round Emilia. 'To us,' he corrects himself.

'You certainly seem to have melted a few hearts this evening,' Kimberley beams. 'Ladies and gentlemen, let's hear it one more time for tonight's winners, Merle and Emilia, who have guaranteed themselves a place on next week's show.'

As they run off the stage waving, Kimberley invites Beth and Gabriel back out to join her and commiserates with them for coming last.

'It's been so much fun,' Beth says bravely. 'I feel really lucky to have had the chance to take part. And Gabe was an amazing teacher. I couldn't have asked for more.'

'It's been short, but definitely sweet,' Gabriel adds. 'We've had two brilliant weeks, I just feel gutted for Beth that there won't be a third. I think she did so well and she's an incredible girl – I know I've got a friend for life.'

'That's so sweet,' Kimberley says, a hand placed over her heart. 'But sadly, folks, that's all we've got time for today. So thanks to our three judges, and to you, our studio audience, for helping us out with the scoring again this week – and to you at home, for tuning in. We hope you enjoyed it as much as we have, and we'll see you again next week here on *Fire on the Dance Floor*!'

The lights go up and the room instantly fills with the sounds of the audience preparing to leave. Minutes later,

Tammy and I are hugging Beth in the reception room, grabbing glasses of the free wine and telling her how devastated we are about her exit from the show.

She assures us she's fine and insists she won't miss the stress of the live performances one bit, which at least makes me feel a fraction less guilty. If she'd said she was gutted, or worse, burst into tears, I think I would have had to tell her the whole ugly truth about my score and her exit.

I notice Aleksis commiserating with Gabriel on the other side of the room and wonder if he also feels like we're to blame, knowing tonight might have been a different story without our secret guarantee to go through. But if he does feel that way, he's very good at hiding it.

Meanwhile, I'm trying really hard not to stare at Merle and Emilia. Now they've admitted they're an item, they're making no effort to be discreet. She's sitting on his lap on the other side of the room, taking selfies of them kissing and clinking glasses.

Noticing me watching them, Beth says, 'I know it's polite to stick around for a bit and be all pro-show, but why don't we skip it today and head straight to the pub? The others will be there already, so what say we just go and get the party started over there instead?'

I suddenly can't wait to ditch my pink and orange ensemble and get away from Channel 6. Even though I'll still need a brave face for our gathering at The Golden Grape, I tell her I'll see her out the front in fifteen.

Chapter 21

Although I manage to keep my guilt about Beth at bay for the rest of the weekend – after she promised everyone at the Grape she wasn't upset about leaving the show – it creeps back into my conscience on Monday morning. As I make my way to the studio, my excitement about learning a new *Fire on the Dance Floor* routine is tinged with a sense that I don't really deserve another chance.

But that sparks the determination to prove I really am worthy of my place in the competition this week. I want to get through to the next round, and I want to do it without any interference.

It turns out Aleksis feels much the same way.

'It does feel a bit like we cheated, even if we don't know for sure that we did,' he says. 'I even thought about withdrawing from the competition this weekend, but eventually decided not to. Better to draw a line under it and move on. Otherwise, we're just letting Merle win.'

There's determination in his voice when he continues. 'So this is what I think we should do . . . we accept what's done is done and we come out fighting. We give it everything we've got this week, rehearse every minute and give the audience no choice but to give us a genuinely high score next Saturday. We'll have to work hard, but I promise to give it a hundred per cent from now on. I'm sorry we got off to such a bad start last week.'

I wave off his apology. 'Let's draw a line under that too. Fresh start this week and I promise I'll work my arse off, too. Please tell me we haven't got the tango, though.'

He holds up an envelope. 'I haven't looked yet. Sometimes I prefer to just see what unfolds rather than planning meticulously. I thought we could open it together.'

I glance up at him in surprise. How different this is to last Monday, when he couldn't even look me in the eye.

I lean towards him as he pulls the card out of the envelope.

'Bachata,' he reads aloud, making my heart sink.

'Oh no.' I slump back against the wall. 'Straight after Merle and Emilia's? We'll never live up to that performance.'

'Hey, give me some credit.' He sounds offended.

'Sorry, that was no reflection on you. It's just . . . '

'Come on,' he says, offering me a hand and pulling me upright again. 'Let's just get stuck straight in. We can do this, you know. We just have to work for it.'

And for the first half of the morning, I manage to brush off my doubts as Aleksis walks me through the basic moves. But as soon as we progress to more complicated sequences, the pressure starts getting to me. The harder I try, the more uncoordinated I seem to be. I can't shake the feeling that I'm never going to be able to deliver the dazzling performance I so desperately want to.

I grow increasingly despondent about how we'll compare to Merle and Emilia. When they danced together, it was intimate and sexy. With Aleksis, despite our earlier bonding moment, I feel like there's still a wall between us – and it shows. I don't know if it's because I'm not totally relaxed around him, just in case he still secretly hates me for what I put Sofiya through. But if we're going to put on a show anywhere near good enough to keep us in the competition, we've got to find a way to break down this barrier.

I think about the turning point in my kizomba rehearsals with Merle. It was after we had sex that everything really fell into place. But that's obviously not going to happen here. It's enough of a miracle that Aleksis and I are being civil to each other. I'll admit he does have a certain appeal now we're not at each other's throats, but I'm not going down that road again.

Aleksis remains patient with me while we go over a few of the steps again, but he must be able to tell I'm struggling. He saves the day just before I have a complete meltdown by saying, 'I'm getting hungry. Do you fancy a quick wander around Brixton Market? I think a half-hour break will do us good.'

I agree that a brief change of scene might get me in a more positive frame of mind for the afternoon. He tells me not to be too hard on myself, it's only day one.

We find a quiet corner in a pop-up café and sit down for coffees and cakes – carrot for him, chocolate brownie for me

– and I notice he gets a fair few looks from the other female customers. I guess Lucy's not the only one who thinks he's attractive. But Aleksis seems oblivious to what's going on around us. His attention is on my cake. 'Want to go halves?' he asks eventually.

I can't help laughing. 'Sure, why not.'

We slide our plates into the middle and he pulls a corner off the brownie with his fork. It makes his whole face light up – which makes me reluctantly admit I can see why people might fancy him. I suppose he can be quite striking. If razor-sharp jawlines and piercing blue eyes are what you're into.

'Wow, that's delicious,' he gushes.

I taste his carrot cake and I'm just as impressed – as well as conscious that cake sharing is something I'd usually only do with a boyfriend. For a second I imagine we're an actual couple, but I quickly shake the thought away. Where the hell did that come from? It's only a cake.

While we drink our lattes, we chat about our interests away from the dance floor and I'm surprised to discover we have a few things in common. We both love long walks in the countryside and lazy Sundays watching animated movies. *Sing* is his favourite and *The Secret Life Of Pets* is mine, but we both have *Up* in our top three.

'Even I welled up watching *Up*,' he admits when I tell him the opening sequence made me bawl my eyes out. I find myself liking the fact that he has a vulnerable side – and doesn't mind admitting it.

We discuss our progress in the studio this morning and Aleksis wants to know if there's anything he can do to help me relax more into the moves he's been pulling together.

'You'll wish you hadn't asked,' I laugh, then instantly regret it because of course he wants to know what I'm talking about. I quickly try to backtrack, but he won't let it go.

'Come on, Kate. It's all on us this week, remember? So if there's anything you think we can do to improve our chances, now's the time to tell.'

I rack my brains for anything else I can say, but when nothing believable springs to mind I end up blurting out the truth.

'It's just that . . . Oh boy, I can't believe I'm going to come out with this . . . It's just . . . well, I may have been told I dance a lot better after sex.'

I kick myself for saying it the second the words leave my mouth. They hang in the air for an awkward moment while Aleksis clenches and unclenches his jaw. I squeeze my eyes shut and wish I'd thought of something more appropriate. When I risk another peek, he can't even look me in the eye.

'Not that I'm saying we should,' I babble, cheeks burning. 'I panicked. I'm sorry. You put me on the spot.'

'I suppose I shouldn't be surprised,' he says eventually. 'It sounds like something that arsehole would come out with.' He hates Merle so much he doesn't even use his name. 'But I hope you realise that's not what makes someone a good dancer. It's about how you feel within yourself, not . . .'

He shakes his head and lets his words trail away, but they leave me berating myself on so many levels as we settle the bill and head back to the studio – for my big blundering mouth, for the gigantic spanner I've thrown in the works just when we were starting to get along, and more than anything else because he's right, and I don't know why I couldn't see it before.

It wasn't the sex that made me a better dancer, it was the fact that for the first time I was able to think of myself as being sexy. So, like Aleksis says, I just need to find that self-confidence again. I promise myself I'm going to try from now on. If Aleksis, who hardly knows me, has faith in me, it's high time I started believing in myself a bit more.

Chapter 22

I surprise myself the next morning by managing not to dwell on my clumsy admission to Aleksis yesterday. Filled with a newfound determination not to beat myself up over things I can't change, I decide I'm not going to feel embarrassed about it.

But just when I'm congratulating myself for not getting hung up on it, it transpires that Aleksis didn't entirely put it out of his mind.

'I've given a lot of thought to what you said yesterday,' he tells me, making me panic for a moment that he's going to suggest we do actually sleep with each other to improve my dancing.

'And what it's made me realise is that a love story between us is exactly what we need to elevate our standing on the show. Merle has already worked out that telling everyone he's got the hots for Emilia will help keep him in the competition. We just need to do the same to get the audience to vote for us – but better.'

My eyebrows shoot so far up my forehead they're in danger of getting lost in my hairline. I know I insinuated that sleeping with him might improve my dancing, but a love story is something of a leap.

'It won't be real,' he clarifies, seeing my alarmed expression. 'It's just about making the audience think it's real – on the show, through social media. They'll lap it up if they think we've really fallen for each other, just like Merle and Emilia, especially after everything that's come before it. Don't you think?'

When I stare at him, speechless, he ploughs on.

'People are naturally curious about other people's relationships. Much as I hate to admit it, the majority of them probably don't care so much about whether we can do a decent bachata. It's reality TV, not the world championships. That's not to say we shouldn't still put on a good show to impress the audience – I'm not about to waste this opportunity to show off my talent now Sofiya has made me see sense. But I think we can both agree it's a popularity contest as much as a dance competition, right?

'So the best way to get the viewers really invested in us, and the audience to go crazy with their scores for us, has to be to give them something off the dance floor as well as on. I reckon it could even make us the show favourites if we really throw ourselves into it. So what do you reckon – are you up for it?'

My mind races, wondering if he's gone crazy. Does he really believe this is a good idea? But he seems so convinced and his arguments are persuasive – plus I can't pretend the prospect of knocking Merle off his pedestal isn't seriously tempting.

'I suppose we could try,' I reply cautiously.

'I think it's the right move,' he says, more decisively now I've semi-agreed to it. 'I ran it by Sofiya too – I hope you don't mind that I did that – and she's on board with it as well. Without wanting to make her sound vindictive, she was quite enthusiastic about us trying to take Merle down a peg or two after everything he's done.'

Another thing I have in common with his sister.

'She'd even like to help, if you agree to it. She said we could put our heads together over at her place later, and come up with a game plan. Just say if that's too much of an imposition, though. I don't want it to feel like we're ganging up on you.'

'No, it's fine,' I tell him, too bamboozled to work out how I really feel about it.

And that's how I find myself pulling up in a taxi outside Merle's former home in Highgate that evening – the Georgian townhouse I've only ever seen in the pictures of him leaving it – in perhaps the most surreal moment since *Fire on the Dance Floor* began. At least the photographers are no longer camped outside it now Merle's marriage split is last week's news.

I wonder if it will still look like it's his place inside, with dance trophies in display cabinets and pictures of him on the walls, or if Sofiya has already removed all traces of him. But it looks just like anyone else's home, with coats hanging up in the hallway and the dishes from that morning's breakfast still sitting beside the kitchen sink.

Sofiya kisses her brother on both cheeks. '*Ćau*, Aleksis.'

'I hope being here doesn't feel too uncomfortable for you,' she says to me by way of greeting.

I tell her I'm slowly getting my head round it and she nods, like she understands. But she doesn't seem at all fazed by the fact that she's about to plot how to cut her estranged husband down to size with the help of his former fling.

'Shall we get straight into it?' she suggests, gesturing for us to take a seat round the dining table and pouring us each a glass of wine.

'I suppose the first question is how to let people know about it,' Aleksis says.

'I hope you don't mind but I've taken the liberty of setting something in motion already,' Sofiya confesses.

'You have?' Aleksis looks at her in surprise.

'Before you got here I was speaking to one of the reporters who hounded me after the photos of Kate and Merle first went viral. I've agreed to do an interview with her. It's happening tomorrow and they'll publish it on Saturday,' she explains.

'But you hate all that stuff,' Aleksis frowns, while I'm blushing furiously at the mention of the photos.

'I know, but I think it will make me feel better to get my side of the story across for once. Everyone sees me as the poor jilted wife, devastated that she's been replaced by a younger model. One of the neighbours even dropped a sympathy note through the door.' She looks horrified by this. 'But it's not the truth and I want people to know I'm happier than I have been for a long time. I want Merle to know it too.'

'In that case, good for you,' Aleksis says.

'I've promised Stella an exclusive – that's the reporter – and it would be the perfect opportunity to get your story out there too. I could drop into our chat that you've developed feelings for each other and that I've given you my blessing. It would be guaranteed to get people talking, what with all the connections between us.'

'It would be good publicity ahead of the next live show,' Aleksis agrees.

'Of course it would be better still if you could get the news out even sooner, to give everyone time to warm to the idea before the show. If it hit the headlines tomorrow, then by Saturday . . . Wait!'

This last word makes me jump and my wine sloshes over the side of my glass.

'I've got an idea,' Sofiya says as I discreetly wipe up the spillage with my sleeve. 'Stella is coming here at eight-thirty tomorrow morning. What if she were to see you two leaving here together just as she arrives? That would give her a news story she could run right away, without having to wait for my interview at the weekend. Imagine the headline – *"Merle's girl spotted leaving the house of his ex-wife with her brother"*. It'd be trending before you finished your morning rehearsal. What do you think?'

'I think this isn't something you've only just thought of,' Aleksis says suspiciously.

'Okay, I admit it, after you confirmed you were both going to come here this evening, I made up the spare room. But it makes perfect sense. This way, you can start getting people interested in you as a couple right away.'

163

'The spare room?' I repeat.

'You wouldn't want anyone spotting you arriving separately in the morning. This way, you can get the ball rolling immediately. And I can lend you all the toiletries and things you might need.'

While I'm still processing this, she adds, 'Then all you have to do after that is make sure you're seen out and about together as much as possible to build on your story. I've done some research on the most likely places for you to get spotted – restaurants, the theatre; anywhere that might get you in the news . . . '

'I only spoke to you an hour ago,' Aleksis exclaims, but there's a smile tugging at the corners of his mouth.

'I hope you don't think I've overreached, Kate,' she says apologetically.

'Not at all, I appreciate your efforts.' I can only hope this sounds convincing. I'm not sure I've really taken everything in yet. It's all happening so fast.

Minutes later, I'm standing beside Aleksis looking at the double bed in the spare room. To me it doesn't look big enough to comfortably sleep two people who aren't in a relationship. And he must be having similar thoughts because he says, 'I'll get her to make up the sofa. I don't mind sleeping down there.'

I agree it's probably for the best.

We've come upstairs to freshen up while Sofiya makes some dinner. She's given us towels and some clothes for us to borrow while she runs our gym kits through the wash, ready for tomorrow.

I turn the plan over and over in my mind as I shower

and get changed. It could backfire spectacularly if we don't pull it off. We'd be labelled frauds – perhaps we'd be better off just carrying on as we are. We could still do okay on the show without all this.

And there's another concern. 'Do you not think it's a bit dishonest, trying to win this way?' I ask Aleksis. 'Like, is pretending we're a couple to get votes any better than the score potentially being fixed to get us through last week?'

'If it had been a hundred per cent above board from the start, I think I'd still want to play by the rules,' he replies. 'But I can live with a few white lies along the way as long as we're dancing to the best of our abilities too. It's just another part of the act.'

'I suppose so. I just hope my acting is better than my dancing.'

'You shouldn't be so down on your dancing. You looked good today and we've still got three whole days before the show. We might need to use a bit of that time to practise looking like a couple, I suppose, but it surely can't be that hard. It's not like neither of us has ever been in a couple before. Here . . . '

He turns to face the mirrored wardrobe, throws an arm around my shoulders and grins.

'See. We already look . . . well, maybe if you smiled a bit more.'

I nudge him in the side and laugh. 'There's a lot to think about, that's all.'

But I can't help thinking we look quite good together as I check out our reflection, so maybe it won't be that hard to convince people we're an item.

The dress Sofiya has selected for me is a perfect fit and when we head back down to the kitchen, lured by a rich waft of garlic, she says, 'Oh, that looks lovely on you. I thought we must be a similar size.'

I return the compliment, telling her the steaming bowls of pasta on the table smell amazing, and she looks delighted. Strange as it seems, she doesn't seem to be harbouring any animosity towards me at all.

'Did you find everything you need in the room?' she asks.

'We just need a sleeping bag,' Aleksis tells her.

'I think you'll be warm enough with just the duvet. It's not cold this evening.'

'It's for the sofa,' he laughs.

He frowns when she doesn't respond. 'What?'

'I just think, if you're really going to make this work . . . I think you need to start acting like a couple right away. I know it's a lot, but you're going to have to look totally comfortable together when everyone is watching you, and I think it will help if you're already used to being close to one another.

'When Stella arrives here in the morning, she needs to be convinced you're two people who've just spent the night together. I can't help feeling the best way to do that has got to be if you really have just spent the night together.'

'I can see how you might think that.' He turns to look at me.

'It sort of makes sense,' I concede.

'Why don't you see how you go,' Sofiya suggests. 'And if it feels too awkward, there's a sleeping bag in the cupboard under the stairs.'

I think this puts both Aleksis and me more at ease.

'Now, Kate, why don't you tell me a bit more about yourself so I can convince Stella I've got to know you and we've become friends. Tell me what made you decide to enter *Fire on the Dance Floor* in the first place.'

I tell her about Lucy sending in my audition tape, to stop me moping about Ed. 'And somehow, miraculously, they asked me to join the line-up.'

'Why miraculously?' Aleksis asks. 'What was wrong with it?'

I describe my Beyoncé moment and he laughs and asks if he can see it.

'Not in a million years,' I shudder. 'Apart from the copy Shane has, it's been permanently deleted.'

'What was the story with this Ed?' Sofiya asks and I instantly wish I hadn't brought him up. Cheating exes is probably the last topic we should get into. But I can't get out of it now.

'He, er, dated me for two years then started an affair with a girl I was working with.' I flinch as I say it, but Sofiya surprises me with her heartfelt reaction.

'I girl *you* worked with? It's not enough that he had this affair, but he had to rub your nose in it as well?' She shakes her head in disgust. 'That's appalling. How did you find out?'

'She told me – eventually. It had been going on for a few weeks by then, but I had no idea.'

'We never do,' she sighs wistfully. 'In the beginning anyway.'

I try not to let on how uncomfortable this makes me feel.

'But your friend stepped in and saved the day. Good for her. We all need friends like that,' Sofiya says. Which makes me wonder if she felt let down by her own when Merle started playing away.

'Are you over him now?' she asks, and for a moment I'm not sure if it's still Ed she's talking about.

'I am,' I say firmly, realising I've barely thought about him since switching partners to dance with Aleksis.

'It sounds like you're much better off without him,' Aleksis says, and I'm strangely touched that he'd care.

'Yes, you've probably saved yourself a lifetime of suffering,' Sofiya agrees. It's the only time I've heard her allude to how much Merle must have hurt her. Then she perks up again and says, 'At least you won't have that problem with my brother.'

Because he can't be unfaithful if we're not really together.

Sofiya then asks about my family – whether I have brothers and sisters and if we're close.

I tell her about them all being in France, which makes me miss them, and she says she relates to that, what with her parents being in Latvia. But she admits she couldn't live in her home town now, having got used to the faster pace of London after twelve years in the city. I know exactly what she means. Surrey seems so sleepy by comparison.

She asks if I know what I want to do career-wise after the show has finished and I admit I haven't got a plan. She confides she didn't have much of a plan herself when she set up her interior design business – she only did it to give her flexible working hours so she could travel to competitions with Merle. But over time she realised she had a flair for it, and now, at the age of thirty, she's in high demand. It explains why the house looks so good.

We talk about *Fire on the Dance Floor* and how we think the other contestants are getting on. Much as I'd like to, we can't avoid mentioning Merle and Emilia again. There's no denying they're a level above everyone else.

'But you've got it in you, too, Kate,' Aleksis says. 'Look how much you improved at the studio today.'

He spent the afternoon showing me how I can add more drama to my body rolls, how to do a head roll without getting dizzy and how to slide my hands down my body in a way that looks suggestive rather than sleazy. By the end of it I did feel sexier while I was dancing – and, like he promised, I didn't need to have sex to do it.

'Well, if Aleksis thinks you've got it, then I know you have.' Sofiya smiles. 'When it comes to dancing, he knows what he's talking about.'

When it gets late and we finally decide to call it a night, Aleksis and I both pause at the foot of our bed.

'So,' he starts.

'So.' I pause. 'Shall we top and tail?'

'We could try that. As long as you don't kick me in the face in the night,' he says.

'As long as you keep your stinky feet away from mine,' I throw back at him.

'They're not stinky.' Then he realises I'm laughing. 'This is a bit awkward, isn't it?'

'A bit. Shall we just get in and stick to our sides?'

'Sure,' he agrees.

'No funny business,' he adds when we've stripped down to our underwear – a vest and shorts set of Sofiya's for me, a pair of Merle's boxers for him – and climbed under the covers.

'Nothing's further from my mind,' I laugh as I turn my back to him, even if his muscular legs didn't entirely escape my notice.

But I don't close my eyes straight away after he flicks off the light. I can't relax, too conscious of being in bed with someone who, until a few days ago, was the last person on earth I could imagine being in this scenario with.

I can tell from the sighs that punctuate his breathing that he hasn't fallen asleep yet, either.

'It was nice getting to know you a bit better this evening,' he eventually says into the darkness.

And I smile, pleasantly surprised, and grateful to him for trying to make this easier.

'You, too,' I reply, only realising as I say it that there's actually some truth in it.

Chapter 23

It takes me a minute to remember where I am in the morning. There's an arm across my middle and a pillar of warmth against my back and for a brief, horror-filled moment I think I'm back at Warren's. I breathe a sigh of relief when I realise it's Aleksis. He must have rolled over in the night and is now hugging me from behind.

I don't feel any inclination to wriggle away, though. To my surprise, it's not uncomfortable having him there. But my eyes fly open when I realise it isn't his other hand I can feel poking me in the back. That's a whole different story. I feel myself go rigid from head to toe, not sure how to extract myself without waking him up.

'Oh shit, I'm sorry,' he suddenly gasps, rolling away from me and sitting up on his side of the bed with his back to me.

My cheeks turn redder than I think they've ever been. 'It's fine, don't worry,' I mutter.

'I'll go and get us some coffees,' he says, sounding flustered as he hastily pulls on a T-shirt.

'White, no sugar?' he asks at the same time that I request exactly that, which makes us both laugh, breaking the tension.

'Coming right up,' he says, and practically sprints out of the room.

I can hear him talking to Sofiya while he's down in the kitchen, although I can't make out what they're saying. When he comes back up with our coffees, I sit up and lean back against the headboard. He doesn't quite look me in the eye as he climbs onto the bed beside me and apologises again for before.

I glance at him and assure him I really didn't mind. Then I panic that it might sound like I'm into him or something and get busy blowing on my drink to cool it down, to try and hide the colour creeping back onto my cheeks.

He takes a deep breath and holds an arm out, inviting me to tuck myself beneath it. 'Shall we start again?' he suggests.

I hesitate, but now he's outside the duvet it doesn't feel so intimate, so I slide myself closer and tentatively nestle against him, conscious of the warmth of his body next to mine.

'Does this feel okay to you?' he checks.

And I realise it does. I don't feel like I need to shy away. So I stop holding my breath and nod. 'Yeah. You?'

He seems to relax, too. 'I think I can handle it. But it's going to be an interesting day today.'

'You can say that again. Coming here was a lot easier than I expected it to be, though,' I admit.

'Oh, Sofiya doesn't hold anything against you. She likes you, in spite of everything. She's got a soft side under that tough exterior, you know. Bit like me.'

He's grinning when I look up at him.

I shake my head and laugh. 'You have your moments.'

'Oh, it's like that, is it? I assure you I'll make a very good fake boyfriend. Not that your ex set the bar very high. I still can't believe what he did to you.'

I wish he hadn't brought it up again.

'Yeah well, I didn't help matters by sticking around afterwards. I won't make that mistake again.'

'If you'd got a swanky job somewhere else you might not have wanted to leave it for the show,' he points out.

'That would have made your experience a lot less complicated.'

'And a lot less exciting. We can have some fun with this, I reckon, if we put our minds to it.'

I look up at him and there's a glint in his eye that makes me think we really could. 'So let's really put our minds to it,' I agree.

Then it's time to get ready for our carefully timed departure from the house.

When Stella is due to arrive, Sofiya watches from an upstairs window so she can tell us precisely when to head outside to ensure we cross paths with her. We wait behind the front door until we hear her shout, 'She's here – go, go, go!' Then we walk out holding hands as she turns onto the driveway.

173

Aleksis catches my eye and smiles, then throws an arm around my shoulder as we walk towards her.

'Čau,' he says as we pass each other, and I glance at her for just long enough to see that her mind is racing to figure out what's going on here. Of course she's yet to find out how Merle and Aleksis are connected, so she must be somewhat baffled as to what Merle's ex-lover has been doing at his estranged wife's house with one of the other dancers. This will be quite the story for her.

'Come on in,' Sofiya welcomes her. 'Never mind those two, they were supposed to be out of here a little earlier, but you know how little brothers are . . . '

We're too far away to hear Stella's reaction.

'Do you think she'll fall for it?' I ask Aleksis, who hasn't removed his arm from my shoulders even though we're no longer in eyesight.

'I don't see why not.'

'I should probably call my parents and forewarn them before they see anything,' I think aloud.

'How do you think they'll react?' he asks.

'Oh, Mum will be all mum-like, I'm sure, and give me a lecture about being dishonest, but hopefully she'll understand it's just part of being on the show. Dad usually goes along with whatever Mum says.'

'You can Skype them when we get to the studio,' he suggests.

'Yeah, I'll do that. They won't be able to give me too much grief if they know you're listening in.'

But it turns out Mum and Dad are out for a walk when I call, so I only speak to Dee, who finds the whole idea hilarious.

'This is so showbiz,' she laughs. 'I hope it works. Keep us updated.'

I promise I will.

We're several hours into rehearsals before an excited Sofiya calls Aleksis. He puts her on loudspeaker so we can both hear.

'It's out there,' she says. 'Look at the *Daily Scene* website. You're officially a couple.'

I grab my phone and find our story.

"*Things are really hotting up on Channel 6's new dance extravaganza Fire on the Dance Floor – and the latest twists and turns are not just in the fiery routines*," I read aloud.

"*Less than two weeks after French bachata champion Merle Picard got steamy in the dressing room with his dance partner Kate Wareing – and was thrown out of his marital home – both he and Kate have found new romances on the show. And in a shocking twist, Kate's new flame, Aleksis Lapsa, is the brother of Merle's estranged wife Sofiya – who has given them her blessing!*

"*Kate and Aleksis were partnered on the show after X-rated photos emerged of her and her original dance partner Merle. Less than a week later Merle admitted he has struck up a romance with his new dance partner, Emilia Harris, who he topped the scoreboard with last weekend.*

"*But in an unexpected twist, Kate and Aleksis have also grown close and were spotted leaving Sofiya's house together after spending the night there. Sofiya confirmed to the Daily Scene that the pair are romantically involved and that she's fully supportive of their union, despite the fact that her husband cheated on her with Kate.*

"'I know many people will expect me to hate her, but I don't blame Kate for what happened. She didn't know me, she didn't know Merle was married and she didn't ask for it to be exposed in the way it was,' Sofiya told the Daily Scene's Stella Barkley.

"Sofiya admitted it was a bit of a shock when Aleksis first came to her with the news, but said she quickly got over it when she saw how happy he was. And it was Sofiya's idea that she and Kate should meet and get it all out in the open.

"'They came to my house and we talked about everything and I found myself really liking Kate,' Sofiya told the Daily Scene. 'I can see why Aleksis has fallen for her. My marriage may be over, but I still believe in love and if Kate and Aleksis find it together, then I fully support that.'"

I look up from my phone and Aleksis looks like he's been holding his breath the whole time I've been reading. He puffs the air out and raises his eyebrows.

'Game on?' he says.

'Game on,' I agree.

Sofiya swings by the studio after lunch to help us get some photos on social media to back up our story. She looks impossibly glamorous, still sporting smoky eyes and forties-esque vintage curls from her interview and photoshoot.

'I couldn't have Merle seeing it and not wondering if he's made a terrible mistake,' she says when I tell her she looks amazing. 'Even if I don't want him back. Stella was delighted, by the way, to be the one to get your story. She's had a tough time making her mark at the paper and said this will help her out no end. I said I'd keep her updated on any developments and in return she said she'd do something for you. She's going to find out who sold them those photos of you and Merle, Kate. I thought you might want to know.'

'Thank you,' I say hesitantly, not convinced I want it dragged up again. I'd just assumed it was someone random at Channel 6 and that I'd never find out exactly who. It's not like someone I know would have done something like that. Unless . . . no, they couldn't have.

Sensing my trepidation, Aleksis brings our attention back to the task at hand. 'Shall we get these photos sorted, so we can crack on with our rehearsal?'

Sofiya takes some of us posing and some of us dancing, but when we flick through them afterwards, we all agree the best is one where Aleksis and I are looking at each other, rather than at the camera, looking completely smitten. If we didn't know better, it could be real.

'Let's get that online, then,' Sofiya says, sending it through to my phone.

And so I post my first Instagram picture in six months, with the caption, '*Busted! We were planning to keep this secret, but now it's out there . . . #aleksislapsa #boyfriend #official.*'

Aleksis replies with a red heart and Sofiya adds a link to the *Daily Scene* story.

'You should share a few of the others too,' she says, handing me her phone. 'The more authenticity you can give this the better, so just heart all the ones you like and I'll whizz them over to you.'

While I'm at it, I upload one I took of Tammy, Liam and

Beth from before the live shows even started. I tag the three of them and caption it, '*I had no idea how much I was going to get out of #FireOnTheDanceFloor. #FriendsForever.*'

Immediately the Fire Dancers WhatsApp chat starts pinging with messages.

'*Is this for real?*' Tammy has written.

She's obviously talking about the photo of me and Aleksis, not the one of the four of us.

'*OMG, this is brilliant news! You look so happy,*' Beth gushes.

And Liam chips in with, '*That's one way to get over Merle.*'

'*It took us both a bit by surprise,*' I write back. '*But it's so different to before. Aleksis is lovely and he just gets me.*'

'*And his sister really doesn't mind?*' Beth asks. The question everyone will be asking.

I look over at Sofiya, who's now helping Aleksis choose a few photos for his own Instagram. 'Make sure you tag Kate,' she reminds him.

It still blows my mind that she can be this friendly towards me after I slept with her husband. I'm not sure I could do the same in her shoes.

'*She's actually pretty incredible,*' I type. '*She just wants the best for everyone. I'm very lucky.*'

'*You deserve some luck after what you've been through,*' Beth says. '*I hope it does all work out this time.*'

Of course there's no chance of that happening, but I don't tell her that.

A flash of sadness hits me then, that it's yet another relationship that won't go anywhere. Even if it isn't real.

But at least I know in advance this time. There won't be any nasty surprises.

'Sofiya's got something else for us,' Aleksis says, interrupting my thoughts. 'It's a dinner reservation at The May Fair hotel for eight p.m. this evening.'

'Stella told me there are always photographers outside and she's promised to run something on you if they get some good pictures,' Sofiya explains. 'It's her way of saying thank you to me for giving her an exclusive.'

'That's doable,' I nod, playing it cool to disguise my trepidation about our plan really getting underway. There'll be just enough time for me to nip home after rehearsals then get back into central London for the meal.

'I've arranged for my friend Dan to be there, too,' Sofiya confesses. 'So he can discreetly take some pictures of his own inside the restaurant. I'll send them on to Stella, so she has everything she needs for her story. All you have to do is look like a couple. It'll be good practice for tomorrow.'

Tomorrow is when the show's camera crew will be filming our video clip for Saturday night's *Fire on the Dance Floor*. And not only will they be capturing the usual footage of us practising in the studio, they'll also be accompanying us on a night out that the producers have arranged, so they've got enough material to fill up the show now there are fewer dancers left in the competition.

Aleksis and I have got lucky and will be doing a rotation in a private capsule on the London Eye, complete with champagne. It shouldn't be too hard to make that look romantic.

'We'd better crack on, then,' Aleksis says, and Sofiya wishes us luck.

'And remember to enjoy yourselves,' she says with a smile.

Chapter 24

Lucy is still at work when I get back to the flat, but I know where she keeps her styling irons so I manage to twist some volume into my hair. I go for neutral colours with my eye make-up, with lashings of mascara, and I team my favourite jeans with a low-cut lace-trim cami and a black tailored jacket.

'Not bad for a thirty-minute turnaround,' I tell my reflection in the mirror as I top it off with bold red lipstick.

Aleksis has suggested meeting in a bar close to The May Fair a bit before eight, so we can arrive there together. I don't know why I'm so fidgety on the Tube journey there, but I can't stop rubbing my hands together, twiddling my hair, tugging my sleeves down over my hands then pushing them back up again. Yes, it's a weird situation, but I'm sure, between the two of us, we can make it a pleasant evening.

At least I no longer feel like I need to hide my face out in public. So much has happened since those photos were published that it really is starting to feel like old news. And if it feels like that to me, despite the turmoil it put me through, it must feel like ancient history to anyone else.

If I do catch anyone staring at me for longer than is polite, with that curious look in their eye, I just smile right at them – and they either smile back reflexively or quickly look away in embarrassment.

I spot Aleksis at the bar as soon as I walk through the door and I'm glad to see he's also opted for jeans. Imagine if he'd gone full suit on me and I'd underdressed. He's matched his with a navy T-shirt and I have to admit he looks good. He reminds me of the catalogue models I used to swoon over as a teenager. I can't help grinning as I walk over, a nervous flutter in my stomach.

He stands up and kisses both my cheeks, then pulls out the chair beside him.

'Do you think we need to kiss properly?' I whisper. 'In case anyone's watching?'

He tilts my chin round so I'm facing the rest of the bar. Not a single person is glancing in our direction.

'I think we're good,' he says with a grin. 'What can I get you?'

He hands me the menu.

'An espresso martini please.'

'The same for me,' he tells the barman and we both watch as our drinks are prepared.

'Don't you feel at all nervous?' I ask. He certainly doesn't look it.

'I don't think we'll struggle to fool anyone this evening. When people see a man and a woman out together, having dinner, they automatically assume they're a couple. It's what everyone does.'

I must look doubtful because he adds, 'I am going to make it look convincing though, don't worry. I can switch it on when I need to.'

'Speaking of which, should we get a photo of us here up on Instagram?' I ask.

'We should definitely do that,' he agrees, and I'm glad to have something to do with my hands.

Aleksis uploads the picture with the caption, '*Cocktails with my favourite @katewareing.*'

After that we drink up quickly because it's time for our next stop, so I leave the bar feeling slightly tipsy. There are only two photographers outside The May Fair as we approach and they both look pretty bored – they're both slouching against the wall and scrolling through their phones. There must not be many celebrity guests expected this evening, which seems to be confirmed when they get disproportionately excited to see us walking towards the entrance.

'A few pictures?' one of them requests.

'Sure,' Aleksis agrees, pulling me closer as we pose in front of them.

Moments later he puts his hand on my bum as we walk into the hotel, which prompts a few more camera flashes. I must be tipsier than I thought, because it makes me smirk rather than wanting to brush it off and tell him to keep his hands to himself. Knowing it's just for show stops it from feeling intrusive.

After another pre-dinner cocktail followed by a bottle of wine with our meal, I'm definitely not sober. But the conversation flows smoothly and Aleksis makes me laugh with tales of his childhood skirmishes with Sofiya, who once painted him blue from head to foot when their parents left them alone for a couple of hours. He also recalls when he stuck an 'I'm a nerd' sticker on the back of her jacket just as she was going out on her first ever date – which the date noticed before she did. They didn't speak for a fortnight.

We order starters and mains, and in between the courses Aleksis holds my hands across the table. At first I have to fight the urge to pull away, but by the time we get to dessert it's starting to feel more natural.

While we're drinking post-dinner coffees, Sofiya forwards us a picture that her friend Dan must have taken, with a thumbs-up emoji. We look deep in conversation and Aleksis's eyes are sparkling. He zooms in on the image and a grin spreads across his face. 'We're nailing this.'

'We are,' I agree. 'You look really into me.'

'I think acting might be what I focus on in my career going forward.'

'Really? You'd rather act than dance?'

I don't know why this surprises me. I guess it's because I've only seen him dancing.

'There are more opportunities. And I can really see myself in a period drama. All those elaborate costumes . . . right up my street. Or maybe a police series on TV. Detective Inspector Lapsa – what do you think?'

'I'm not sure I can picture you in uniform. I'm too used to seeing you in sequins. You'd make a good baddie though, especially when you do that look.'

'What look?' He seems mystified.

'You know. The one where people can't tell what you're thinking. It's so unnerving.'

He laughs at this. 'And there I was thinking that was my sister's speciality. What do you think, then – the next Bond villain?'

'I could see that.' He'd be perfect.

He shakes his head, but he's still smiling. 'I think I'm more Bond, personally. Suave, sophisticated, good with the ladies.'

'Is that so?'

He gives my hand a suggestive squeeze. A small part of me – the drunk part, I presume – wants to think it's not part of his act. But before I can analyse this, he asks me who I'd play if I could be the lead in any movie. The first thing that pops into my head is Julia Roberts in a *Pretty Woman* remake.

'So you like an older man,' he teases.

'I like how romantic it is,' I correct him.

He raises an eyebrow. 'I didn't have you down as the romantic type.'

I can only assume he's basing this on my behaviour with Merle.

'Then you obviously need to get to know me better.'

'Fair,' he laughs. 'So let's say we're making the film of your life. What's the plot going to be?'

'Girl goes on to become world class dancer after beating the odds to win reality TV show with her talented partner?' I suggest.

'Ambitious, I like it. And who's going to play us? I can see a bit of Emma Stone in you, I think.'

'I'll take that,' I smile. It's been said a couple of times before, and it's just as flattering coming from him.

'And Chris Hemsworth for me?' he says.

'I was thinking more the guy who plays the terminator in the second movie. The liquidy one, not Arnie obviously.'

'I'll take that,' he fires back at me. 'From what I recall he did look pretty good in uniform.'

We carry on bantering until the bill arrives and when it's time to leave, we jump into a taxi together outside the hotel in case any of the photographers are still around – not that we see any. But it only takes us as far as the nearest Tube station as I'm heading south and Aleksis is going north.

'I thought that went really well,' he says.

'Me too.'

And in the pause that follows, it strikes me that it hasn't felt at all like we were pretending to like each other. I wouldn't even be sad if the evening wasn't coming to an end yet. I can't help wondering if he feels the same way.

But Aleksis steps back and says, 'See you tomorrow then, bright and early?'

'Absolutely.' I make it sound breezy. 'See you in the morning.'

I was obviously reading too much into it. And what on earth was I thinking anyway? I imagine he's just as surprised as I am that we got on so well in spite of everything.

There's another surprise waiting for me when I pull my phone out of my bag to let Lucy know I'm on my way home – a message from Warren is waiting on the screen.

'*Looks like someone got an upgrade,*' he's written under

a screenshot of the photo Sofiya took of me and Aleksis. He's added a laughing face, but it still makes me squirm uncomfortably. We probably should have had some kind of conversation after our one-night stand, just to clarify that's all it was.

'*I'm sorry I didn't warn you,*' I type, wincing. '*It wasn't planned.*'

Well it was, of course, but he doesn't need to know that.

'*Relax, no hard feelings,*' he assures me. '*The guy's hot. I'd do exactly the same in your shoes. I like you though, Kate. I hope we can still be friends.*'

I breathe a sigh of relief and tell him I'd like nothing more. We're bound to see each other again while Lucy's dating Aiden, and that will be a lot less awkward if we're both on the same page.

'*The guy's hot*', though? I flick to Instagram to look at the photo of me and Aleksis again. It is a flattering shot and it's got a lot of likes. The other pictures Sofiya took also have plenty of red hearts. I suck my breath in when I notice the number of people following my account has risen to over two thousand. In a day. That surely bodes well for our plan.

Thankfully, the comments are mostly positive, saying how good we look together and how happy we look. One or two say how jealous they are of me getting with Aleksis. Ha, if only they knew.

Lucy is waiting up for me when I get home, wanting to dissect the evening with me before she goes to bed.

'So you got on really well, made each other laugh and even Warren can see he's hot,' she summarises.

I roll my eyes. 'He was funny and charming, but he was also acting,' I remind her.

She grins mischievously. 'Well, for the record I think he'd be crazy not to try and make it official.'

And while I assure her that would never happen, I can't help thinking how much I enjoyed his company.

Chapter 25

By the time I get to the studio the next morning, Stella's second article has appeared online. True to her word, she's run a piece on my night out with Aleksis and it's accompanied by the photo of his hand on my bum outside The May Fair, as well as several more that Dan must have taken inside the restaurant. He's done a good job – they do look legitimate.

The story doesn't say much, other than to point out that our relationship is going from strength to strength and that we can't keep our hands off each other, followed by another plug for the show and the exclusive chat with Sofiya at the weekend. I wonder if Merle has seen it and if it will bother him in the slightest. Or if he'll see straight through the charade.

A quick check on Emilia's Instagram on the way here told me she now has thirty thousand followers and counting. There are pictures of her and Merle at rehearsals and going for coffee, with Emilia dressed up to the nines and both of them looking like models. It's hard not to compare them to me and Aleksis and feel like we're coming up short. It still stings just a little to see Merle with Emilia, too.

But thankfully there's not much time to dwell on it, because Sarah, Steve and Andy are already outside the studio with their camera bags when I arrive. It's time for the first really big challenge to get underway. Looking loved-up in a photo or at a restaurant isn't that hard, but convincing people who we're interacting with will be a lot less straightforward.

'Hi again,' Sarah greets me as they pile through the door with their equipment. 'Over there, same as before,' she directs her colleagues. 'Where's Aleksis? Did you not arrive together?'

'Er, he stopped off for coffee,' I improvise, although I'm not sure how I'm going to explain it when he turns up without any. But luckily I don't have to, because he arrives a few minutes later hidden behind a giant bouquet of flowers and the coffee is instantly forgotten.

'What the—'

'For you.' He grins, and holds up the bucket in his other hand. 'They let me take this to put them in.'

'That's so sweet,' Sarah says. 'And this will be a great prop for today's clip too. It's given me an idea. Can we film you walking in with them again?'

Once she's captured Aleksis's grand entrance, she gets us to perform a few steps of our routine with one of the stems clutched in my hand. I sweep it up in the air and bring it down in front of my chest. Aleksis takes it and

190

pops it between his teeth, spinning once before coming back to face me so he can pass it to me mouth to mouth.

It's meant to look sexy but when our eyes meet, ready for him to pass the flower, I can't help sniggering, which sets us both off with the giggles and the flower drops to the floor. It's not exactly what Sarah had in mind, but she decides to keep it anyway, because she thinks the audience will like it.

After that she fishes around in her bag and finds some lipstick.

'I have another idea,' she says, which makes me laugh again and simultaneously fills me with dread. I'm not sure I can take many more of her ideas. But what follows I really like.

'Today, we decided to liven up our little studio,' Aleksis says to camera, getting him a thumbs-up from Sarah. We're kneeling side by side on the floor, with the mirror to the side of us so Andy, who's filming, can't be seen in the reflection.

'We've noticed some of the other studios look a little more glam than ours, and we didn't want it to feel inferior,' I explain.

'We bought it some flowers,' Aleksis takes over, shooting me a grin then looking over his shoulder at the bouquet in the bucket behind us. He grabs my hand and pulls me to my feet.

'And we're going to add some wall art,' I say, producing two lipsticks from my pocket and handing him one. He draws a trio of daisies on the mirror and looks over at me. I add a few balloons on strings and look back at him.

He adds some love hearts then reaches down and plucks a flower from the bucket, which he tucks behind my ear.

Not in the script!, a voice screams in my head. He shoots me a wink that makes my heart do an unexpected flip.

He turns back to camera. 'Much better,' he grins. Then to me, 'Although I hope you have some tissues or we might get in trouble with the owners later.'

I may well find myself in trouble, I think, *if he keeps this up.*

After that Sarah films a bit more of us dancing and talking about how our week is going so far. Then, when she packs up to leave, she reminds us that we need to be at the London Eye at seven-thirty p.m. sharp for our evening filming.

'They've given us two rotations,' she explains. 'We can work out the best angles on the first one and capture anything we missed on the second. You could bring the flowers. It'll be nice for continuity.'

'Sure,' Aleksis agrees. 'We'd better crack on then. We'll need to finish a bit early if we're going to have enough time to go home and freshen up.'

When we're alone, he admits the flowers were his sister's idea – she thought they'd help sell our story. She was right, but I can't help feeling disappointed. I'd quite liked the idea that they were a gift from Aleksis. Who doesn't like having flowers bought for them?

Aleksis tells me there are a couple of extra moves he wants us to add into our routine this morning.

'The first one starts like this,' he says, pivoting me round by the hips so I'm facing away from him. He presses his chest against my back and for the first time I'm conscious of every part of his body touching every part of mine as he leans into me to make my body roll forward, before lightly pulling me back towards him till my bum is resting against his thigh. He then nudges me forward again before spinning me back to face him.

It's simple, but sensual and makes me think of sex. With Aleksis. Which instantly makes my cheeks flush with colour. This is not how I'm supposed to think about him. It was Merle who made moments like these seem erotic, not Aleksis. Thankfully he doesn't seem to notice how much I'm blushing.

'Yep, that works,' he murmurs, his face full of concentration. This isn't having the same effect on him, then. 'And now . . . '

He takes both my hands again and this time, rather than turning me, he turns himself, steps in front of me and pulls me in tight behind him, so my arms are around him and my boobs are pressed against his back, my hands on his chest. This doesn't help with my X-rated thoughts. He uses his back to roll my body this time and again I'm acutely aware of our closeness. What is wrong with me today? I need to get a grip on myself.

'Excellent,' Aleksis says, still oblivious to the effect he's having on me. He must think my palms are sweating because it's warm in the studio. 'We'll put them in at the end just before the back drop. Let's do them both again a few more times, then we'll go from the top.'

I have to work as hard at maintaining my composure as I do at perfecting the moves. Can he really dance like this without feeling even the tiniest stir? It certainly appears that way, but I don't know how he manages it. As for me, it quickly becomes my favourite rehearsal with him so far.

When it's time to go and get ready for our evening on the London Eye, Aleksis suggests meeting at Waterloo station twenty minutes before our rotation, so we can walk over there together. On my way back to Balham, I wonder if I can wear the same outfit I wore last night. It's my favourite and the one I'm most comfortable in. But as I've already been photographed in it, I opt for a dress instead – a floaty floral one which I top off with gladiator sandals and a denim jacket. I find myself hoping Aleksis likes it.

But he doesn't even notice me when I first arrive at Waterloo because he's busy posing for a selfie with two teenagers, who seem very excited to have spotted someone from the telly. I watch him indulging them, pulling silly faces for their photos, and he doesn't seem remotely put out by the intrusion.

It throws me off balance for a moment. I can't help smiling at how goofy and unguarded he's being. It's so different to the rigid, unapproachable Aleksis I first encountered in Shane's office.

When he does finally see me, his face lights up, like he's pleased to see me. It makes my own smile grow wider, like I'm pleased to see him too. It dawns on me that I'm looking forward to spending another evening with him and that I won't just be going through the motions. Which isn't part of the plan at all.

He waves me over and the teenagers beg for a few more pictures, with me in as well this time. I cheerfully oblige, letting their enthusiasm boost my confidence. Then, spirits high, I slip my hand into Aleksis's for the walk to the London Eye. Just to keep up appearances, of course.

My mood is elevated even further by the glass of champagne that's thrust towards me as soon as the door of our capsule closes behind us.

At one end there's a makeshift bar, topped with several bottles of Veuve and manned by a smartly dressed waiter. At the other end there are two high stools alongside a table decorated with candles and bowls of nibbles. The rest of the floor has been left clear so Sarah, Andy and Steve can move around easily and put their lights wherever they might need them. They discreetly stack their bags behind the bar.

'We'll just film everything today and edit it down afterwards,' Sarah explains. 'We'll be circling round, but just ignore us as best you can. I'll probably get you to move occasionally too, to get the best background. Does that sound okay?'

'All good,' Aleksis nods.

'Good, and I hope you don't mind, but I'm going to grab a drink for us three, too. Bit cheeky I know, but it's on the company expenses so . . . '

'Get stuck in. It's not like we're going to get through all these bottles ourselves,' Aleksis says.

'Then we're happy to help,' Sarah laughs.

We spend much of the first rotation looking out at the views and pointing out the various things we've spotted as we sip our champagne. It's the perfect evening for it, with blue sky as far as the eye can see. Aleksis moves his chair next to mine and puts his arm round me, which makes me smile. It's enough to make me forget all about the cameras.

By the time we start the second rotation, we're both a bit tipsy – and so are the camera crew. Sarah asks us to perform a section of our routine in the middle of the capsule – just a teaser, as we don't want to show too much of it ahead of the actual dance. Then she decides she wants to film the whole thing.

'I'm wondering if we can have it playing on the screen on Saturday while you perform it live,' she says. 'It could look really nice if the timing's right.'

'Sure, we can try that,' Aleksis agrees.

But we abandon it after a few attempts. Even keeping our steps really small there just isn't enough room in the capsule.

'It looks great though, from what I've seen,' Sarah says.

'Thanks,' I grin. 'Aleksis is pretty good at making me look like I know what I'm doing.'

He rolls his eyes. 'She's better than she realises.'

'Well, I'll be backing you two on Saturday,' Sarah says, a slight slur in her voice.

This gets a laugh from Aleksis. 'I bet you say that to all the contestants.'

'Some more than others. Ooh, I probably shouldn't be admitting that. Shh, don't tell anyone!'

'Perhaps you should slow down on the champers?' Andy suggests with a raised eyebrow.

'Nah,' he and Sarah say in unison, turning back to the waiter for refills.

Before we get back down to ground level, Aleksis receives a text from Sofiya. He shows me the screen.

'*When you're done there, can you do drinks, Charlotte Street Hotel, nine p.m.? Stella has set it up,*' her message says.

'That okay with you?' he asks.

'Of course.' I send a silent thank you to Sofiya. 'Let's make a night of it.'

But before I can get excited about spending the rest of the evening alone with him, he asks Sarah, Steve and Andy if they want to come with us.

'Count me in,' Sarah agrees. 'I've got my drinking head on now. I'm happy to go for another.'

I swallow my disappointment as Andy adds, 'Yep, I'll come for one.'

'Oh, go on then,' Steve laughs. 'I don't want to be left out.'

And although the five of us crammed round a table, chatting noisily over cocktails, doesn't quite fit in with the romantic picture I thought Aleksis and I were supposed to be creating, it still gives Stella a story. Her piece the next morning shows our giggling group arriving at the hotel together then sitting in the window, drinking and laughing. Aleksis has his arm round my shoulders again and is even caught on camera kissing me on the cheek – one of my favourite moments of the evening.

Underneath the photos of our little gang, there are pictures of Merle and Emilia in the window of a neighbouring restaurant, looking super serious at their candlelit table. I imagine Stella's original intention was to pitch us directly against each other with a comparison piece on our body language, restaurant choice and clothing. Instead, she's ended up dubbing me and Aleksis the fun couple and Merle and Emilia the aloof ones in a piece called "*Battle of the Ballroom Beaus*", which is quite all right with me.

"*Fire on the Dance Floor favourites Merle Picard and Emilia Harris, and Aleksis Lapsa and Kate Wareing might be used to competing against each other on the show, but the two recently formed couples came within inches of a showdown off the dance floor last night as they both hit the town in London's Fitzrovia for a much-needed break from rehearsals,*" the piece begins.

"*While Merle and Emilia settled in for a quiet meal at The Ninth, Aleksis and Kate enjoyed a raucous night out across the street, throwing back cocktails with the show's camera crew at the swanky Charlotte Street Hotel.*

"*Merle appeared to be deep in conversation with Emilia, who looked stunning in a figure-hugging black dress and matching Louboutins as they enjoyed their Mediterranean feast. Aleksis and Kate, meanwhile, who were more casually dressed, laughed and joked with their companions and posed for photos with fans as they let their hair down for the night, proving just how popular they've become on the show.*"

There are more photos of our respective evenings as well as some stills from the show before the story continues.

"*Last week Merle and Emilia dominated the scoreboard in the Latin dance contest thanks to their sizzling bachata, while Kate and Aleksis narrowly avoided eviction. But it didn't appear to have dampened their spirits as Aleksis tenderly kissed Kate in the hotel bar.*

"*The two couples left Fitzrovia within moments of each*

other, but luckily did not cross paths. So who will survive when they come face to face on Fire on the Dance Floor on Saturday? Tune in at seven p.m. on Channel 6 to find out."

I scroll back up and study the photos. Merle and Emilia look intense and serious. Aleksis and I look relaxed and laid-back, but still like a couple. And the piece feels like a win as we sound far more friendly and fun-loving than Merle and Emilia – which, it turns out, is exactly what Aleksis was hoping to portray when he invited Sarah, Steve and Andy to join us.

I flick to Instagram and see that my number of followers has risen to 6,403, which feels huge, until I check up on Emilia and see her account has passed 42,000. I put my phone away with a sigh, telling myself it doesn't matter as long as Aleksis and I deliver a knockout performance on Saturday night.

Chapter 26

Our final day of rehearsals goes really well. By the end of the afternoon Aleksis thinks we're ready to give Merle and Emilia a decent run for their money and I'm over the moon that it's all come together so nicely. The fact that we've made the headlines three days in a row is a huge bonus – with Sofiya's interview still to come out tomorrow.

'It's been a successful week.' Aleksis grins, and I can't help smiling back. 'We just need our good fortune to continue for a little while longer and for the audience to back us tomorrow, and we're more than halfway there.'

'Should we go out again tonight, do you think?' I ask as we pack up for the day. 'See if we can make it four consecutive days in the news?'

'We should rest tonight, so we're fresh for tomorrow. Tonight, I'd suggest a healthy dinner, a hot bath and an early night with a good book.'

I know he's right, but I find myself wishing we could spend one more evening together. Even with all the press and all the practice sessions there are no guarantees the audience will keep us on the show, and I don't want to even think about the possibility that last night really could have been our last. I'm not ready for my *Fire on the Dance Floor* journey to be over – not when I've just started feeling really good about it.

It seems like a lifetime ago that Lucy practically had to drag me kicking and screaming to my first meeting with Shane at Channel 6. Did I think I'd even make it past week one back then? I thought it was worth trying, but I didn't think it was likely. But when I think about how much I've progressed since then, it starts feeling like anything could be possible – something I never expected to find myself thinking. So I want to stay in the competition now and . . . and yes, if I'm honest, around Aleksis, too.

The more I think about this, the more worried I become about the fast approaching live show. So much so that Aleksis receives a garbled text from me just before midnight, admitting I've started panicking that neither my dancing nor our fake romance will be enough to get us through. He replies straight away and offers to meet me an hour before we're due at Channel 6 so he can help calm my nerves. It's going to take a hell of a pep talk.

Over coffee the next morning he reminds me how positively Sarah reacted to what she saw of our routine and assures me my dancing is every bit as good as Emilia's.

'As for our relationship, we just need to do exactly what we've been doing for the last few nights and no one will question it, not that we'll give them any reason to. They'll be far too busy worrying about their own agendas to be wondering about ours.'

I knew he'd be the voice of reason, and apologise to him for letting myself get so worked up about it.

'It's an unusual situation,' he says, full of understanding. 'But remember, we're in a really good position this week. Our routine is strong and we've had all the media coverage over the last few days. I think we should be feeling confident about tonight, and Sofiya's interview will be the icing on the cake.'

'The interview!' I can't believe it slipped my mind. 'I forgot to pick up a copy.'

'Don't worry, I grabbed one on the way here,' he says, reaching into his bag.

But when we pull the supplement out from between the folds of the newspaper, it's not Sofiya staring off the cover at us.

It's Merle.

Chapter 27

'What the . . . ' I start, as Aleksis hastily flicks to the feature inside.

He lays it flat on the table to reveal a sultry shot of Merle on the *Fire on the Dance Floor* stage underneath a giant headline that says, *"I've made mistakes, but I won't let that hold me back."*

"Fire on the Dance Floor's Merle Picard exclusively tells us about his marriage split, finding new love and keeping his eyes on the prize," I read the words underneath aloud in disbelief.

Aleksis turns the page and there's another full spread, the words wrapped around another smouldering image of Merle as well as a photo of him and Emilia dancing. There's a smaller one of me doing the kizomba with him in week one, too.

I skim through the questions, which are mostly about his love life, and his answers all follow the theme that while he hasn't always made the right choices, he's determined to move forward, find true happiness and show the world how talented he is.

He says he was as horrified as anyone else when the photos of me and him were printed and claims he regrets hurting his wife. He ends by saying he's in a much better place now and that he hopes Sofiya and I are too. And at the bottom there's a footnote saying, "*To hear the other side of the story, don't miss our exclusive chat with Sofiya in tomorrow's paper*" – and the byline is none other than Stella bloody Barkley.

'I can't believe she's done that.' I slump back in my chair. 'I thought she was on our side.'

'It looks like she's not on anyone's side,' Aleksis frowns. 'I don't think this will undo all the other coverage we've had this week, though. It's just a setback. I still think we can do this. We're not going to let him win.'

He puts his arm round my shoulders for the walk to Channel 6, but when Olivia greets us in the lobby, she tells us we're the first to arrive. So much for making a grand entrance.

Tammy turns up next and she's so fired up about her performance today she can't wait for the live show to get started. She doesn't seem at all resentful about our coverage in the press, which is a relief, and her positivity is infectious, so we're chatting away merrily when Merle and Emilia eventually stride into the room.

While Emilia completely ignores our little group, Merle looks straight at me and doesn't look away until I break eye contact. It sends a little shiver through me. Why does he always look like he knows exactly what's going through my mind? Like he knows something's off with me and Aleksis, like he can tell how much effort it's taking to keep my cool. I turn my gaze back to Aleksis and remind myself that even if he is faking our romance, I know he's got my back.

Beth and Liam's dance partners are the last to arrive. They're no longer in the competition but the *FOTDF* bosses want to add a group performance starring all the professional dancers to the following week's show, to fill in the time left by another couple being voted out.

Olivia kicks off the usual rounds of hair, make-up, costumes and dress rehearsals. This time, the waiting in between is made more bearable by the fact that Aleksis stays with me for most of the time, maintaining the pretence of our relationship. He persuades Olivia to send us to the costume department at the same time and we emerge in matching outfits – him in a sheer red shirt and me in a red sparkly corset, black trousers for him, black sequinned leggings for me.

'Snap!' he laughs, and we hold hands on the way back to the reception room.

Merle and Emilia don't hide away in his private dressing room today and I catch him watching me more than once across the reception room. It feels like he's trying to catch me out, but I know I'm just being paranoid. I do my best to ignore him, but when Olivia tells everyone it's time to head to the studio for the live show, it's a relief to be away from his questioning gaze.

'Feeling okay?' Aleksis checks. And I nod. If nothing else, we'll surely be the most improved couple after last week's salsa. He pulls me close and kisses the top of my head, I'm sure to reassure me. Instinctively I turn my face up to his and kiss him back, brushing my lips across his cheek. He doesn't shy away. Filled with pre-show adrenaline, I think we both forget for a moment that our relationship isn't real.

As Kimberley kicks off proceedings, Aleksis stays close beside me. I have to force myself to pay attention as she gives everyone a quick reminder of who's left in the competition and how we all did on last week's show.

I'm not thrilled to be reminded of Merle's hypnotic bachata or my less than spectacular salsa, but at least they're only short clips. Then Kimberley banters with the judges for a few minutes before inviting Tammy and Elijah to join her on the stage, to see how they've progressed since last week and how they enjoyed their night out watching *Hamilton* at the theatre.

After their video clip has played, they get into position for their salsa. And Tammy is just brilliant. Their performance bags them a respectable 8.6 from the audience.

'Now that's how to dance the salsa,' Kimberley gushes. 'What an incredible start to the show. I can tell it's going to be an electric night tonight. Ladies and gentlemen, please put your hands together once again for Tammy King and Elijah Gill!'

They exit the stage to a loud round of applause and we all clap Tammy on the back as she squeezes back in between us. She looks delighted. But with Merle and Emilia up next, I wonder how long for. I have no doubt they will raise the bar even higher, especially when

Kimberley announces that tonight they'll be dancing a raunchy rumba.

The clip of their rehearsals is all lingering looks and smouldering eyes and their night out is at a burlesque show, to really drive home what a sexy couple they are. Not that they need to. Emilia's outfit this evening is half dress, half sequinned bikini and doesn't leave much to the imagination. I reluctantly have to admit she looks incredible.

And it's not hard to imagine the intimacy between her and Merle once they start dancing, as he bends her backwards with his hands on her waist till only their hips are still connected, then lifts her high up into the air before sliding her slowly back down the whole length of his body.

I brace myself for a flare of jealousy as it stirs up memories of my own passionate encounters with him. That used to be me. If things had turned out differently, that could still have been me. But although watching them transports me be back to our Kensington studio, to Merle undressing me, to what would follow, I find I no longer ache for it quite as intensely. Before I can delve into the reasons why, Olivia moves in next to me and Aleksis with her clipboard and whispers, 'You two are up next.'

'What? No!' I hiss, as a roar erupts from the crowd, interspersed with whoops and wolf whistles, signalling the end of Merle and Emilia's dance. 'You said Theo was going to be after Emilia. We're on after Theo,' I remind Olivia.

'I know, but Shane's just changed the running order. Don't ask me why, but he wants you to go next.'

'We can't!' I desperately don't want to dance straight after Emilia. 'We, er, we . . . '

'Don't worry, the sound and lighting guys have been given a heads-up and your videos are all set up and ready to roll,' she says. 'Right, here come Merle and Emilia, you're up, off you go!'

And as we run out to join Kimberley, Aleksis firmly gripping my hand in his, I realise I've missed both the judges' comments and Merle and Emilia's score, so I have no idea what we're up against.

'Oh, this is just adorable,' Kimberley swoons, placing a hand on her heart as we watch the playback of Aleksis drawing his flowers on our studio mirror.

'Love really is in the air here tonight, folks,' she says to the audience as he puts his arm round me in our capsule on the London Eye.

'After last week's performance from Merle and Emilia we all know how steamy the bachata can be. Let's see if the same sparks are flying for Kate and Aleksis as they bring us their own version of the bachata this evening. Ladies and gentlemen, give it up for Kate Wareing and Aleksis Lapsa!'

She backs away, leaving the two of us in the spotlight. Aleksis steps towards me and sweeps my arms up above my head then guides them gently down and round his shoulders.

'We've got this,' he whispers. Then our song starts playing and our dance begins.

It's not like the salsa, where I could channel my nervous energy into the physical demands of the routine, so I take a deep breath to calm my nerves and pretend it's just me and Aleksis in our own private bubble, where nothing matters but him, me, the music and the choreography. It does help me relax, but I don't know if I remember to smile.

We must deliver a convincing performance though, because the audience makes as much noise for us as they did for Merle and Emilia. The second our music stops, they're clapping and cheering, and I turn round to see two of the judges are on their feet.

'Sensational,' Mariana declares.

'Simply stunning,' Sophie agrees. 'And what a huge improvement from your performance last week. It was elegant, romantic, sensual, all the things a bachata should be. It was beautiful. Well done.'

'I agree,' Jacques says. 'I'll be honest, I didn't think anyone could top last week's bachata, but that was smooth, delicate, emotional. I couldn't take my eyes off you. And I think, from the reaction, that the audience agrees.'

'What a fantastic response from the judges – and the audience,' Kimberley beams. 'And what a different story to last week. But is it enough to get Kate and Aleksis through to the semi-final? Audience, it's time for you to submit your scores. Did you feel the love on the stage tonight? Or was it all a bit too staged for your liking? Let's find out!'

The dial on the scoreboard leaps up the chart then wavers for a few seconds before finally settling on 9.1. A huge grin takes over my face, and Aleksis picks me up and spins me round before setting me down and kissing me full on the lips. But I'm so blown away by our near-perfect score that it barely has time to register.

'Another superb result!' Kimberley cheers. 'That puts you just a tenth of a point behind Merle and Emilia this evening. Congratulations! That's enough to get you through to next week's semi-final. But let's not forget, there are still two more couples to dance tonight, so there's still time for someone else to steal that top spot. Could it be Dean with his cheeky cha-cha? Or Theo, who'll be raising temperatures with his fiery Argentine tango? Ladies and gentlemen, let's find out, but first let's hear it one more time for Kate and Aleksis!'

And our moment in the limelight is over for another week. I'm so elated about scoring 9.1 that I'm not even upset about finishing behind Merle and Emilia. I can't believe we got so close to them. I don't know how much of an influence our fake romance has had, but it can't all be down to that. Perhaps Aleksis was right – maybe I have finally found my feet on the dance floor.

Being guaranteed a place in the next round doesn't stop me feeling nervous watching Theo and Dean dance, though. I'm desperate for Tammy to stay in the competition – we've been supporting each other since day one. To my relief, neither of them beat her 8.6, but it's Theo and Daniele who come off worse, bagging just 6.2 in the audience vote.

'Ah, that's too bad,' Kimberley says at the end of their dance. 'Come on over and tell us how you feel.'

'I'm obviously gutted, but there was always a high chance this would be the week that did it for me,' Theo says.

'Yes, the Argentine tango is definitely getting a name for itself as the great eliminator,' Kimberley agrees. 'Theo, we're so sorry to see you go, but it's been fantastic having you on the show. We hope you've enjoyed it.'

He plasters a smile on his face. 'I've loved every minute.'

'And that's all we've got time for tonight,' Kimberley says, turning back to the audience. 'Theo and Daniele are out of the competition and now only four couples remain. Can anyone knock Merle and Emilia off the top spot? Aleksis and Kate certainly came close today. And let's not forget Tammy and Elijah were only half a point behind them. Can Dean up his game and upset the pecking order next week? Find out next Saturday, when we'll be back with more *Fire on the Dance Floor*!'

And that's another show done.

As Olivia leads us back through the corridors to the reception room, I hear Theo mutter something to Dean about some of us having had an unfair advantage this week. I'm pretty sure he's referring to me, but I don't react. I don't doubt I'd feel exactly the same way in his shoes, but I'm not going to allow him to burst my bubble.

Aleksis grabs us a glass of wine each and raises his glass. 'Well done, you,' he beams.

'Was that real?' I gasp, still in disbelief. I don't think I've blinked once since we came off the stage. I'm referring to the whole evening – to our dance, to the judges' comments – but Aleksis thinks I'm just talking about our score.

'The score was definitely real this week.' He grins. 'I didn't want to worry you before we danced, but they told me earlier that last week's arrangement was a one-off.'

I want to fling my arms round him and squeal. That means we did it, just us, exactly like we wanted. But I'm distracted by a flurry of movement as Beth and Liam come bounding towards us.

'Surprise!' Beth says. 'Hey, Tammy, get over here! You guys were both amazing tonight. We loved your bachata, Kate, and your salsa was so energetic, Tammy.'

'Thanks,' Tammy beams. 'I'm still on a high. I just love it. I don't want it to ever end.'

'Yeah, I haven't come back down to earth yet either.' I give them both a hug. 'It's great to see you guys.'

'Olivia told us we needed to come back here after the show tonight,' Beth explains. 'I think she's got something to tell us. It's kind of weird being back in this room again, though – it brings back all the excitement of being on the show. And the terror. I'm so glad I can just live that part vicariously through you guys now.'

Olivia bangs her clipboard and asks for our attention.

'Hi everyone, if I can just have a few minutes of your time, thank you. Firstly I just want to say well done to everyone tonight – and commiserations to you, Theo. But there's also good news for you, in that we want you back on the show next week. All of you, in fact – so you too, Beth and Liam.

'As you know, we've been planning to feature all the professionals in a showpiece on next week's *Fire on the Dance Floor*. But we've been monitoring the comments about the show on social media, and what the viewers want is to see more of the contestants dancing, too. So the showpiece will now feature all of you – professionals *and* contestants – and the dance we've selected is the rueda.'

There's a collective murmur around the room.

'For those of you who don't know what a rueda is,' Olivia raises her voice to make herself heard, 'it's a partner dance that is danced in a circle – a wheel – with a caller calling out instructions for you to follow. A lot of the steps are similar to what you've been learning over the last six weeks, so you'll have most of the basics, but there will still be a lot to learn and there isn't much time. So we're going to need to ask you all to give up a bit of your personal time to come in for rehearsals, so we can make it look really good by next Saturday.

'We want to get started on it straight away, so we're proposing that everyone comes back here tomorrow and we'll practise right here on set. It's bigger than most of your individual studios so it makes sense to do it here. I know Sunday is usually your day of rest, but we don't want to eat into your personal rehearsal time too much. We're proposing a full day tomorrow, starting at nine a.m., then three evenings next week – Tuesday, Wednesday and Thursday, with each of those sessions starting at five p.m.

'It's a lot of extra hours, but we think it will add another great element to the show. And for those of you who are still competing next week, you'll still have plenty of time to practise your individual dances, so there shouldn't be too much of an impact on that. This is going to be really exciting for everyone and for the show, and we think the viewers are going to love it. Any questions?'

'Did you say nine a.m. tomorrow?' Tammy checks.

'That's right. We want to make this look perfect.'

'There goes the big night out at the pub,' Tammy groans quietly.

'We can still go for one,' Liam says.

'You'll come for a quick one, won't you?' Beth asks me. 'I know we've got an early start, but it would be great to have the whole gang there again. You could come too, Aleksis. We can squeeze an extra chair round the table.'

'Sure, why not,' he replies, surprising me, because I thought he'd want us to go somewhere where we might get photographed, even if we do have to be up at the crack of dawn.

I know Lucy will be delighted to have the chance to suss him out. I might even be a tiny bit delighted myself, that we'll get to toast tonight's success together, and that he's willing to hang out with my friends.

Inevitably one drink turns into two as we get stuck into discussions about our performances this week and what's coming in the week ahead. We watch clips of people dancing the rueda on YouTube to see exactly what it is we'll be doing, and it does look like it's going to be a lot of fun. But with the couples swapping partners after virtually every move, I realise this means I'll be dancing with Merle again tomorrow, albeit in brief spurts, and I'm not sure how I feel about that.

It's not until I catch myself stifling a yawn that I look at my watch and realise it won't be long before the landlord's calling last orders. I show Aleksis the time. 'We should probably get going soon if we want to be fit for tomorrow.'

'Yeah, I'm ready to call it a night,' he agrees. 'We'll need extra energy for all the additional rehearsals this week.'

'I'm trying not to think about it,' I admit. 'But I'm still glad we came out. I would have been too hyped up to sleep if I'd tried to go straight to bed. I hope you didn't get too heavily grilled by Lucy. She can be really nosy.'

He smiles. 'It was fine, we had a good chat.'

She must have been on her best behaviour for once.

My thoughts drift back to the week ahead. 'I hope we've got an easyish dance for our next individual performance, with all the rueda moves to learn too. Have you looked yet?'

He taps his pocket. 'I've got the envelope in here. Do you want to look now?'

I nod and he slides the card out, making sure no one is watching.

'The cha-cha,' I read quietly. 'Is that good for us, or bad?'

He thinks about it for a moment. 'It's challenging, but I think we're up to the task. We'll just have to work really hard if we want it to look spectacular.'

'We're going to need it to look spectacular if we haven't got time to be seen out and about this week. We'll no longer have that advantage.'

'I'll come up with something good, don't worry. And we've still got Monday and Friday nights for going out. Plus, if we keep up with the Instagram posts we'll hopefully stay on everyone's radar.'

He gives me a quick hug, then seems to remember the rest of the gang might be watching and kisses me full on the lips for the second time this evening. And this time it definitely registers. It makes my heart flutter.

'I'll see you bright and early,' he says with a smile, before heading for the door. I can't take my eyes off him as walks away.

'I saw that,' Lucy teases, snapping me back to attention.

'Just making it look realistic,' I tell her, although I'm no longer sure I believe it.

'It was cool of him to come to the pub with us,' she says. 'I didn't expect him to be so down to earth. I thought all professional dancers might be dickheads like Merle, but he blended in really well.'

'He's very easy to be around.' Easier than I ever could have imagined, in fact.

'Well, that should help you with getting out of bed for your early start tomorrow,' Lucy laughs.

I feign a look of horror at the reminder. But I'm not at all horrified to be getting a bonus day with Aleksis. Even if Merle is going to be there, too.

Chapter 28

Nine a.m. comes around all too quickly. It feels like I've only just left Channel 6 when I make the journey back to Hammersmith.

I've made an effort with my hair and make-up. I tell myself it's in case they're planning to film us today. But I know it's also because I want Aleksis to think I look nice. Merle too, much as I hate to admit it. I just hope I can trust my body not to react when I feel his hands on me again.

I grab a newspaper to read on the journey and this time Sofiya's interview with Stella has been printed. She looks gorgeous and comes across well, without a trace of bitterness. She talks about the early excitement of meeting Merle, how she adored watching him perform and how she thought they'd be together forever. Then she admits their marriage was nearly derailed twice by his affairs, and that she found the strength to move past them because she still loved him.

"But when I saw the pictures of him with Kate, I just knew I couldn't go through it again. And as soon as I decided that, it was like a weight had lifted from my shoulders – a weight I hadn't even realised was there."

Then Stella asks Sofiya about the first time she met me.

"My brother was so angry about her and Merle. I'd kept the other infidelities from him, so it came as a shock. In some ways I think he even felt responsible – I wouldn't have met Merle if I hadn't been at a dance competition with Aleksis. But he was taking his anger out on Kate and that wasn't fair. So I went to the studio to help them clear the air. And I found myself, unexpectedly, liking Kate a lot. She reminded me of myself when I first met Merle, swept up in the excitement of the dance world and brave enough to take a chance on romance when it came along. Once my brother stopped being so hot-headed, he started seeing it too."

Stella asks how Sofiya felt when Aleksis admitted he'd developed feelings for me.

"He didn't want to tell me at first. He didn't want to upset me. But he didn't want to lie to me either, so they came to mine for dinner, so we could get it all out in the open. And it was lovely to see how easy they are around each other and how they make each other laugh. It made me aware Merle and I hadn't laughed like that for some time. It's hard to find the connection they've got. When it happens, you've just got to follow your heart."

And this is followed by a plug for the following week's show.

I wonder if Merle has seen it and if he has, how he feels about being exposed as an even bigger love rat. And if,

218

deep down, he's sad that Sofiya isn't standing by him this time. But it's business as usual in the *Fire on the Dance Floor* reception room when I arrive. He's engrossed in a conversation with Daniele and Valentina and couldn't look more composed. I do my best to ignore him.

Despite the early hour, the atmosphere is charged – this is something new for everyone. I grab a coffee and join Beth, Liam and Tammy, who are already sipping steaming cups.

'Did you stay much later last night?' I ask. If they did, they're wearing it well.

'I left just after you,' Tammy replies. 'I decided to follow your good example.'

'I saw it through to the end,' Liam admits. 'And the landlord said he'd save the same spot for us next week, if we want it. I think he was pretty pleased when he saw all the empties on our table.'

Aleksis arrives, kisses both my cheeks and asks if I got a good rest.

'I wouldn't have turned down another hour in bed, but I'm fine. You?'

'I was a bit restless, thinking about today and our choreography for the week, but I'll survive. I think that must be our rueda teacher over there,' he says, nodding towards a petite girl with long dark hair who I haven't seen before.

Olivia introduces her as Ros, and as she looks around the room at each of us, I notice her pausing when she gets to Merle – the effect he has on everyone. But when I follow her eyes, he's not looking at her, but at me. It feels like time stands still as he holds my gaze.

'We'll give you a few more minutes to finish your drinks then we'll head to the studio and get started,' Olivia announces, breaking the spell.

It turns out Ros has a big voice despite her small frame, so once we're in the studio she quickly has us all forming a circle in pairs. As even the basic moves involve switching partners, I'm swiftly passed from Aleksis to Theo to Gabriel and then to Merle. And just like before it feels like I've been hit by a bolt of electricity as soon as his hand touches my back. So I'm not in control of it, then.

His eyes find mine and his lips curl up into a smile, but there isn't time for either of us to say anything as I'm already moving around the ring to Dean and Liam, then Elijah and back to Aleksis.

'Good,' Ros says. 'Now let's move on to something more complicated.'

Soon we're adding claps, spins and jumps, and it gets pretty chaotic as we start switching partners, not just with the couple next to us but the one next to them, as well as reversing the direction in which we switch. We go wrong several times, but Ros corrects us then gets us to practise over and over until we get it right.

Then the turn patterns start getting technical and we really have to concentrate. Not just on where our arms and legs are meant to be – but on remembering the names of the moves, which are all in Spanish, so that we know what to do when Ros calls something out. It's not easy but it's exhilarating, and I'm not the only one who breaks into a smile when we successfully put a few sequences together in a row.

We don't stop for two and a half hours – when Ros announces a fifteen-minute rest and drink break – and I realise I haven't even had time to think about Merle. I've whizzed past him multiple times, been back with Aleksis seconds later, and passed by everyone else in between.

'I don't know why I haven't done this before,' Aleksis grins as we head to the drinks machine together. 'I love it.'

'Me too.' I feel just as animated. 'There's so much to take in, though. I feel like I need to make notes.'

'It's a steep learning curve. We'll definitely need the extra practice days they've booked us in for.'

'Kate.' Merle's voice behind me makes me jump and my heart rate trebles as I spin round to face him. 'Can I have a word?'

I look back at Aleksis and his whole demeanour has changed. His jaw is clenched and the animosity rolls off him in waves. When his eyes meet mine, I can see how much he wants to give Merle a piece of his mind. But instead he shrugs and leaves me to decide whether to talk to him.

'What's up?' I ask Merle, sounding as suspicious as I feel.

'In private?'

Aleksis shakes his head and fires him a warning glance before turning away with a sigh. I watch him stalk across the room to join Tammy and Elijah, where he stays with his back to us. I consider following him, but curiosity gets the better of me. I want to hear what Merle has to say.

'So *now* you decide you want to talk to me?' It annoys me that I sound so snippy.

He puts his hand on my back and steers me further away from everyone else, and that familiar electricity radiates out from his fingers. The spark shouldn't still be there, but my treacherous body has its own ideas.

'I thought it was time we made our peace,' Merle says earnestly as I battle to ignore the fizz in my veins. 'I know it hasn't been easy. I have wanted to talk to you, honestly I have, but I wanted to protect you. I didn't want to give anyone here anything more to talk about. I didn't want to make your life more difficult.'

I scowl at him and wait for him to continue.

'I thought I was doing the right thing. But now, being around you again, it's made me realise that was a mistake. It's really good to dance with you again, Kate. It's reminded me how special it was before. It really meant something. I miss it – all of it.'

I stare at him wide-eyed. I don't know what I was expecting but it certainly wasn't this.

'You had a wife,' I hiss, struggling to keep thoughts of our studio days at bay.

'I didn't want to tell you and scare you off. I didn't want it to stop. Especially not the way it did. We had a good thing, Kate, didn't we? Don't you miss it too?'

It would be so easy to tell him I do. But it only takes a glimpse of the grimace on Aleksis's face and the withering look on Emilia's to bring me back to my senses.

'What exactly are you doing here, Merle?' I snap. 'You're with Emilia now and I'm with Aleksis. I don't know why we're even having this conversation.'

'But you're not, though, are you?' he says, placing his

hands on my shoulders and looking me straight in the eyes. 'I see you together and you're not really together. Not like we were. Not like we could be.'

I shake myself free, not quite believing what he's suggesting and not wanting him to think I'd even entertain the idea. Thankfully, Tammy chooses that moment to come to my rescue.

'Hey Kate! I need your help a minute. Sorry, Merle, I'm going to have to steal her away.'

She grabs my hand and pulls me towards the ladies' loos.

'Everything okay?' she checks.

'It was nothing.' I wave it off. 'He just wanted to say sorry for everything that happened.'

'As long as that's all he wants. You know you can't trust him,' she warns.

And she's right, of course. But I can't pretend I didn't feel the tiniest flicker of temptation – and it's left me rattled. *Why?* Because I thought I was stronger than that and that I'd never let him get under my skin again.

And there's something else, too. The mere suggestion of it feels disloyal to Aleksis, even though we're not really together.

I do my best to put it out of my mind for the rest of the day, but it stays in the background despite Ros giving us plenty to think about. By the end of the session, I feel mentally drained and it's a relief when Aleksis suggests we don't hit the town afterwards. All I want is a hot bath and my duvet – and some time to try and work out how I'm feeling. I even turn down a quick drink with Beth, Liam and Tammy.

Back at the flat, Lucy perches on the edge of the bathtub while I soak in a sea of bubbles so she can hear how my day went and, more importantly, what it was like to dance with Merle again. I tell her about our exchange.

'But Tammy interrupted before he could say anything more, so it was left with him having more or less suggested we could pick up where we left off,' I sigh.

'Would you want to?' she asks, sounding surprised.

'I know I shouldn't. But he's just that one who you know with every fibre of your body is bad news, and yet you want him anyway. I mean, why would I not want to have amazing sex with the hottest man I've ever laid eyes on?'

'Erm, because he ghosted you afterwards, he's with someone else now and because you've become friends with his wife?' she points out.

'I know all that. But then when he's standing in front of me, I forget about all of it and just remember the sex. The annoyingly fantastic sex. It's infuriating.'

Lucy pats my shoulder and stands up to leave. 'I think I can predict where this might be going,' she says. 'Just make sure you don't end up getting hurt.'

Chapter 29

At our cha-cha practice the next day, Aleksis admits he spent the rest of the evening thinking about how to get us more press coverage ahead of the next live show, now the rueda practices will take up most of our free time this week.

'Sofiya's going to check in with Stella to see if she has any recommendations for Friday night,' he says. 'Although I'm not sure how likely the *Scene* would be to feature us on just another date night. It would probably have to be something a bit more newsworthy than that. I've been racking my brains.'

'We could always move in together,' I laugh. And in the silence that follows I wish I could eat my words. I'm not sure he realises I was joking. He must think I'm insane.

But then he says, 'It would get people talking,' and it's my turn to properly consider it. It would certainly give Stella another exclusive that would put us ahead of the game again. Which is what we both want, isn't it?

'I think we should do it,' Aleksis says decisively. 'There's a spare room at mine – you could come and stay there. We just won't tell anyone else that's where you're sleeping and they'll never know any different. What do you reckon?'

What I reckoned was that he wouldn't take my flippant suggestion seriously. I can't move in with Aleksis, can I? But I suppose it's only for a couple of weeks, so we could probably make it work. We spend so much time together now, a little more shouldn't be too difficult. Not for me, at any rate.

I decide to throw caution to the wind and tell him I could be talked into it.

'You could bring your things to the studio tomorrow morning and we could go back to the flat straight after the rueda session,' he suggests, his enthusiasm building. 'I could get Sofiya to meet us there and take a few pictures of us arriving, which she can send to Stella. I'm sure she'll be happy to help.'

'If we're going to do it, we would need to make sure everyone knows about it,' I agree.

He takes this as my consent and starts typing a text to Sofiya to ask if she's free for camera duties. I could still change my mind and tell him not to send it, but I don't. And Sofiya replies immediately to say she thinks it's a great idea.

It's followed moments later by another message to say Stella is also on board. I can't help wondering if I've just thrown myself into yet another *Fire on the Dance Floor* frying pan.

But for once I can read Aleksis's expression and he looks

delighted we've found a way to keep our names in the headlines. Until his phone pings again and all the joy drains from his face.

'What is it?' I ask in alarm.

'There's some other news from Stella and I don't think you're going to like it,' he says.

'Tell me,' I urge, steeling myself for whatever might follow.

'She's found out who sold those photos of you to the papers.'

Which I wouldn't have thought was that significant if his forehead wasn't so deeply creased. My apprehension grows as I'm forced to seriously consider that it might have been someone I know. And then Aleksis confirms it.

'It was Liam,' he sighs, and it feels like all the air has been sucked out of my lungs. My friend Liam? Who's always been such a sweetheart, bigging up the rest of us even after he went out of the show?

I reach for the ballet barre to steady myself as I try to make sense of it. I just can't imagine Liam being the one who stabbed me in the back.

'Is she absolutely sure?' I eventually splutter.

Aleksis rests a comforting hand on my arm. 'I'm sorry. It must be a shock.'

It's more than that. I can barely get my words out. 'But why? What did I ever do to him?'

'I don't think it was because of anything you did. According to Stella, he was paid five thousand pounds.'

'Five thousand pounds!' I feel my blood starting to boil. 'I mean, that makes more sense – it's a lot of money – but . . . '

I can't get my head around it. I can't imagine anyone being that cruel to someone they know, let alone Liam. How could he have done this, then had the gall to carry on as if he'd done nothing wrong? When I see him tomorrow, I'm going to . . . I don't even know. Give him a piece of my mind for a start – that's the least he deserves. In fact, I'm not going to wait till tomorrow. I'm going to have this out with him right now. I grab my phone and storm out of the studio.

I pace up and down the corridor while I wait for him to answer my call, but he doesn't pick up. Infuriated, I decide to post a message in the Fire Dancers chat instead. After all, the others deserve to know what their so-called pal is like, before he does anything similar to them.

'*I've just found out who took those photos of me and Merle and sold them to the press,*' I type furiously. '*Liam, you two-faced prick, how could you? You even pretended you were concerned about me afterwards. I guess you thought I'd never find out, right? Well, you were wrong. And now everyone else knows what a lying piece of shit you are too. I can't believe I ever considered you a friend.*'

Beth replies first. '*OMG Liam, is this true? Did you really do that?*'

'*Oh fuck,*' Tammy writes. '*Why, Liam? What were you thinking?*'

'*I'm sorry,*' comes his simpering reply. '*I had a moment of madness after I got kicked off the show. It was my only chance to still get the money for the gym. I didn't think about the consequences. And then it was too late to undo it. I'm so, so sorry.*'

228

'*Your only chance?*' My anger flies off the scale. '*There are a billion other ways you could have got the money for your stupid gym – and none of them include ruining my life. You put me through hell. I thought I'd never be able to show my face again. In a million years I never imagined the lowlife behind it would be you.*'

He starts typing again but I realise there's nothing more he can say that I want to know. Fighting back tears of rage, I block him and remove myself from the chat. The fact that it was him – a friend – is almost as bad as the pictures being out there in the first place. How could he betray me like that?

I storm back into the studio and throw my phone into my bag.

'Anything I can do?' Aleksis asks softly.

'Not unless you've got a bottle of vodka hidden somewhere in here,' I reply, only half joking.

'I can offer you a lukewarm coffee and a KitKat?' he says. And he sounds so genuinely upset that he can't offer me anything stronger that my fury dissipates a little. It reminds me there are some good people in the world.

'Can we just change the subject?' I request, suddenly wanting to throw myself back into our cha-cha practice and forget everything else. 'I don't want to waste any more time thinking about it.'

'Of course,' he nods. And we rehearse until it's time for me to go home and pack a suitcase for the big move tomorrow.

Lucy is unexpectedly enthusiastic when I tell her I'll be staying at Aleksis's place for a few weeks. I thought she might question the wisdom of it, even if it does give her and Aiden the Balham flat to themselves for a while.

'You never know, he might get so used to you being there that he doesn't want you to leave,' she says, with a twinkle in her eye.

I pretend to be insulted. 'And there I was thinking you might miss me around here.'

'Of course I will. Who else is going to leave toothpaste in the sink and forget to take the recycling out?' she teases.

'Aiden,' we say simultaneously and burst out laughing.

Chapter 30

My legs start to ache before I'm even halfway through the next day's cha-cha rehearsal. The footwork is so fast and the timing is really hard to grasp. The thought of an ice bath has always filled me with horror, but I'm starting to wonder if I might need one if I'm going to survive the week.

'I am pushing you quite hard,' Aleksis admits. 'We could do a slower, easier version, but I know you can do this and it will look so much better this way.'

He promises we'll do a longer stretching session at the end of the day.

From time to time my concentration slips when I glimpse my suitcase in the corner of the studio. It gives me that flash of excitement that always comes before a holiday. I know I'm not going to a fancy hotel in the Caribbean, but I can't wait to see what his apartment looks like and keep wondering how it will feel being there. Will it make us feel more like a couple? Do I *want* us to feel more like a couple?

Aleksis politely suggests that I keep my eyes on my reflection in the mirror, to help me focus and so I can see when my posture and positioning are just right. And watching myself makes me realise what a long way I've come since the start of the competition. Six-weeks-ago-Kate was like a gawky teenager compared to how I look now. Seeing how much I've improved makes my confidence soar.

True to his word, at the end of the session Aleksis makes sure every muscle is properly stretched out before we make the journey to Channel 6. Even so, I'm relieved when we manage to get a seat on the Tube. Sitting down for fifteen minutes feels like bliss.

It doesn't last, though. Before we reach Hammersmith, we find ourselves in an impromptu photoshoot thanks to a mum who recognises us and asks if she can take a photo of us with her daughters. It attracts the attention of the other passengers in our carriage and soon there's a queue of people wanting their picture taken with us. I don't think half of them even know who we are, they just don't want to risk missing out.

We're still laughing about it when we arrive at Channel 6. It was a brief but welcome reprieve from my growing anxiety about seeing Merle again after what he said to me on Sunday – and Liam, now his true colours have been revealed.

As soon as we walk into the reception room, Liam is out of his chair and heading towards me, but Aleksis holds a hand up in warning and Liam stops in his tracks. It makes me like Aleksis even more.

'Are you okay?' Beth asks when I join her and Tammy. 'This must be so awkward.'

'As long as I pretend it never happened, I can just about deal with it,' I assure them.

Beth squeezes my arm. 'We're both here for you.'

I tell them I appreciate it, then Olivia announces that now everyone is present we can head to the studio and get started.

To my surprise, I don't let either Liam or Merle get to me for the first hour or so of the rehearsal. I keep reminding myself that I'm strong and I can rise above whatever has come before. Liam does say sorry the first time we're paired together, but I ignore him. I'm determined not to let my anger bubble up to the surface. It helps that I'm only with him for a few seconds at a time before I'm passed to the next dancer, so he can't say anything more.

I'm feeling pretty pleased with myself by the time we stop for a drink break – but just when I'm silently congratulating myself for my maturity, all hell breaks loose. It starts when Liam tries to approach me again.

'We have to talk about this, Kate,' he says, blocking my path this time so I can't dodge him. 'I want to apologise. I know what I did was wrong and I want to make it up to you. I wasn't thinking straight at the time and I've been feeling awful ever since. I've been wanting to say something ever since it happened, but I didn't know how.

'Now you know, I just want to make it right. I want to give you the money they paid me for the photos. It was a lot – two thousand pounds. You should have it, it should be yours. You're right, I should have found another way to get my gym. I don't want it to be founded out of this.'

'Five,' I say sharply.

His face blanches. 'I beg your pardon?'

'Five thousand.' I poke him in the chest to emphasise each word. 'You're not trying to make it right, you're trying to make yourself feel better and keep some cash for yourself. You really are disgusting.'

His demeanour changes from earnest to affronted. 'I'm trying to say sorry.'

'You're trying to make yourself look like less of a shit,' I snap.

'You're hardly perfect yourself,' Liam fires back, losing his temper. 'What kind of person sleeps with a married man just to win a dance show?'

'Fuck you!' I yell, aware that everyone is looking at us now.

Then Aleksis pushes himself between us. 'I think you should walk away now,' he warns Liam.

'Or what?' Liam gives him a shove as I jump out of the way.

Gabriel and Elijah rush over as they square up to each other, and Merle takes my arm and pulls me further away.

'Kate,' he says, concern in his voice. 'What's going on? Are you okay?'

'It's nothing,' I reply, not wanting to talk to him, of all people, about the leaked photos. But my body is shaking with fury – as well as shock at how quickly things have escalated – and I want nothing more than to get away from the sound of Gabriel begging Liam and Aleksis to calm down on the other side of the room.

So when Merle suggests we step outside for a moment, to take a breather until whatever it is blows over, I don't even question it. I follow him just to get away from the tension in the studio, from the shock of screaming profanities in someone's face for the first time in my life.

I let him lead me to his dressing room, as if in a daze, and when he's closed the door behind us and turned to face me, I simply stand there as he tucks a loose strand of hair behind my ear. He doesn't say anything, he just looks me straight in the eye and I stare back at him, almost willing him to make this nightmare go away.

And then suddenly we're kissing and I can finally forget about the drama down the corridor, about the photos, about Liam throwing me to the wolves, about Aleksis, about having to keep up appearances, about pushing myself to my limits, about absolutely everything. It's not until Merle starts rolling my top up that I snap myself back out of it.

'Stop!' I gasp. 'Stop! We shouldn't be doing this. God, what was I thinking? I shouldn't have come in here. We need to stop.'

'Even if we both want it?' he says, his voice thick with desire. 'I want you, Kate. I've always wanted you.'

I feel like I'm on fire – my body's crying out to be seduced – but I manage to stay in control.

'No, Merle.' I shake my head and push him away. 'I'm moving in with Aleksis tonight. This can't happen again.'

Then I dash from the room, praying nobody sees me and jumps to the wrong – or even the right – conclusion.

The concerned look on Aleksis's face when I walk back into the studio makes me feel terrible. Liam is on the opposite side of the room, getting a talking-to from Beth and Tammy.

'I'm sorry,' I apologise to Aleksis. 'That shouldn't have happened.'

I know he'll assume I mean the confrontation with Liam, even if it's not what I'm referring to.

He puts his hand on my arm. 'It's understandable. Are you okay to continue?'

Our eyes meet and I can see from the worry etched on his face that he genuinely cares. The realisation makes me feel even worse about kissing Merle. Even though we're not a real couple I feel like I've cheated on him – and worse still, at a time when he was trying to defend me.

I silently kick myself for allowing Merle to exploit the situation – I have no doubt he knew exactly what he was doing when he took me to his dressing room. I'm not saying I played no part in it, but I just wasn't thinking straight.

And now I can't stop wondering what it means for me and Aleksis. If he found out, I don't doubt it would spell the end for our arrangement. And given how desperately I don't want that to happen, I think what that probably means is that I'm no longer going to have to try so hard to convince people I have feelings for him. But now's hardly the time to start thinking I might like him for real.

'I'm fine,' I tell him, doing my best to keep my voice even. 'I just needed to let it all out, I think. But what about you? I really am sorry you got dragged into it.'

'All good here,' he assures me. 'Liam has apologised to me. He doesn't want to cause any more trouble.'

'Shame he didn't feel that way two weeks ago,' I mutter bitterly.

'Right, can we get back to it now?' Ros directs the question to the whole room. 'Everybody ready? Everyone calm now?'

There's a chorus of yeses and we get back into our circle. Aleksis gives me an encouraging smile as the music starts up again and I offer a weak smile back to disguise my guilt.

Merle sneaks me knowing looks for the remainder of the rehearsal and lets his hands linger on me longer than necessary whenever we pass each other in the rueda, but I don't rise to it. Liam avoids eye contact with me altogether, while Beth and Tammy fire a few curious glances my way, which I pretend not to notice. Emilia doesn't wipe the scowl off her face all evening and I wonder if she can guess what Merle and I have done. But I tell myself she can't possibly know.

When Ros announces we're done for the day, I can't get away from everyone fast enough. I grab my suitcase and race for the door, telling Aleksis I'll wait for him outside. I don't want either Merle or Liam to corner me again and I don't feel like answering any questions from Beth or Tammy. I'm not sure I trust myself with the answers.

Why, why, why did I go to Merle's changing room with him? I must have known what would happen. I'm furious with myself for my moment of weakness, for letting him think he had the upper hand – and for letting Aleksis down.

I take deep breaths and try to force it out of my mind. I don't want Aleksis to realise there's anything wrong, and I need to psych myself up for seeing Sofiya when we get to his apartment. I'd die if she ever got wind of what just happened. If she even suspected it.

'That was eventful,' Aleksis says, when he finally catches me up.

'I just want to get out of here,' I reply. I want to forget the whole evening ever happened.

'I'll book an Uber,' he says. 'It's too late to be messing around with Tubes.'

I force a smile onto my face, but I'm not sure it reaches my eyes. A feeling of wretchedness hangs over me for the whole journey, until Aleksis tells me we're turning onto his road.

'Here we are,' he says brightly, as we pull up outside a grand red-brick mansion block that looks like something out of a period drama. Sofiya is on the doorstep and waves her camera in the air by way of greeting.

'You live here?' I ask, staring at the giant windows and manicured flower beds.

'I do.'

And I'm not surprised he says it with a grin. I finally stop brooding about Liam and Merle and focus on the task at hand. I need to pull myself together pronto if we're going to make this look convincing.

Aleksis helps by draping his arm round my shoulders as we walk to the front door. It feels so familiar there now that I manage to relax as Sofiya snaps away. Then the door is opened and we're inside possibly the nicest apartment I've ever seen.

'Wow!' I gawp open-mouthed at the vast living space with giant works of art on the wall. 'This is not what I expected at all.'

There's a plush four-seater sofa, deep pile rugs, ornate

sideboards and a huge modern chandelier hanging from the ceiling. I slowly spin round to take it all in.

'What did you expect?' Aleksis asks, sounding amused. 'A big empty room with a mirrored wall and a barre?'

'I don't know – a bit more of a lad pad, I suppose,' I admit.

'With a ten-year-old armchair, an Xbox and a projector wall?'

'Something like that.'

'Not really my style,' he says, laughing. 'Although Sofiya may have had more to do with the decor than me.'

'It needed updating when our parents moved out,' she explains. 'When they moved back to Latvia, they said Aleksis and I could stay here if we wanted to. I was in my own house with Merle by then, so Aleksis got it all to himself. But he definitely needed my help with the decorating.'

'I don't think I would have wanted to leave if I lived somewhere like this,' I tell them. I can just make out an impressively spacious roof terrace through the double doors at the end of the room – my absolute dream.

'You should see the house in Latvia,' Sofiya laughs. 'Right, time for me to get out of your hair. I want to get these pictures edited and sent over to Stella, so she can run them tomorrow.'

Aleksis sees her out then gives me a tour of the rest of the flat, from the large, bright kitchen to the smaller, cosier bedrooms, which each have their own bathroom. Aleksis has an art deco velvet headboard decorating his bed, and framed black and white photos of dancers on his walls.

The guest room has an elegant wrought iron bed frame and a beautifully restored antique wardrobe.

He puts my suitcase on the bed and says, 'I'll leave you to make yourself at home. Come and find me when you're ready.'

I lie down next to it and close my eyes, wanting just five minutes of peace after the stress of the evening. But when I open them again, the room is dark and the rest of the flat is silent. I grope towards my suitcase and retrieve my phone from the side pocket, squinting at the sudden brightness from the screen.

'It can't be,' I whisper, as my eyes grow accustomed to the glow and I discover it's just after three a.m. I thought I'd be spending my first night here staying up late and chatting to Aleksis, getting to know each other better, not falling asleep without even saying goodnight.

But it will have to wait till breakfast now – Aleksis won't still be up at this time – so I quietly move my suitcase to the floor, climb back under the covers and go back to sleep until sunrise.

Chapter 31

The apartment looks just as spectacular when I venture out of my bedroom the next morning. But despite the uber-stylish furnishings, it still feels homely. I try to imagine what it must be like to wake up here every morning. It's a far cry from the shabby rugs and chipped work surfaces I'm used to.

Aleksis emerges from his room, stifling a yawn. He's wearing nothing but jogging bottoms and I quickly look away before he catches me checking out his abs. Now that I think I might genuinely like him, it's like I've finally given myself permission to find him attractive. But I don't want him to know. It would only make things awkward.

I had wondered if he might feel uncomfortable with me being here, like I'm intruding on his personal space. But the fact that he's wandering round half-dressed suggests he's perfectly at ease with it, and I can't help thinking his self-assurance makes him even more likeable.

'Did you sleep all right?' he asks.

'Like a log,' I nod. 'Sorry, I just passed out as soon as I lay down. I only meant to rest for a few minutes.'

'No problem, you obviously needed it.'

He lines up a box of eggs, some mushrooms, a pepper and some tomatoes on the counter. 'Would you like an omelette?'

'Ooh, yes please.'

All I've had since yesterday lunchtime is an energy bar and a bag of Maltesers, and now I've seen the food I realise I'm ravenous.

'With all the trimmings?' he asks.

'Yes please,' I say again, feeling nothing like his fake girlfriend as I watch him making us breakfast.

Once again I have to check myself, but at least it must mean our plan is working if in trying to convince everyone else of our story, I've started falling for it myself.

My stomach rumbles as soon as the smell of cooking fills the air and I'm not sure the omelette lasts more than sixty seconds on my plate, but I still feel like I could devour a three-course meal afterwards. Thankfully Aleksis is on the same page because he makes us toast as well, and follows it up with yoghurt and fruit salad. A breakfast designed for another busy day.

Before we head to the studio, Stella video calls us to get some quotes for her latest story. She peppers us with questions about the first time we met, when we realised we wanted to be more than dance partners and whether we were worried we'd moved in together too quickly.

'It will seem quick to some people, but Kate was coming here most nights anyway, so it just felt like a natural step,'

Aleksis fibs. 'And this way I get to wake up to this gorgeous smile every morning.'

He winks at me, which makes my heart do a somersault. I try to convince myself it's down to the nerves of doing this interview.

'You're making me blush,' I tell him, one of the few things I say which is true. 'But yeah, we were together almost twenty-four hours a day anyway, so it made sense. It already feels like home.'

Stella asks us if either of us have noticed any bad habits in each other around the house.

'Leaving the loo seat up,' I tell her, glancing at Aleksis again.

'Filling the plughole with her hair,' he adds, looking back at me with a challenge in his eyes.

'Throwing his clothes at the laundry basket, not in the laundry basket,' I fire at him with a grin.

'She always burns the toast when she does the breakfast.'

'I do not.'

'Thank goodness for extractor fans, that's all I'm saying.' I shake my head in mock indignation.

'Have you had any big rows about anything?' Stella asks.

'No,' we both confirm.

'We get on really well,' Aleksis adds.

'Not even about Merle? I'm sorry but I've got to ask, was there not even the tiniest cross word about the fact that Kate slept with your sister's husband, Aleksis? Sorry,' she apologises, visibly cringing.

'If you let yourself be concerned by other people's pasts, you would never be with anyone,' he says. 'Everyone makes mistakes, but that doesn't define them. Of course I was angry on Sofiya's behalf when I first found out what Merle was doing, but in my family, we deal with our anger very quickly. It's not healthy to hold on to it and let it eat away at you. Sofiya has no hard feelings towards Kate, so there was no reason for me to stay upset about it. As Sofiya herself said, Kate had no idea he was married.'

'And Kate, have you never felt awkward about what happened with Merle?' Stella asks.

'Honestly, I thought Sofiya would hate me – Aleksis too. But they couldn't have been nicer about it and I now count Sofiya as a friend. And Aleksis, of course, as a lot more.'

The lie comes so easily, now I've apparently started feeling like it would be no bad thing if it were true.

'And with just ten days to go till the final of *Fire on the Dance Floor*, how are you feeling about that, Kate?' Stella asks.

'We've still got this week to get through, but if we make it through to the final we'll be delighted.'

'It would be amazing to be the show's first ever winners, but we'll be happy with any stage we get to,' Aleksis adds. 'Whatever happens, we'll come away with more than we started with, so it feels like we've won anyway.'

I realise the prize money has barely crossed my mind with everything else that's been going on. I think about it now: how it would save me from ever falling back into a rut, and how I long for that safety net. But if having Aleksis in my life is what I get out of the competition instead, would I even care if I didn't win?

For a moment I try to picture what will happen to us

after the show. We've got this weird and wonderful experience binding us together now, but will he still want to see me when he no longer has to? Or, because of the way it all started, will we just close the door on it and never look back? A week ago I wouldn't have cared. But now . . .

Stella interrupts my thoughts with another question. 'What's it like on set, with Merle there too?'

'We don't have much to do with each other,' I reply quickly. 'We're either off rehearsing or at costume fittings, but when we do cross paths we keep it very professional. You just have to get on with it. We've only got five weeks on the show – and that's if we get through to the next round – so I just want to make the most of it and have the best time I can possibly have.'

Which hadn't really sunk in until I say it out loud. There's so little time left and I do want to enjoy it. What's the point in ruining it by fighting with Liam and worrying about Merle?

After a few more questions about whether I've lost weight through all the rehearsing (a bit) and whether I'll keep dancing after the show (I hope so), Stella wraps things up and Aleksis closes his laptop.

'That went well.' He smiles. 'We're pretty good at this.'

The way he looks at me when he says it makes me wonder if the boundaries have started blurring a bit for him as well.

'I guess it's time to update my parents again,' I think aloud, and he agrees he should probably do the same.

'I've decided I'm going to talk to Liam today too,' I tell him.

He looks surprised. 'Really?'

'I don't want the rest of the week to be negative, so I'm just going to accept his apology then let it go.'

Just saying it out loud makes it feel like a weight has lifted.

'That's quite the U-turn, but good for you,' Aleksis says with a smile. 'You can't change it, so if you can put it behind you that can only be a good thing, right? What about Merle?'

'What about him?' This comes out a little more sharply than I intended, and my cheeks start burning.

He looks at me quizzically. 'I just wondered if that extends to him as well.'

'We've done all the making up we need to,' I reply curtly, still furious with myself for what happened in his dressing room. I quickly excuse myself to go and call my family before Aleksis can ask anything else about Merle.

When Mum pops up on my screen, sporting a deep tan and a contented smile, I decide not to mention Merle or Liam or anything that might wipe the glow off her face. I stick to telling her how much fun the rueda practice is and how gorgeous Aleksis's apartment is, before admitting I'm going to be living in it for a while.

But although I hurry to explain it's just to keep our names in the media, I should have known my own mother would be able to read me like a book.

She looks at me fondly. 'If you say so, darling.'

Chapter 32

I talk to Liam before anyone else when I arrive at Channel 6 after another day of cha-cha practice. I want to get it out of the way before we get stuck into the rueda – and while I'm still feeling pumped up from seeing Stella's latest story online. Aleksis and I have done a good job of sounding loved-up, which has boosted my confidence no end. If I was watching the show I'd definitely be interested in our story and keen to keep us in the competition.

Liam couldn't look more relieved when I tell him I've decided to forgive him for selling the photos and that I just want to forget all about it. He apologises again, as well as for what he said yesterday, and again offers to give me the money he was paid for the pictures – all of it this time – to make amends.

'Let's just leave it at that for now,' I say, offering him my hand.

'Sure,' he says, shaking it. 'But for the record, I do feel terrible about it.'

Beth comes running over when she sees the handshake, with Tammy trailing more tentatively behind.

'Does this mean you guys are friends again?' Beth asks.

'We're working on it,' I confirm.

'Oh yay! I hated that everything got so messed up.'

I think we all breathe a sigh of relief as Ros gets us to partner up so she can run through everything we learned yesterday before introducing some new moves.

This time I smile back when Merle shoots me his knowing looks, which I think is me being grown up, but which he seems to interpret as encouragement, because when we finish rehearsing three hours later – having opted to go straight through without a break and finish earlier this time – he corners me in the corridor when I'm on my way to the ladies before leaving the studio.

'I couldn't stop thinking about you last night,' he says, his eyes searching mine.

'Don't, Merle,' I start. But before I can tell him I'm not going to do this dance with him again, he strokes my cheek and adds, 'I know you're feeling it too.'

And no matter how much I want to deny it, my resolve wavers yet again. Because when he's standing there in front of me, my body still yearns for him to kiss me. But I cling on to my last shred of willpower.

'You should be saying this to Emilia.' It's meant to be said with conviction, but my voice sounds far away, and not like my own.

'She doesn't make me feel this,' he says, taking my hand and pushing it against his trousers, so I can feel him growing hard. An image of us having sex pops straight into my mind, right here in the corridor, my back against the wall, my legs round his waist . . . but I pull my hand away. This is not happening again.

I don't do it quickly enough, though.

'Kate? Merle? What's going on?' Emilia's voice shrills from behind me.

I spin round to face her, my face reddening as her expression tells me she knows exactly what was going on.

'Nothing,' I hastily assure her, turning to Merle to back me up. But he just smirks and stays silent.

'Jesus, Merle,' I mutter as I push past him and escape into the bathroom. I slam the cubicle door shut behind me and put my head in my hands, furious with him – and with myself. How can my self-control still yo-yo around him, when I don't even like him any more? It's maddening. And why the hell did Emilia have to choose that exact moment to come looking for him?

I wonder how the conversation in the corridor is going, but when I emerge from the bathroom Merle and Emilia have gone. My heart sinks when I get back to the reception room and see her talking to Aleksis. I join them apprehensively.

'Hi, I'm ready when you are.' I keep my voice light as I touch his arm.

'Sure, let's go,' he replies tersely, avoiding my eye. 'See you tomorrow, Em,' he adds, kissing both her cheeks before heading for the door.

'See you tomorrow, guys,' I call out to Beth, Tammy and Liam as I follow him out. He strides ahead, leaving me half-jogging to keep up.

'I guess she told you then?' I ask, dreading the answer but needing to know.

He stops abruptly and turns to face me.

'How could you?' he says, sounding so disappointed it makes me want to cry. 'After everything we've been working towards, how could you risk throwing it all away like that?'

'But it really wasn't anything,' I protest weakly. 'It was just Merle trying to persuade me to get together with him again, that's all.'

'You had your hand down his trousers,' he snaps.

'It wasn't—' I'm silenced by the anger in his eyes.

'How do you think Sofiya will feel about this?'

My heart sinks. 'You're going to tell her?'

'I don't know what I'm going to do. I need time to think.'

'I know it looked bad but, honestly, nothing happened.'

'Let's just talk about it later,' he says, ending the conversation.

We don't speak again for the whole cab journey home. I keep my head down and just scroll through my phone. My Instagram following has really spiked after the news that I'm now living with Aleksis. Suddenly more than twelve thousand people want to know more about me. I try not to let that terrify me.

I text Lucy to see if she's around for a chat later, but she doesn't reply. She's probably with Aiden, having a lovely time, and for a second I allow myself to feel jealous. I'm glad she's so happy, of course I am, but today it just reminds me what a shambles my own love life has been lately. I wonder if I'll ever get it right.

Back at the flat, Aleksis goes straight off to his room for a bath and tells me to help myself to whatever I want in the kitchen. I should be starving, but the strained atmosphere has killed my appetite, so I grab a glass of wine, which I drink too quickly while I beat myself up for being such an idiot – again.

I'm working my way through my fourth glass and am far from sober when Aleksis finally emerges from the bathroom. He looks sexy with his wet hair glistening and his skin flushed from the hot water, which only makes me feel more forlorn. Why couldn't it be him who was into me instead of bloody Merle? Why can't I just end up with a nice guy for once? I feel my eyes getting watery with a combination of alcohol and self-pity.

'What's wrong?' Aleksis asks irritably, clearly still angry with me.

'I'm fine,' I reply unconvincingly.

He pours a glass of water and hands it to me, attempting to extract the wine glass from my other hand at the same time, but not before I manage another slug.

'I'm not going to tell Sofiya, okay?' he says. 'It won't help anyone.'

A tear escapes and rolls down my cheek.

'Don't do that.'

I look away, but he can tell I'm crying.

'Hey,' he says more gently. 'What's that for?'

'Because I'm making such a mess of this,' I sob. 'I don't know why. I don't know if it's because I've just been convincing myself I'm okay with everything – with Liam and Merle and the photos and everything – when really

I'm not. Or if it's the pressure of the show. But it's too much. I'm crumbling.'

'You're being hard on yourself. You've had a lot to deal with.'

'But I could have dealt with it so much better. I kissed him,' I confess, my tears in full flow now. 'Merle, I mean.'

His body stiffens.

'Not today. At the first rueda practice, after it all blew up with Liam. He made a move on me and for a couple of seconds I kissed him because I wasn't thinking rationally. I was so angry with Liam and I was just caught up in the moment. It made me feel awful and I wish it hadn't happened. It was so stupid and now I feel like I've ruined everything and you probably hate me.'

'I don't hate you,' he says quietly, but he's standing so still I can tell he's shocked.

I'm vaguely aware I should probably have saved this revelation for a conversation with Lucy, but I plough on anyway, fuelled by wine and regret.

'I nearly ruined all our hard work. And for what? For a stupid kiss with an awful man who has no idea how to treat other people. I don't want to waste my time on someone like that. I don't want to be sneaking around grabbing secret kisses with someone who's just biding their time till something better comes along. That's not what I want.'

'Perhaps it's time to start thinking about what you do want,' he suggests.

'I want this.' I wave my hand between the two of us. 'To be with someone nice, who makes me feel good about

252

myself and makes me laugh. I want *this*, the bloody fairy-tale.'

'But this isn't real.' He says it gently, like he's trying to soften the blow.

'I know.' I sniff, rubbing my eyes and smearing mascara across my cheeks. 'And that's what makes all this so much worse.'

The pause that follows is so long I think Aleksis must be trying to think of a polite way to tell me he regrets letting me move in and would like me to leave. I could hardly blame him. And my heart sinks when he eventually he says, 'Look, if we're going to do confessions tonight, I've got one as well.'

I can't believe we haven't even managed to make it through the second night.

'Let's just say, I really don't like the thought of you with Merle, okay?' he says softly, like he's not sure he should be admitting it. 'And it's not just because of Sofiya.'

I peer at him through puffy eyes, not sure if I've heard him correctly.

'The thing is, I know we're just pretending to be in a relationship, but it doesn't always feel like it. And when Emilia told me what she saw, it's not so much that I was angry with you for putting our plan at risk, but more that I was worried about how it would change this.' He pauses. 'Change us.'

I suck in my breath. So he's been feeling exactly the same way I have? It sounds that way, but I need to be sure. I shake my head, trying to clear the wine fog that's settled over me. 'Are you saying what I think you're saying?'

He takes the water glass from me and sets it down on the counter, then he tilts my chin up and kisses me lightly on my lips.

'This is what I'm saying,' he confirms.

Then we kiss again, for much longer time this time. And when we finally break away, I can't stop staring at him, not trusting myself to speak. He wipes the moisture from under my eyes and asks, 'So, is this okay?'

And I'm not sure if the room is spinning from the kiss or from the wine as he sways in front of me. But the next thing I know, there's daylight creeping under my bedroom curtains and I'm under the duvet, on my own, fully clothed, with no idea how I got there – unsure if I imagined the whole thing.

Chapter 33

I grope for my phone, trying to keep my sore head as still as possible, and groan when the screen tells me it's only six-thirty a.m. There's no chance of getting back to sleep though – my mind's already racing.

The last thing I remember clearly is confessing to Aleksis that I like him, but the next part of the evening is frustratingly hazy. I'm only sixty per cent certain he said he has feelings for me too – and even less sure we kissed. But I wouldn't have dreamed it up, would I, just because I want it to be true?

With no recollection of what happened afterwards or how I got to bed, it's entirely possible my mind is just playing tricks on me. But I don't think I'm under the covers in all my clothes because Aleksis doesn't like me. I think it's because he isn't Merle and therefore wouldn't dream of taking advantage. But does that mean he wouldn't kiss me, either? I groan into the pillow in frustration.

The mystery is solved when I eventually drag myself

out of bed to go and look for some painkillers. Aleksis emerges from his room and kisses me full on the lips as he passes me in the kitchen. His breath is minty and his skin is soft – he's already brushed his teeth and had a shave. It makes me wish I'd put some make-up on and done something about my bed hair.

'How's the head?' he asks with a grin.

'Getting there,' I reply, holding up my water glass. 'I have to admit, the end of the night is a little vague.'

'You drank almost a whole bottle of wine on an empty stomach, threw yourself at me then promptly passed out,' he summarises, sounding amused.

'I threw myself at you? That's not how I remember it.' Not that I remember it.

'I'm kidding,' he says, laughing as he slides an espresso in front of me. 'It was perfectly mutual.'

'So we did kiss?'

He nods.

'And I passed out straight afterwards?'

'Kind of during.' He chuckles. 'I'd like to say I made you weak at the knees but I'm not sure I had much to do with it.'

'Oh God, I'm sorry. And I got to bed how?'

'Kind of a mutual effort again. I took your shoes off. You tried to put your pyjamas on without taking your jeans off. In the end you decided to sleep in your clothes. You were out cold before I'd switched the light off.'

'I really know how to impress a guy,' I mutter, cringing at the thought of it.

'But at least we both know where we stand now,' he says,

with a sparkle in his eyes. 'No more pretending, if that's still okay with you.'

'That is very okay with me,' I confirm.

Then he leans in and kisses me again and I stop thinking I'm going to wake up at any moment. This is really happening. Me and Aleksis, no longer faking things, kissing every time we pass each other as we get ready to head to our studio, lacing our fingers together as we sit side by side on the Tube, enjoying how it feels now it's not just for show.

I'm still on cloud nine when we arrive in Brixton, half an hour behind schedule. I'd completely forgotten today was our day for filming our latest segment for the show.

'I'm so sorry we're late,' Aleksis apologises to Sarah, Steve and Andy, who are already set up and ready to go. 'We got held up,' he adds, shooting me a grin that doesn't go unnoticed by Sarah.

'No harm done,' she says, with a knowing smile.

'What have you got in store for us today?' Aleksis asks.

'Well, when I was filming Merle and Emilia yesterday, I found this old yoga mat.'

My heart lurches as she holds up the mat I once had sex on with Merle.

'It gave me an idea.'

'Of course it did,' Aleksis says, while I hold my breath in terror.

'I'm going to get you to do some yoga together,' she says, and I feel my shoulders relaxing again. 'It'll probably look better if you don't get it all completely perfect.'

And we don't, but not because we're not trying. It's

mostly because we keep getting the giggles. I think our new relationship status has made us both giddy.

The first pose isn't too difficult. We sit facing each other with our feet touching, our legs bent and holding hands. Then we lean outwards so we can straighten our legs in the air, our feet still connected between us, and we hold that pose for a minute. So far, so good.

Then Sarah gets Aleksis to lie down on the mat with his feet in the air. She instructs me to push my hips against his feet and lean my body over so I can put my hands on his and he can lift me off the floor into a flying position. I can't help thinking it's a bit different from the last time I had a man lying under me on this mat.

'Don't drop me,' I warn, as I sway in the air above him.

'Trust me, I'm not going to drop you. I'm underneath, remember?'

Next, I'm supposed to let go of his hands and let my torso flop down towards the floor while he balances me with just his feet.

'I can't,' I squeal. Just trying to let go with one hand makes me wobble uncontrollably. 'Hey, stop laughing. I'm falling. Put me back down. Aleksis!'

He manages to propel me back to standing before I face-plant on the mat.

'Sorry. Your face was a picture.'

'I'd like to see you try it.'

'Come on then, you get down here,' he challenges.

'I'll never be able to lift you . . . '

'There's still one more position to try,' Sarah interrupts with a smile.

This one has us standing side by side and holding hands, then crouching into a deep squat and trying to sit down at the same time as each other without any of our hands touching the floor. I lose my balance immediately and end up with my legs over my head. After that we're supposed to rock back up into the squat position, but after several failed attempts we're laughing so hard we have to abandon it.

'This is brilliant,' Sarah says. 'We'll cut that one into the middle and finish up with the first one to make it look like you've given up for an easier pose. That works perfectly – thanks guys. Right, let's see a bit of your rehearsal then we can chat about how your week is going. My impression is it's going pretty well.'

Sarah wraps up just before lunchtime, leaving us with a good few hours of cha-cha practice. My goal for the afternoon, set by Aleksis, is to really master the breaks among the faster sections of the footwork, which need to be precise to look good. By the end of the session, I think I'm getting it right just over half of the time.

'Do you think I'm going to be ready?' I ask as we pack our dance shoes away.

'We've still got one full day,' he reminds me.

When he sees the crestfallen look on my face, he adds, 'You're going to be fine. Just think about last week. The difference between Thursday and Friday's dancing was huge. It'll be the same tomorrow. It's a pity we can't skip the rueda this evening, though. So you could give your legs a rest.'

If only! But exhaustion isn't the only reason I'd like to skip it. I'm worried Emilia might want a confrontation and I don't want to be at the centre of another scene. I've brought enough drama to the show already.

'Come on, let's get it over with,' he says, 'then I'll cook us something nice back at ours afterwards.'

And I roll the word 'ours' round and round in my head on the way to Channel 6, liking the way it sounds.

Chapter 34

I'm surprised to see Merle and Emilia chatting and laughing together when we walk into the reception room, like yesterday never happened. There's not a hint of tension between them. I guess that means Merle has managed to convince her nothing was going on between him and me, which is a relief, but it makes me feel sorry for Emilia. I have no doubt she's heading for heartache.

They seem equally surprised to see Aleksis and me holding hands and looking completely at ease with each other. Merle's eyes travel unsubtly from our smiling faces to our interlocked fingers and he looks at me with a frown. Then I get caught up in a round of hellos with Beth, Tammy and the rest of our gang and manage to forget about it.

By now our rueda is looking good. Throughout the evening, Sarah pulls each couple to the side in turn for a quick chat about it. She'll be creating an edit of our conversations to be played on Saturday's show.

I'm rarely with Merle for longer than a few seconds at a time while we're rehearsing, but there is one awkward moment when we're standing together while Ros tells us about a new move she wants to add to give our rueda more flair.

'So you're still choosing Aleksis?' he says quietly.

'Shh, Merle,' I hiss. 'I'm listening to Ros. But yes, I'm very much with Aleksis.'

'And there's nothing I can do to change your mind?' he asks.

'Nothing,' I tell him, really believing it this time.

'Merle, do you want to come and do the demo with me?' Ros asks pointedly.

He gives me one last probing look before he joins her in the middle of the circle.

'Right, for this move, men, I want you to dip back and touch the floor with your right hand then come back up to standing,' she instructs. 'When we turn here . . . ' she takes Merle's hands and walks him through the steps, 'this is where you use the momentum to propel away from your partner. It looks hard, but it's not as long as you keep the tension in your arms. Everyone got that?'

'Got it,' we chant as she returns Merle to my side.

'Good. Right, we're into the last hour. Let's get this absolutely perfect,' she demands and we're off again. I can't help noticing Merle seems to be looking in her direction more than mine for the rest of the session.

'I'm pooped,' Beth confesses when it's finally home time. 'I don't know how you lot are managing with all your other training as well.'

'Let's just say early nights are the new going out,' Tammy sighs.

'Oh, I was just about to suggest going out for a burger instead of heading home for food,' Aleksis says to me, laughing. 'What do you reckon? It'll be quicker than me cooking.'

I'd been looking forward to an intimate dinner with just the two of us, but my mouth salivates at the thought of a plate of greasy carbs. 'As long as there are chips – lots of chips – I don't mind.'

He takes me to a tiny family-run café near his flat, which only has five tables. As I take in the mismatched chairs, terracotta walls and dim lighting, the owner greets Aleksis like a long-lost son.

'Don't worry, the food's better than the decor,' he tells me with a wink. 'Grab yourselves a table and I'll bring over some menus.'

'It really is,' Aleksis says. 'You won't find a better burger relish anywhere in London. I've been trying to get him to give up the recipe, but he won't tell.'

'Do you come here quite often?'

'At least once a month. He keeps threatening to do the place up, but I selfishly don't want him to. I don't want it to get too popular.'

He's right about the relish. It's tangy and sweet and a perfect complement to our juicy, tender burgers. I wolf mine down in minutes, only wondering afterwards if I'm going to look bloated when I get undressed later – if Aleksis is indeed going to see me naked later. It's been a full-on day and we've hardly kissed since this morning, so even though we're going home as a real couple for the first time, I don't know what to expect from the rest of the evening. It's uncharted territory.

Now that I've started thinking about it, though, I can't help picturing him in his boxers; my hands against his warm, smooth skin; his mouth on mine; his arms wrapped round me . . . and I think he must be having similar thoughts because he pushes his leg against mine under the table and shoots me a grin.

'Shall we pay up and get out of here?' he asks and I quickly agree.

His hand brushes against mine as we amble back to the flat, and I smile to myself as I weave my fingers between his. When I look up at him, he's smiling too. Then he shakes his hand free, throws his arm round my shoulder and pulls me in close, so our bodies are pressed up against each other. When I look up again, both our smiles have grown wider. It's all I can do not to break into a jog.

He leans in to kiss me when we reach the doorstep and I fight the urge to whoop. Unlike this morning, there's no tentativeness. His lips are soft and his tongue is curious. It's everything I want it to be.

When I grip him tighter, he responds with an increased sense of urgency. He nibbles my bottom lip and lets his hands slide lower down my back. It's no longer the cool breeze ruffling my hair that's making me shiver.

He breaks away to unlock the door, then we pick up where we left off as soon as we're in the hallway, kissing, touching, testing out our new dynamic. We stay like that for a long time, savouring the moment it seems we've both been waiting for all day.

When I reach up to push his jacket off his shoulders, he shakes it off his arms and leaves it on the floor where it's fallen. Then he leads me into the kitchen and lifts me up onto the work surface, so we can carry on kissing without me needing to stand on tiptoes. The lift is effortless, drawing my eyes to the defined muscles in his arms. I can't believe I didn't notice them from the beginning.

I run my hands over his biceps and down his chest, eventually finding my way up under his T-shirt. He steps back and yanks it off, then tugs mine free from my waistband. I lift my arms so he can pull it up over my head. When we kiss again, I can feel the heat radiating from his body as he cups my face in his hands then drops them down to my boobs. My legs are wrapped loosely around him and he pushes himself gently against me, the smallest gesture, but filled with such promise.

I reach behind me to release the catch on my bra and slide it from under his fingers so they're directly on my skin. His touch is firm, making me sigh into his mouth. His lips only leave mine so he can dip his head to run his tongue over my nipples, his breath tantalisingly hot on my skin.

Eventually he lifts me off the worktop and carries me through to the bedroom, my legs tighter round his waist now, our breathing heavy. He sets me down on the mattress and lowers himself over me, supporting his weight on his elbows, his eyes finding mine. Our bodies grind softly against each other as our mouths meet again.

When I roll on top of him and wiggle forward till my

265

breasts are hovering above his face, he groans with pleasure as he stretches his neck up to suck first one nipple then the other. Then I slide back down to kissing level and our hands creep lower, his fingers trailing across the front of my leggings as I push mine inside his waistband. I can see he's already straining against his trousers.

I roll my leggings down and kick them off, then guide his hand back between my legs, loving the feel of his fingers through the lace of my knickers. It doesn't take long for them to find their way inside.

What follows is so different from my recent experiences. Less rushed, less frantic, less noisy – but no less passionate. Aleksis is slow and deliberate with his hands and his tongue, turning me on so much that when he finally enters me I think I'm going to come on the spot. But I stay on the brink while he slides in and out in a steady rhythm.

When his thrusts start gathering momentum, I feel the exact moment when I pass the point of no return. But even when I lose myself to him in a trembling, gasping flurry, he doesn't stop, stretching my orgasm out until he finally lets himself go. His jaw muscles clench as he shudders above me.

He lies with his arms around me afterwards, his whole body pressed against mine, and I feel so close to him, emotionally as well as physically. It makes me wonder why I ever got so hooked on Merle – it was exciting, but he never made me feel safe and cared for like this. Looking back now, I realise there was no warmth, no affection. But this is different. It feels like something. And I know I'll never be tempted by Merle ever again.

Chapter 35

When I wake up the next morning, we're nose to nose on the pillows. Feeling me move, Aleksis opens his eyes.

'*Čau.*' He grins.

'*Čau* to you.' I smile back.

'That was quite a night,' he says.

'Yes it was,' I agree, my smile widening.

'No regrets?'

'Absolutely none.' And I roll on top of him and kiss him to prove my point.

I'd like to say I manage to exhibit the same level of patience he showed the night before, but he's already erect and I can't wait to feel him back inside me, so I hoist myself up till I'm sitting on him, then I guide him in, enjoying the satisfied groan it draws out of him. He grips my hips as I rock backwards and forwards, never taking his eyes off me. Then he raises himself to a sitting position too, so we can kiss while I ride him. He groans

267

again when I lean back and arch myself into him, pushing him deeper.

'Oh, Kate, I'm going to come,' he breathes, and this time he doesn't hold back. He crushes me against him as he orgasms and I can feel him pulsing inside me.

Afterwards he rolls me onto my back and runs his tongue from my buttocks to my clit in long, luscious licks until it tickles so much it almost hurts. But just when I think I can't take any more, he pushes his fingers inside me and I finally climax, his name escaping from my lips in a gasp, a Cheshire cat grin breaking out on my face as the dizzying tremors subside.

'Do we have to go to the studio today?' I ask, trailing my fingers idly across his chest.

'We probably do, if we want to get through on Saturday night,' he says, smiling.

'I could happily stay here all day.'

'It's very tempting,' he agrees. 'But sadly, we've got a big day ahead of us.'

On top of our rehearsal, Channel 6 has arranged for all the remaining couples in the competition to attend a movie premiere in the evening to build up some buzz for the show – filling our only free night of the week, but saving us from having to think of our own way to generate more press coverage.

'To be continued?' Aleksis asks hopefully.

'Hell yeah,' I laugh, already looking forward to round three.

At the studio, I work harder than ever on refining my steps and by the end of the day we agree there's nothing more we can improve. I finally look like a bona fide dancer, just like Aleksis said I would. I give myself a silent pat on the back – what a momentous achievement. It makes me think we've got a really good chance of getting through to the final tomorrow.

I try not to dwell on that fact that if we do go through, with the salsa, bachata, kizomba and cha-cha already ticked off, there's a one in three chance we might land the dreaded Argentine tango for our last dance. The merengue would be less alarming, but it's not a style I've really warmed to. The rumba's the one I most want to perform. It might be as challenging as the tango technically, but I feel more of a connection to it for some reason.

Back at the flat after rehearsals, I get straight to work on my hair and make-up, ready for the premiere. I want to look my best.

Earlier, when I told Aleksis I wasn't sure I had anything appropriate to wear, he offered to ask Sofiya if I could borrow something of hers, explaining that her wardrobe is full of red-carpet outfits that she never wears. 'She'll be delighted to see one of them getting some use,' he said.

Initially I was reluctant, but I didn't want to cut our rehearsal short so I could run out and panic buy something, so I agreed to let her help me out.

And when she drops by with a suitcase of dresses for me to try on, I'm so thankful I did. Among the selection is a silk skater-style dress with a teal and navy animal print that fits me like a glove. I feel unbelievably sexy in it.

Aleksis tells me I look gorgeous. And he looks so hot in his midnight blue suit with a plain white T-shirt underneath that it takes my breath away. I don't know how I didn't see how attractive he is when Lucy first pointed it out.

It doesn't take Sofiya long to notice something has changed between the two of us. Probably because neither of us can wipe the smiles off our faces. Within minutes of being in the flat, she correctly concludes, 'You're not faking this any more, are you?'

My heart pounds while I wonder if she's going to be okay with it.

'I'm not even going to ask what gave it away, but you're right,' Aleksis confesses. 'We've decided to do this properly.'

'That's fantastic,' she exclaims, and I could cry with relief. 'To be honest, I'm surprised it took you so long. You're so well suited.'

Yet again her magnanimity amazes me.

'We know that now,' Aleksis says with a radiant smile that makes me glow inside.

His phone pings to let him know our car from Channel 6 has arrived. It will take us to a meeting point near the cinema where we'll join up with the other contestants, so we can travel to the venue in a convoy and arrive all together. Shane thinks this is the best way to guarantee us some column inches in the newspapers.

The plan is to synchronise our exits from the cars and stand together on the red carpet to give us more pulling power. Then once we're inside, we've been told we can do what we like.

I text Lucy while we're in the car. The last couple of days have been such a whirlwind I haven't even had a chance to fill her in on the developments with Aleksis. She's going to go nuts.

'*Sorry I've been quiet. It's been crazy trying to fit everything in. Good crazy though. Something exciting may have happened . . .*'

'*With Aleksis?*' she guesses immediately.

'*Yes, with Aleksis.*' I can't help smiling. '*We may have slept together last night.*'

'*Shriek! Is he your boyfriend now?*'

'*No! It's way too soon to put a label on it.*' Not that I'd mind. '*We've literally hooked up once. Well, twice if you count this morning too. It was really good though and I really like him.*'

'*Full details when I see you after the show tomorrow please! Is Aleksis coming to the pub too?*'

I promise her we'll both be there, then look over at him to check he's still real. He smiles back in a way that makes my heart do a little dance.

Our simultaneous arrival at the cinema does get the attention of the paparazzi, as Shane had hoped, and the cameras flash as we converge on the red carpet. I don't know if he does it on purpose, but Merle positions himself next to me, putting his arm round my waist below Aleksis's arm round my shoulders as we pose for photos. It makes me uncomfortable, but I can hardly shake him off with so many eyes on us.

When one of the actresses from the film arrives, our little group is moved along and guided inside to the cinema's bar area, where we're offered champagne cocktails. I spot Kimberley Ross in a smart white trouser suit and recognise several other famous faces from TV shows. Everyone looks impossibly glamorous, which makes me even more grateful for Sofiya's dress.

It's hard to ignore Merle as he air-kisses his way round the room like a pro, so I'm relieved when the screening finally starts and I can lose myself in the film for a couple of hours. Thankfully, it's much easier to stay out of his way at the after-party, because it's in the cavernous lobby of the hotel next door.

There are hundreds of guests, waiters wandering through the crowd with magnums of champagne, and acrobats dangling from the ceiling. Several bars line the perimeter and there's an impressive selection of canapés on offer, but the highlight for me is a chocolate fountain the size of a swimming pool. My five-year-old self would have been beside herself.

It's attracted quite a crowd, but I squeeze in with Aleksis and we help ourselves to a skewer of juicy strawberries. He pulls out his phone so he can take a picture of us dunking our fruit for Instagram. But while he's trying to get the shot, chocolate drips off his skewer, leaving a long, sticky trail across his T-shirt.

I can't help laughing. 'I'm surprised that wasn't me, for once.'

He tries to wipe it off with his finger, but the smear gets even longer. 'I'd better find the loos,' he says, rolling his eyes.

And it's while I'm waiting outside for him that I scroll through the latest headlines on my phone and see the love triangle stories that have started popping up online analysing our body language in the red carpet pictures of me sandwiched between Alexis and Merle.

'You've got to be kidding me,' I mutter as I click on some of the links. One has even gone so far as to suggest I'm still in love with Merle and just pretending to be with Aleksis to gain popularity on the show. If that were still true, it would have had me analysing every move we've made to see what gave us away.

'What's up?' Aleksis asks when he emerges from the gents and clocks the look on my face. I hand him my phone and his reaction is much the same as mine when he spots Merle's arm round me in the photos.

'What the hell is he playing at?' He sounds exasperated. 'He must have known how that would look.'

'It did feel deliberate,' I agree.

'He's such a tosser.'

And I agree with that too.

We both look out at the hubbub surrounding us, perhaps subconsciously checking to see if Merle is in the midst of it, but if he is I can't see him. I'm not sure I feel like rejoining the party, though.

'How do you feel about getting out of here?' I ask. 'It's getting late and I don't want to give the make-up girls too much work to do tomorrow, trying to cover up the bags under my eyes.'

'Good idea,' he agrees, then points at the giant wet patch on his T-shirt. 'I'm kind of soggy anyway.'

'Then we need to get you out of those clothes as soon as possible.'

He grins back at my flirty smile. 'I'll get us a taxi.'

His T-shirt has almost dried by the time we get home, but it's still discarded within seconds of us walking through the door. This time when he scoops me up onto the work surface so we can kiss more comfortably, we don't end up in the bedroom. He pushes my skirt above my waist right there on the counter.

I lean back so he can help me wriggle free of my underwear and he nudges my legs wider and finds my clit with his thumb, bringing on that blissful feeling that I'll never get tired of, intensifying it with his fingers just when I think it can't get any better.

I want to kiss him, touch him, take my dress off, run my fingers through his hair, but my arms are behind me, supporting me. And before I have a chance to push myself upright, he bends forward and hooks my legs up onto his shoulders, bringing his head down between my thighs. I collapse back onto my elbows, drop my head back and close my eyes. The way his tongue makes me feel, it's like it was made just for me.

I don't push myself back up until he draws himself up to standing and eases my legs down from his shoulders. I reach for him as he steps in to kiss me, tugging at his belt buckle as he trails his fingers along my thighs.

When he breaks away to free himself from his trousers, I unzip my dress and pull it up over my head. I watch him step out of his boxers and kick them away, then he moves back in front of me, tugging lightly at my hair as his tongue finds mine again.

He slides my hips closer to the edge of the counter, angling himself towards me, and I gasp as he grasps my hips and enters me. I reach up and cling on to his back as he starts pumping against me, my breasts squashed against him as I kiss his neck and nibble his ear, moaning as my orgasm creeps ever closer.

I can feel his breath on my skin, hot and heavy as our bodies crash against each other and I can see the concentration on his face. He's so close, too.

When he pushes his hand between us and finds my clit with his thumb again, I'm completely lost. It feels like my whole body has turned to jelly and I can barely hold on to him as I come. He buries his face in my hair and climaxes moments later, gasping and juddering as he lets himself go.

We stay there for some time afterwards, locked together and regaining our composure.

'I think I might need to lie down now,' he eventually says with a grin.

'We do have a big day tomorrow,' I laugh.

He lifts me down to the floor and kisses me one last time. 'Then let's make sure we're ready for it.'

Chapter 36

Being at Channel 6 feels a lot less daunting with Aleksis beside me. I feel even more upbeat when I learn Emilia has landed the merengue for tonight's live performance. To me, it's the least watchable of all the dances. I'm optimistic the audience will prefer our cha-cha.

It's brilliant having the whole gang back in the reception room – it makes for a much livelier atmosphere. Beth has shaken off her nerves and is looking forward to dancing again, Liam is back to his usual cheery self now we've called a truce, and Dean and Theo look thrilled to be reunited.

The day follows the usual format of rehearsals, make-up and costumes, except that there's extra time set aside for one more rueda practice. This time, Merle keeps whatever thoughts he's having to himself. I take that to mean he's finally accepted he can't come between me and Aleksis.

I can't help noticing a bit of tension between him and Emilia, though – and that he seems to be exchanging more than a few meaningful glances with Ros. But that's not my concern.

The rehearsal goes without a hitch – and thankfully it's just as polished when we perform it in front of the live studio audience to kick off this week's show.

'Bravo!' Kimberley shouts at the end. 'What a brilliant way to get things started here at *Fire on the Dance Floor*. It's certainly got me in the mood for a party. Well done, everyone, thank you so much for that. And how nice it is to see all the old faces back in the room with us this evening. Beth, Theo and Liam, thanks for joining us again. And Gabriel, Daniele and Valentina as well, of course.

'Come over here and join me, guys,' she beckons them over, 'while the others go off and get ready for their individual performances. Beth, tell me how it feels to be back on our fantastic stage again. I have to say, that looked like so much fun.'

'It's a bit nerve-racking when everyone's relying on you not to mess it up, but it's such a buzz when it all goes right,' I hear her say as the rest of us rush off to get changed.

Aleksis and I are dancing first this evening, so we race down the corridor to Layla, Hannah and Kelly, who are waiting to give us a speedy makeover. It's amazing what they can do with three minutes – one outfit off, another on, hair whipped up into a sleek up-do, a layer of hairspray, an extra slick of eyeshadow and lipstick and we're back by Kimberley's side, ready to watch Sarah's edit of our cha-cha lessons and yoga practice.

'Ladies and gentlemen, it's time to see what our four remaining couples have got in store for us tonight,'

Kimberley says. 'And we're expecting more blazing hot performances as they battle it out for a place in next week's final. First up, hoping to ignite the dance floor, it's Kate and Aleksis, who'll be dancing a cheeky cha-cha for us this evening. And they've been working on their core muscles this week in a bid to put them in the strongest position. Let's take a look.'

Our video clip gets the laughs we were hoping for, then Kimberley directs us to the middle of the stage for our dance. For the first time in the competition, I'm not utterly terrified. I know the routine by heart and I feel good in the swishy white dress I'm wearing. It's sexy – held together on one side by a series of glittery straps that show off flashes of skin in between.

My newfound confidence obviously shines through in my dancing – because even though the two minutes fly by in the usual blur of music and adrenaline, when Aleksis reels me in for the final spin, which ends with us facing each other and looking into each other's eyes, I know it couldn't have gone any better. There wasn't a single step that didn't feel exactly like it should.

Aleksis kisses me as the cheering begins. He knows we've just done our best dance to date, too. I can see it in his eyes.

'The audience are on their feet!' Kimberley shouts. 'What a reaction! Judges, what do you think of that? You must be as blown away as the rest of us by that incredible performance. Mariana, let's hear from you first . . . '

'All I can say is . . . I loved it!' she shouts. 'What I love most about this kind of show is how much you can see people like Kate grow and improve week on week. Kate, you should be so proud of yourself tonight. You've come such a long way since this short competition started. And Aleksis, that's a credit to you, too – that you can produce such a beautiful performance from someone who until two months ago had never set foot on the dance floor. It was wonderful to watch; so full of energy. Fantastic.'

'Sophie, anything to add?' Kimberley asks.

'I agree – what a huge improvement this is from your very first night on the show. I think the bookies might even be revising their odds after that performance. I'll be amazed if this doesn't see you two through to the final because you would absolutely deserve your place there.'

'And Jacques?' Kimberley prompts.

'I loved it and I want to see more. So I really hope you are in the final next week because I think you've got even more to offer. I know how I'd be voting tonight if the vote was with us, and I'd give that performance a perfect ten.'

'Did you hear that, audience – a perfect ten!' Kimberley shouts over another round of cheering. 'Congratulations you two, you must be thrilled. But of course it's not the judges who have the final say on whether you stay in the competition – so, audience, it's over to you. It's time to decide Kate and Aleksis's fate. Do you want to see them back for one more week? If so, go high! It's time to submit your scores.'

'*Lai veicas*,' I whisper to Aleksis, which makes his whole face light up.

'You remembered!'

'My pronounciation might be a bit off, but . . . '

'It's perfect,' he says, as the dial shoots up the scoreboard.

And for a moment I think we might get that coveted ten. My heart feels like it's going to burst right out of my chest in anticipation. But I'm not disappointed when the dial settles on 9.6 – it's the highest score of the competition so far.

'A personal best,' Kimberley beams as Aleksis picks me up and spins me round. My face no longer feels big enough for the grin that's taken over it.

'And not only that but the top score of the series so far, which will surely secure you a place in the final. We'll soon find out, ladies and gentlemen, because it's time to crank up the heat and bring out our second couple. So please give it up one more time for Kate and Aleksis, and let's welcome back to the stage Dean Mason and Jessica Young!

'Tonight they'll be bringing us a coquettish kizomba – the third kizomba of the series so far. Will it be the dance to take them through to the final? It's time to find out. Ladies and gentlemen, it's Dean and Jessica!'

Aleksis wishes them luck as we pass them on our way off stage, but it turns out luck is not on their side, with Jacques branding their routine uninspiring and the audience awarding them 8.4, which, although respectable, leaves them vulnerable. I feel bad for Dean – I can see he's disappointed – but at the same time a thrill runs through me as Aleksis and I squeeze each other's hands. This means we're through. We're going to be in the final.

It means we can relax as we watch Tammy and Elijah's Dominican bachata, which has faster footwork and is more vivacious than the sensual bachatas Emilia and I chose to perform. But I still hold my breath as the dial wavers on the scoreboard after her dance, praying it stops high enough to put her through too.

She's delighted when she also secures a personal best, with a score of 9.2 – but it's bad news for Dean. With only the show favourites, Merle and Emilia, still to dance, his time on the show is fast running out.

When Kimberley has finished congratulating Tammy and Elijah, Merle and Emilia take their place on the stage. Emilia is wearing a silver bra top and a tiny white ruffled mini skirt that makes my dress look conservative. Merle is also all in white and the tightest trousers imaginable. There probably isn't a woman in the room who isn't thinking about how taut his buttocks are. It feels like they've already won before they've even started dancing.

Their merengue is error-free, as I think everyone would expect after their previous performances, and the judges are as enthusiastic as ever afterwards. But somehow it leaves me a bit cold. I can't quite put my finger on why. Maybe it's just a bit too perfect.

The audience start a slow clap as the dial on the scoreboard begins to creep up towards the top of the scale. But it doesn't move nearly as fast as I imagine Merle would like it to and the whole atmosphere in the room seems to change when it comes to a stop on 8.1. There's a collective gasp from everyone watching. Merle and Emilia – the favourites since their first dance together – are out of the competition. I'm absolutely stunned – though not, I imagine, as stunned as Merle is.

'Well, I don't know about you, but I'm gobsmacked,' Kimberley says over the hum of chatter that's filled the room. 'After such praise from the judges I did not see this coming. Guys, come on over here and join me. I can see from your faces that this has come as a shock. I can only imagine how devastating it must be to go from two weeks at the top of the scoreboard straight to elimination. Tell us how you're feeling.'

'I don't know what to say,' Emilia admits, her voice breaking slightly. She clears her throat. 'I thought it was one of our best performances – we worked so hard and put so much into it. The judges' comments were so positive and I thought our score would reflect that. I don't think either of us expected our journey to end here.'

'I'm not sure any of us did,' Kimberley says sympathetically. 'And Merle, do you have anything to add?'

'The audience were wrong,' he says bluntly, looking furious.

When she realises he's not going to add anything further, Kimberley quickly moves things along. 'It's clear emotions are running pretty high here tonight, ladies and gentlemen. So would you please put your hands together one more time for the couple leaving the show this evening, Merle Picard and Emilia Harris.'

Emilia manages a small smile and a wave as she follows Merle off the stage.

'And that's just about all we've got time for tonight,' Kimberley says. 'After Merle and Emilia's shock departure, we now know which three couples will be competing to win twenty-five thousand pounds in next week's final.

Congratulations to Kate and Aleksis, who were a class act tonight with their unparalleled score, and to Tammy and Elijah, and Dean and Jessica, who will all be back to battle it out one last time next Saturday.

'What a rollercoaster it's been, with Merle and Emilia looking set to hold on to that top spot, but then reminding us that nothing's ever guaranteed on *Fire on the Dance Floor*. We'll be back with more surprises at the same time next Saturday, so we hope you'll join us right here on the dance floor to find out who'll be crowned our very first *Fire on the Dance Floor* champion.'

Then it's the usual hustle back to the reception area for the dancers – the pats on the back, the congratulations, but alongside it all my mind's still reeling about Merle and Emilia. I can't believe they're out. Sofiya will be delighted.

Aleksis grabs two glasses of wine and passes me one. His eyes are brighter than I've ever seen them.

'We couldn't have wished for a better outcome,' he gushes. 'You were so good out there tonight. *Priekā*! Cheers!'

I swell with pride at the compliment. 'We actually did it – top of the scoreboard. But Merle and Emilia . . . I'm so shocked.'

'You outperformed them, you totally deserved it,' Tammy says, as she helps herself to a drink. 'So cheers to us, Kate. We've only gone and got ourselves into the bloody final!'

I laugh and clink my glass against hers. Then Olivia arrives and requests our attention so she can 'share some exciting news with us all'.

'I won't keep you long. I just wanted you all to be the first to know that as a result of the hard work you've put into the show, it's exceeded all our expectations and we've just been given the go-ahead for a follow-up series next summer,' she beams. 'So thank you, everybody, for the part you've all played in making that happen.'

As I follow her eyes around the room, I notice Merle and Emilia aren't among us. I don't imagine they feel like socialising. I'm sure I wouldn't if I were them.

'While I don't doubt the three remaining couples will pull out all the stops for the grand final next weekend,' Olivia continues, 'we've decided to add a little extra incentive for the professional dancers, to make sure we really go out on a high. So Jessica, Aleksis, Elijah, keep this in mind: whichever one of you wins next week is going to be guaranteed a place in next year's line-up. So if you fancy another stint on *Fire on the Dance Floor*, you know what you've got to do.'

They beam at each other and nod. Challenge accepted.

'And for the remaining contestants – Kate, Tammy, Dean – we want to do something a bit different with your filmed segments for this last week,' Olivia says. 'We want to show you in your real life, away from the dance floor – with your family or where you work – to give the audience a chance to really get to know you. So if you could have a think about that and we'll be in touch with you all on Monday to hear your ideas and schedule in a filming day for each of you.'

We murmur our assent and I try not to panic as she thanks us for our time and tells us she can't wait for next Saturday. I don't have a job and my family are in France. I can't film at the old flat with Lucy because everyone knows I'm living with Aleksis, and I'm not part of a sports team or a book club or anything else that could work for my video clip.

'Don't worry, we'll think of something,' Aleksis assures me, as if reading my mind. 'We'll put our heads together tomorrow. Let's just enjoy the rest of this evening first.'

'The Grape is waiting,' Tammy reminds us.

'Then lead the way,' Aleksis says.

Dee video calls me while we're en route to the pub and when I answer she's squeezed in between Mum and Dad on the screen.

'Congratulations,' they all shout.

'You were wonderful, darling,' Mum adds.

'Top of the class,' Dad says. 'You must be over the moon.'

'You've already seen it?' They usually have to wait till it's on catch-up.

'We Skyped with Auntie Irene so we could watch it live on her telly,' Dee explains. 'It was a bit hard to see but we got the gist.'

'Ah, you guys. I'm absolutely delighted. Me, in the final! Whoever would have thought it?'

'We all had faith in you,' Dad says.

'We knew you could do it,' Dee agrees.

'And is everything else okay?' Mum checks. 'At the flat and everything?'

'Of course. Aleksis is the perfect flatmate,' I smile.

Now's not the time to tell her how much more he's become, even if she suspects it. She's had enough insight into my love life of late and I don't want to answer the inevitable barrage of questions that would follow, either.

'Glad to hear it,' Mum says. 'Right, we'll leave you to it then. We know you'll want to get on with your celebrating. We just wanted you to know how proud we all are of you. Talk to you soon, love.'

'Flatmate?' Aleksis repeats, raising an eyebrow as I slip my phone back into my bag.

'With benefits,' I grin, sliding my arm round his waist and pulling him close.

'I'll take that,' he laughs, putting his arm round my shoulders. I think we're both thinking about the benefits for the rest of the walk.

Chapter 37

'Check you out, Miss Finalist,' Lucy says when we arrive at the pub.

'It's bonkers, isn't it?' I laugh, giving her a hug. 'I can't even describe how it felt when I saw our score. It's such an adrenaline rush you barely even register it.'

'I knew you could do it,' she beams. Then her eyes light up as Aleksis slips into the chair next to mine and kisses me.

'Congratulations,' she says to him, and I know she doesn't just mean for winning tonight's show. Given half a chance she'll no doubt tell him what a lucky man he is to have snared me. She must be dying to find out how the two us made the leap from faking our romance to doing it for real.

'Did you enjoy it?' Aleksis asks her.

'It gets better every week. I can't wait for the final – it's going to be epic.'

'Speaking of which, I've got our last envelope in here,' Aleksis says to me, patting his pocket.

'Ooh, open it now,' Lucy urges, before I have time to reply.

'Yes, go on,' Beth says from across the table. 'Let's see what you've got.'

'You weren't all supposed to hear that,' Aleksis laughs. 'It's meant to be a secret.'

'We won't tell.' Beth looks round at everyone. 'Will we?'

My eyes meet Liam's.

'Promise,' he says. 'I'm not going to mess up again.'

'I'll share if you share,' Tammy offers. 'I've already looked at mine with Elijah.'

'Okay, fine,' Aleksis laughs. 'Let's do it.'

'So, Elijah and I will be dancing . . . ' She performs a drum roll on the table. 'The rumba! Which is exactly what I was hoping for. There's an extra surprise in the envelope too, but I'll leave that for you to read for yourselves. Okay, your turn.'

I hold my breath as Aleksis opens our envelope, conscious this narrows my possibilities down to just the Argentine tango and the merengue, and gutted that I'm not going to get the chance to learn the rumba myself.

Before he starts speaking his eyebrows shoot up, which I don't think is a good sign, especially not when it's accompanied by a long pause that I don't think is for dramatic effect.

'The Argentine tango,' he finally reveals, his eyes finding mine.

My hands fly up to my mouth. 'No!' Of all the dances, why did our last one have to be that one?

'And there's more,' he says. 'We'll also perform another dance of our choice.'

'That's the extra surprise,' Tammy explains.

'That's a lot to learn,' Beth frowns, voicing my immediate concern.

'It can be one of the dances you've already done,' Tammy clarifies. 'A previous favourite, it doesn't have to be something new. I'd love to do our merengue again, even if it didn't get us a great score – although now it's put Emilia out of the competition Elijah will probably have other ideas.'

I can't even think about what my favourite has been. I'm still reeling from the tango news. But Aleksis tucks the envelope back in his pocket and insists we don't even think about it until tomorrow. 'Tonight is for celebrating,' he says resolutely.

And I do manage to push it to the back of my mind and immerse myself in the banter for the rest of the evening. But as soon as we're alone back at the flat, my anxiety comes flooding back. Landing the tango just feels like such a rotten break when things have finally started going our way.

'Try not to worry,' Aleksis assures me, wrapping his arms round me and kissing me. 'Look how far you've come in just a few weeks. It's not going to be the struggle it would have been back at the beginning.'

'But it's the Argentine,' I fret, searching his face for reassurance.

'And you're a really good dancer now. You've just got to remember to believe in yourself,' he says with a smile.

I close my eyes and sigh, still not fully placated.

'Look at it as a vote of confidence,' Aleksis says. 'Shane won't want the final show to look anything less than spectacular, right? So they wouldn't give us this dance if they didn't think we could do it justice.'

It does make sense when he puts it like that.

'There's no rueda taking up our time this week, so we've got plenty of time to prep. And don't forget, I pulled off a pretty decent tango on the opening show, so you're in good hands. We can start pulling some ideas together first thing in the morning,' he promises.

'Thank you.' I smile, finally comforted. 'I needed to hear that. I'll stop stressing about it and try to be more relaxed.'

'For that, I already have an idea.'

He takes my hand and leads me out onto the terrace. A light breeze caresses my skin as he pulls me in for a kiss.

'I've always wanted to have sex out here,' he whispers, and a smile creeps onto my face.

When he lifts his top up over his head, the tango is suddenly the last thing on my mind.

Chapter 38

Aleksis has me holding on to the kitchen counter and working through a series of footwork drills the next morning, while he sits at the table and works on our choreography. Every now and again he comes over to correct something I'm doing and we end up kissing for a while. It makes the drills much more interesting.

Over lunch we discuss what we should do for this week's video clip and conclude a family Skype from Auntie Irene's house is the best option. Hopefully Sarah will be able to come up with a way to make it fun to watch. She usually does.

We also decide to go with a repeat of our bachata for our second dance in the final, with a couple of moderations to give the audience something new to see. Although this week's cha-cha got us our highest score, we both agree it's too soon to do it again – the audience might find it boring.

By this point, Aleksis has worked his ideas for our Argentine tango into something more concrete, so we

291

spend the rest of the afternoon on partnerwork. He walks me through the whole routine first, so I can see what we're working towards, then breaks it down into smaller sections to help me fully understand the mechanics of the dance. It quickly becomes apparent it's going to take a lot of work to master the art of the leg flick without kicking him anywhere delicate.

Our plan is to get the tango locked into our memories first, then have a bachata crash course at the end of the week. We stick at it till dinner time, and it's only then that I check my phone and discover a string of missed calls and voicemails, from a number I don't recognise.

'Kate, it's Olivia from *Fire on the Dance Floor* again,' the most recent message says. 'Can you call me back urgently please. Doesn't matter what time, I'll be waiting to hear from you.'

She picks up straight away when I type in the number she's left and starts speaking before I've even said hello.

'Oh Kate, thank goodness I've got hold of you. Can you and Aleksis be at Heathrow Airport at seven-thirty on Tuesday morning? I've got three tickets on hold for a flight to Toulouse, coming back at seven-fifteen in the evening – so you can go and see your family. I know it's short notice, but as soon as Sarah suggested it, we knew it would look great on the show. She'll go with you, of course, so she can film it.

'We'll have a car pick you up at the other end to take you to your sister's, so you'll be there in time for lunch and home in time for bed. Does that sound okay? Can I get it all booked in? Shane really wants this to happen.'

'What is it?' Aleksis asks, seeing my body stiffen and my eyes go wide.

'Olivia wants us to go to France for a day,' I explain, my mind already racing. 'On Tuesday. To film us with my family.'

He considers this for a moment then says, 'That sounds feasible.'

'But what about rehearsals? That's a whole day of practice we'll miss.'

'I'm sure we could squeeze a bit in – at the airport, when we get back, whenever we can find a few spare minutes.'

'We'll lose so much time, though.' I can hear the rising hysteria in my voice. 'And what about this?' I gesture from him to me. 'I haven't told them.'

'I think we should do it,' he says decisively. 'They should at least meet the man you're living with, don't you think? We can call them this evening and tell them everything. Well, maybe not *everything*.'

I clearly don't look convinced because he adds, 'I think it'll be a good thing, us going there. It might even stop them feeling so bad about not being here while you're doing the show.'

'Is that a yes, then?' Olivia interrupts. I'd forgotten she could hear what we were saying. 'The tickets are on hold for another hour and I don't want to lose them. There was limited availability so we might not be able to get any more.'

I promise to call her back as soon as I've checked it with Mum, Dad and Dee.

'Are you absolutely sure about this?' I ask Aleksis while I text Dee to find out if they're free to join us on a Skype chat.

'A hundred per cent. This is exactly the kind of thing that will make the audience feel like they've got to know you, and if that means they vote for us on Saturday's show, I'm all for it. We'll have to thank Sarah for suggesting it.'

'Do you think she just wanted a day down in the south of France?'

'I don't doubt it, but who can blame her? It was that or a suburb in Manchester,' he laughs. 'No offence to your Auntie Irene.'

'Dee's firing up her laptop now, so brace yourself,' I warn him.

'I'm good with parents, don't worry,' he assures me.

I don't know how good they'll be with him, though, once they discover we're not sleeping in separate beds any more. Given what happened last time, I'm not sure how Dad's going to react to the news that I've got involved with another dancer.

But before I can let him know Aleksis is no longer just my flatmate, Mum's already telling him how delighted she is to meet him and how he's been her favourite from the beginning, and thanking him for looking after me on the show.

'I'll be there in a minute,' Dee yells from somewhere off-screen. 'Just sorting out the monsters.'

'We've been finding it really inspiring,' Mum says, still focused on Aleksis. 'We've even talked about taking dancing lessons ourselves, once we're back in the UK.'

'You've talked about that,' Dad says. 'I don't know one foot from the other.'

She pats him on the hand. 'That's why you go to lessons. So what's your last dance going to be? We're dying to know.'

'It's the Argentine tango,' I tell her. 'My worst nightmare.'

'I'm sure it can't be that bad,' Mum says.

Aleksis fires me a grin. 'That's what I keep telling her.'

'We've already got the champagne on ice,' Dad admits.

'No pressure then, Dad!'

'Sorry, love. We're just really excited.'

I roll my eyes in exasperation.

'Perhaps you can just be excited about our other news instead,' I suggest.

'What's that, love?' Dad asks.

I tell them about the proposed trip to France,

When she's established I'm actually serious, Mum exclaims, 'That would be wonderful!'

'We'd love to see you,' Dad agrees. 'And the kids will be over the moon. We can meet you at the airport.'

'We'll have a driver to bring us over from the airport,' I explain.

'Then we'll have extra time to get everything ready here,' Mum says.

Aleksis tells them they don't need to go to any trouble.

'I'll want to do my hair,' Mum says. 'And find Dad a new shirt.'

'What's wrong with my shirts?' He sounds perplexed.

Dee appears on the screen before Mum has a chance to answer.

'Sorry about that – Nathan's being a right pain today. What's this I hear about you coming to visit? Did you say you're flying over on Tuesday?'

I explain the plan again and Dee goes straight into organising mode – what we're going to eat, what she needs to buy, how she's going to get the kids to behave while we're there.

'It's only a flying visit,' I remind her, but suddenly I can't wait to be there. Hearing them all so eager to see me makes me wonder why I ever hesitated.

'Then let's make sure it's a good one,' Dee beams. 'It'll be great to meet you in person too, Aleksis. You can tell us how much of a pain my little sis is being during rehearsals. She's never liked doing what she's told.'

'She's the perfect student. We're working really hard, but still managing to enjoy ourselves.' He kisses me on the cheek, which doesn't go unnoticed by my sister.

'On *and* off the dance floor?' she asks, smirking, and I can feel my cheeks flushing. It's time to fess up.

'You could put it like that,' I nod.

'Amazing. I bet that's easier than pretending,' she laughs. 'You can tell us all about it when you get here.'

'We will. But right now, we should probably get back to Olivia and let her know she can go ahead and book the flights. I'll text you from the airport on Tuesday morning to confirm everything's on time, okay? And all being well we'll see you around midday.'

'Can't wait,' Dee says.

Aleksis is smiling when I end the call. 'They seem lovely,' he says. 'Maybe after this we should fly to Latvia and meet my parents too. After the competition's finished, I mean.'

'Really?' My stomach flips with excitement that he wants this to happen.

'They'd love to meet you. They're pretty laid-back too. I think you'll like them. And where they live is really beautiful. Do you fancy it?' He looks hopeful.

I answer him with a kiss. Knowing this isn't going to come crashing to a halt as soon as the show is over makes me happier than I think I've ever been.

Chapter 39

Monday flies by in a whirl. We get to the studio at eight, our earliest start yet, stay till it closes at six and are tucked up in bed by nine-thirty, because we have such an early start for our morning flight. Not that we go to sleep right away. Theory has it that people sleep a lot better after an orgasm – and we're both more than willing to test that theory.

'Ugh, make it stop,' I groan, when my phone alarm starts ringing at four-thirty a.m.

'Five-minute snooze?' Aleksis suggests.

'Can't we make it fifty?' I snuggle closer to him.

'If you keep doing that we'll miss the flight,' he warns.

We reluctantly drag ourselves out from under the covers when the second alarm goes off.

'Still think this is a good idea?' I ask through a yawn.

'Come on, cold shower and we'll feel much more lively,' he suggests.

I settle for lukewarm – I can't face an icy blast this early.

298

It doesn't take us long to get ready. Other than our dance shoes and our phone chargers we don't have anything to pack, and neither of us wants breakfast at this hour.

'I quite like having no luggage,' Aleksis says as our taxi whisks us through the deserted streets of London to the airport. 'I'm so used to having to cart a load of suitcases around with all my dance gear inside.'

'It does feel liberating. I can totally see the appeal of having a little place abroad and having everything you need there so you don't have to lug a bag back and forth.'

'I'd better make sure you win that final then,' he laughs. 'We can practise on the plane if it's not too busy. I can't imagine anyone else is crazy enough to be travelling this early in the morning.'

But the flight is almost full and the aisles are too narrow, so instead we pass the time watching dance videos on his phone.

Sarah is first out of the car when we get to my sister's house, so she can film us arriving. The dog bounces round her feet while my parents smother me in a hug. Then my niece and nephew charge me and knock me right over, which looks even more fun to the dog, who weaves among us trying to lick our faces.

Mum is left to introduce herself to Aleksis while Dee tries to rescue me from the kids, Pete shoos the dog away and Dad grabs Sarah's camera bag from the car.

'I'll return at five,' the driver tells us before pulling away, probably relieved to be escaping from the chaos that's unfolding.

Nathan and Daisy shriek with excitement and try to get

Aleksis to dance with them in the driveway. Pete herds the dog back into the house and Mum sets about getting drink requests from everyone. She gets a bit teary as well. 'It's so lovely to see you. I'm so sorry we haven't been there for you.'

'We've been through this, Mum. It's absolutely fine. I've got Lucy and Aiden, plus Beth and Tammy, and Aleksis of course, so it's all good.'

'I know, but—'

'Mum, it's fine. Come on, let's get inside and show Aleksis and Sarah around.'

The kids are already tugging Aleksis towards the stairs and arguing over whose room he should see first.

'And then we'll show you the garden and you can go in our swimming pool,' Daisy says proudly.

I turn to look at Dee. 'Swimming pool?' I'm sure she would have mentioned it if they'd had one installed.

'Paddling pool,' she clarifies. 'They do like to exaggerate.'

Once the kids have finished giving Aleksis a tour, they turn their attention to Sarah. They want to be filmed, then shown how to use the camera, then have a go at filming themselves. Sarah takes it all in her stride.

Mum and Dee have really gone to town with lunch. There's a delicious selection of salads, quiches, cheeses and cold meats, with Mum's traditional apple tart for afters. I'm completely stuffed by the end of it.

'Will you come in the pool now?' Daisy asks Aleksis.

'I'd love to, but I don't have any trunks with me,' he smiles.

'You can borrow Dad's. Dad, Aleksis can borrow your swimming trunks, can't he?' she pleads.

300

Pete looks from Aleksis to himself. 'I'm not sure they're going to fit, love.'

'I'm not sure I'm going to fit, either,' Aleksis points out, looking at the water-filled inflatable ring in the garden. 'But I can sit at the side while you go in. How does that sound?'

'I think that will be okay,' Daisy says in that serious voice children put on when they want you to know who's boss.

She grabs his hand and half leads, half drags him outside. He shrugs at me as he goes, but he's laughing at the same time.

'He's very handsome,' Mum observes when he's out of earshot, which makes Dad roll his eyes. 'I hope he's treating you nicely. Not like that other one.'

'He couldn't be nicer.' Then I tell them about the premiere and our rehearsals, and show them some photos of his flat on my phone.

'Looks like you've landed on your feet there,' Dee grins.

'It's only temporary, but yeah, no complaints.'

When our lunch has settled, we clear the dining room furniture to one side so Aleksis and I can get a bit of tango practice in. The floor is tiled so it's not bad for dancing on, but it gets pretty cramped when everyone piles into the room to see us in action. There definitely isn't space for us, six spectators and a camerawoman. The kids quickly get bored, though, so Pete takes them back out into the garden.

When I mess the routine up for the fifth time, Dee realises I'm struggling to concentrate and herds our parents out of the room, too. Out in the hall I hear Mum say, 'But they're only here for a few more hours.'

'Yes, but they need to rehearse, just for a bit,' Dee says. 'Let's give them an hour or so then we'll drag them back out for tea and cake before they have to go.'

'Your mum's so sweet,' Aleksis says as we listen to their retreating footsteps. 'It's a shame we can't stay longer. I think she's loving having you here.'

'Careful what you wish for,' Sarah says from across the room. She walks towards us, holding out her phone.

'What's this?' Aleksis asks, taking it from her.

'It's a text from Olivia. Our flight home's been cancelled. She's trying to find us another one, but there might not be anything till tomorrow.'

I look at Aleksis in alarm. 'But we have to get back – we can't miss any more rehearsal time.'

'She says she'll call as soon as she's managed to sort something out,' he says.

'I guess we just carry on practising here till we hear from her.'

But my concentration is even worse while we wait for news, and I know I must be covering Aleksis in bruises while I try to get my leg flicks right. Not that he complains.

'Just remember to wait till your knee is touching mine before you kick up,' he advises.

'Got it,' I nod, though I'm not sure I have.

When Sarah's phone finally rings, she puts Olivia on loudspeaker so we can all listen in. Olivia confirms that she can't get us on a flight back till the same time tomorrow evening – which means we're going to lose another whole day in the studio.

'I'm sorry it's not better news,' she apologises, then tells

302

us we don't need to worry about finding somewhere to stay – she'll look for a hotel nearby and text us the details when she's booked it.

Aleksis thanks her, then does his best to stop me freaking out.

'We can make this work, Kate. We've got our makeshift studio here, we've got our shoes, we've got our music, Olivia's sorting us out a place for us to sleep. All we need is a couple of toothbrushes. So why don't we go and see if your sister has any spares and if not we'll nip out to buy some. Then we can come back here and practise for as long as we need to. It'll be fine, I promise. What about you, Sarah? Is it going to be a problem for you not getting back till tomorrow?'

'They'll have to send Steve and Andy out on their own to film Dean and Jessica, but other than that no, no problem. I might have to put in a few extra hours in the editing suite when we get back, but if it means I get to sit in the sun with a beer all day tomorrow while you rehearse, I can't say I'm too upset about it.'

'We might start wondering if you sabotaged the plane,' he laughs. 'Okay, let's go and ask about those toothbrushes. And maybe Dee can recommend a local restaurant we could all go to for dinner later. If we're going to be sticking around, we might as well make an evening of it.'

We find Mum and Dee sitting in the shade on the terrace, watching Dad and Pete having a water fight with the kids.

'Are you done already?' Mum asks hopefully when we join them.

We tell them about the flight cancellation and I can tell

Mum is trying not to look too pleased that we no longer have to dash off so quickly.

'You don't have to stay at a hotel, though,' Dee says. 'You should all stay here. We could do a barbecue.'

'You don't have any spare rooms,' I point out.

'You two can have mine and Pete's room, Mum and Dad are in the guest room, Sarah and I can have the kids' rooms and Pete can pitch a tent with the kids in the garden. They're always going on about camping out here overnight. They'll be ecstatic and we've got the weather for it.'

'Pete might not be so keen,' I point out.

'And it wouldn't feel right kicking our hosts out of their own bed,' Aleksis says.

'Pete won't mind at all. It's only for one night and the kids will think he's Superdad for the rest of the week. I'll be perfectly comfortable in one of the kids' beds. What about you, Sarah?'

'Sounds good to me.'

'What time is it now? Three-thirty. Perfect. Mum, why don't you and I pop down to the supermarket to pick up some nice meat and salady bits, and I'll get Pete to dig the tent out. Dad looks happy chasing Nathan and Daisy around, and Kate and Aleksis can get some more practice in. Then I'll get Pete to fire up the barbecue around sixish – that'll keep him happy. What does everyone reckon – does that sound like a plan?'

'If you're sure you don't mind,' Aleksis says. 'It would be nice for Kate to get to spend some more time with you.'

'Then it's decided. Pete!' she calls, and when she's got

his attention, she says, 'Can you grab the tent out of the shed please, love? There's a problem with the flight so everyone's staying over. Me and Mum are going to nip to the shops to get some stuff for the barbie.'

'Oh right, who's sleeping in the tent?' he asks, before the penny drops. 'Ohhhh, I see. Right, come on then, kids! Who wants to help me put the tent up?'

They squeal with delight when they realise what this means.

Sarah disappears off to let Olivia know we don't need hotel rooms after all, leaving Aleksis and me alone back in the dining room, where we finally make some progress with our tango. By the time the first wafts of barbecue smoke catch our attention, I've memorised the first half of the routine and we've started working on the second. We're a bit behind schedule, but our cancelled flight no longer feels like a catastrophe.

Chapter 40

It's a balmy evening and we join the others in the garden for a glass of rosé while the barbecue coals heat up. The kids are already in the tent doing a jigsaw, and when the first sausages are ready, they beg to be able to stay in there to eat theirs.

'Okay, but no greasy fingers on the sleeping bags,' Dee warns. 'I'll be watching you!'

Sarah gets her camera out again. 'I've already got plenty to work with and I think it's going to look great, but this is too nice a setting not to include as well. It will finish the montage off perfectly.'

'You haven't even asked us to do anything daft yet,' I tease.

'There's still tomorrow,' she warns.

Dad asks her how long the final edit will be.

'Only a few minutes. But you can pack a lot into a few minutes.'

They start chatting about how she'll decide what to include and what not to, and Dee turns her attention to Aleksis.

'So how do you rate your chances for the weekend?' she asks. But I don't hear his answer because Mum is already talking to me.

'You look like you've lost weight. You are looking after yourself, aren't you – eating enough, getting enough sleep?'

'Of course I am. But I'm dancing eight hours a day, so I'm bound to lose a little bit. Don't worry, it'll come straight back when *Fire on the Dance Floor* finishes.'

'I'm so glad you decided to go on the show.' She smiles. 'It's something you'll remember forever. I love watching you on that screen. You look so beautiful.'

'Thanks, Mum. I'm really glad I'm doing it too. It's been so nerve-racking at times – and exciting and terrifying and pretty much everything in between. But there's never going to be anything else like it. And I got to meet Aleksis, too.' I lower my voice. 'I really like him, Mum. I think he might be a keeper.'

Her smile gets wider. 'He does seem lovely. And he's slotted right into our madhouse, which must say something about him.'

'It's been a bit of a whirlwind, but I just love being with him,' I admit, glancing over to check he's not listening.

Dee and Aleksis have finished talking and are looking right at us.

'Oh, hi.' I feel my cheeks flushing. 'Anyone need a top-up?'

I reach for the bottle in the wine cooler, only to discover it's empty. I stand up quickly. 'I'll go and grab another one.'

'Let me help you with that.' Aleksis follows me into the kitchen.

'So you think I'm a keeper, do you?' he asks when we're inside.

'You weren't meant to hear that. I thought you were talking to Dee.'

'Don't be embarrassed. It's a nice thing to hear.' He pulls me towards him for a kiss. 'I might just feel the same way,' he whispers. And I swear I actually feel my heart swell.

I stay on cloud nine for the rest of the evening. Pete supervises bedtime for the kids, who've worn themselves out running around all day, then the rest of us chat, laugh and drink into the early hours until my own eyes start to droop. Aleksis and I have been awake for nearly twenty-four hours – it's time to call it a night.

I stifle a yawn when we're alone in the bedroom.

'Exhausted?' he asks.

'Yes, but still horny,' I laugh.

We kiss and start undressing each other, but my sister's bed lets out an almighty squeak as we lie down on it and wriggle towards each other.

'We'll wake the whole household up if we try to have sex on this,' Aleksis whispers, and as if to prove his point, the bed creaks loudly again as our weight shifts on the mattress.

'We should have taken the tent,' I reply in between kisses. 'We could have got up to all sorts in there without anyone knowing.'

'The power of hindsight,' he sighs. 'Is there somewhere we could go? The bathroom maybe?'

'What if someone needs the loo?'

'The garden then?'

'The kids might wake up. Argh, this is going to kill me. Let's go to the bathroom. I reckon we'll get away with it if we're quick.'

He smiles. 'We're not usually very quick.'

'Special exception tonight?'

He doesn't need asking twice.

The rest of the house is quiet, which hopefully means everyone else is asleep. We creep down the hallway feeling like naughty teenagers, with towels wrapped around us just in case anyone does happen to be up.

As soon as the bathroom door is closed behind us, I whip the towels away and sit on the edge of the bath, pulling Aleksis towards me so I can take him in my mouth. His breathing gets heavier as he watches me making him hard, his hands playing with my hair as he rocks gently towards me.

'Oh Kate,' he whispers as I tease him with my tongue, making his whole body shudder. He moves his hands to his thighs and I can see him squeezing them to help himself stay in control.

He slowly backs away and drops down into a crouch in front of me, spreading my knees wider so he can run his tongue across my clit, over and over. Just the thought of having sex with him had already turned me on, but he still makes sure I'm as aroused as he is before he draws me back up to my feet.

I turn my back to him and bend forward, my arms supporting me on the side of the bath, and he nudges my legs further apart as I push my buttocks towards him, then he enters me from behind, sliding in slowly, which makes us both moan.

'Shh,' we whisper in unison, stifling our giggles.

But I gasp again as he pulls back slowly then thrusts deeper. I can't hold it in if he's going to keep doing that.

'Be quiet,' he laughs.

'I can't help it,' I say over my shoulder. 'It feels too good.'

'Try putting this between your teeth.' He hands me my new toothbrush and I shake my head, laughing, but I try biting down on it, which works for a few seconds until another open-mouthed moan sends it clattering into the tub, giving us both the giggles again.

'There's no way no one heard that,' he says.

'I don't care any more, just don't stop.' I wiggle my hips suggestively and it's all the encouragement he needs.

He pounds against me quickly, until he's clinging on to me and squeezing me against him, a slightly strangled noise escaping from his throat as he tries to come without making any more sound.

When he withdraws, he moves alongside me and makes me climax still bent over the bath, the fingers of one hand deep inside me and his other hand underneath me, rubbing my clit until the world around me disappears in a dizzying blur. I definitely don't stay as quiet as I intended to.

Chapter 41

At Dee's insistence we spend most of the following day in the dining room working on our routine, joining the others for a long lunch and again at the end of the afternoon to say goodbye before our drive back to the airport. My eyes well up a bit in the back of the car as I watch them waving us off. Apart from the slight wobble about the flight cancellation, it's been such a stress-free stay, with so much love and laughter. Now it feels like we're heading back into a tornado.

Aleksis puts a comforting arm round me and kisses the top of my head, and I snuggle up against him, trying not to think about the pressure we'll be under for the next few days. But while we're waiting to board our flight at the airport, I spot a *Fire on the Dance Floor* story trending in third place on the news feed on my phone – and it sends my anxiety through the roof.

"*Shock shake-up as Dean forced to quit FOTDF and Merle returns,*" the headline reads.

'What the hell?' I hastily click through to the story.

"*Fire on the Dance Floor's Dean Mason has been forced to withdraw from the show just three days before the final after spraining his ankle during training,*" the story begins. I nudge Aleksis and get him to read it with me over my shoulder. It says Dean has been advised to rest for at least two weeks to avoid permanent damage, so the producers are bringing back Emilia and Merle – the show favourites before their unexpected departure – to take his place.

There's a quote from Emilia that says, "*Merle and I will be at a disadvantage coming into it this late, as we've missed three days of training, but we're going to do our very best to give the audience the best performance we can.*" And one from Dean, saying, "*I'm absolutely gutted, but I've got to do what's right for my body.*"

The article concludes, "*It's certainly a tough break this far into the competition but, sadly for Dean, the show must go on. You can find out how the other couples get on in the Fire on the Dance Floor final this Saturday at seven p.m.*"

'That jammy bastard,' I fume. Why does Merle always seem to land on his feet?

'It doesn't change anything,' Aleksis says firmly. 'Yes, he'll be tougher competition than Dean, but we're well on the way with our routine and they haven't even started theirs yet. We've still got two full days and a bit of time on Saturday before the show. We've still got as good a chance as we had before.'

'I know. It's still annoying, though. I thought we'd seen the last of him.'

'He would have been around anyway, even if they weren't competing,' Aleksis points out. 'There's bound to be some kind of everyone-on-stage celebration when the winner is announced. There always is.'

'I guess so.'

I notice Sarah hurrying towards us, balancing out her camera bag with a giant duty-free bag in the other hand.

'Come on, you two, it's the last call for our gate. We don't want to miss this one as well.'

'Shit, we didn't notice the time. Here, let me take one of those,' Aleksis offers and we set off at a jog.

There's no one else at the gate when we arrive, apart from one member of staff at the desk, who looks like she's packing up.

'Hurry,' she says when she sees us. 'You can still make it.'

We scramble to show her our passports and tickets then race down the tunnel to the plane once we've been cleared.

'Take your seats quickly please,' the stewardess instructs.

But because the plane is already full – we're the last ones to board – there's no space in the overhead lockers for Sarah's camera bag and there's no way it's going to fit under the seat in front. The duty free can just about be squeezed in there, but the camera bag is far too bulky.

'I'm going to have to take that,' the stewardess, who has followed us up the aisle, tells her.

'Take it where?' Sarah asks. 'It's full of valuable equipment.'

'It'll have to go in the hold. There's no room for it here.'

'I really don't want—'

'It'll be perfectly safe there, I assure you,' the stewardess cuts in. 'So if you'd like to take your seat, the flight is ready to depart.'

'Are you sure we can't squeeze it in one of the overhead lockers?' Sarah pleads.

'As you can see, we're a full flight,' the stewardess says impatiently. 'And before you ask, there isn't anywhere else to put luggage in the cabin. But it'll be fine in the hold. We'll take good care of it, I promise. Now can you take your seats, please.'

'I'll just pull a few bits out quickly.'

Sarah reaches for the bag at the same time the stewardess grabs it. 'Please! You're holding up the flight.'

Sarah relents and lets the stewardess win. 'Fine. But there's some very expensive equipment in there so please be careful with it.'

The stewardess doesn't reply as she struts back to the front of the plane with the bag.

'What a bitch,' Sarah mutters as we slide into our seats.

'She's just doing her job,' Aleksis says. 'Don't worry, that case is really sturdy and it's got a decent lock on it.'

'I was going to do some work on the flight, though. And now I can't because I stuck the laptop in there with the camera.'

'You'll just have to talk to us,' Aleksis grins. 'Sorry!'

Sarah rolls her eyes and smiles, but I can tell it stays in the back of her mind for the rest of the flight, even though she banters with us until we're back in London.

In arrivals, Aleksis offers to wait with her at the carousel.

'Oh no, I don't want to hold you two up. Get yourselves

home. It's been a great two days though. Your family are lovely, Kate. I felt really at home there.'

'Ah, thanks.' I give her a quick hug. 'I hope you're not here too long.'

Aleksis puts his arm round me as we walk to the taxi rank. There's no one else waiting, so we're on our way within minutes.

'I've been thinking,' he says, as we hold hands in the back seat. 'For our second dance, maybe we shouldn't do the bachata after all.'

'So what, the cha-cha instead? The audience did love it. And it is a bit more fresh in my mind.'

'Not the cha-cha, either. I was thinking of the salsa.'

'The salsa?' I splutter. Surely he's not serious. 'But that was our worst dance.'

'I know, but we're in such a different place now. You've improved so much and, if I remember rightly, things were a little strained between us when we did it last time. I'm still sorry about that.'

I shake my head to show it's forgotten.

'But if we do it again now,' he continues, full of enthusiasm, 'we can show everyone how far you've come since the show started. And no one will be expecting it – they'll expect us to pick one of our best dances – so it'll be a big surprise. It'll show them how confident we are, that we'd pick our weakest performance and turn it into one of our best.'

'Would we, though?' I bite my lip, struggling to remember anything good about our first effort. 'I was terrible last time,' I remind him.

'Which was mostly my fault. It'll be different this time. We'll make it more fun; a bit more Cuban. I think a really upbeat salsa will give the audience something to really get behind.'

I can see how much he wants me to love the idea, but I'm still not convinced.

'How about I show you what I've got in mind when we're back in the studio tomorrow and you can see how you feel then,' he suggests. 'But bear in mind that Merle and Emilia will probably repeat their bachata, because that's what got them their best score, so the audience will probably appreciate it if we do something different.'

I hadn't thought of that. 'Okay,' I relent. 'Show me tomorrow. But if I'm still terrible . . . '

'You won't be, I promise.' He gives my hand a squeeze. 'I know this is the right move, I'm sure of it.'

We're interrupted when our phones ping simultaneously.

'*You're not going to believe this,*' Sarah has written to us both. '*That bloody stewardess didn't tell anyone to put my camera bag on the plane, so it's still in bloody France. I'm absolutely fuming. I'm sure she did it deliberately.*'

I exchange a worried look with Aleksis.

'*They can't send it over till tomorrow now, then I'll have to schlep all the way back to Heathrow to pick it up. Like I haven't got enough to do. I can't believe she just left it in the corridor. I told you she was a bitch.*'

I grip Aleksis's hand. 'It will make it back here, won't it?'

I think I'd have a nervous breakdown if we had to give up more rehearsal time to squeeze in a trip to Auntie Irene's now.

'It'll be fine,' he reassures me. 'They know where it is, so they'll just send it on the next flight. Which means for the next forty-eight hours we can just rehearse solidly and nothing else.'

'Nothing at all?' I ask with a suggestive smile, pushing my doubts about the baggage handlers aside. Well, it can't be all work and no play.

'Maybe the odd thing,' he laughs, and I suddenly wish the taxi would get a move on.

Chapter 42

Aleksis shows me his salsa plan in the studio the next day and I can see why he thinks it's a good idea. It's a clever mix of snappy spin sequences and light-hearted charm – and it's not so different from our first routine that I don't think I can learn it in the little time we've got left. I agree that we should go for it and we work on it until lunchtime before switching back to the tango for the rest of the day.

Sarah rings just before the studio closes to warn us her camera bag has still not made it back to the UK. She's been told it won't be here till Friday at the earliest.

'What's the problem?' I ask, feeling my stress levels go up a notch.

'I wish I knew. I'm guessing there's an issue with luggage travelling separately from its owner or something like that. They're not being overly helpful.'

I try to sound less panicky than I feel. 'Does that mean you might have to fly back out there and collect it?'

'There isn't time. With Merle being so particular about his filming, I'm expecting to be completely tied up with him and Emilia now. Olivia has made a suggestion though, which we think might work as a contingency plan. I said I'd run it by you.'

'Go on,' I say, praying it doesn't involve either me or Aleksis flying back to France.

'We were wondering if we might be able to persuade the airport to release the bag to your sister – then hopefully she could pick it up, download anything that's still on the camera to my laptop and ping all the files over to me. We can sort out how to get the actual camera back here later, when it's not so urgent. Do you think she might do that?'

'I can't see why not. It's only an hour's drive, so I'm pretty sure she'd be happy to.'

'Do you want to check, and if she says yes I'll get Olivia to sort it with the airport?' Sarah asks.

'Of course, I'll do it now.'

And thankfully, Dee agrees straight away – on the proviso that I send her a thank you case of wine.

I give her Olivia's number, so they can liaise about the arrangements, and tell her she's a lifesaver.

'It sounds like we can go home this evening and completely relax now,' Aleksis says when I've ended the call.

'Don't you think we should be seen out and about somewhere? We haven't been in the news all week.'

'I don't think I've got the energy,' he admits. 'Unless you want to see photos of me falling asleep in my dinner.'

'But that only leaves tomorrow night – the night before

the final.' Even I can hear the worry in my voice. 'Wouldn't we be better off relaxing then?'

'I think we'll be fine to do something tomorrow evening. It doesn't have to be anything crazy and by then we'll have recovered from France a bit more. Tonight all I want to do is have a hot bath, I don't know about you.'

A long soak does sound appealing – a moment of calm before the storm.

'Let's take it easy tonight and I'll get Sofiya to ask Stella if there's anywhere she can recommend for us to go tomorrow,' Aleksis adds.

'Fingers crossed she comes up with something good.'

Back at the flat, tempting though it is to squeeze into Aleksis's bath with him, we each run our own, so we can stretch out and let our muscles loosen up. While I'm soaking I text Lucy and tell her I've got some big news to share with her.

'*You're pregnant??*' she writes back.

'*Noooo!*' I can't help laughing at her tendency to jump the gun. '*I'll have you know we are keeping the condom companies very much in business! But Aleksis got on really well with my family while we were in France – so he's invited me to Latvia to meet his parents after the show!*'

'*Ooh, sounds serious . . .*'

I can feel the butterflies in my stomach as I tell her I think it might be.

'*Just let me know when to buy my hat!*' she replies.

And this time I don't tell her off for getting carried away.

But thinking about life after the show reminds me we've only got one day left in our tatty little studio together. I've

320

grown quite fond of it and realise I'm really going to miss it. I can't believe how quickly the time has flown since our first rehearsal there. In less than seventy-two hours, my *Fire on the Dance Floor* journey will be over – when it feels like we're only just getting started.

I wonder if Aleksis is brooding about it too, so I wrap myself in a towel and pad down the corridor to his bathroom to find out.

'Mind if I join you?' I ask through the door.

'Not at all. Come on in,' he calls out.

I walk in to find him up to his neck in foam.

'Want to jump in?' he asks, pulling his legs towards him to make room.

I step into the water and it creeps dangerously close to the top. He releases the plug until there's room for me to sit down – facing away from him so I can lean back against him with his legs round my sides.

'This is nice,' he says, wrapping his arms around me. 'I could stay here for hours.'

'You'd shrivel up,' I laugh.

'Oi.'

'I don't mean down there. Although we could take extra steps to make sure that doesn't happen.'

'What do you have in mind?' I can tell he's smiling as he says this.

I move his hands to my breasts, no longer interested in a conversation about the fast-approaching *Fire on the Dance Floor* finishing line. 'We can start here.'

He caresses them and kisses my neck. 'I think I can manage that.'

But when he tries to slide his hand further down, he discovers he can't reach in this position. 'Hm, what do we do now?'

'What about if I do this?' I shuffle around to face him, lean back against the other end of bath and put my feet up on either side of the tub. His eyes widen and his lips curl into a grin. 'That could work.'

He slides one foot towards me and strokes me with his toes. Then he splashes onto his knees and says, 'I want to go down on you.'

'You'll drown,' I gasp as he plunges his face into the water.

When he comes up for air, he admits it wasn't one of his better ideas.

'Maybe we should just do this after the bath?' I suggest.

He pulls the plug immediately and fires me a wicked grin. 'I think we're clean.'

He cocoons us in a towel while we're drying off and I can smell the soap on his skin as he presses his body into mine and kisses me, pushing his tongue into my mouth and biting gently on my bottom lip. I can feel him swelling against me as I run my hands up and down his back, down to his hips and onto his buttocks, and my nipples tingle in response.

My skin is still damp as he leads me through to the bedroom, leaving the towel where it's fallen on the floor.

On the mattress, he pushes my arms above my head and kisses me everywhere. He nibbles my ears, brushes his lips against my cheeks, runs his tongue down my neck and takes my nipples in his mouth. Then he moves lower and finds that sweet, sweet spot between my legs that makes all my other thoughts melt away.

'God, I love that,' I murmur, propping myself up on my elbows to watch. If someone found a way to bottle this feeling they'd be a billionaire.

Before he makes me come, I reach down and lift his chin up till his eyes meet mine. For a second he looks worried – if I'm enjoying it, why would I want him to stop? But he relaxes when I beckon him back up the bed, licking my finger and sucking it flirtatiously before rubbing it across my nipples and beckoning again.

He climbs up on top of me and I wrap my legs round his back, reaching down to guide him inside. When he crushes his mouth against mine as he grinds himself against me, I can taste myself on his tongue.

I cling on to him tighter, consumed by the feeling of his body on mine, his hands in my hair, the tingling inside me. I'm vaguely aware of my nails digging into his bum when a particularly strong thrust tips me over the edge and makes me cry out as I climax, but I can't loosen my grasp.

'Oh fuck,' he mutters as his own orgasm tears through him.

Then we both burst out laughing from the sheer release of it as he drops his head down onto my shoulder and lets his body relax against mine. We lie there, breathing heavily, neither of us wanting to move.

'We might need another bath,' he says eventually, rolling aside and idly trailing a finger through the light sheen of sweat that's settled on my chest.

'I think we'd end up right back here again,' I laugh. 'Not that I'd mind.'

'You're probably right.'

But we stay where we are, lying with our legs intertwined and satisfied smiles on our faces.

A twinge of uncertainty creeps in behind my smile though, when my thoughts drift back to *Fire on the Dance Floor* and how little time we have left on the show. There's just one more day in the studio, then the final, then everything's going to change – just when I've got so used to being with Aleksis round the clock that it's hard to picture things any other way.

It seems incredible that our stilted introduction in Shane's office was less than four weeks ago, given how I feel about him now. But no sooner than I've admitted to myself that I could happily spend every waking moment with him, I'm going to have to readjust to normal life again – and I can't even imagine what that's going to look like.

Chapter 43

'*One day to go!*' Liam has written in the Fire Dancers chat when I check my phone over breakfast. '*Hope your routines are coming together, K&T. Can't wait to see them.*'

I'd been hoping for news from my sister, but I know it's too early, even though she's an hour ahead in France. I just want to know the camera bag has been successfully reclaimed. It would be nigh-on impossible to cobble together a new video montage now – there's not enough time.

Beth wants help deciding what to wear on Saturday. Aleksis was right – all the eliminated dancers are going to be back on set to create a party atmosphere, but as they're not competing, they're not going to be dressed by the costume department.

Tammy tells us her mum and sisters are fighting over who's going to come and watch the final. Her sisters think they'd benefit more from being on TV, while her mum says it should be her and Tammy's dad cos they're older and might not get another chance.

'*Can't the show make an allowance and squeeze a few extra people in for the final?*' Liam asks. '*If they're worried about it giving you an unfair advantage, they can just not give the extra people a keypad.*'

Tammy admits she hadn't thought of that and says she'll talk to Olivia to see if she can sort something out.

I put my phone away then, so I can focus on the day ahead, but it's a struggle not to keep checking it every five minutes on the way to the studio. I'm not going to be able to relax until I've heard from Dee. I'm desperate to know if her airport mission has been a success, but my phone remains stubbornly silent.

By mid-morning, when there's still no news, I buckle and impatiently dial her home number. She'd have to be back by now if it had all gone to plan. But it rings out with no answer, and there's no response from her mobile, Pete's mobile or Mum's mobile either.

'Where are they all? Why are they torturing me like this?' I moan to Aleksis.

Even Sarah hasn't been in touch, and she must be having kittens about the AWOL footage by now if it's not back in her possession.

'I'm sure we would have heard from her if there was a problem,' Aleksis says. 'They'd have to be talking to us about replacement footage by now if they hadn't got hold of it. Your sister is probably just busy doing all the uploads and Sarah's probably talking her through it.'

He sounds calm and rational – the exact opposite to how I feel. My body is jittery from the stress.

When the phone finally rings, I nearly jump out of my

skin. I break away from Aleksis mid-dance and sprint to my bag, praying for some good news. But it's Aleksis's phone, not mine, and his sister's number is on the screen. His eyebrows shoot up as he listens to what she has to say.

'I'm putting you on loudspeaker,' he says eventually. 'So Kate can hear this too.'

'I was just letting Aleksis know that Stella has come up with an event tonight that's guaranteed to get you back in the headlines,' she explains. 'It's a good one.'

This momentarily puts the brakes on my growing panic about the camera. 'What is it?'

'Eden Shay is putting on an exclusive gig at a pub in Brixton ahead of the launch of her new album and there are lots of celebrities going, so there'll be lots of cameras. You'll need to be there at six-thirty sharp if you're going to make the red carpet, but it's really close to your studio.'

'As in *the* Eden Shay?' I check, thinking I must have misheard. 'Like, bestselling artist of the last decade Eden Shay?'

'Exactly,' she confirms. 'Stella was still feeling bad about my interview getting bumped for Merle's, so when she spotted Merle's name on the guest list that gets circulated to the press to make them want to send photographers, she called in a favour to get you two an invite.'

'Are you serious?' I didn't think it would be possible to top last week's film premiere, but I love Eden Shay.

'I am. And this would even the playing field somewhat, so I hope you'll agree to go. The last thing you want is Merle and Emilia splashed all over the internet tomorrow instead of you.'

'Just try and stop me!' I gush. 'And please pass on a massive thank you to Stella from me. This is a dream come true.'

I look up at Aleksis to check he's as keen as I am, and he confirms it with an enthusiastic grin. Then he hits his sister with such a cheeky request that I'm surprised she doesn't decide to keep the tickets for herself.

'Any chance you could swing by the apartment to pick up some clothes for us and bring them down to the studio this afternoon? It'd save us having to trek halfway across London and back and cut our rehearsal short. You know where I hide the spare key.'

Amazingly this makes her laugh. 'I suppose so, seeing as you asked so nicely. But you'll owe me big time.'

'Don't I know it,' he replies.

'I'll chuck in some towels and soap as well, if you like. I presume there are sinks there that you can use to freshen up. And do you want me to bring a couple of my dresses again, Kate? In case there's something you like the look of.'

I'm sure she'll have something gorgeous. 'I'd love that, thank you.'

'Great, then I'll see you around five-thirty.'

Aleksis tells her she's a legend, then puts his phone back in his bag. And our rehearsal goes much better for the following couple of hours. With the gig to look forward to, Dee and the camera bag are temporarily forgotten.

It's nearly two by the time my own phone pings – this time with the news I've been waiting for all day. I whoop as soon as I see the text from Olivia.

'We've got it,' I read out to Aleksis. 'Your sister's really gone the extra mile. We'll organise a little something to say thank you.'

'Thank goodness for that,' Aleksis laughs, high fiving me then pulling me in for a kiss.

'I think I might cry. It's such a relief.'

'Don't do that,' he says. 'Let's celebrate with a quick lunch break, then we'll switch to the salsa again. You've been brilliant this week by the way, in case you didn't already know. Despite all the disruption, you're picking up both routines really well.'

'It's because I'm enjoying it. This salsa might even be my favourite dance. I wouldn't have said that four weeks ago.'

Four weeks ago, I would have dug my heels in and flat-out refused to dance it again in the final. How different things are now. How different I am.

Sofiya arrives bang on time, and drops off a suitcase full of the things we need to get ready. After we've splashed ourselves clean in the sinks, got changed and I've speedily done my hair and make-up, we check ourselves out in the mirror – and I have to admit, I'm impressed. You'd never guess we'd thrown it all together in under an hour.

I've selected a short white prom dress with a sheer embellished layer over the top. The white underlayer has a strapless bodice and a flared skirt, while the sheer layer adds delicate streaks of silver to the skirt and an intense swirl of silver to the bodice that creeps up onto each shoulder. It's stunning. Aleksis has opted for pale grey trousers and a crisp white T-shirt, which complement the dress perfectly.

'Your sister has such good taste,' I smile.

'It runs in the family,' he says and pulls me towards him for a kiss.

It's only a ten-minute walk to the gig and when we arrive we're instantly swept up in a flurry of camera flashes and fans calling out to us for selfies. We pose with a few, then stop in front of the waiting paparazzi, who ask us to turn this way and that so they can all get their shots in.

There are more than I expected, but when I later spot high-profile models, Premier League footballers and TV stars inside the pub, I realise why. We're among red-carpet royalty. I can hardly believe my luck.

I catch a brief glimpse of Merle and Emilia on the other side of the room, but it's a big enough venue that we don't cross paths. And once Eden Shay walks out onto the makeshift stage, no one is looking anywhere but at her.

There's something mesmerising about her as she thanks everyone for coming along. It's that stage presence you just can't explain. And even though she only sings six songs, chatting in between about what inspired each one, it's one of the best gigs I've ever been to. I've never been so close to the front before. I could almost reach out and touch her.

I can't stop raving about it when we find ourselves back out on the street just over an hour later. 'I wish we could go back in and watch it all again. That last song has brought me out in goose bumps.'

Aleksis puts his arms round me when he sees me shivering.

'I don't want to go home yet, do you?' I ask, as we watch

a soap actress slip out of the venue and climb quickly into a waiting car.

'Not really. It's too early for bed and we won't gain anything by trying to squeeze in any more dance practice now.'

My eyes follow the car as it speeds away. 'Where do you think she'd go, if she fancied an after-party?'

'Mayfair?' he suggests. 'We could always head that way too and treat ourselves to some fancy food at Nobu.'

It feels like a fitting way to round off such a brilliant evening.

But there are no free tables at short notice on a Friday night, so we end up squeezing into an Italian restaurant close by, for a less extravagant but equally tasty feast.

Still on a high, we kiss all the way home in the taxi. And back at the apartment our upbeat mood continues. We pour ourselves a nightcap and take it to the sofa, still jabbering on about our favourite parts of the evening, as well as the other bands we'd like to see in such an intimate setting.

Aleksis idly traces the hem of my skirt with his fingers while we're talking, until eventually they find their way under the folds of material. A knowing look passes between us and we both put our drinks on the coffee table without another word.

We move closer together and he runs his hand up my thigh. When he reaches the lace of my knickers, he hooks them to one side and reaches inside. I lean back and smile, impressed that he always manages to find just the right spot.

After I've raised my hips so he can help me wriggle free of my underwear, he swings me up onto his lap so we can kiss while he touches me. As our tongues meet I can feel him stirring through his trousers beneath me.

He tucks his hands under my bum and lifts it until I'm kneeling in front of him, his mouth now level with my clit, and I pull my skirt out of the way so he can open me up with his tongue, the waves of pleasure instantly making me light-headed. He grips the backs of my thighs to hold me steady.

I lean my arms on the back of the sofa so he can let go of my legs to undo his trousers, and somehow he manages to push them just far enough out of the way with his mouth never leaving me. I lower myself onto his lap and he enters me from below, his hands caressing my breasts through the material of my dress, his trousers caught up round his ankles, neither of us wanting to interrupt the flow to finish undressing.

As we rock against each other he brushes his lips across my cheeks and I kiss his neck. Then our mouths meet again, his tongue seeking mine hungrily.

I push myself up into a crouch, plunging him deeper inside me and he uses his hands to help me bounce. I can feel how hard he is inside me, but just when I think he's about to come, he lifts me away so that I'm standing between his knees, wriggles closer to the edge of the sofa and puts his tongue back on my clit, the bliss all mine again.

When he feels my legs wobble, he spins me round and brings me back down onto his lap, this time unzipping my dress and tossing it aside before he reaches for my breasts and then enters me again. I watch his toes curl each time I rise and fall above him.

'Oh Kate,' he gasps, his body starting to buck under me. He clings to my hips while he comes.

Barely recovered, he moves a hand to my clit, and my orgasm isn't far behind his.

'You've made me hard again,' he murmurs, as my jerks slow to quivers. Which won't get any complaints from me.

We move to the rug, and if I ever thought multiple orgasms were a myth, I don't any more. The first one has barely subsided before the second one is ricocheting through me, courtesy of his tongue. I couldn't have asked for a better end to the night.

When we finally curl up in bed and he pulls me into his arms, I realise I've gone the whole evening without giving a second thought to the *Fire on the Dance Floor* final tomorrow. In fact, there's only one thought racing round my head as I close my eyes – *I think I'm falling in love.*

Chapter 44

It's not even six o'clock when I jolt awake in a panic about our Argentine tango. I may have managed to put it out of my head yesterday, but there's no such luxury this morning. This is it – the last hurdle. My adrenaline is already pumping.

I half want to wake Aleksis up so he can take my mind off it again, but I leave him snoozing. At least one of us might as well be properly rested.

When he finally stirs, just after seven, he kisses me good morning.

'So, the big day, eh? Are you excited?'

'No,' I admit.

'Let's just enjoy it. I know there's a lot of pressure, and we really want to win, but I still want it to be a good experience for you. So let's just have fun and whatever will be will be, okay?'

'Okay,' I agree. 'But I do want to win, though.'

He laughs. 'Of course you do.'

I'm more nervous than ever by the time we get to Channel 6. I don't think my heart will stop racing all day. But if Aleksis is having any last-minute nerves he doesn't show it – as, I suppose, you'd expect from a professional.

We say hi to Elijah, the only other person in the reception room when we arrive. I hope more of the others turn up before Merle and Emilia do. The awkwardness between us will be a lot less obvious with everyone else around to deflect attention from it.

'I saw the photos from the Eden Shay gig – they look great,' Elijah says, without a hint of jealousy. 'I bet Merle will be annoyed though.'

In all the stories that have appeared online this morning, photos of me and Aleksis have been included right at the top with the other big names at the event. Merle and Emilia are much lower down, alongside a handful of former reality stars.

'I think I'd be pretty unimpressed, too, if I were him,' I admit. 'I don't know how we got to be so prominent. Not that I'm complaining, of course.'

'Perhaps they missed the news that he's back in the show,' Elijah shrugs.

'I'm sorry you didn't get to join us,' Aleksis says. 'My sister sorted our tickets out. I don't know how Merle managed to swing his.'

'Hey, no problem. Tammy might be a bit gutted – but more about missing the gig than the press coverage, if I've learned anything about Tammy.'

And he's absolutely spot on. When she joins us not long afterwards, she couldn't be happier for us – although she does request that I buy her a ticket for Eden Shay's tour if I win the £25,000 prize tonight. I tell I'd be delighted to.

I'm relieved it hasn't created any animosity. It would be even harder going into the final if there was that to contend with as well.

When Merle and Emilia eventually walk into the room, it instantly puts me on edge. Luckily, Olivia is not far behind them.

'Hi everyone,' she says. 'This is it then – the grand final! You'll all have extra time to practise in the main studio today, seeing as you've got two dances this week instead of one. The rest of the contestants will be joining us later this afternoon as they don't have anything to rehearse. Merle, Emilia, do you want to head to the studio first as you've had the least practice time together this week? The rest of you, if you can just hang fire for the moment, and we'll sort out costumes and so on shortly.'

And that's the last I see of Merle until two hours before the live show, when I find myself alone in the reception room with him while Emilia is with the costume girls, Elijah and Tammy are rehearsing and Aleksis is in the bathroom.

'Kate,' he says, walking over to join me.

'Merle,' I reply warily.

'We might as well keep each other entertained, *n'est-ce pas*? While no one else is around.'

'I guess so.' Although I'm not at all sure it's a good idea.

'There's something I wanted to show you, anyway.' He unlocks his phone and hands it to me. 'Remember this?'

I watch in horror as the video of us dancing the kizomba starts playing, with my blindfolded, naked body pressed up against his fully clothed one. What once seemed so erotic now just looks tacky and embarrassing – and feels so violating. My cheeks flush red with humiliation and anger. 'You promised to delete that, Merle.'

He snatches his phone back off me before it occurs to me to try and delete it myself.

'I thought it might come in useful. And as it turns out, I was right. I was pretty much guaranteed to win this competition until last week, but now you and Aleksis have got yourselves all over the internet and he's managed to drag a half decent dance out of you, it's not so certain. I need to tip things back in my favour.'

I swallow back a creeping sense of dread.

'So here's the deal,' he continues. 'If you throw your chances of winning tonight, I won't upload this video online. And then everything will be back as it should be.'

'And how exactly would you propose I do that?' I snap.

'However you see fit. Mess up your dance, come clean about your showmance with Aleksis—'

'It's not a showmance.'

'All the more reason to keep this private, then,' he counters.

I stare at him, my mind racing. Would he really stoop this low just to get a place on next year's show?

'You don't have to agree right away,' he says, standing up to leave. 'You've still got two hours to think about it. But I know what I'd do if I were in your shoes.'

Then he walks away, leaving me reeling.

I slump back in my chair, chilled to my core. I've worked so hard to get this far in the competition, I don't want to throw it all away now. I don't want to let Aleksis down, either. But when I think back to the night when the pictures of me and Merle went viral, it makes me shudder. Could I bear the humiliation of more naked images of me circulating online for all eternity? Images which my parents, friends, future work colleagues, and one day even my children might see? And not just photos this time, but a full bloody video.

Panic rising, I dig my phone out of my bag and dial Lucy's number.

'Everything okay?' she asks, instinctively worried. 'I didn't expect to hear from you this close to the show.'

'Something's happened and I don't know what to do,' I admit. Then I take a deep breath and tell her everything – how Merle filmed me without telling me, lied about deleting it, and how he's now using it to blackmail me.

Her outrage is instant. 'How dare he? And now he's trying to intimidate you with it as well? This is not right, Kate. You've got to put a stop to it.'

'But how?' I wail.

'Isn't revenge porn illegal? Tell the producers what's he's done. Tell *everyone* what he's done. He should be thrown off the show for this. It's disgusting.'

'But how can I prove it? He'd probably just say I was making it up to get rid of him.'

'Then there must be another way.' She thinks for a moment. 'What does Aleksis have to say about it? He's known Merle for long enough – he must have an idea of how to pull him back in line.'

'I haven't told him,' I say, miserably. 'I don't want him to know about the video.'

'He'll find out anyway if Merle posts it.'

But the thought of telling Aleksis makes me feel nauseous. And what will he be able to do anyway? Merle isn't going to back down just because Aleksis tells him to.

'The stupid thing is, there's every chance I won't win tonight anyway,' I sigh. 'I know I've managed to get pretty decent at dancing, but I've still got to get through the Argentine tango.'

'Maybe, but please don't let it be Merle who decides it for you. I want to see you give the performance of a lifetime tonight. And afterwards I want us to celebrate it, win or lose, and for you to be proud of all the amazing things you've achieved in the last two months. And you won't be able to do that if you just give in to him, will you?'

She's right, of course. I've come too far to just give up on it all now. So I ring off, having promised I'll find a way to get it sorted.

I look up to see Aleksis arriving back from the gents, closely followed by Olivia, who tells us we're up next for rehearsals. As we walk to the studio, I can tell from the way he keeps looking at me that he knows I'm agitated, but I wait till we're alone before I tell him why.

His expression turns quickly from concern to fury as I relay the details of my exchange with Merle, and before I can stop him he's striding back towards the door, fists clenched with rage.

'Wait!' I call out after him. 'We need to figure out the best thing to do.'

'I'll deal with it,' he says over his shoulder, and images of him and Merle throwing punches at each other flash through my mind.

'No, wait,' I yell again and this time the urgency in my voice stops him in his tracks. He turns back to face me.

'This is my problem and I need to be the one who makes it go away,' I say firmly, a surge of determination flooding through me. 'But thank you.' I smile, touched by his eagerness to protect me. 'I'll be back as soon as I can.'

Then I slide past him and into the corridor, with absolutely no idea what I'm going to do next.

I don't make it further than the first corner though, because – hang on a minute – isn't that my dad walking towards me from the opposite end?

'Dad?' I ask, completely bewildered. 'What on earth are you doing here?'

'Oh!' He looks startled – and then guilty. 'It was meant to be a surprise.'

'It's certainly that,' I reply, wide-eyed. 'But seriously – you're here? Is Mum here, too?'

'There you are!' Mum's voice rings out from behind me. 'Oh Kate, it's you. Hello, darling. Sorry, it was meant to be a surprise.'

'So I keep hearing. Will someone tell me what's going on?'

'You'd better let your sister explain,' she says. 'Come on, follow me. Come on, Jim.'

'Dee's here too?' I ask as I hurry along behind her, momentarily forgetting my Merle predicament.

She pushes the door to Shane's office open without knocking and inside are Dee, Pete, Nathan and Daisy. Dee is sitting at the desk doing her make-up while Pete wrestles Daisy into a clean dress and Nathan waits his turn.

'Auntie Katie!' Daisy squeals, breaking free and throwing her arms round my legs. 'We've come to watch you do the dancing.'

'So I see,' I say, hugging her back. 'But how?'

My question is aimed at my sister, who shoots me a sheepish grin.

'Surprise! You're not supposed to know we're here until the actual show, but I guess it's too late for that now.'

'Explain,' I demand.

'Well, when you asked me if I could collect the camera bag, a little idea popped into my head – what if I were to fly it back here in person to ensure it made it safely back to Channel 6? That way there'd be no risk of them not getting it back in one piece. I ran it by Olivia and she thought it was a great idea – so I asked if she would do me a favour in return and bring the whole lot of us over, so we could support you on tonight's show.'

'And she agreed?'

Her smile gets even bigger. 'I didn't think for an instant she'd say yes – it was just a silly suggestion – but the next thing I know she'd discussed it with the producers, got the green light and booked us all on a flight on Friday morning.'

'So you've been here since yesterday?' I can hardly take it in. Now it makes sense why none of them were answering their phones all morning.

'Yep, we stayed at Mum and Dad's last night. Then we snuck in here a couple of hours ago and the plan was to surprise you live on tonight's show – oops! Now you'll just have to pretend you're surprised.'

I don't think it'll be too hard to make it look convincing – I'm pretty sure I'll still be in shock.

'I don't know what to say. I mean, this is amazing. I can't believe you're all here.'

'Just tell me I'm a genius,' she laughs. 'And come over here and give us all a hug. We're absolutely bursting with excitement. It was so hard not to tell you.'

After Mum has wrapped her arms round me, followed by Dad, then Dee then Pete, I tell them I'd better get back to rehearsals and that I can't wait to catch up with them properly later. I keep my Merle dilemma to myself – I don't want to drag them into it – but more than ever I don't want to have to mess up my performance on the show tonight. Not now my whole family has flown all the way here to watch it.

As I back out of the door to a chorus of 'good luck's and 'love you's, it strikes me that the only way I can make my problem go away is if I can get hold of Merle's phone. If he hasn't got the video, he can't use it. But it's not like I can just bowl into his dressing room and he'll hand it over.

If he isn't in there, though . . .

I race towards the costumes room and get there just in time to see Emilia emerging in her latest ensemble – a gold swimming costume with some tassels hanging down to create a very mini miniskirt. She looks amazing. Merle really doesn't deserve her.

I falter for the briefest moment, my mind flashing back to that day when Ed's new lover devastated me with the news that my boyfriend was a snake. I hate the idea of inflicting that kind of pain on anyone else. But Emilia has a right to know what Merle's really like. The question is, will she believe me?

She eyes me suspiciously as I take a deep breath and ask for a quick word.

'I really need your help,' I tell her.

'It's a bit late now,' she says, presumably thinking I mean with my dancing.

My palms prickle with sweat as I confess the real reason, all the while silently praying I've judged this correctly. I'd want to be told if I were her, wouldn't I? I'd want to know what my partner was capable of.

She looks away and shakes her head when I finish talking. I don't know what she means by it and I can feel my heart pounding. Is she angry with him? With me? Does she think I'm winding her up? The seconds drag on as I wait for her to respond.

Eventually she turns back to me with a look of resignation in her eyes. My heart jolts when she says, 'What do you need me to do?'

Chapter 45

I wait at the end of the corridor while she's in the dressing room with Merle, peering anxiously round the corner and desperately hoping she can lure him out of there. The plan is for her to persuade him to go back to the studio for one last rehearsal, after she saw me and Aleksis return to the reception room and realised the studio would be empty. She promised to lay it on thick.

It feels like she's in there for hours and it's torture not knowing what's going on. If she doesn't manage to get Merle out of the dressing room, I'll have only moments left to decide whether to ignore his threat, give the show my best shot and let him release the video, or whether to let Aleksis down and let Merle win. I change my mind every few seconds – I can't bear more humiliation, I'll go along with his scheme; Merle can do his worst, I won't be beaten like this.

I jump out of my skin when the dressing room door finally opens and I hear Emilia telling Merle to hurry up. I pull my head back out of sight as she tells him, 'We'll have just enough time to run through them both one more time, if we're quick.'

As soon as the coast is clear, I sprint towards the dressing room, pulling the door closed behind me the second I'm inside. With shaking hands, I call Merle's number from my own phone, praying he hasn't taken it with him without Emilia noticing. I'm screwed if he has – I haven't got a plan B.

When I hear it ring, I don't think I've ever felt more relieved in my life. I fight back tears as I quickly locate it and send a silent thank you to Emilia as I pull it from his bag. When I have it in my hands, such a surge of happiness washes over me that I have to steady myself on the dressing table. I've got it. My nightmare is over. I switch it to silent, bundle it into a wodge of tissues to disguise it and slip quickly back out into the corridor.

Aleksis finds me in the reception room less than a minute later, his brow furrowed with worry and confusion. 'Emilia practically chased me out of the studio. She said you needed me back here.'

He sounds upset, but his eyes light up when I discreetly show him the phone in among the tissue and realisation dawns.

'Nice work,' he says, a smile breaking out on his face.

'I'm going to take it outside now and get rid of it for good,' I tell him.

He asks if he can do the honours – and once we've found a sheltered spot seems to take great pleasure in crushing it under his heel before dropping the pieces in the trash.

'No more video,' he says defiantly, and I don't think three words have ever made me happier.

He reaches for my hand and gives it a squeeze. 'Nothing can stop us now.'

'Let's go out there and smash it,' I agree, suddenly raring to go.

It's not long before Olivia is leading us back to the studio for the very last time and Kimberley is getting the show underway.

'Ladies and gentlemen! The judges are ready, the contestants are poised, the dance floor is waiting, and I think we all know what that means . . . Yes, that's right! It's my pleasure to welcome you to the electrifying final of *Fire on the Dance Floor*!'

Beth and Liam are sitting at a table next to the judges' desk with Gabriel and Valentina. Theo and Dean are at the table beside that with Jessica and Daniele. There's a glass of wine in front of each of them. I wish I could run over and glug some down to calm my nerves.

'We've got an exciting night ahead of us, with just three couples left in the competition, dancing for the chance to win twenty-five thousand pounds,' Kimberley says. 'Tonight they'll each be performing two dances – one that was allocated to them at random and another that they've chosen for themselves – but it'll be up to you, the audience, to decide who wins the prize money and who goes home with nothing.

'There will be no elimination after the first round of dances, meaning all three couples will be battling it out right to the very end. Will Emilia and Merle seduce us with their stylish

346

salsa? Will Tammy and Elijah make our hearts race with their ravishing rumba? Or will Kate and Aleksis break the *Fire on the Dance Floor* curse and tango all the way to the top? I don't know about you, but I can't wait to find out!'

Until this moment, it hadn't occurred to me that Merle and Emilia's allocated dance might be the salsa, so despite dropping our bachata to avoid a potential clash, one of our dances is still going to be the same as theirs. It feels like a bad omen, but how earth-shattering can theirs be when they've only had a couple of days to learn it?

'But first,' Kimberley continues, 'let's say hello to our three fantastic judges – Mariana, Sophie and Jacques. Welcome back! Are you excited about the night ahead?'

'I can't wait to see what the dancers pull out of the bag tonight,' Mariana says. 'There have been some incredible performances on the show so far and I think all three of the remaining contestants have the potential to win.'

'They've all raised their game week on week, so I'm expecting some exceptional choreography from all three couples,' Jacques adds. 'I'll be looking for creativity, technique and most of all that *fire* that just brings the dance floor to life. And I just want to say good luck to everyone.'

'And Sophie . . . '

'Obviously we know what their allocated dances are, but even we don't know what each couple has chosen for their freestyle option, so there are surprises in store for all of us tonight. Bring it on!'

'Thank you, judges,' Kimberley says. 'And tonight we're also welcoming back former contestants Beth, Theo, Liam and Dean and dancers Gabriel, Valentina, Jessica and

Daniele, who are all here to lend their support to our three finalists. It's great to have you all here tonight – you all look gorgeous.

'And now it's time to really get this party started. So let's bring out our first couple of the evening, Tammy King and Elijah Gill, who are ready to rock our worlds with their rousing rumba. Tammy and Elijah had us out of our seats with their Dominican bachata last week. Let's see if they can get us on our feet again. Take it away, guys!'

She moves out of view as Tammy and Elijah run into the middle of the stage, and Aleksis clutches my hand as they sail through their routine. When Kimberley asks the judges what they thought at the end, they're full of praise.

'Your best dance yet!' Mariana declares. 'The lines were sharp, the timing was spot on. I think this dance really suited you, Tammy. Really well done.'

Then it's time for the audience to reach for their keypads and you can almost feel the tension in the room as the dial flickers across the scoreboard. When it settles on 9.4, the room erupts in cheers.

'A new personal best!' Kimberley shouts. 'What a great way to start the show.'

'I'm absolutely delighted,' Tammy beams.

'We couldn't have asked for more,' Elijah adds.

'It's certainly going to be a tough act to follow for our next couple,' Kimberley says. 'Especially as Merle and Emilia have had just two days to prepare this next dance after they stepped in to replace former finalist Dean, who sadly had to withdraw from the competition this week with an ankle injury.'

She pauses to allow the camera to zoom in on him. He points at his support boot then rubs his fists under his eyes as if he's crying, then shrugs and breaks into a grin to show the audience he's not really upset. Although I'd be willing to bet he is.

'But we're sure they've given it their all,' Kimberley continues. 'So let's get ready to be swept away by their saucy salsa. Ladies and gentlemen, please welcome to the stage . . . Merle Picard and Emilia Harris!'

Aleksis grips my hand even tighter as they run out onto the stage. Emilia's barely-there outfit glistens in the spotlights. Merle is wearing black trousers with a strip of gold down the side of each leg. His sheer black shirt is open to reveal his tanned torso. They remind me of a Chanel perfume advert.

The music starts and it's quickly apparent their salsa is going to be more than good. Merle leads Emilia through spin after spin and it's so fast I feel dizzy just watching it. They throw in some athletic lifts and some crazily complicated armwork and I start really fretting about how our routine will compare. Ours is nowhere near as technical – this is another level. It makes me wonder why Merle ever had any concerns about not winning. I'd even vote for them myself.

The audience erupts with whoops and whistles when the dance is over and Kimberley has to quieten everyone down so the judges can be heard.

'You had so little time to prepare, and yet you made it look like you've been dancing together your whole lives,' Jacques says. 'It was so powerful; so intense. Emilia, I truly believe you could have a future in professional dance if you want it.'

He fans himself with his hands. 'I think you've brought me out in a hot flush.'

'Now I don't know whether to apologise or thank you,' Emilia laughs.

'And now it's time to find out whether our audience members are also feeling the heat after that performance,' Kimberley says. 'Audience, grab your keypads and let's see how fired up Merle and Emilia's sensational salsa really got you!'

The dial whizzes straight up the scoreboard, bagging them a 9.7 – a new show record.

'That's the top score of the series so far,' Kimberley shouts. 'Congratulations! Well done, both of you. That's amazing. Tell us how you're feeling.'

'I'm feeling like we maybe should have spent less time preparing our previous dances,' Emilia says, which gets a laugh. 'But seriously, we worked so hard these last two days, so it feels fantastic to be rewarded for all the hours we've put in. I'm absolutely thrilled.'

'Ladies and gentlemen, put your hands together one more time for Merle and Emilia,' Kimberley says, kicking off another round of applause.

My heart starts pounding as the minutes turn to seconds before it's my turn to face the judges. With 9.7 to beat, the pressure is really on.

'Remember what I said,' Merle whispers as he passes me at the side of the stage, but I ignore him, safe in the knowledge that he's no longer a threat.

'And last but not least in this first round of dances, we have last week's top scorers Kate Wareing and Aleksis Lapsa, who tonight will be trying to beat the *Fire on the Dance Floor* curse with the final Argentine tango of the series,' Kimberley announces. 'At least I'm assuming no one has picked it for their freestyle performance.'

'But will Kate and Aleksis follow in the footsteps of Beth and Theo, who were both knocked out of the competition by this dance, or can they beat the odds tonight and tango into the lead? Ladies and gentlemen, it's time to find out. Please make some noise for . . . Kate and Aleksis!'

The lights go down around us, leaving us illuminated on the stage, and I swear you could hear a pin drop in the studio. My pulse thumps in my ears. It would be so easy to let the thought of all the people out there, watching us from the darkness, overwhelm me – not to mention however many have tuned in at home. I wonder if Aleksis can feel the tremor in my knees.

But just when I think my legs might give way altogether, he catches my eye and fires me a wink that makes the corners of my mouth start to lift. Not quite a smile, but a sign that I know I can trust him. And as I take a deep breath, I remember that I can trust myself too.

'You look gorgeous,' he whispers. 'I didn't get a chance to tell you earlier.'

And this time I do smile as I realise I feel it too. My hair is loose and tumbling around my shoulders, and my backless scarlet dress reaches the floor but is split to the waist on one side, leaving half my skin on display.

It's the sort of dress I used to think only Emilia could

pull off, but today it feels perfect for me. So instead of trying to bat away the compliment like I would have done in the past, I let it uplift me. And in doing so, I start believing that our tango really could be the winning dance for us. Because if you put your mind to it you can achieve anything, right?

I'm vaguely aware of applause as Aleksis starts leading me through our routine: dipping me slowly to the floor, drawing me back up sharply, then holding me steady as I run my leg up his. There's more cheering as he lifts me into a spin with one of my legs round his waist, and a gasp as our legs tangle and untangle with increasing speed. But it's only when he's spun me in towards him then dramatically dipped me with one leg extended forward between his, in perfect timing with the end of our song, that I really absorb the noise from the audience. It gets even louder as Aleksis breaks into a grin and pulls me up into a kiss.

It's a good while before Kimberley can make herself heard.

'Thank you, everyone. Wow, what a reaction! I think it's safe to say we were all blown away by that. But let's hear from our judges. Jacques, tell us what you thought of Kate and Aleksis's tango.'

'I think the audience reaction says it all. That was unquestionably the best Argentine tango we've seen all series,' he declares. 'The variation in the tempo, the complexity of the footwork, the way the music was used to accentuate the drama of the lifts and dips . . . it was extraordinary. You should be very proud of yourself tonight, Kate. That was exceptional.'

I'm completely speechless.

'Thank you,' Aleksis jumps in for me. 'We really appreciate that, especially coming from you, Jacques.'

'So, audience, it's the moment of truth,' Kimberley says. 'Can Kate and Aleksis tiptoe to the top spot, or are they about to dip into second or third place? Please pick up your keypads and let's find out.'

Chapter 46

Aleksis wraps both his arms around me as we watch the dial jump into action and seconds later he's spinning me in the air as the audience awards us 9.7. I can't believe it. In a million years I never would have anticipated scoring so high on the most difficult dance of the series.

'Another 9.7!' Kimberley shouts over the cheering that follows. 'Congratulations! That puts you in joint first place ahead of the freestyle dance.'

I finally find my tongue.

'I knew Aleksis had put together something special, but I just thought, I don't know, because two other people got eliminated after their tangos . . . I'm in shock. Delighted though. Aleksis really is an amazing teacher and I'm so happy our score reflects that. He's just the best.'

'That's so sweet! Really well done, guys,' Kimberley says. 'So audience, you've seen one dance from each of our couples, and Kate and Emilia are tied at the top, with Tammy just three tenths of a point behind in third place, which means there's still everything to dance for. So without further ado, let's bring Merle and Emilia back onto the stage to find out more about their week, as well as what winning would mean to them.'

I avoid eye contact as we pass each other on the stage, but I can sense Merle is glaring at me. He must be wondering what I'm playing at. I keep my eyes on Aleksis, determined not to let Merle burst my bubble after our amazing comments from Jacques.

'That was so good.' Tammy pats me on the back as I reach the side of the stage.

'I told you you could do it,' Aleksis adds, giving me a hug. 'Come on, we've got to go and get changed for our next dance. Good luck for your freestyle, Tammy, if we're not back in time.'

Kelly bustles us into the costumes room and within two minutes I'm out of my red dress and into a shimmering blue and green mini dress. While Hannah gives my hair a quick spritz and Leyla adds some turquoise glitter around my eyes, I steal a few glances at the TV monitor that tells them how much time they have to work on us – and see that Emilia and Merle are reviving their breathtakingly hot bachata.

To maintain suspense, the audience scores are collected afterwards but not divulged, so Kimberley can do a big reveal after all three performances. But judging by the audience reaction, it must be high.

I catch a glimpse of Tammy's at-home video while Leyla gives my face a last dusting of bronzer. Her parents' house is so crammed with aunties, cousins and neighbours she can barely get through the door. But it's only when Aleksis and I are backstage again that we discover she decided to repeat her merengue after all – her favourite dance rather than her top scorer.

'I have to say, the atmosphere is absolutely electric up here on the stage this evening,' Kimberley is saying. 'Ladies and gentlemen, give it up one more time for our merengue masters Tammy and Elijah. And now let's give another warm welcome to our final couple of the night – Kate and Aleksis!'

I'm sure I can pick out Lucy's voice among the cheers as we join Kimberley on the stage.

'This week Kate and Aleksis jetted off to France in between rehearsals for a surprise visit to Kate's family,' she says. 'And here's a glimpse of their impromptu French vacation . . .'

At the end of the video, which is a lovely reminder of our trip, she compliments my sister on her gorgeous home and makes the audience laugh by inviting herself along when we next go down there.

'I think all our hearts were warmed by the delight on your family's faces when you surprised them with that visit, Kate, so we've decided to recreate that mood in the studio tonight,' she smiles. 'So before you start your final dance, here to watch you perform in person for the first time ever in the competition, all the way from France, it's your sister Dee, your brother-in-law Pete, your niece and nephew Nathan and Daisy, plus your mum Carol and dad Jim.'

And I'm so grateful I knew this was coming because otherwise I would have burst into tears as they all run out to join us on stage.

When our giant group hug finally breaks up, Kimberley asks Dee how it feels to be here supporting me.

'We're loving it,' Dee says. 'We've been watching it all on TV of course, but this is so much more exciting! I really hope they win.'

'Well on that note, it's time for us to see Kate and Aleksis in action for the very last time,' Kimberley says. 'Guys, if I can ask you to head to the centre of the stage, and the rest of you, follow me. Ladies and gentlemen; for their final dance, Kate and Aleksis have chosen the salsa – a brave move after their first attempt, which nearly saw them leaving the competition. But a lot has changed in these last few weeks. Let's find out if their salsa style is one of them.'

She steps out of the spotlight with my family in tow and we get ready to begin.

Aleksis smiles at me. 'Remember, just have fun with it.'

I promise him I'll try.

Where Merle and Emilia's salsa was all about speed, lifts and spins, ours is all about tricks and giggles. Aleksis does as many spins as I do, dips to the floor and spins me by my knees rather than my waist, then pops up and spins me using his feet rather than his hands. He ducks under my arms, making it look unexpected, then folds my left hand towards my shoulder, raises my elbow to his mouth and plays my arm like a trumpet, which never fails to make me smile.

We break apart for a solo section where it looks like we're trying to outdo each other and I'm relieved that I don't mess it up. Then there are a few final spins before he drops me into a dip . . . and my last ever *Fire on the Dance Floor* performance is over.

The volume of the cheering as he pulls me to my feet and kisses me tells me he judged it exactly right – the audience loved it.

'That was adorable,' Kimberley gushes. 'Let's go straight to the judges and hear their reactions.'

'It was cute, but I don't know if it was enough,' Jacques says, which draws a gasp from the audience and feels like a spear straight through my heart.

'I mean, there's no denying we're seeing a very different Kate to the one who dragged her heels through a more serious salsa just a few short weeks ago,' he continues. 'But I can't help feeling this routine has forgotten what the show is about – *fire* on the dance floor. To me this was more of a gentle hug.'

'I disagree!' Sophie interrupts, lifting my spirits again. 'You two took a huge gamble choosing to redo your salsa tonight and I, for one, think it paid off. It was charming, fun and flirtatious. I love the chemistry between the two of you. Look how much fun they were having! Look how they were bouncing off each other! It may not have been a sizzling salsa, but I still felt the sparks flying.'

'Thank you, judges. Quite the split opinions there,' Kimberley says. 'But how will our studio audience feel? Do you want Kate and Aleksis to blaze their way to the top, or are their dreams about to go up in smoke? Ladies and gentlemen, for the last time, please pick up your keypads and enter your final scores of the series.'

After the judges' comments I genuinely have no idea

how this is going to go. Was it not the right move picking a light-hearted final dance? Should we have repeated our bachata after all?

At least we won't be kept in suspense for long.

Kimberley invites Tammy, Elijah, Merle and Emilia back out onto the dance floor.

'Guys, this is it,' she says. 'It's now time to find out who is the first ever winner of *Fire on the Dance Floor*. But before we reveal our first ever champion, I'd like to say a huge thank you to our three judges, Mariana, Jacques and Sophie, who've shared their opinions and their expertise with us over the past few weeks, and to everyone else who's been working so hard behind the scenes to make all this possible. And to you, the audience, of course, for supporting us over the last five weeks. We've had an absolute ball making the show and I'm delighted to be able to tell you that *Fire on the Dance Floor* will be returning for a second series next summer, and that's all thanks to you.'

This sparks more whooping from the audience.

'As we get ready to reveal the final scores for each couple, let's have a quick reminder of all this evening's action. First we saw Tammy and Elijah dancing the rumba, which they followed up with their favourite dance, the merengue, and they currently stand in third place with 9.4.

'Then we had Merle and Emilia wowing us with their salsa, which put them, momentarily, in first place with a massive score of 9.7 – and they followed that up with another amazing performance of their sultry bachata.

'But Kate and Aleksis equalled their score when they broke the *Fire on the Dance Floor* curse with their beautiful

Argentine tango, which also bagged them a 9.7. Then they entertained us with their own take on the salsa.

'With less than half a point separating all three couples, anyone could be walking away with the twenty-five thousand pound prize tonight.'

'Go Tammy!' someone shouts from the audience.

'Emilia!' another voice calls out.

'Kate!' someone adds, then everyone is shouting for their favourites until Kimberley manages to quieten them all down again.

'And now, the waiting is finally over. It's time to announce who will be crowned tonight's king or queen of the dance floor. Can I have a drum roll please.'

The band obliges and it feels like my heart is thumping at the same speed.

'In third place,' Kimberley says, 'after scoring a respectable 8.9 for their snappy merengue, giving them a total of 18.3, it's Tammy and Elijah. Hard luck, guys, but absolutely well done for making it this far in the competition. You did such a brilliant job, you really did. It could have been anyone's night tonight and I'm sorry it wasn't yours, but we've loved having you along for the ride. Tammy and Elijah, everyone – our third place finalists.'

They give each other a consolatory hug and wave to the audience, who respond with a long round of applause. Aleksis squeezes my hand and my heart beats even faster.

'Well, I can tell you,' Kimberley says, when the audience has simmered down, 'that it's been a closely fought battle between the two remaining couples, and there is a tiny margin separating them.'

She pauses to let the tension build even further.

'In second place, with a fantastic score of 9.8 for their chirpy salsa, giving them a grand total of 19.5 . . . it's Kate Wareing and Aleksis Lapsa. Commiserations, guys. I'm so sorry it wasn't your night tonight. But you were both amazing and we really hope you've enjoyed your time on *Fire on the Dance Floor*. Ladies and gentlemen, please put your hands together and show your appreciation for this year's runners-up, Kate and Aleksis.'

Aleksis kisses me on the top of my head then holds my hand up in the air as the clapping fills the studio. It's hard to describe what's going through my head in that moment, but seeing the crowd giving us a standing ovation goes a long way to making up for the frustration that Merle has come out on top yet again.

'And that means, of course, that we have our first ever *Fire on the Dance Floor* champions!' Kimberley says, and another round of whoops commences. 'After bagging an incredible 9.9 for their racy bachata, giving them a whopping score of 19.6 – ladies and gentlemen, I give you the show's winners, Emilia and Merle!'

A row of indoor fireworks explodes across the back of the stage and gold confetti tumbles down from the ceiling as Merle bows to the audience and Emilia looks genuinely shocked. I force myself to clap, even though it pains me to do so. It's galling having to cheer for Merle, but I don't want to look like a bad sport.

'They captivated us right from the start and were simply a cut above tonight with two incredible performances,' Kimberley beams. 'Deserved champions, I think you'll all agree. Congratulations, guys. You must be delighted. Emilia, tell me what this win means to you.'

Before she has a chance to speak, Merle jumps in with, 'We've loved every minute, haven't we? What a month it's been. And to know I'll get the opportunity to do it all again when the show is back next year – I can't wait.'

'Thanks Merle,' Kimberley says. 'And Emilia, you've just won yourself a whopping twenty-five thousand pounds! Do you have any idea what you might do with it?'

'I haven't even allowed myself to think about it until now. I wasn't expecting this at all. But I'm so grateful to the show for everything it's given me – the whole experience, the new skills I've learnt, the laughs and now this.'

She places one hand over her heart and smiles radiantly.

'And a new boyfriend of course,' Kimberley adds with a wink.

'Oh no, we've broken up,' Emilia corrects her, and it's Merle's turn to look shocked. 'As of now,' Emilia clarifies. 'It turns out he isn't the person I thought he was, so now the show is over, so are we.'

Kimberley is momentarily thrown by the awkward silence and thunderous look on Merle's face that follows, but she quickly recovers.

'I'm sorry to hear that. So, er, moving quickly on, why don't we hear from our other couples now? Kate, Aleksis, how are you feeling now you've had a moment to breathe after tonight's result?'

'I'm not sure it's all sunk in yet,' I admit – not just the result, but Emilia's knockout blow to Merle too. 'I can't quite believe it's all over.'

It briefly crosses my mind that Sofiya will be disappointed we didn't win, but the devastation I anticipated for myself hasn't come. We gave it our best shot and we were good. I can't be too downhearted about that. And Merle getting his comeuppance is an excellent consolation prize.

'I'm just sorry I let her down at the end,' Aleksis says, shaking his head.

I look up at him in surprise. 'You didn't let me down. This has been one of the best experiences of my life and I'm so happy I got to share it with you.'

'You two are still a couple then?' Kimberley checks with a nervous laugh.

'Absolutely,' I confirm.

'Thank goodness. And Tammy, Elijah, quickly over to you – we hope you've enjoyed your time with us too?'

'It's been brilliant,' Tammy replies, wearing a gigantic smile. 'And if anyone at home is thinking about giving it a go, I'd thoroughly recommend it.'

'You took the words right out of my mouth.' Kimberley says. 'Because if any of you watching here or at home think you've got what it takes to impress our judges and our live studio audience, all you have to do is fill out our online application form and submit a short video to tell us why you think you should be joining us on the dance floor next year. And it could be you up on this stage ready to walk away with twenty-five thousand pounds!

'And that's just about all we have time for tonight,' she concludes. 'Don't forget you can watch all your favourite dances again on our website, and remember to look out for the announcements about the next series. Once again,

I'd like to thank all our contestants and our professional dancers for taking part, and huge congratulations to Emilia and Merle, our *Fire on the Dance Floor* champions!'

Chapter 47

On the way back to the reception room, Aleksis asks if I'm okay.

'I thought I'd feel a lot worse than I do,' I admit. 'I'm actually proud we did so well, even if we didn't win. I'm sorry you've missed out on a place in next year's show, though. I know you must have wanted it.'

'They haven't said they *won't* have me back. You never know, they may decide to stick with all the same pro dancers, for consistency.'

'They'd be fools not to ask you. Although I'd be jealous of the lucky girl who got to dance with you. I'm really going to miss it,' I sigh, realising just how much as I let it sink in that this really is the end.

'I could always get you up at the crack of dawn tomorrow and start teaching you the samba,' he suggests.

'Er, no. I'm sure we can find other ways to entertain ourselves.'

'I don't doubt that,' he laughs, and the smiles stay on our faces for some time after that.

Steve, Sarah and Andy are already holding half-empty champagne flutes when we join the post-show drinks. The costume and make-up girls are lined up at the makeshift bar, Olivia is clinking glasses with Tammy, Beth and Liam, and even the three judges have popped in to toast the show's success.

We grab our own celebratory fizz and I scan the room one more time. Emilia is with Theo and Dean. The professional dancers are all present, chatting in small groups. The only people missing are Kimberley and Merle. I can't help wondering if that's a coincidence. I wonder, too, if he'll ever guess what happened to his phone.

Shane arrives and works his way round the room, thanking everyone for their contributions. 'You lot have made me a very happy man these last few weeks,' he says when he reaches me and Aleksis. 'Thanks for being part of it.'

Tammy comes over and raises her glass to mine.

'I think we've earned these. What a night!' She can't stop smiling. 'It's a shame we didn't win, but fair play to Emilia for pulling it out of the bag like that. She was so good. I'm still planning to party my socks off though. Do you think the landlord at The Grape will let us have a lock-in later? I'm up for a session.'

'He might be persuaded if we get over there soon and plant the idea in his head,' I nod.

'We'll come to the pub with you,' Sarah says. 'If it's an open invitation.'

'The more the merrier,' Tammy replies. 'I might even invite Emilia, as long as she brings her winnings with her.'

But Emilia politely declines. I suspect she's got something far fancier in mind for her victory party.

As we leave the Channel 6 building for the very last time, I well up a bit at the thought that we'll never be back in that velvet-seated room, in the warren of corridors or on the heart-stopping but magical stage. But as soon as we get to The Grape I'm swept up in the jubilation of all our friends and family who are already gathered there for our *Fire on the Dance Floor* farewell.

'Here she is!' Dad shouts. 'Grab a prosecco! I've put a couple of bottles on the table. Help yourselves.'

'Don't mind if I do.' Tammy grins. 'Thanks, Mr Wareing.'

'You were robbed tonight, sweetie.' He pulls me in for a hug. 'We all thought you were brilliant.'

Lucy waves at me from across the room, where she's chatting to my mum, Dee, Beth and Liam.

'I can't believe that twat got to win after all,' she says when I join them for more hugs. 'It's so unfair.'

'I'm already over it,' I assure her, looking at all the smiling faces around us. 'I can't complain when I've come away with all this.'

Seeing my family mingling with friends new and old makes my heart swell. It still feels like a celebration despite Merle and Emilia walking away with the crown.

'It's my show highlight,' I smile. 'Although that feeling you get at the end of a dance when the audience starts cheering and you know you've smashed it comes a very close second.'

'So what's next?' Beth asks. 'Has *Fire on the Dance Floor* given you the bug?'

'Tammy might have her heart set on presenting a music show, but there'll be nothing so nerve-racking for me,' I laugh. 'I need to get a job pretty swiftly so I can afford my rent, but I want to make sure it's the right job this time. I won't just settle for anything.'

'You'll figure it out,' Lucy assures me. 'Pity you won't get to blow that twenty-five thousand on a round-the-world trip first, though . . . '

'You could still do that,' Liam interrupts, and we all turn to stare at him, probably all wondering the same thing – how?

'If you want to, that is,' he says. 'I know you've said before that you don't want it, but I still want you to have the money from, you know, before. I haven't spent it and I really think it should be yours.'

My skin prickles at the reminder and I shake my head. 'Thank you, Liam, but I can't. It wouldn't feel right.'

'It doesn't feel right for me to have it either,' he persists. 'But if you take it, I get to feel like less of a dickhead, you still get to travel – everyone's a winner.'

Beth, Dee and Lucy's heads all snap back towards me, to see my response. I think they're all holding their breath.

'What about your gym?' I ask. In spite of everything, I don't want to be the one who stops him from getting it.

'The thing about that is,' he breaks into a grin, 'I've just found out I've got a place on *The Cube* next month, so I think I'll be sorted. Of all the ones I applied for, it's the one I really wanted. I'm absolutely over the moon.'

'That's amazing,' Beth shrieks. She claps him on the back. 'Congratulations.'

'Thank you,' he laughs. 'I've already set up copies of the games all over my house and I've got a few weeks to practise so I'm feeling confident. So please take the money, Kate, seriously. It's yours more than it's mine and I really, really want you to have it. Please?'

'I think he wants you to take it,' Lucy says.

'Take it,' Beth agrees.

'Take it,' Tammy nods.

I look at each of them in turn and they all start nodding furiously.

'Fine,' I sigh, rolling my eyes. 'I'll take it.'

And everyone cheers.

'So does that mean you're planning on running off on me?' Aleksis asks from behind me, making me jump. I hadn't realised he'd moved into hearing range.

And my heart lurches at the thought of it. Because even though it makes perfect sense to jet off now, before I get back into the rat race, I'd hate not to see him for months – even if he promised to wait for me.

'I'm not about to jump on the next plane,' I tell him.

'It would be a good time to go, though, now it's getting into autumn. I hear Australia is lovely at this time of year, especially in the run-up to Christmas.'

And with those words, my world turns a little darker. The show finished less than two hours ago and already he's putting us as far away from each other as is humanly possible. Perhaps I should have seen this coming but, like a fool, I let myself believe he's not another Merle, just stringing me along to try and win the competition. I so wanted him to be different.

'I'm sure it's great,' I shrug, silently berating myself for opening myself up to heartache yet again.

Oblivious to my misery, Aleksis cheerfully adds, 'What do you reckon, a month or two in Sydney in November and December? New Year's Eve fireworks on the Harbour Bridge?'

A tear escapes and rolls down my cheek and Lucy discreetly pulls the others away to give us some privacy.

'What's that for?' Aleksis asks in alarm. 'I thought you'd be happy.'

'I don't want to go to Australia,' I sob, all the pent-up emotions of the day suddenly flooding out of me. 'I know it hasn't been long, but I really thought me and you . . . I thought this was the beginning of something. I actually believed I was going to meet your parents.'

'And you will,' he laughs, brushing the moisture off my cheeks. 'I obviously wasn't explaining myself very well. I wasn't suggesting you go to Australia on your own. Before we left Channel 6 this evening, I got an offer to join another pilot for the show over in Sydney. I wasn't quite sure how to bring it up until you started talking about going travelling. I was trying to ask you if you might want to come with me.'

I eye him warily. 'Seriously?'

'Seriously. I was even wondering if we might be able to squeeze in a couple of weeks in Thailand before it starts – so I can get a natural tan instead of all this lotion.'

My lips curl up into a smile as a wave of relief floods through me. 'You mean you don't really love that shade of orange?'

'Hey, I could still change my mind,' he warns. 'I'll have quite a lot of training to do once the show starts, but we'd have evenings and Sundays together. You could hang out on the beach or go off and explore while I'm working – we can work those details out later – but I would love it if I could have you there with me.'

Any attempt I might have made to play it cool at that moment flies straight out of the window as I fling myself into his arms.

'I'll take that as a yes,' he laughs, kissing me and hugging me back.

Then he releases me so he can tap his glass against mine. 'Farewell London. Australia here we come!'

Acknowledgements

To my friends Catherine Usher, Melanie Francis, Kate Bates, Kevin Fuller and Zoe Stormont, huge thanks for taking the time to read my early drafts and giving me such overwhelmingly positive feedback. It spurred me on and gave me the confidence to look for an agent and a publisher.

To Anne Perry and Meg Davis at Ki Agency, I'm so grateful to you for believing in *The Dance Deception*, for finding it a home and for providing me with the knowledge, patience and support every first-time author needs when navigating their way through the publishing process.

And to Thorne Ryan and Rachel Hart at Avon - not to mention the rest of the team - I can't thank you enough for your boundless enthusiasm, for helping me shape *The Dance Deception* into the best version of itself and for giving it a cover I absolutely love. You've made a lifelong dream come true.